The Maste
Downsland

by

Peter Chegwidden

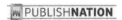

www.publishnation.co.uk

North Kent, the latter part of the 18th century

Disowned and disinherited by his family for marrying the girl he loves David Grayan leaves their wealth and status behind. With what little money he has he embarks on various business ventures that eventually reap dividends and earn him his fortune. He buys a handsome house with large grounds in North Kent. A philanthropist, he employs many more people than he needs to, funds a school and medical facilities for local villagers and enjoys the respect of the country folk. But he is largely shunned by his own class particularly for his unconventional views and practices.

Then tragedy strikes.

Pregnant with their first child his beloved wife, Marie, dies in childbirth leaving David Grayan a heartbroken, bereft and sorrowful character. Unable to come to terms with his dreadful loss, he throws himself into his business affairs and retreats into a dark, solitary state where even his few close friends cannot help him, an emotionally broken man.

At this juncture a new maid, the young Sarah Brankly, starts work at his Downsland Hall. But can a mere maid, a lowly servant, provide any medium by which he might emerge from his darkness into the light? And could he love again?

However, there are serious matters awaiting David Grayan that will weigh heavily on his darkened soul and require his intervention; matters of family and friendship, matters that will challenge his beliefs, matters that will plague his every step.

Prelude

"In this I expect to be obeyed."

It wasn't unusual for Sir William Grayan to bellow when angry and do so in his rich, deep baritone voice, although such action was normally reserved for the servants, and was normally undeserved.

A man of power and privilege, Sir William liked to exercise his authority but this morning was finding it difficult to do so with his eldest son who now stood ready to defy him.

Lady Grayan sat quietly, her sad eyes betraying her fears. Mother and son studied each other as Sir William continued:

"Marry a merchant's daughter indeed. Who the devil do you think you are sir?" And Sir William prepared to storm from the room, his face red with fury and screwed up with rage, only to be brought to a sudden halt by David Grayan's firmly spoken words.

"My mind is made up sir. I will marry Marie Haskerton and that is my final word."

Marie Haskerton he had met by chance. She stole his heart without a second thought. But he would be marrying 'beneath himself' as he was all too often reminded. Marry a merchant's daughter? His father had bellowed those words at him four times in a row, adding more and more contempt and venom each time he spat out 'merchant's daughter'.

They were deeply in love before she was acquainted with the truth about David Grayan's position in life and society. He had deliberately kept it from her as he did not want her love if she was a woman who sought a husband for his wealth and status. He had a second reason: he would no longer be heir to the family fortune if he married her, for his parents would never agree the match.

The evening he explained all this to her was the occasion she swore undying love and devotion, saying she would dwell in poverty providing she had him always. They embraced and kissed with a passion and fervour they had not shared before, and

2

wept tears of joy openly and happily as they clung to each other with determination and commitment.

Now father and son had reached an impasse.

David would not entertain an arranged marriage with Lady Fitzgower and that was an end to it.

Lady Grayan closed her eyes and wrung her hands in her lap, dreading what must follow, the anxiety etched in her face. Her husband resumed his rapid departure, his only words directed at a footman who did not open the door quickly enough. Lady Grayan spoke, quietly, purposefully.

"You will rue this day, David. You will be disinherited, you will be forbidden to meet or communicate in any way with me and your brother and sisters. Will you hurt me so? Will you tear my own heart to pieces? Will you so willingly destroy your family?" Eleanor Grayan was shaking with distress as her emotions overwhelmed her and the tears fell, softly, silently, and her voice vanished into nothingness as she sought to control herself.

David Grayan was inwardly moved. Was he really ready to put love for a woman above family loyalty and break his mother's heart? He knew the answer, knew it too well.

He walked from the room without another glance at his mother. He and Marie were married that autumn and David was disinherited and rendered a family outcast.

***

With enough money of his own, and a small dowry from his new father-in-law, he bought a small cottage in north Kent where they would see hops and fruit growing, and from where they could enjoy distant views across the waters of the Swale to the isle of Sheppey.

It was a cottage where his dreams took shape and from where those dreams were made manifest. His business interests expanded and proved successful for the most part. And thus it was that his wealth grew aplenty. They moved into a much larger home, had servants for the first time, became farmers and grew richer still.

3

In all this Marie stood shoulder to shoulder with her husband, for David held unconventional views with regard to the parity of men and women, doing so in the belief that convention and society was wrong and that men and women should be regarded as equal in all things, an opinion widely considered the work of a heretic, a madman, a fool.

"Imagine what talented minds might have been at work," he expounded once to Marie, "if we had allowed women scope for their ability. What celebrated architects, engineers, surgeons, leaders in government and commerce, even military leadership we could've experienced, and all for the better."

They never lost touch with the basic skills of working the soil, rearing animals, carrying out their own repairs wherever they were needed and creating simple buildings for their livestock and equipment. They worked together all hours, and took that aptitude into later life when they employed local people and toiled alongside them.

The Grayans longed for a family they seemed doomed not to have. Marie comforted him and told him time would tell and they should put their trust in God to deliver them a child. He loved her all the more for it even though he did not believe in her God or her God's ability to provide a baby.

With time, and greater success, they moved to a grand house with a widespread estate, and Downsland Hall swiftly came to witness God's blessing when Marie announced she was with child.

Philanthropists by nature they now employed more on the estate and in the house than they actually needed. The largest village nearby, Westlingstead, was given a school and Henry Barrenbridge, a physician and long-time friend of David's, arrived to set up a medical practice, and so the welfare of their workers, their families and other local people was well catered for, much to the Grayans' satisfaction. For that was what they sought, also openly encouraging those in their employ to better themselves.

Here at Downsland Hall they entertained those that were important to David's businesses, as well as Marie's family and their own few true friends. There were no balls or lavish banquets for the cream of society to revel in for it was not their style and they were despised for it. Society looked down upon them generally and kept a reasonable distance, the exception being the handful who felt they had some advantage to gain by retaining token friendship.

Together they designed their gardens and landscaped the estate in which they often worked side by side with those they employed. Local people were permitted to visit the grounds, which set a prominent neighbour, the Hon. Geoffrey Malter, into a frenzy of discontent.

"You can't let that rabble loose at your home," he once ranted to his wife, "they'll steal and get above themselves and then cause trouble elsewhere. It's a disease that needs eradicating before it takes hold. Whatever next."

In time Marie Grayan did less and less physical work as her pregnancy developed. It had been a most wonderful summer and as September and autumn approached with onrushing urgency, Marie's time also drew nigh.

Chapter One

The shadows in the walled garden were longer now as the sun crept nearer the horizon every day as it made its way across the blue September sky. It had been a pleasant enough place to sit during hot summer days and evenings and Marie Grayan had often done so, but now the shadows were falling on the seats by late afternoon, so it was a less attractive proposition.

She gave thanks to God for his gracious mercy and generosity in granting them a child, and did so several times each day especially now with the birth approaching. She still liked to stroll in this part of the garden as she believed she was closer here to God, and there was rarely anyone else to disturb her reverie. Today one of the gardeners, Thomas, was busy in one corner unaware his mistress was close by. She did not trouble him and returned to the house at a sedate pace.

She knew her husband had reason for great sadness, for today he had learned his mother had died and he would not be permitted to attend the funeral. He had shown her the letter. His father had written without compassion and bluntly blamed him for his mother's demise.

The only line of communication he had with his family had been established with his younger sister Hester. David was able to write to her at a friend's address from where she would reply, her friend posting each letter. Hester and David shared a special bond, for he had often looked after her when she was little more than an infant, and more than once shielded her from their father's wrath, enduring a terrible beating on her behalf.

They had decided how they would write to each other before he left home. She had to take even more care now as she had married and her husband would not have countenanced her behaviour. David was an outcast, a traitor, Charles Handlen had pronounced, and his wife did not doubt his commitment to his hatred in the least.

Handlen came from an affluent family and was otherwise dedicated to the pursuit of pleasure. Hunting, gambling, a mistress in London, Handlen dabbled in whatever he could regardless of expense. Hester often wrote about his profligate expenditure, his time wasting, and the fact she knew he was with his woman when he should've been at home.

She tolerated all this because she had no choice and it sickened David to imagine her despair and unhappiness. But that was a woman's life, dictated by conventions society had developed to suit itself. He knew that Hester, like her older sister, had to wed whomsoever pleased their father, and it pained him ceaselessly that he had freed himself and now revelled in a degree of joy and freedom denied his beloved sister.

Marie felt his pain.

She had been spared such a match. Indeed, both she and her own sister Mary and elder brother Henry had been able to marry for love, both couples being frequent visitors at Downsland, as were her parents. Her father's business had prospered over the years and he and David had become engaged in two joint ventures that had borne considerable fruit. It pleased Marie no end, and she could foresee no limits to this gladness.

As she entered the room David rose and was swiftly at her side, guiding her into her favourite chair with tenderness and concern, asking after her well-being. She did not require such attention but kept such considerations secret, immersing herself instead in the warmth of his love that engulfed her just as it always did. A smile lit her face and he felt his own love surge through his body as he gazed upon the eyes that had beguiled him the first time they met.

"Thomas was busy in the walled garden but I did not disturb him. I'm sure he would've enjoyed some pleasant conversation but he would've detained me at length and it was getting cold." A gentle laugh emerged from her lips, gentle and affectionate, not mocking. "He adores his work and I don't think he will ever stop, but he loves talk far too much. Perhaps I'm being unkind. He is well and truly in advanced years and I expect he has his aches and pains." She saw the vexed expression on David's face. "I'm sorry, I know you have much to worry you."

"No, no, I think it better to discuss other matters. Mama is dead. I cannot pay my respects as I should wish. It must be left as it is. I have no regrets about my behaviour. It was my father's intransigence that led to the consequences. To the best of my

7

knowledge Lady Fitzgower remains unmarried and without prospects, whereas I have the finest wife imaginable and have known the beauty of love, deep and perfect, and the success it can bring to a couple." Marie smiled knowingly.

"I am still sad for you. Will you reply to your father?"

"I have already done so. A brief note of condolence ignoring the vile slur he has heaped upon me."

"And will you write to Hester?"

"Yes. As you know I have to send my letters to a friend of hers as I would not want to put her at risk. Charles and my father are men from the same mould."

"Do you know much of Charles's mistress?"

"Only what Hester knows, and that is precious little. I'm sure he attends her as he sees it as a fashionable pastime, one beloved of and practiced by his fickle friends."

"I am pleased you have no mistress David."

There was no disguising the pleasant humour in her voice.

"No need of one Marie. You are my whole world, my whole life." He stood and moved to her side, softly kissing her forehead as she grasped his hand and held it to her bosom, her eyes closing as his words echoed around in her mind and she felt his other arm on her back, bringing intense feelings of devotion to her heart.

"I'll ring for some tea if you wish it, my love." She nodded her agreement and watched this precious man, this cherished gift, cross the room.

"Yes, I'd love tea. And then I shall write to papa and inform him of your news."

***

Hester Handlen had much on her mind as she crossed the road on the way to her friend, Margaret Cheney. This was the most pleasurable of diversions in a life devoid of delight. A dutiful wife, Hester took each day as best she could and had no dreams, no ambition, no hopes to brighten her outlook.

Charles had arrived home late last night, taken her to his bed, lustily, drunkenly making love to her before collapsing on the floor snoring heavily. She hadn't seen him since breakfast that morning. Tonight they were to attend a ball near Canterbury and she would arrive on his arm, indeed his dutiful wife, and smile at those who must be smiled upon, dance with whoever might ask her, make conversation as required, and return home with her husband who would then satisfy himself with her. Swiftly, horribly, violently.

The dutiful wife.

She thought back to the last event they had attended, just a week ago. A banquet in London. She had thoughtlessly talked of matters Charles did not wish her to mention. In the bedroom he had stood over her and shouted his displeasure and anger while removing her clothing in the roughest manner imaginable. Then he had whipped her, the punishment completed by the customary act of savage intimacy while she writhed with pain.

The dutiful wife.

David did not believe women should have to submit to such duty. The duty of love and devotion, freely given yes, but not a duty of convention or for that matter convenience. David did not believe women should be the playthings of husbands, let alone reckless, mindless husbands who treated their wives with utter contempt, sometimes beating them into submission.

What dreadful consequence might befall her if Charles learned of her correspondence with her brother? She had never written to David about the beatings lest he should take unwanted revenge on her husband. That would lead to terrors anew.

Today she would write about her mother and try to explain why she felt so little loss, for so surely she felt numbness rather than sorrow. It was as if she somehow attached blame for her situation on her mother who had, after all, been as helpless as she was. It was life, and it was the way their kind lived it, accepting the situation no matter how unpalatable. How she envied David, and how she envied Marie. What a happy, trouble free marriage they had, and now a child in the offing, any day now, to complete a blissful picture.

Envy indeed.

Yes, she would write at Margaret's and try to tell her brother her true feelings for their mama, when she would've preferred to write of her hatred for her father, for Charles, and for society, for their class, and for her own misery from which there was no escape.

The maid showed Hester into the withdrawing room where she and Margaret embraced and joyously exchanged the pleasantries of true friends.

A few days ago Hester had told her the story of the whipping while the tears flooded down her friend's cheeks into her lap, Margaret's tear-sodden face transfixed in cold disbelief and sheer horror. Margaret had experienced an arranged marriage but love had grown, for Albert was a man of great kindness and they had come to treasure each other. Now she felt wretchedness for Hester's situation, just as she had come to feel repulsion for Charles.

She left her guest alone for a few moments to read David's latest letter, written before their mother's death.

He wrote about the dreams he shared with Marie for their first born, he wrote in glowing prose about the late summer in the garden and how the plants enriched their very existence, he wrote about another success in business, he asked after Margaret and Albert, and he commented on her social life as she had outlined when writing a week ago. Now her own tears fell. Quiet sobs, sweet little teardrops slowly making good their escape and slipping from her eyes.

If only she could tell him. If only she could. He wrote hoping she was enjoying the events she must attend, for she had given him the belief that she was happy doing so and gained much gratification from them. If only she could tell him. And she knew she would now write and say that, yes, she had loved every minute.

***

"I could be a maid at Downsland."

The announcement, delivered with a certainty and assuredness typical of the girl, did not surprise her mother who smiled in acknowledgment and continued with her chores as if no words had been spoken.

"They are a fine couple, so why not? I would be no trouble to them. I'll not be wed. No man will ever come for me...." This time her mother interrupted.

10

"That's foolish talk. Fair young lady you are. Do for a fair young man, you wait and see, you wait and see."

"What man wants a barren wife?"

"A man who will love you for yourself. And he will come for you, he will come, wait and see."

"Oh mama, mama, bless you, but I am quite resigned....."

"You should not be so. Hold on to your dreams, hold on to your hopes. Never let go...."

"Anyway mama, I would be no bother at Downsland. I am told the maids attract too much attention from the men folk working there so a maid without prospects should be welcome."

This time they both smiled.

"Sarah, and how pray are you going to come by such a position?"

"I will go there and ask to see Mr Grayan, or his wife if he is indisposed." She stood with her hands on her hips and a look of fortitude on her youthful face. In such a pose she looked every inch a determined girl of seventeen years that would not be mistaken for someone older and wiser. Her mother laughed at her, but it was a loving humour, respectful without being scornful, and it was recognised by her daughter who smiled in return.

"You think me foolish mama?"

"No my child. No I do not. You may go with my blessing and try your good fortune. But remember that your papa may prefer you to remain here tending our animals." She did not look at her daughter. She didn't need to.

Here was Sarah, headstrong, with the arrogance of youth who, though she did not feel disposed to admit it, still harboured many dreams and entertained ambitions that must surely be beyond her. If she wanted to go to Downsland she would go, and she'd be strong enough, forthright enough, to ask to see the master. But her mother knew she would not go. Sarah Brankly would not leave them.

Possessing no looks that might readily appeal to a man the poor child had suffered terribly at the age of seven, having a tumour cut from her in an operation that might have killed her at the time. The drastic surgery had taken the womb with it, but fortunately she recovered within a year and was now free of pain although she still walked awkwardly, an outcome of the healing process after that wretched butcher of a surgeon had worked on her.

Without the operation she would've died in agony. It was a chance her parents had to take.

She had watched her three elder sisters grow and leave the nest, all married to the handsomest of men, or so it seemed to Sarah. And, of course, she longed for her day to come. As the years had passed, and her siblings were courted and wed one by one, she came to realise that her day would never dawn and that her dreams, the dreams of many a maiden, would come to nought.

The sadness slipped by largely unnoticed by her family, for it was only when she was the only one left in what had been the girls' bedroom that she cried herself to sleep, praying silently for her own man, prayers she knew would go answered.

She read books when she could come by them, improved her education by any means whenever an opportunity presented itself, and had allowed acorns of aspiration and purpose to develop slowly within her. If she could, she would make something of her life, make the best of what the fates had thrown at her, and one of those acorns might yet grow into a strong oak. Sarah would continue to believe in herself. What she had lost could be replaced by something quite different, and she determined that should be the case.

***

"Most unwise Roger. I heartily recommend you have no part in it."

David Grayan was addressing his good friend Roger Culteney who was staying at Downsland for a few days, always a most welcome and entertaining guest, much loved by both David and Marie.

The two men had become friends when David was forced from the family home and remained close despite the fact Roger relied too heavily on an income from his own father, and was inclined to spend it all too easily. He had been encouraged to invest in one or two of David's own ventures and had been well rewarded by their success, but his attention to business detail did not match that of his friend and consequently lost money on ill-fated schemes.

He'd been describing one in the hope that David would join him in a particular investment and had been notably unsuccessful in persuading his shrewd host that this company had a sound future. On the contrary.

"Roger, it's impossible. They will simply pay you a handsome dividend to encourage you to put more money into the affair, when all they will be doing is paying your dividend straight from the cash of new investors. And so it will go on until there's no more money coming in and then the whole nonsense will collapse, the proposers long gone and wealthy, and people like you left with nothing."

"David, I have such a feeling about this. You really should reconsider....."

"Heed my words, Roger, and forget this..."

"But David, there's money to be made here, mark my words."

"Roger, no more on this. Let's be done. You will be a fool to embark on this, and I will not join you."

Roger sighed and finished his wine. He was offered more and accepted at once.

"If you will not join me then I shall do this alone, and you will be amazed I dare say when it bears fruit."

"I shall be amazed if it does. Pocket any dividends and do not re-invest. If you must lose, then lose only your first stake. Is your father investing?"

"Good heavens no. Wouldn't dream of mentioning it to him. He's had enough of my money-making schemes."

"And that, dear sir, is because they nearly all go the same way. Changing the subject, tell me, what news of Lily Cowans?"

Roger threw his head back and let out a soft cry that could've been misunderstood for one of anguish. David laughed.

"Oh David. She loves me, she loves me not. Confounded woman cannot make her feelings clear to me and I don't want to look a fool and declare myself and be laughed at."

"If only you adopted the same attitude to money..."

"She is the fairest of the fair. My goodness, my love for her is boundless, but does she look to me in the way a woman should look at a man under consideration? No David, she does not."

David laughed some more.

"Declare yourself man. If she rejects you then all is lost. If she accepts you then you have won this fair maiden with the advantage she will marry with an appreciable dowry." It was Roger's turn to laugh.

"Hang you David! But by God you're right. And even if she rejects me I can always imagine she is coy and indicating I should come again later. I had forgotten all about a dowry, but you are so right my dear friend..."

"Roger, Roger, never for one moment would you forget what might be a sizeable dowry!"

"Then let's drink to my proposal to Miss Cowans and to her father's generous benefaction. I shall indeed declare myself on my return to Dover."

Glasses were raised, the two men toasting good fortune in whatever guise.

"Save your money for the wedding tour Roger."

"I shall give much thought to what you have said and may even save my money. Lily is worth it I am sure of it."

"Good. Now let's join Marie whom I know is looking forward to more of your conversation and wit Roger."

The two rose and made their way forth arm in arm, touching briefly again on the loss of David's mother and the unfortunate situation surrounding it.

September was becoming a month of pleasure and anticipation but unbeknown to those at Downsland a calamity lay in wait when the autumnal sunshine would be replaced by a cold, bleak darkness, with pleasure expunged and expectation lost.

And it would mark the arrival of disruptive storms and appalling emptiness to fill the lives of some, bringing changes that would be neither welcome nor palatable, the discordant states of affairs having far-reaching effects on others.

The summer had brought warmth, a good harvest and the promise of a sound future. Summer had thus been deceitful and led those who had enjoyed its long days to falsely believe the goodness and contentment would last and be unassailable.

Chapter Two

Henry Jennings heard the first creak and stepped smartly to one side as the tree gave way and with great drama toppled towards the ground, a victim of the work Henry had done with his axe at its foot. The young Jed Maxton had already moved to safety on Henry's instructions knowing the end was nigh.

The two usually worked well together but today Jed's enthusiasm was irritating the older man, and doing so for two reasons. He was trying to impress Agnes Byrne who was watching with clear admiration etched in her face and, secondly, he was chopping so violently that he had not always struck the right place or done so at the correct angle.

Keen to demonstrate his strength to Miss Byrne, and succeeding in gaining her approval, Jed had not been demonstrating his concentration to Mr Jennings who sent him a notable distance from both tree and girl.

Agnes had started at Downsland as a maid but now worked full time in the grounds under the control of Henry Jennings. Showing a natural propensity for an outdoor existence her desire to work there came to the attention of Marie Grayan who encouraged her to try her hand at activities always executed by men.

The men grumbled and did their best to dissuade her from following such a path, often giving her tasks she had little chance of completing. But Agnes confounded them by doing these jobs well, and in time won the men over. They knew full well master and mistress had strange ideas and thought it best to tolerate these madnesses as best they could in the vain hope that people such as Agnes would tire of the ventures and return from whence they came.

Agnes Byrne didn't tire.

By and large Henry Jennings coped with this situation despite secretly harbouring a grievance against the Grayans in that they had planted this demon in his midst, and he did not agree with it, believing it not to be a woman's place.

At this precise moment the thoughts of Agnes and Jed were far removed from their work and more closely allied to each other, and that was another devilment for Henry to deal with, for it interfered with the smooth running of his field of operation.

On one occasion, when they were alone, Agnes had teased Henry and flirted wickedly, and he had scolded her for her impudence and ordered her away. Let her practise her feminine wiles on Jed, for he was certain that they would be wed in time. It was another reason he did not like women around him when he was about his work. Too much of a distraction. She had looked smart and elegant in her maid's uniform. Why not stay indoors where she belonged?

But he had to admit that the rough clothing she now wore could do nothing to hide the fact she was a girl blossoming into adulthood with a rare abandon and subtle promise. Jed had arrived at his side as a horse galloped briskly down the track near them.

"Twas young Robert Broxford riding at pace," he declared, puzzled by the event, "and I'm wondering where he's a-going at such speed. Must be some errand."

"Yes, but unusual for all that Henry." Jed was musing on the occurrence, for he knew Robert well and was aware he was occasionally despatched with messages, though rarely required to treat them with such urgency. But a thought came to him.

"Might be going for the physician Henry. Might be mistress's time."

"Ah yes," his companion sighed as if some great light had been shone upon a dark scene, "you could be right at that Jed. You could be right."

Within minutes, as they gathered up their tools leaving the tree trunk where it had fallen to await cutting up tomorrow, they witnessed a carriage being driven from the estate with some haste.

"Y'right Jed. If you ask me it's the mistress's time and the coach will be for her family," Agnes added as if to shed even more light on the situation. Jed nodded but Henry was unable to let the matter pass without an admonishment.

"Not for you to speculate, missy. Best hold your tongue." She managed to look dismayed although neither man believed she truly was, and she certainly did not look admonished, especially when she smiled at Jed as soon as Henry's back was turned.

***

Some days had passed since Roger Culteney had departed Downsland and he had spent his time extracting more money from his father by various fraudulent means. He was now setting about the business of investing it against David Grayan's best advice.

Culteney was tall and slender, slightly stooped, with a shock of unruly auburn hair which was at odds with his overall appearance, he always being smartly attired and otherwise well groomed. He possessed what could be best described as a long, narrow face with a long, narrow nose and bold brown eyes that darted about as if to doggedly miss nothing.

He cut a very different figure to that of his friend.

David had a rugged square face, not decidedly handsome yet impelling in its appeal. He was thick set, not always smartly dressed, and sported a crop of curly light brown hair that had delighted Marie from the outset. Although usually in good humour he had a serious side and did not relish the foolishness of others or abide it with any great tolerance. Nonetheless he felt clear in mind he had won his gentle battle with the feckless Roger Culteney.

However, despite seeming to agree with Grayan's suggestion, he had returned to Dover for the sole purpose of increasing the amount he had for investment as he remained convinced the scheme was destined to be extremely profitable. He had no intention of calling upon Lily Cowans.

Presently he was in London signing away a notably large sum of money.

A quantity belonged to Dr Henry Barrenbridge, another old friend who had, at Grayan's request, set up a practice that incorporated a small hospital not far from Downsland Hall. Culteney had, during his visit, managed to encourage the doctor to participate. Barrenbridge was reluctant at first, even suggesting they ask David his advice, whereupon Culteney swiftly responded that he had already done so, thus misleading

17

the physician into believing the man's blessing had been given, when it had not.

Bewhiskered Henry Barrenbridge had earned the respect of local people. A jovial and cheerful disposition sat comfortably with his rotund appearance, and his skill as a doctor and surgeon had been widely recognised and appreciated. He had two assistants, James Parry-Barnard and Judith Pearland, both seeking to advance themselves in medicine. The latter, formerly a nurse at the practice, showed all the attributes of becoming an excellent physician whereas the former lacked commitment coupled with no lack of laziness.

Parry-Barnard was a young man who believed he knew everything about medicine when in fact he managed to demonstrate he knew so little. Pearland had the disadvantage of being a woman, albeit a very capable one. Patients loved her as a nurse but were wary of her as a potential doctor.

The building they worked in was small and cramped but it sufficed. There were two small consulting rooms, a tiny ward with four beds, a room used for operations, the apothecary store, kitchen (two ladies from the village came to prepare food) and two rooms which were used as offices, and for meals and rest. There was little rest taken. Barrenbridge, energetic and zestful, bustled about with purpose at all times and was adored by all who came in contact with him.

In his fifties and a single man by choice he had taken lodgings in the village of Westlingstead and had formed an attachment with the widowed landlady who took it upon herself to cater for his every need. She was every bit as rotund and merry as he was, and worshipped him as a man as well as a physician.

Parry-Barnard came from a privileged background and had his own lodgings in Faversham, a decent ride away and therefore a good and safe distance from his place of employment. Pearland was a local girl, born and bred in Westlingstead, and had come to the attention of Marie Grayan who then promoted her medical prospects much to the consternation of Parry-Barnard. Barrenbridge tolerated the situation, confident she had no future in his field.

There were three other girls who worked as nurses and a man who came in occasionally to attend to the accounts and other matters. The practice served several villages and settlements as well as all who worked at Downsland, and it attracted patients from further afield such was the reputation built there.

Henry was attending to a young child in the hospital when Robert Broxford arrived and summoned him. Leaving his assistants to tend to the sick, particularly the young boy who was seriously stricken, he gathered up his bag and other items and caught hold of master Doubleday in the front garden. The boy did all the odd-jobs, the clearing up, the emptying of chamber-pots, the gardening and so on, and despatched him to fetch the horse and cart with all due haste.

He also gathered up one of the nurses, Grace Gandling, and in time set off in pursuit of Broxford riding ahead. Gandling was a local woman in her mid-thirties, unmarried, who had proved to be the kind, caring and dedicated nurse Barrenbridge needed. Utterly reliable, she brought comfort easily to the afflicted for it was her very nature to do so. She had precious few other capabilities and had never garnered the attention of a man, and seemed all the happier and contented for it.

They travelled with alacrity, for Marie Grayan's time had indeed come.

***

In Eltham Mr and Mrs Haskerton were enjoying conversation and musing on whether their latest grandchild would be a boy or a girl.

"I say a boy," proclaimed Daniel Haskerton with some confidence.

"And I say a girl," his wife replied, "as I rather like the name Charlotte, which is the one they have chosen for her."

"I didn't know that, m'dear. What name for the boy, then?"

"As far as I am aware they are undecided. Like me Marie is certain it will be a girl."

"Perhaps they will call him Daniel after me." Haskerton sported a broad grin which his wife noticed as she looked up from her sewing. She returned the smile. He continued:

"She's a lucky girl, m'dear. Excellent husband, excellent."

"Luck did not come upon it Daniel. He is a remarkable man and he has made his own fortune with our Marie at his side and now they live as the well-to-do should, her future secure. You forget they met when he had nothing to commend him, but Marie believed in him and has supported and encouraged him. Their children will do well in life you may be sure."

"Georgina m'dear, I do not forget, and I cherish the day they met. I meant lucky in the sense that David recognised her as a woman who would understand him and who was therefore suitable in all respects. He did not wish for a wife who wanted elevation in society and attendant wealth, nor one who would be content with a secondary role to her husband...."

"I hope, my dear, you do not include me in your description." Both laughed quietly. She continued.

"I have accepted my role as your wife as dictated by custom, and you have accepted me as your wife on the same basis, and we have loved and been happy and successful. I do not agree with David's revolutionary ideas any more than you do Daniel."

"I know my pet. And I know we are both pleased Marie has done so well for herself."

A maid entered and curtsied.

"Message from Downsland Hall Sir." He took the envelope and read the contents.

"From David. It's Marie's time. The doctor has been sent for and a coach is sent for us. Come my dear."

There was no apparent haste, no anxiety. They rose and made their way slowly upstairs, Georgina giving instructions to the maid, these being primarily to fetch the housekeeper without delay. The servants would pack their belongings but Mrs Haskerton would supervise. Mr Haskerton went to his study to collect any items he might need knowing that his own stay at Downsland would be brief. Business would call him back.

He wrote a brief note to the office manager and had it sent by messenger upon the instant. His wife busied herself with their housekeeper and the arrangements for departure. Within the hour they were on the road. Henry Barrenbridge and Grace Gandling were already at Downsland and in Marie's company. David Grayan had left the bedchamber and was downstairs pacing

20

about like a caged animal until a maid, Ginny Perkins, came upon the scene.

He had always liked Ginny. She had a childish waif-like appearance that belied her twenty six years, and had been with them for the last seven of her life. He invited her to sit and engaged her in conversation. She was nervous at first, constantly fiddling with her apron, looking everywhere except at her master, but gradually came relaxation and with it she found her voice.

After a while they were talking gaily and enjoying each other's company. It helped occupy his mind and it ate away at the time, and that was what he wanted.

And so the scene was set. The sun moved unceasingly towards its destination on the western horizon and this simply beautiful September day swept into its eventide, casting longer shadows across the estate so beloved of the Grayans and bringing with it the chill of an early autumn night.

The day nature created had no drama of its own to present to the people. The drama belonged solely to the people themselves but it was still nature that provided the medium, the conduit for drama and tragedy here at Downsland Hall.

***

The lights were being lit by the servants as David Grayan lifted himself wearily from his chair and bade Ginny leave him, thanking her for the company he'd craved. Henry Barrenbridge had once more come downstairs to issue reports and again gave no sign that there was to be any problem. Patting his friend upon the shoulder he smiled confidently.

"She's well and all is proceeding as expected David." No further words were needed from either man. Without lights the room would've been in near darkness for the day was spent and the night would have to be their companion as time continued to flow unabated. The Haskerton's had not yet arrived.

"Everything is well. Everything is prepared. We're ready. It is up to nature now, my boy." David did not answer, not even with a nod, and looked away, fretting like any good father awaiting the first born.

Ginny Perkins crossed the floor on her way from one place to another, and did so without a glance at the two men. David took no notice but Henry observed her gentle, silent glide as she passed by and then was gone through the door, carrying out whatever duty had befallen her.

The men were disturbed by a single scream from upstairs. Henry responded at once and leapt up the stairs two and three at a time. David's heart was in his mouth. He was throbbing with anguish yet knew it would be like this and knew he must endure it, for Marie must suffer it far worse than he.

And again time moved on inexorably.

He paced and paced, his hands sweating. He declined drinks offered by the maids, never forgetting his politeness and the courtesy with which he treated his staff.

Later he heard soft footsteps on the stairs and no other sound. He rounded the corner and saw the physician making his way down. Both stopped and stared at each other and David shook with fear and horror. His friend's face had a story to tell and it was a story David was not prepared for, a story that was far more serious than he could ever have imagined.

All Henry could say was "I'm sorry David. I'm sorry."

***

The Haskertons were sitting together looking at nothing in particular, just holding hands. No words, just the sound of their steady breathing. Georgina's tears had long dried. They were downstairs sharing the pain and the absolute quiet with just the flicker of the lights for company.

Upstairs David Grayan cradled baby Charlotte and watched the tiny movement of her lips as she inhaled and then exhaled. What a pretty picture she made. He couldn't really have imagined what a newly born infant might look like but if he'd had any expectations Charlotte would've exceeded them.

Then he looked across to Marie lying in the bed. She was the most beautiful woman he'd ever known and at present she appeared lovelier than ever with her head resting on the pillow. She encapsulated all his dreams, she was love, she was everything, she was his driving force, she was his very heart. And now she had given them a baby daughter to complete the picture. But that picture lay in ruins, torn asunder.

He had been kept from the bedchamber for a few moments until they had cleared up, so he did not witness the last dread struggle and agony when Charlotte arrived and Marie passed from one life to another, or the terrible state it had left her in.

Now he saw only beauty and lifelessness. The merchant's daughter who had captivated him, taken his heart, taken his love and given so much in return, and who shared this most enchanting and fabulous marriage and the boundless love that grew with it. He saw happiness that demons were now tearing apart. He saw joy that death was trampling into the ground.

The room itself was now eerie, as if there were no lights, just a magnificent presence providing dull illumination, and he knew Marie's soul was there to look after him and Charlotte, and he took strength from it.

It was cold there, but he did not feel it. Their baby gave him warmth. Henry had told him the child might not live, so he clung desperately to this cherished treasure and willed her to survive for Marie's sake that she might be his new dream, his new beginning.

He looked again at his wife. He had kissed her when he entered, kissed those loving lips, now incapable of response, yet still felt the passion they always stirred in him. But that passion was freezing over in a way he didn't want to try and explain for he had no understanding of such feelings. His mind was swamped with memories and he felt dizzy as each picture swayed before him, each picture mingling with the one before and the one after, and becoming little more than a blur in which the colour black was getting stronger.

Grace Gandling had handed him Charlotte and now sat in a remote part of the room in quiet contemplation, ready should the baby require assistance and ready should David be overcome by the emotions welling up inside him.

The onrushing tide of hurt was beating at the barriers of his heart and an appalling storm was developing in his head, and all he had to control himself was the small bundle in his arms. What bliss was she, what blessed salvation. Dear Charlotte. He found himself hoping Marie would wake and they could share this sweet ecstasy together, hugging their very own creation, a true family at last.

His hopes were continually dashed, shattered and laid waste. Marie was dead. His love and his whole life, dead. He wanted to cry to relieve the agony but the tears would not come, for they were frozen as Marie's loving heart must be now. He would've given anything to share an embrace and the warmth of her kiss, and he wanted to cry out and scream to her God for one last chance, one more moment with his darling.

He wanted to destroy everything he had built, as Marie's death had destroyed the temple of adoration they had built and worshipped at. He wanted to condemn her God.

His shoulders heaved. He longed to trample down the gardens they had created then realised his wife would not have wanted him to do that, for where else could her spirit roam? If he destroyed her world as her death had ruined his, he could not expect to find her spirit by his side and that he yearned for now more than anything.

Charlotte was the slender path to the future. He must not let her go, he must love her, love her, help her strive for life, and let her light his new dreams which were forming even now in his mind. He simply had to have something to hold on to or the desolation would run him to ground and obliterate him. Now, now, now, he must hold on.

In time the storm abated and he allowed the silence to wash over him as Marie slipped into the darkness engulfing his emotions. She was so beautiful and irreplaceable. He was losing her and he knew her spirit must travel away now it had comforted him and brought him to peace through the maelstrom of despair and heartbreak he had suffered. The tempest was done and the tears came at last. She had helped him through. She had.

Marie's spirit had carried him across the grasping, suffocating waves of fear and deprivation and allowed him to revel in his memories even as his loss had delivered him into the arms of misery.

Slowly he rocked back and forth, cradling their daughter to his bosom, as he sank further and further into the mire of anguish. The tears were gone now. He stared at Marie's white and lifeless face and saw nothing but the exhilaration of their time together. He tasted the nectar of love and wanted to recall her sparkling eyes, her cheery smile, her gay and carefree disposition that had smitten him before they were wed, and which continued to enthral him through their marriage.

All that was gone. Gone forever. Paradise wrecked. It was all gone now. Quite done with. He sat motionless staring at Marie, cuddling his infant, all he had left, and he lifted her and softly kissed her forehead. Then he sat in silence and his own darkness again contemplating the emptiness as the minutes ticked by.

And within the hour poor Charlotte followed her mother to the next life.

Chapter Three

Over a year had passed since Marie Grayan had died. David had carried the tiny coffin that bore Charlotte when mother and daughter were buried.

People came from far and wide to mourn the loss.

His father had written a dreadful letter saying that it was all he deserved for killing his mother, and employed expressions such as an eye for an eye, and that it was to be hoped Marie might rot in hell while David suffered eternal damnation.

It was to be the last time father and son corresponded.

Hester had attended the funeral briefly, for her husband was busy with his mistress and she knew he would be engaged for some time. It was a gesture David appreciated for the act of bravery it was and he hoped she would not be revealed and taken to task for it.

Marie's death was not the only tragedy. Six months later there was an unnecessary death in Westlingstead.

Charles Brankly had been taken ill and was attended by James Parry-Barnard who prescribed an immediate operation. Brankly died on the operating table the young doctor too inexperienced to correct a failing on his own part. Barrenbridge, who had been temporarily away at the time, knew only too well what had happened once he had the chance to question Parry-Barnard and examine the corpse.

In truth Parry-Barnard's diagnosis was partly wrong and he did not have the requisite skills to carry out the surgery. With great reluctance Barrenbridge decided not to disclose the very shortcomings that had cost Mr Brankly his life.

It was left to Brankly's distraught wife and young daughter to run the smallholding they had in the village. It was a task they were used to but now carried it through in sombre mood, uncomplaining despite the additional burden of the work Mr Brankly normally executed. They were a close family and their loss was the greater because of it.

Henry Barrenbridge had otherwise received some welcome news in the form of an appreciable dividend on his investment which he reinvested on Culteney's suggestion. He could see a most princely return on his money in the not too distant future.

David Grayan had an unexpected visitor. He had become reclusive in the year following his loss and rarely entertained, preferring his own company often shut away in his study or walking alone in the grounds, but this visitor cheered his aching soul.

He was astonished when a maid announced his sister. The maid, Ginny Perkins, the one who had kept him company that evening before the sorrowful event, was one of very few of those he employed that he had occasional discourse with, and although it pleased her it saddened her also. He was not the man he was. He was morose, his conversation stilted, his bearing cold and unfeeling. Yes, he was pleasant enough with her, kind as he had always been, interested in her and her life, but there was now the absence of depth and vivacity to his exchanges with her.

David hurried and embraced his sister and smothered her with all the affection he could muster.

"Is anything wrong, is anything wrong?" he asked with great urgency. She leaned back in his arms.

"No my darling brother, well, nothing that need disturb either of us." He let go his grip and led her to a seat, sitting right next to her, his eyes pleading for the answer.

"Charles is away on some business and those who have brought me will not betray me. I know who my loyal servants are. I must tell you David, father is desperately ill and may not recover. I understand that will be of no concern to you. His demise will not bring you back into the family, nor will it release me to see you more often.

"But I thought you should know as nobody else will inform you. However, that is not the sole reason for calling upon you. I am with child and I am worried. I long for the companionship of a child, to have a reason for living, to have something precious to hold and to love, but I am worried about Charles."

"Surely Charles will leave you to bring up your son or daughter as you see fit?"

"I have not told you this, and do so now not because I seek your vengeance which would only make matters worse, I assure you. I plead with you to take no action on my account."

"Hester, Hester, what have you to tell me? What is it?"

"Charles is a monster David. When he perceives I have not been a dutiful wife by his definition he beats me..."

"Beats you? I will kill him, I swear..."

"No David. For my sake take no action I beg you."

Brother and sister held each other, David overcome with concern. Hester continued.

"He can be savage, but the marks are not left where they may be seen. My maid tends my wounds when I bleed. I am most concerned that one of these beatings may harm my child or worse still kill it. You of all people David, will understand my plight."

"Indeed I do, but why have you never mentioned this before?"

"For fear you would confront him. That I could not allow you to do."

"But what can I do now?"

"If need be would you shelter me here? For I would leave him and face the scandal to protect my child."

"Of course my darling Hester, of course."

"You would have your chance to confront him. But I beg you to wait until father has died. Dear David, how often you saved me from beatings at my father's foul hand. How little you could've realised the husband he chose for me would carry on his evil work."

David was stunned by what he had heard.

"You will be welcome and safe here. And you must bring your trusted maid and any other loyal staff. I will look after them and pay them, they need have no fear."

"Oh David, my treasure, bless you for your kindness. I am sorry to impose after your own great sadness. You must miss Marie a great deal."

"Every minute Hester. My whole world has gone. Charlotte would've celebrated her first birthday recently. I often wonder what she would look like today, as I wonder what future she might've enjoyed." His voice trailed away as the memories overtook him and left him bereft.

But Hester had no further time to call upon. She must be away and home well before her husband might return. David understood though it pierced his heart to see her go so soon especially now he had heard her story. He stood on the steps as

28

her coach departed and watched its progress through the estate until it had vanished from view. Even then he continued to watch and persisted with this vigil for several minutes more, observed only by Ginny Perkins on the steps behind him.

She was seeing a broken man, and she found herself aching for his distress. Of course, she had no idea about the news Hester had brought that seemed to afflict him more, but she knew the situation through truth and gossip, that they were not allowed to meet nor correspond. Yet she knew they wrote to each other. What a painful relationship indeed.

Ginny came from a large family who lived on the outskirts of Maidstone to the south-west, and family events were much looked forward to. She met her brothers and sisters when the chance presented itself, which was often, and frequently saw her parents. And here was her master in grief for his loss made all the worse by the severance from his own family and the fact his favourite sister was forbidden to see him.

At that moment he turned and saw her. Flustered, for she had no reason to still be there, she curtsied and fled swiftly indoors, leaving him to return his gaze to the way the coach had gone. In truth he had not a thought for the maid. He did not recognise her and cared nought for her presence. He was still stunned by what Hester had said, and his emptiness in his sad empty world felt like a mighty weight upon his heart.

So many thoughts tangled up in this mind. Poor Hester being abused and beaten, the knowledge she had kept it from him, images of how he believed Charlotte might have looked, Charles Handlen reeling from the blows as he attacked him, Marie comforting her husband after sad news had been imparted as she had done so often....

So many thoughts. And with that he turned slowly and made his weary way indoors and on to his study where he would stay for as long as possible.

***

Roger Culteney was drinking in the *Dover Castle,* a coaching inn at Teynham, and was on his way to Downsland Hall having left London earlier in the day. Sitting alone he was fretting over his friend.

He'd expected him to recover from his bereavement much sooner, but far from recovering David Grayan was sinking faster than a rock thrown into a deep river. Culteney had little understanding of the loss of a dearly loved family member and thought Grayan would soon be looking for a new wife with the promise of children to follow. It was all very black and white and all very simple.

To a man like Roger Culteney the best cure for David's sadness would be to enjoy the company of a woman. Perhaps David had seduced one of his maids. An easy answer for Culteney who had availed himself of the pleasures of a young girl at his father's home. Molly, her name was, and she was a delight being no more than fifteen and unaware of the elation of intimacy. He thought back to that afternoon when he swept his arms around her uniformed waist and she surrendered to his searching lips.

He smiled as the recollections warmed him. She was so innocent. Buxom for one so young, her soft fulsome body had thrilled every sense he possessed. Molly looked appealing in her maid's uniform and even better out of it. There was a maid at Downsland that he believed had caught his friend's eye; maybe he had taken a drink at her well of pleasure, maybe he had.

At Westlingstead Henry Barrenbridge was also thinking about David Grayan but viewing the position in a very different light. It hurt him that as a friend of long standing as well as being a medical man he could arrive at no answers and provide the man with no comfort. Unlike Culteney he had never considered for a second that David had any intention of remarrying, certainly not in the foreseeable future, and knew that the master of Downsland Hall showed no interest in that direction.

It would not have occurred to him that David would not have seduced a maid for he had far too much respect for those who worked for him, and for that matter such action would be to soil Marie's memory, especially if undertaken in the home he had shared with his late wife. Barrenbridge would've been horrified and disgusted to learn of his friend Roger Culteney's solution to despair and sorrow.

30

No, today Henry was deep in thought, worrying himself about David's mental state and the toll it was surely taking on his health. The man looked grey and drawn, pain etched in his face, and he was all too often untidily dressed as if he had given up caring. Henry's own immense despondency was that his friend now rarely set foot in the gardens which Marie had loved. Yes, he walked the estate at length, a solitary figure, head down with eyes that saw so little, but he didn't venture into the gardens he and Marie had designed and created.

He'd asked him about it once.

"I always believed Henry, that Marie's presence would be with me in those gardens but I have not felt her there at all. I know now she does not inhabit them and I am wasting my time looking for her there. Why does she not come to me Henry? Why does she not come and find me?"

Henry was lost for answer.

On his last but one visit to Downsland the physician had once more found the man in his study, surrounded by papers relating to his business interests, his face a blank. He had not even looked up when greeting Henry and had only done so when he politely asked if he would forgive him, but there was considerable work to be completed. Would he mind calling again when perhaps conversation could be had?

He returned as requested one evening but found David difficult to talk with for the man said few words and appeared engrossed in his misery from which there seemed, to Barrenbridge, no immediate chance of escape. He had tried to coax him but his efforts were in vain, and he left soon afterwards and had not been back.

Handing him his hat, cloak and cane, Ginny Perkins had quietly asked after her master. Henry, to his eternal discredit, snapped that it was none of her business, but he at once pulled himself up and apologised to the maid and asked forgiveness for his rudeness.

"He ... he ... he is well my dear, but has a deal on his mind. His work is vital, we all understand that, and he is encumbered by it at present. Look after him my dear. Once again I am sorry for my harsh words."

Ginny curtsied but did not answer. She should not have asked in the first place and he was right to take her to task over it. She was surprised he had apologised.

Roger Culteney's visit had been no different.

Fortified at the inn he'd made his way to Downsland and was left to enjoy his own company while Grayan, having greeted him and nothing more, slunk off sullenly back to his study and to work.

His visitor wandered around downstairs, then, with boredom approaching, strolled across to the gardens and explored them, appreciating the remaining blooms this warm October day without recognising what he was looking at. He recalled how Marie had loved it here and how hard she and David had worked to bring these from imagination to reality.

After a pleasant talk with one of the gardeners he set off again around part of the estate and there found a group of three villagers taking the air and being thrilled by the scenery. He actually frowned on the Grayans' idea of throwing their grounds open to whomsoever might want to walk there but on this occasion stopped to speak to the group. In this he was partly driven by the presence of a comely young woman, presumably the couple's daughter, who returned his polite smile in a manner that pleased him.

Lily Cowans never smiled at him like that in spite of all the time he had known her.

Roger loved the company of women rather more than being with men and the conversation today, being light and gay, made the meeting with this lady all the more agreeable. She smiled often and made knowledgeable comments about Kent and the immediate area around Downsland, and this delighted Roger who was quite certain he was falling in love.

The only drawback was that the gentleman was a basket-weaver and he and his daughter were therefore lowly peasants, the latter not truly worthy of his designs. This gave Culteney a moral dilemma, for she was a prize but in his opinion well below his social status. But surely a passing diversion, a brief amusement could be countenanced? Love could be pithy.

He was content that he had loved the maid Molly but only insofar as his love for her lasted as long as the time they spent together. He'd left the wretched girl with child, damn her, and he'd had to pay for her silence by ensuring she was adequately provided for after the birth. So his love for her had only survived until she revealed her situation.

Noting this family lived nearby, and close to Henry Barrenbridge's lodgings as it turned out, he said he would call, if that was convenient, and maybe select something to purchase. This clearly cheered the father as if he was sensing that more business might be available by this medium. It also brought the first smile of the meeting from his wife, who had expressed a wary disposition thus far, and produced a muted squeal of happiness from the daughter.

Lifted by this encounter he made his way back to the Hall with a spring in his step and found David waiting for him.

"Not that I approve of letting the people in as you do David, but by God I met a family, he's a basket-weaver, who were uncommonly decent and amusing to talk to. Fine daughter too, very fine."

His host did not look up and sat with a scowl on his face while clutching his glass of wine but not drinking.

"David my dear friend, you are such a sad figure, what can I do to improve the situation?"

"I mean no offence Roger, but there is nothing to be done. Please accept me as I am or leave me alone."

"David, no offence taken I assure you, but I am concerned for you. It has been over a year now..."

Grayan bit back at him, almost growling.

"It is an eternity for me Roger. A day, a year, a lifetime. It makes no difference. Marie is dead and I cannot find her spirit here. Ye Gods, I have looked. I rarely visit the graves. What can going there do? Her spirit is not to be found there amongst the dead. Tell me where I may find her and I will go straight to her." He hurled his glass across the room startling his friend.

"I thought she would be here with me every day but she is not. We stood side by side in life. Why not in death?" He rose quickly and trudged from the room. "I'll see you at dinner. I have more work to do."

Roger sat up abruptly, disturbed by the outburst, and then decided he must go and see Barrenbridge urgently. There was enough time this afternoon and he was going to see precious little of David before the evening. He would ride off now.

***

Her father had taught her to read and write and to add up from an early age, and she had then spent some time at school adding further improvements to her education.

Sarah Brankly was presently sitting, pen in hand, diligently making some entries in the ledger her late father had kept. Alongside were some notes she was making. Her mother was preparing some food and every now and then watched her daughter, her face filled with pride. A young woman of business was Sarah. Thank God! She kept the accounts, something her mother could not have contemplated, but then her father had brought her up to be capable of doing precisely that.

How sad that she should be brought to this so soon.

The death had created a vast hole in their lives, but they had made the most of their condition and pressed on as best they could. Sarah really was excellent around their smallholding, the tiny farm that had been the father's world and in to which his wife and their children had been admitted through love. They owed it to him to maintain it.

There was no choice. It was their livelihood and its success was the difference between living and starving. But it had not been a good year. They had striven hard but there had been problems not of their making with the crops, and they had not been able to sell as much as they'd hoped. Sarah was frowning with seriousness and concentration as the figures gave increased evidence of a bad year.

Catherine Brankly had been able to call upon the assistance of her brother Edmund, a widower whose flock had left the nest and who was, quite frankly, at a loose end and rather lonely. He had willingly given his time when he could and his help had been much appreciated. Catherine was thinking about her brother when she spoke to her daughter.

"Sarah, your uncle Edmund is lonely. All six children now gone and him widowed over four years now. What do you think about him coming to live with us? He could sell his home and that might provide something for us all to fall back on when times are hard, and he's been very good when he's been at work here."

"Mama, is this a matter uncle Edmund has raised?"

"No my child, he has not. And I wouldn't suggest it without asking you, and I wouldn't suggest it to him if you disapproved." Sarah was deep in thought.

"What you have said mama, makes good sense." She tried to look as serious as she supposed she should look. A grown woman, a mature lady. Her mother smiled inwardly for Sarah was still her little girl and here she was in adulthood, assumed or otherwise, taking on the role of head of the household with all the authority she could muster. "We should give it thought and not proceed with too much haste."

Ah, the wisdom of so few years! For all that, her mother was proud of her and pleased she was adopting this attitude, but such pride always had to be tinged with sadness for the lass who longed to be wed with no likelihood whatsoever of such joy being achieved.

"Uncle Edmund would be good company for me later when you are married and away." Mrs Brankly forever spoke with sustained optimism about her daughter's future even though she knew it was a hopeless cause. Unfortunately Sarah could see this and realised her mother's words were intended to cheer but not to predict what might be.

"Mama, I will always be here for you. You and papa were always here for me and it is my heartfelt pleasure to serve you and do so with all the love I possess. But I too would welcome uncle Edmund for he is a bright fellow and the best of company. Yet I counsel against a hasty decision. Let us think and talk further."

***

Also thinking very carefully was Thomas Evershen.

He paid no attention to the meagre meal before him. His wife had done well with what little there was available and he ate with enjoyment as he watched his daughter opposite. Clara could bewitch a prince with her beauty. He glanced at his wife. How did we ever create such loveliness when we are so ugly? Clara

35

was eating ravenously but studying her plate so he was able to concentrate his eyes on her vivacious face.

Aye yes, she could bewitch the King himself!

She had bewitched that dandy, that fop at Downsland today. Buy something from me? What would a gentleman, that popinjay, buy from a bumpkin like me? I am a basket-weaver. No strutting peacock would want what I make. But he might want a closer acquaintance with my enchanting daughter, for that is his sole reason for speaking to us. His kind avoid us.

So let us think. He would not marry Clara for all her beauty. So what else might he do? The devil's work I'll be bound. Take his entertainment and take his leave. The devil indeed. No man will use my Clara in such a fashion.

But supposing I allowed him some licence there? Perhaps Clara could keep him waiting with the promise of gifts to come and perhaps I could take some financial advantage in the meantime. He has money, plenty of money and I would not want much. And once Clara has surrendered he would want to keep his secret and that too must be worth some money. I will take her aside and advise her of her duty in this.

She has always listened to me and done my bidding. I have kept her from the greedy hands of men not worthy of her fair splendour and she detests me for it. To permit her to run to the arms of a real gentleman, a man of wealth; why, I should have her blessing! But she must know that she may only encourage him at this stage and I will explain that in detail.

Clara looked up at the end of the meal.

"Papa, eat up for we have finished. Are you not hungry?" He smiled in reply.

Hungry for money, my precious gem, and you must do the family well in that respect.

***

The Haskerton's visits to Downsland were increasingly infrequent these days, for they found poor welcome and even less companionship, and their stays were dogged by David's absences and his unpleasant manner.

In the early days following their daughter's demise they had invited him to their home only to find themselves rebuffed and not always in a courteous style. Hurt by his attitude they assumed he was suffering his bereavement so wholeheartedly that it had washed away his politeness, and they forgave him.

But were they not suffering too? Marie was their daughter and they had lost her as well as their grandchild. Were they not to be comforted in their grief? Over a year gone and there was no reviving David Grayan. He had been utterly destroyed and his remnants left to perish in the Kent countryside where once he shared the sunshine of love and shared his ecstasy with the common people, with his friends and with his new family.

Henry Barrenbridge sat with Roger Culteney and once more discussed the remarkable man who had been their friend, and his fall into the pit of purposelessness that had left him bare, stripped of all the good things he had been. Naked of compassion, feeling, good conscience. Naked of decency, taste and courtesy.

Whereas Barrenbridge was struggling to find answers and was worried sick by Grayan's behaviour, and wanted the intercourse with Culteney to continue lest they stumble on a way forward, his visitor was keen to depart, anxious no doubt to find the alluring basket-weaver's daughter.

And in due course Sir William Grayan died, his passing not mourned by anyone at Downsland Hall.

Chapter Four

The second anniversary of Marie Grayan's death is approaching.

It has been a poor summer with most farmers complaining bitterly about the weather. Too much heavy rain has taken its toll and there have been few warm days for crops and people alike to enjoy.

David Grayan's sister, Hester Handlen, has recently given birth to twin boys and did not need to call upon her brother's hospitality. As she grew with the babes inside her, husband Charles spent an increasing amount of time with his mistress and left Hester alone. There were no more beatings for he was rarely there to administer them, and they socialised together less and less as the time drew nigh.

He took no interest in his sons, or for that matter in his wife, beyond giving instructions the boys were to be raised to be obedient, honest, diligent in their studies and a credit to their parents. It had been decided that Edward, first to appear, was the elder and therefore the heir, and was to thus take priority in all issues. There were nannies but Hester kept her infant children close to her and vowed it would never be any different.

Charles, of course, had other ideas but had not expressed these to his wife. Let her nurture them through infancy and then he would appoint a governess and Hester must then release any grip she presumed to have. He was not going to let her have any influence over Edward and George. She had, for now, done what was required of a dutiful wife and in time she would be expected to have more children, for that was her prime role.

In Kent the atrocious weather had matched the mood of David Grayan.

He had shed private tears when his sister's letter came to proclaim the good news, and how he ached to see her and her lovely boys. He wrote one of his longest letters in which Hester was confident she had noticed a revival of spirit, such were the splendid words he chose. But she could not be sure.

Otherwise Grayan, when seen about the estate, looked as thunderous as the clouds, and his staff avoided him when possible. He had been known to growl noisily when something displeased him and he had shouted reprimands at various people if he believed they were not doing their jobs properly. He even shouted once at his housekeeper, the redoubtable Mrs Forbes, who told him if he did it again she'd be off. He ordered her to pack her things and be gone.

Eleanor Forbes had been at Downsland as a senior maid when the Grayans purchased the property and was confounded if the master was going to speak to her like that, and told him so. He relented at once, apologised profusely and begged her to stay. Downsland functioned well because Mrs Forbes ran a tight ship and was a thoroughly organised person, imposing a strong level of discipline yet in a kind, caring way, something that had attracted the Grayans to her.

They appointed her housekeeper almost at once, the previous incumbent unwilling to serve under the unconventional couple, and she had made a remarkable success of the post. But she did not like the way things were going.

In May she had been required to comfort the distraught Ginny Perkins. David had upbraided her over some shortcoming or other, yelling an objectionable tirade and threatening her with a beating that would 'leave her in pain for days'. This was not the David Grayan they had known, and the occasion was particularly sad for Ginny. She had kept well out of his way ever since but wished she could find a way to relieve his suffering, and knew she could not.

Before last Christmas Roger Culteney, in an impetuous act typical of the man, and with no forethought for the consequences, ran off with the basket-weaver's daughter and married her.

Encouraged by her father he had paid her an immoderate amount of attention determined to reap her fruits, and looked upon the matter as a contest in which he would be the eventual winner.

As soon as his own father heard the news of the marriage Roger was sent for and, in a stormy meeting, found his well of money about to run dry. In this he was unconcerned as he was able to assure his bride he was about to come into a fortune with his investments ready to mature.

Presently they lived in rented accommodation in Whitstable, which Roger hoped was sufficiently distant from her father in Westlingstead. He sold a few of his shares to give them an income of sorts but Clara Culteney rather imagined that in marrying into a wealthy family she would benefit both socially and financially and it was not proceeding in that direction.

Her own home, with servants, was the least of her plans. The elopement had been a gloriously romantic affair in which she deliberately defied her father and thwarted his own scheme to make money from the arrangement. He had not intended her to marry the cad, merely make it advisable for Culteney to part with a small quantity of what Evershen assumed was a fortune.

The marriage was, in truth, not going well with Clara impatient for the trappings of prosperity.

And then, as David had predicted, the major enterprise collapsed with Roger losing all his money. He decided against telling Clara in person, writing her a lengthy letter which he left at their home while she was out, and gathered up his belongings and fled.

Thomas Evershen took his daughter back, whipped her, and set about devising a loathsome design for locating and dealing with the scoundrel, obtaining money the chief objective. He was aware Clara's husband was a friend of David Grayan. Unlike most villagers he detested Grayan and all he represented, believing the man looked down upon them all and graciously provided advantages, such as the school and hospital, so that he might be worshipped.

Yet his expenditure was minuscule, in Evershen's opinion, compared to his mighty wealth. Could Grayan be persuaded to find Culteney and perhaps even settle a debt for poor Clara? If Grayan paid up an appreciable amount would it be necessary to pursue the errant husband? Probably not.

His daughter needed some compensation for her loss, her appalling treatment, and as her father he should receive any monies forthcoming.

He would find a way of tackling Grayan.

Coming to terms with a different loss was the physician, Henry Barrenbridge. He'd been all but ruined when the firm Culteney had promoted collapsed. He'd been on the verge of proposing to his landlady but had withdrawn in the knowledge he now had no means of supporting her. It was one more worry. There were just his earnings from the practice at present and it would take a long while to rebuild his resources.

With a heavy heart he had abandoned trying to help his friend, thinking that David might be so far into his hopeless descent that his demise might be unstoppable. He visited Downsland on occasions but was barely regarded as a friend, more an inconvenience. Was David hoping his own death might reunite him with Marie? He had constantly complained to Henry in the early months that he could not locate her spirit close to his side, nor find it in the gardens she loved, nor in the estate where they had walked and worked together. Barrenbridge was more concerned for his health than ever before, and could recognise all the signs of a man in self-inflicted decline. David was not eating properly, was too heavily engaged in his businesses, fretting over accounts and orders, and pining endlessly for a love lost.

It was a bad mixture. The man was exhausting himself.

The Haskerton's had fared no better in the efforts to come to their son-in-law's aid, and during the summer had regrettably reached the conclusion that writing was all they had left to offer, completely discarding any hopes of seeing David. Their sorrow was all the worse for it was their own daughter who had perished and their torment was magnified by David's behaviour, and their grieving made no less bearable.

By themselves they had come to terms with the tragedy and cherished happy memories of the Grayans and agreeable times spent altogether at Downsland Hall, memories that had rendered them sad for many a month after the death. They frequently travelled to the graves of Marie and their grandchild Charlotte and found paying their respects consoling where in the early days the visits had merely served to enhance their misery.

But for David Grayan there appeared to be no merciful release with the passage of time, his own misery compounded day by day.

***

Sarah Brankly looked about her and around all she could see of her part of the North Downs.

For once it was a good enough day and the weather was being kind. It was too late to help some of the crops and she felt nature was laughing in her face, smirking at the trouble it had caused. She had another reason to be annoyed and resentful.

Her uncle Edmund had indeed moved in with them and done so shortly after Christmas when there was snow upon the ground and the nights were freezing. She had agreed to the plan without reluctance but was now regretting her decision. By March he had sold his own modest cottage and now they had money to offset a poor year on the smallholding and maintain a good standard of living.

But it had made them beholden to him and Sarah did not like that.

In fact, he was prone to remind them periodically of their good fortune, emphasising the difference his presence made to their lives, to which Sarah's mother would heartily agree and bless him for all he had done, praising him for his selflessness. He had gradually taken on the role of head of the household and therefore also controlled work carried out on their tiny farm.

When he began disallowing Sarah to do certain tasks she had always completed she became angry, and her mother was required to step in to prevent an altercation. Her mother had taken to criticising her behaviour, often in front of Edmund, and had threatened strong action on two occasions, warning her against further transgression. Edmund had nodded approval, once adding rather unnecessarily that his own children had been discouraged from repeated bad behaviour by painful means.

The last straw was when, with her mother's permission, he took over the ledger and, having studied her work, suggested she had not produced her accounts with accuracy and it was a good job he was able to correct them. She could not look to her mother for support and Edmund was counting on that, for Mrs Brankly had never had any dealings with them and knew nothing about them. But Sarah knew they were accurate.

She had lost a vital part of her life, her world, and she was far from happy. He was supplanting her intentionally and in her mother's eyes he could do no wrong. How she missed her dear beloved father. He would not have stood for this.

One evening, alone in her room with nothing to do, she hatched a scheme, a plan she had only half-heartedly aired about two years before. At the time she had dismissed it and it was long forgotten, for her father was still alive and her world was complete, and she was busy about the smallholding in so many ways. She was essential to it. Now she was only needed to do whatever Edmund bid, menial responsibilities of no consequence, and it bored her and irritated her, nothing she did being of any value.

She knew what she must do.

Sarah Brankly would seek employment at Downsland Hall. But what terrible stories had emerged since Mrs Grayan had died two years ago! Mr Grayan was now a monster, a dark, evil person who stomped around Hall and grounds, haunting it like a malignant ghost, frightening all who worked there.

And yet, and yet .... he had been regarded as a remarkable and learned man with many superior ideas, a true philanthropist who had done so much for Westlingstead and all the settlements around, and provided much needed employment for so many. She had mourned her father but with the passage of time she had coped with her loss. Surely Mr Grayan must be over the worst and not the black animal people painted.

Her dear friend Ginny Perkins had been a maid there for years and had always said how kind and friendly he was. He had revolutionary beliefs too! Men and women as equals? But hadn't he demonstrated that by the way he and Mrs Grayan lived and worked together, very much equals? After all, they often worked alongside those they employed. And her friend Agnes Byrne had been able to follow her own course and work in the grounds where she loved her life. The Grayans had made that all possible. Revolutionary definitely.

Agnes, she knew, had an understanding with fellow woodsman Jed Maxton, a young lad from Lenham who had proposed, so Agnes said, while they were chopping down an old dead tree. They should be married next spring.

Ginny spoke less of her master these days, discreetly avoiding awkward conversation on the subject, but was clearly moved by

Mr Grayan's plight. Agnes tended to join in the gossip and tittle-tattle and thought him a sinister person. Ginny was older and wiser and tried to remember the numerous good things about the man rather than pay heed to rumour and story-telling. She had kept him company the evening before his wife died, and how convivial it had all been given the nervous state he was in.

She was quite upset by his behaviour but attempted to excuse him, yet was still perplexed over his outburst at her, so full of bile and venom, so unlike the man he once was. She granted him her silent forgiveness, for she felt it was the least she could do.

Sarah considered her situation and weighed up the best means of going about her undertaking. Two years ago she would've walked up to Downsland Hall and asked to see master or mistress, but there was a bleak cloud shrouding the place regardless of whether she preferred to think well of Grayan or no. Ginny said he spent innumerable hours in his study, was now and again seen walking the grounds, and only rode out when he had business to transact or one of his enterprises required attention.

Nowadays his only visitors, and rare ones at that, were his associates in commerce and trade, and customers who needed to be impressed with a stay at his fine house. Even then, Ginny had said, he ensured they were well entertained but he was aloof and engaged only in modest conversation, retreating to his study as soon as they departed. She had not been convinced that all those whose business he sought were as influenced by the man as they should've been, and that could be harmful to his trading prospects.

The more thought Sarah gave the matter the more assured she became that Ginny was the medium by which she might hope to access Grayan himself. She resolved to call upon her friend at Downsland on the morrow. First she would speak to her mother but do so when they were alone.

The next day Edmund was busying himself first thing in the morning, trying to appear important and in Sarah's eyes failing, as he fussed here and there, gave his niece her orders, pretended to make entries in the ledger and finally took himself to the pig shed. Sarah sighed with relief.

She was doing the washing with her mother.

"Mama, I wish to seek employment at Downsland. Uncle Edmund is managing quite well here and is very good company for you, and I am required less and less other than by you, my dear mama. I am given to understand there may a vacancy. Maids leave because they marry and also because they cannot abide the master.

"I would have as good a chance as anyone. The money would be very helpful as I could give some to you and save a small amount for my future, whatever that may be. There is bound to be a post spare...."

"Sarah, I need you as you realise full well. Look, we are doing the washing. Then we must bake, and then we must sweep the house. My brother is very capable and can manage the smallholding quite well. There is a place for you here, my darling, and I would miss you so very much." Sarah crossed the floor and hugged her mother, but was not to be deflected.

"Mama, I would come and see you often. It may be possible for me to live here and attend the Hall for my duties there..."

"Oh what nonsense child. Walk there and back and work yourself to a standstill in between, and come home to assist me? What folly."

"It is not folly. I am young and strong and able and have need of more to occupy me, a desire to learn and must have a new quest to satisfy my yearning for achievements."

"Sarah, no more of this. You will stay here where you are loved and help me as you do now."

"What's all this then?" Neither woman had seen Edmund enter and his loud interjection took them by surprise.

"It is nothing dear brother. Nothing at all."

"Uncle, I wish to gain employment as a maid at Downsland and mama will not permit it."

"Hold your tongue Miss. This is not an issue for your uncle."

"Tell me anyway," Edmund commanded as he took a seat at the long table where they ate their meals. Mrs Brankly looked hurt but decided against intervening. There was no point for Edmund would obviously side with her and put Sarah in her place. There was little to worry about.

However, the intercourse did not work out as she'd hoped, for much to her surprise Edmund was delighted and, rising from his seat, he gave his wholehearted support for Sarah's exercise.

"Splendid idea Sarah. Capital, capital. Attend to it as soon as you please and I wish you every good fortune. Of course you must stay at Downsland; your mother is right, you cannot walk to and fro for each duty. I am informed maids are often in demand as they cannot work with that unpleasant oaf." He laughed with contempt, an empty laugh which Sarah recognised as evidence his support was not what it seemed on the surface.

Nonetheless she felt she had gained what she wanted and would go to Downsland later. Her mother was smiling and that confirmed her view that Edmund was not promoting her idea at all and that her mother thought she had won.

"I shall go when I have finished helping mama with the chores and we have had some food."

"Yes that's right m'dear. You go and we will see you tonight on your return. By the by, as you are not yet of age your earnings, assuming your appointment is granted, will come to us, you do know that?" Edmund had cut right through her and her mother's smile of satisfaction did not improve her temper. But she controlled herself.

"Yes of course Uncle. I had hoped a little might be mine to save, but I will forego it if you so decide."

"That's it m'dear. All your money will come to us if you please, and if you are a good child I will make a gift of a few coins now and then."

His sinister and patronising comments pained Sarah for she was not aware of this aspect of the man, and she was rapidly concluding that she might easily hate him, that he was now revealed as a repugnant person who had poisoned her life and was trying to do so with her relationship with her mother. It hardened her tenacity. She would get this job, she would.

But it would not be at the expense of her love for her mama.

***

"Ginny I ask for no more than five minutes with the master."

46

"Sarah, I will speak to Mrs Forbes and commend you. Another maid left last week and I am sure Mrs Forbes will appoint you. The master is not involved."

"I would like to see him for I have much to impress him with, as you know...."

"Sarah, Sarah, you want to be a maid, that is all. Mrs Forbes sees the maids."

"Ginny would you not try for me?"

"If he dismissed the notion Sarah, then Mrs Forbes might not be able to take you on, don't you see?"

"I will take that chance. Please help me Ginny. Please."

Sarah's forceful presentation was persuading her friend but against her better judgement.

"This man is not the monster people say he is, surely?"

"I believe he is not Sarah, but he is also not the man he was and will not look kindly upon my intervention."

"Are you afraid Ginny?"

"Not afraid, but as concerned for you as for myself. He is not a man to be interrupted by trivial matters, if indeed he ever was."

"He will not think me trivial."

When her friend arrived at Downsland unannounced Ginny Perkins had been granted half an hour to speak with Sarah and the two had repaired to her room. Being a senior maid she had a second floor room with a pleasant enough outlook across the vegetable garden to the woodlands beyond. The Grayans took the welfare of their staff to heart ensuring all rooms were spacious, comfortable and well furnished, with senior maids granted their own rooms which featured views not normally afforded elsewhere to mere servants.

Once you had risen to higher seniority you might get a room with a view over the gardens, and the housekeeper, Mrs Forbes, had accommodation at the front of the building from where she could see the pick of the summer and autumn blooms. Sarah knew that if successful gaining employment she would have to share and probably have no view whatsoever.

Now Ginny looked at her with a glance of equal disbelief and admiration. Several years younger than herself she possessed an arrogance that did not actually seem misplaced, and yet it gave her a strength of character that Ginny knew she would need if

47

ever she came face to face with the master. Not think her trivial? Why no, but what *would* he think of her? She almost wanted to discover! But it was out of the question.

"I do not think you trivial, but you must understand dear Sarah, Mr Grayan simply does not have time for minor matters and may reject you out of hand."

"Let's go now!" Ginny shuddered at the thought of such a project.

"Why Sarah, it's impossible. Now stop being foolish."

"Foolish I am not. I am determined. Oh please help me Ginny, please, please."

Her pleading was melting Ginny's doggedness, but she hadn't quite surrendered.

"And what if I am dismissed on the spot? How would you feel if he beat me?"

"He can beat me in your place, I shall insist upon it. And I will not allow him to dismiss you."

Ginny could not help but laugh. The folly of youth. Had she been like that when young? She could not recall but perhaps she had.

"Yes, I will take you. You have won me over, and if necessary he can beat us both!"

And so they made their way towards his study, a place where they were forbidden unless on a mission of urgency connected directly with the master, a place some staff felt was a cauldron of evil populated by pixies and elves bent on mischief, such was the reputation of David Grayan when he was shut away there.

Heart pounding Ginny knocked firmly at the door.

"Enter." A bellowed cry thrust its way through the solid door and shook both girls. Gingerly they made their way inside and Sarah had her first look at Grayan. He was hunched over a desk full of papers that were in such disarray she was sure they must fall at any moment, and wished she did not cause their cascade by virtue of a sudden movement. He was unshaven, his collar undone, his hair uncombed. He had the appearance of having dressed in haste.

"Yes?" he growled noisily as if angered by the interruption, which Ginny presumed he probably was.

48

"Sir, if you please sir. May I introduce my friend Sarah Brankly, also of Westlingstead, who seeks work as a maid and begs for a few moments of your time. I'm sorry sir. I know I shouldn't be here and will accept the consequences, and we will leave upon the instant...." Her voice trailed away as he looked up with such a cold and sneering expression that Ginny might have been driven from the room without further words. It was fearsome.

But his face softened as he returned to his papers, and his voice softened too, and became one of resignation rather than annoyance.

"I do not appoint maids. See the housekeeper Ginny. Go now." It was Sarah who spoke in response.

"I wish to see *you* sir. I will not keep you. I have much to offer as I will explain and would like the honour of being appointed by you. I know of you as a remarkable man and know you will appreciate what I have to say." She felt nowhere near as brave as she sounded, and Ginny was sufficiently bemused to be ready to run from the study. Sarah continued. "It is a pleasure to meet you sir. I have heard so many good things about you. The privilege is mine."

David Grayan sat back in his chair and took in the sight before him.

"Speak girl, then be gone. Go to my housekeeper. *Speak.* Let me hear what you have to say and be quick. I have no time for this, but you have found me in good humour and I will listen." Ginny was far from convinced that the words 'good humour' could be applied to the master with all reasonableness, and was all but reduced to tears in fear.

If Sarah was of a similar disposition she showed no trepidation, moving to the front of his desk with a brisk step.

"I have run a smallholding with my parents. When my father died I took over all responsibilities and have worked with animals, crops and fruit alike, made the accounts and conducted all matters of business and money and correspondence. I wish to better myself and know by your reputation sir, that you will encourage those who wish to improve themselves. I can read and write and enjoy books especially those that have assisted my education.

"Now my widowed uncle has now moved in with us and, with my mother's agreement, runs the farm.

"They are happy for me to come to you now I have less to do at home. I will offer you this, sir.

I will work as a maid here for two weeks without pay so you can judge me. I ask only accommodation and food. If I prove satisfactory you may decide to retain me, otherwise I shall leave when required to do so."

This revelation shocked Ginny who stood open-mouthed a few paces behind Sarah. Grayan looked up again. His anger, if it had been present, had clearly subsided, and his expression had a warmth about it Sarah noticed, whereas Ginny, still nervous, did not. He reached forward and grabbed a piece of paper from the desk and waved it at Sarah.

"Do you know a man named Evershen?" He made it sound like an accusation rather than a question. "Lives in Westlingstead."

"Yes sir, that is I am acquainted with him. He is a basket-weaver and I have purchased goods from him, and occasionally he buys food from our farm."

"He has a daughter, Clara?"

"Yes sir. She attended the school with me, but I do not know her well. I have not seen her for some while and assume she has married and moved away."

Waving the paper in the air he continued.

"According to Evershen she eloped with a friend of mine, Culteney, married him and he has now deserted her, Evershen seeking redress on her behalf now she is back home in your village. Here, read this letter and tell me how I should respond." He thrust it forward and Sarah accepted it with alacrity, stepping back and studying it. The main part read as follows:

'*My daughter is home with her family devastated by the behaviour of a man you may consider to be a good friend. Her reputation is in shreds. She is a degraded woman. I am certain you cannot support Mr Culteney.*

Therefore if you have any knowledge of his whereabouts I would be grateful of any intelligence you may be able to pass to me. I believe my daughter is entitled to a reasonable settlement

50

and I intend pursuing that on her behalf. If I cannot trace this deplorable man my poor daughter will face destitution and utter ruin. I think a payment of some sort is due, and I trust you would not wish a friend to treat a woman so poorly and escape unpunished.

I appeal to your goodness, your renowned integrity, to help me correct to some small degree the appalling wrong inflicted on my innocent daughter, and permit me to take whatever measures are necessary to find and deal with Mr Culteney.'

Sarah read the whole letter twice and made up her mind.

"Sir, I believe he is asking you for the money. He hopes you will see it as a matter of honour and settle accordingly. As Clara is not of age I imagine any money you send will go directly to Mr Evershen and that may be his intention. I would not have written the letter in this fashion and I believe he has unintentionally showed his hand, not the hand of a gentleman.

"I would reply that, regardless of whether or not I consider Mr Culteney a friend, his behaviour is not my responsibility and that Mr Evershen must continue his search elsewhere. If you know where Mr Culteney is sir, and he is a true friend, then you may wish to pass the address to Mr Evershen. Equally you may wish to keep the fact from this man."

Shaking visibly, her heart throbbing in her chest, she handed the paper back. He had not removed his eyes from her face and now, quite suddenly, he roared with laughter and rocked back in his chair.

"Miss Brankly, you have it right. I am sure you have it right. Go and see Mrs Forbes and ask for your job; tell her I commend you. And you will not work for me for nothing. You will be paid from the day you start." His laughter subsided but she noticed a bright glint in his eyes, eyes that at once left her face and stared at a bewildered Ginny just behind her.

"Ginny Perkins. You have been disobedient. You are forbidden to come here as you know. And to have the impertinence to bring a stranger into my home and into my private quarters. Intolerable." Then he laughed again just as Ginny was about to faint, overwhelmed by all that was happening and now by a stern reprimand. Sarah turned. Her friend, being of small stature, looked like a frightened child fearing everything terrible that might befall her by way of punishment.

"But I forgive you Ginny, I forgive you. I remember the evening my wife died and you kindly sat and talked to me when I was in such a state over the birth. Yes, kindness indeed. Bless you for that. And I also know you are one of a handful who do not think me a madman and ogre.

"Yes, you might be surprised, but I keep my ear deep to the ground. I know what goes on and what is said. You defend me and I am grateful. Bless you for that too. On this occasion my gratitude to you has saved you from dismissal, but I must also tell you that I do not know what we would do without you. Best not to find out, eh?" His voice had become a hoarse whisper, but there was gentleness and compassion in his words, and he smiled with such grace and warmth that both girls were moved.

"Go now. Go to Mrs Forbes. As a new maid, Miss Brankly, you will be permitted nowhere near me. Remember that." His smile had vanished and his head was down, once more scrutinizing his mass of papers. The girls retreated with haste and sought out the housekeeper, Ginny more than relieved she had survived the encounter, Sarah as happy as anyone could be.

A new chapter of her life was opening and she would use it as a stepping stone to whatever good might come of it in the times ahead.

Chapter Five

It is November. After a miserable summer the weather relented during the autumn to provide some delightful days and acceptable evenings but now the first chill of winter is upon Kent. Sarah has settled into her new post at Downsland Hall and shares a room with another new maid, Esther Hammond. They have become good friends.

Her mother was far from pleased when she arrived home that day two months ago and announced with great pride that she had seen Mr Grayan himself and he had appointed her. She could not keep a smile from her lips which only served to infuriate her mother more. Edmund had approved but consoled his sister by saying they would now be able to afford someone to assist with the household chores.

And so it was that Clara Evershen, using her maiden name, found employment there on three days a week. Sarah liked to think that she was, in effect, paying the girl's wages bearing in mind what she knew of the poor girl's circumstances. Unbeknown to Sarah Mr Evershen had sworn dreadful oaths of vengeance when he received Grayan's reply and had resolved to pursue Culteney to the ends of the earth, and despatch David Grayan along the way if he possibly could.

He would find a way of dealing with the master of Downsland Hall.

In the meantime Roger Culteney has paid a visit to Grayan at the invitation of the latter. He has taken some tracking down but was easily persuaded to call, being without funds and disowned by his father and, presumably, under an obligation to his estranged wife.

Hester Handlen dotes on her twin boys. They are growing and she loves them dearly. Her husband is not yet any bother to them, preferring to spend most of his time with either mistress, he now having secured a second as a means of avoiding boredom. Hester is not aware that their money is fast running out.

The Haskertons write occasionally to David and receive short, simple replies, but that is their only contact, and they are saddened by the situation.

The medical practice thrives, which helps restore some of Henry Barrenbridge's coffers, but Judith Pearland is restless wishing she could qualify as a physician and knowing such progress unlikely. She is not assisted by the attitude of some villagers who cannot accept she is as capable as anyone of tending to their health. James Parry-Barnard is, in contrast, sought after, often at the expense of Pearland but she knows he is not as proficient as she is. It is very frustrating.

But shortly she will have her chance.

***

Sarah had written to Clara expressing her joy at hearing she was helping her mother and hoped she was happy there. The exercise had a two-fold purpose, for its main reason was genuine and clear, but it was also written with the expectation that Clara might reveal more of her recent past.

Her reply was read with eager eyes but proved disappointing. Sarah knew from her mother that Clara's absence for some months had been explained by claiming she gone away to help a relative in Ramsgate and was therefore using her maiden name, Evershen, with no suggestion of an elopement and marriage being made. Her letter was interesting enough and proposed a meeting of the two at some point in the near future. Sarah decided that might be a more productive medium to obtaining information.

What had added entertainment and fuel to Sarah's fertile mind was that Roger Culteney had stayed at Downsland for four days earlier. She had glimpsed him more than once and concluded that poor Clara was well rid of him, for he certainly had no attractive features either physically or in manners, the latter being truly demonstrated when, near to where Sarah was polishing, he spoke abruptly and harshly to Ginny giving her a smart slap on her rear as she turned to leave.

"That was despicable," she said to her friend later in the day. "You should report him."

"Sarah, that will not do. Put such ideas from your mind or you will lose your post. He is a guest of the master and I overstepped the mark, he was right to reproach me, I had not done my duties correctly, to his liking. We do not report guests to anyone. You're in service now so learn quickly."

"I was upset for you dear Ginny. There is a man I would not wish to marry or wish upon my worst enemy."

"There are many like him Sarah, believe me. I do not gossip but I have heard he may have mistreated a woman he had an understanding with, but I will not share the rumours that are usually attached to the story. Just remember, hold your tongue and know you are a better person."

Sarah did not need to hear the rumours.

Poor Clara, seduced and ruined, her chances of a good match lost forever.

Culteney had been involved in one very lengthy meeting with Grayan during his stay, and there had been raised voices sufficient for servants to hear, heated arguments indeed. Sarah did not doubt that the visitor was suffering for his vices but was unaware he was also being trampled into the ground about his failed investment which had brought Barrenbridge close to ruination.

The outcome of the meeting was that Grayan told Culteney to see Evershen, apologise, and suggest an amount in final settlement. Grayan would underwrite this scheme if Evershen was never made aware of it, and would give Culteney a single payment himself, enough to enable him to live far away from Kent and never return to the county. He could then make his peace with his father and possibly return home.

It took two full days, and further arguments before he agreed and on the final day called on Evershen. A deal was struck, so he told Grayan, and the payments were arranged. But he had been nowhere near Evershen and had betrayed his loyal friend for personal gain hoping to pocket all the monies to be paid.

***

As November drew towards its close the fuller effects of winter were being felt across the county. On this particular day high winds had presented problems in the estate and one young tree now hung precariously over the main drive, its main trunk broken, its upper branches snapped.

Henry Jennings and Jed Maxton were struggling in the wind to which scything rain had been added, an unbearable combination, and making little headway in their efforts to cut away the offending elements before they could tackle the trunk. Jed had climbed up to saw away one overhanging branch when he lost his footing. As he slipped sideways the saw tore along his arm and then the branch, to which he was now clinging, gave way and he crashed to the ground, the piece he was cutting falling on top of him. Henry dashed over and lifted the bough, pulling off his coat to wrap around Jed's bleeding arm. He looked around him and caught sight of Nathanial Browers the other side of the track and bellowed with all the might he could muster, but his voice was carried away by the wind in the opposite direction.

In despair Henry believed his only chance was to leave Jed and go to Nathanial so that help might be summoned, but before he could set off a rider appeared at his side and leapt from the saddle.

"Praise be, it's the master," cried Henry, who followed Grayan to Jed's side and saw the man throw his own cloak over the prostrate figure.

"Stay and try and stem that bleeding Henry. I'll ride to the house and send back a carriage to take him to the physician. I fancy there is no point getting Barrenbridge here; Jed may need surgery and they have all the medicine they need at the hospital. I'll get Nathanial to assist you."

With that he mounted and rode across to the other groundsman who promptly raced over to Henry.

The carriage was there in minutes and the men gently lifted the stricken Jed inside, departure being immediate with Grayan riding alongside. Both Henry and Nathanial were with Jed on their master's orders and doing their very best to control the bleeding and make the young man comfortable. He was no longer screeching in pain, issuing strange squealing noises instead, and he was not responding to any words that were said. Henry thought he might die at any moment.

***

The weather did not inconvenience Thomas Evershen busy in his workshop, although he cursed it for the howling noise the wind produced, as he cursed the rain that was dripping through the roof to one side. It did not stop him working and he had work to attend to.

Never out of his mind was the vexed question of Clara's downfall and how he might extract money from either Culteney or Grayan. He was making some egg baskets to fulfil an order for a farmer near Doddington but he was relying heavily on instinct in his efforts as his mind was pounding with raw anger and frustration.

He'd paid out some precious money in pursuit of information about Culteney but he might just as well have thrown it in the river. At least Clara, in her desolation, had some employment and was bringing him a small income. The right course to money had to be taken with Grayan. It was the only way open to him. But how?

As his twisted, bitter mind wrestled with the dilemma a vision came to him. It could be of no value yet it would not release its grip on his ruminations. Eventually he sat back and pondered this new development. Mrs Brankly's daughter worked at Downsland now, and she and Clara knew each other and had recently corresponded. Could that be a possible route to anything that might bring money from David Grayan?

His mind eased. Nothing would come to him, but give it time, give it time. Nurture it and give it time and something may grow. With that he relaxed, smiled wickedly, and returned to the half made basket in front of him. He felt better. It was as if he had unravelled a great mystery that had baffled the cleverest of men and it pleased him, and it enabled him to concentrate on his work, happy in the knowledge the answer would come to him. In such a condition he paid no heed to the sound of a coach rushing past.

***

David Grayan had ridden on ahead and dismounted by the hospital. He was dismayed to discover Barrenbridge had gone to

57

Folkestone and Parry-Barnard was attending upon a wealthy private patient in Hawkhurst. Judith Pearland greeted him, gave him the news and told him to bring Jed straight to the room they used for operations. Grace Gandling was on duty and summoned at once, Pearland giving her a string of orders which she seemed to absorb without difficulty. Grayan watched this fevered activity with a sense of despair and fear of time being wasted rushing over him.

"Who can I send for? Where is another doctor?" he shouted. Judith Pearland stood before him and placed her hands on her hips.

"I am a doctor all but qualified. If Jed is as bad as you say there is no time to go elsewhere. Now mind out of my way and let us prepare. If you wish to be useful sir, please help nurse Gandling." And with that she was gone leaving Grayan open mouthed.

Nevertheless he did help Gandling and then the coach drew up and Jed was brought in, barely conscious.

"I want one man to accompany us and offer whatever assistance he may; the rest please wait out here. There is no more time to lose." David Grayan stepped forward to answer Pearland's call and the door was closed behind him as she began examining the patient. He made to ask a question but was prevented by a raised hand. "Please do not speak, just do as I ask sir."

***

News of the accident had spread like a rampant disease and came to the ears of Agnes Byrne, Jed's intended, who screamed once and then fainted.

Sarah Brankly was nearby and rushed to her aid, lifting the girl bodily in her arms and conveying her to a couch. Her strength impressed Esther Hammond who had been close and who also ran to help.

"You're so strong Sarah...."

"I am used to lifting animals Esther, and Agnes is a young lady, a light weight I assure you. Now get some water, some to drink, some to wash with, a towel if you please, and ask Mrs Forbes for some smelling salts." Esther was away like the wind.

Gradually Agnes revived and was tended by the girls under Eleanor Forbes's direction.

"Jed, Jed, Jed," she wailed, "Is there any news? How will we hear? I must go to him, I must go, please help me, I must go...." And the tears came in floods as Sarah clasped her to her bosom and hugged her tight.

"We will hear soon enough. The hospital is too far. The master is with him and will send word you may be sure...."

"No, no, I must go to him. Please let me have a horse, please, please, please. Oh for pities sake please let me go..." And again the agony besieged her and tore her apart.

Mrs Forbes spoke, quietly but with tender firmness.

"Agnes you may go when we hear. You are in no fit state to ride and the weather is atrocious. You must do as I say. There is nothing you can do for Jed. He is in the right hands in the right place and they will do their best for him. Has not Dr Barrenbridge the highest reputation as a surgeon? Leave matters to him, I beg you. We all feel for you Agnes, and we understand your passion in this, but I beg you to stay in our care."

Agnes wept bitter tears but nestled closer to Sarah in a gesture of surrender. What Mrs Forbes had said was correct, as she knew full well, but she loved Jed more than life itself. He was everything to her and she could not bear to lose him now. He was her very being, he was the air that filled her lungs, he was the joy that filled her heart, she could not lose him now, not this most wonderful of men. How badly might he have been hurt? She could not stop the pain rising within her and hammering all her senses, and more tears flowed as she cried out in helpless angst.

The weather showed no signs of easing, the rain beating on the windows, driven there by a reckless wind. There was no silence to be had anywhere. Another maid appeared.

"Beg pardon ma'am, but there's a lady to see master. I've told her he's not at home but she's asked to wait."

"Did you tell her the master might return?" Mrs Forbes sounded annoyed.

"Yes ma'am I did. Did I do wrong?"

"No Nancy, not at all. I'll come and see her. Take me now. What name did she give?"

"Miss Cowans ma'am. Miss Lily Cowans."

***

The patient was lying still and quiet and being subjected to a very thorough examination. There was grave intensity with which the examination was being executed, ensuring that everything that might require attention was noted and that anything that did not was dismissed.

Once the detailed scrutiny had been completed the patient was able to rise and dress. She invited her physician to join her for tea. The diagnosis had been simple. There was nothing wrong with her but she was a wealthy woman, so James Parry-Barnard prescribed a harmless medicine for a non-existent minor ailment which he hid with words that might have been Latin but weren't.

Lady Fitzgower was overjoyed especially when he offered to return two weeks later to ensure her problem had cleared up. Harriet Fitzgower was advancing in years yet still possessed the magic to entice a man, particularly one who was himself from a fairly wealthy family of status, as Parry-Barnard was. Her eyes had betrayed her. They twinkled for him and teased him.

Now they were taking tea. He noted her remarkable good looks having already noted that she owned gifts that a man might find entertaining and gratifying. The elder daughter of a Duke and Duchess, Lady Fitzgower remained unwed which surprised Parry-Barnard but gave him a degree of hope that he realised might be misplaced.

Unbeknown to him she had been disappointed by a man he knew well, David Grayan. She had never loved him but knew that the uniting of the two great families was of primary importance. Besides, he was a strong, healthy and handsome man who, while he had no other obvious appeal to her, would ensure her children were of fine sturdy constitution, thus guaranteeing the family line would be in secure hands. She could not understand why he should abandon her for a merchant's daughter, someone without position, over something so ridiculous as love, and allow himself to be disinherited. She was well rid of him.

But other suitors had there been none.

Now there was this rather fetching doctor. An excellent background and standing that might tempt her parents to agree a match. Lord Parry-Barnard was known to her father and although, as the third son, James would not inherit the title he was still a good prospect. And he appeared to be a very good doctor.

She might not have thought so if she had realised James Parry-Barnard had lied about his qualifications and should not have been anywhere near her. But he was tired of the practice at Westlingstead, tired of waiting for the chance to qualify, and wanted to move up in society. Lady Fitzgower represented that opportunity.

He should not have been engaging private clients. Henry Barrenbridge frowned upon it but needed his presence greatly so permitted a certain leeway provided it did not interfere with the arrangements at the hospital. With Barrenbridge away he should not have left Westlingstead but Lady Fitzgower's urgent summons had suggested she was all but at death's door.

They had met when James's father had recommended his son to the Duchess over another minor ailment, easily remedied, and he had secured the position of their physician. He was encouraged by a grateful Duke to add rather more to his bill than he'd intended and realised he was upon the ladder of success.

***

"*Agnes, Agnes, Agnes,*" cried Esther as she dashed along the corridor. "Come quick, come quick. The master has sent the coach to bring you to the hospital. Jed is as well as might be expected. *Oh come quick, the coach awaits.*"

A breathless Nathanial Browers arrived to urge immediate action.

"Oh Nathanial, has Dr Barrenbridge saved him?" Agnes pleaded as she grabbed her things and was handed a cloak by Sarah. Nathanial was cautious.

61

"Time will tell, young missy. He has much recovering to do. I cannot say in all conscience."

"I am ready. Sarah, will you not come with me?"

"I ... I ... I ... I am not sure I am permitted .... Yes, I will come. I will find a cloak."

Esther was awake to necessity and had fetched a cloak in no time, and the two girls hurried to the front where the coach was waiting. The weather attacked them from all sides, the rain soaking them, the wind chopping them about. They climbed aboard and the coach was under way.

"Oh Sarah, Sarah. I knew Dr Barrenbridge would save him. But am I wrong to hope he may recover?"

"He is an excellent physician and surgeon, Agnes, but you should prepare yourself. We do not know what has happened. He may not be well enough...."

"I am certain he is. He cannot desert me now. I will not allow it. Please dearest love, be strong for I am coming, I am coming."

The journey seemed long and the ride bumpy and uncomfortable, not that the latter consideration was of concern to the girls. Agnes was beginning to wonder what she might find. Would Jed be crippled and maybe badly so? She would still love him; that would never change, in fact she might love him more if that were possible. The story they had been told was that the saw sliced through his arm and the branch had landed atop him when he fell, so he might have lost his arm and suffered broken bones. It did not paint a pretty picture in the girl's mind and she started to fret and suddenly clung to Sarah almost with violence.

Sarah knew only too well the torture she must be enduring as she thought back to that day when Parry-Barnard had fought to save her father. Perhaps he was assisting Dr Barrenbridge with Jed and the thought cheered her, and she involuntarily gave Agnes another hug, a hug of hope.

And so it was with mixed feelings that they arrived at the hospital, Agnes gingerly alighting. She had begged to go to Jed's side, longed for this moment, and now it was upon her there was caution. Would she be able to face the truth, whatever it might be?

They were greeted by David Grayan. Both girls curtsied but remained silent. His face told a pitiful story and they were afeared for his news.

"Agnes, Jed is alive but he has been badly hurt. He lost too much blood but he may yet be saved. His arm is broken but, so I am told, will heal together with the cut made by the saw." He noticed Agnes wince and grab Sarah's arm for support. "He has two broken ribs, they should also heal, and a broken foot which may give him trouble. It is thought it has been too badly damaged to heal properly, but it should not seriously inconvenience a young man." Agnes supplied a watery smile and nodded as the words sank in.

"Jed may owe his life to Henry Jennings who did much to stop the bleeding. Without his swift action Jed might have lost his life there and then. Jed is asleep now but you will be able to see him. A warning. He has other minor injuries including cuts to his face but these are not serious wounds. He must be left to rest. All we can do now is pray I'm afraid."

Agnes lowered her face, eyes red from the tears. It was Sarah who spoke.

"Sir, thank you for all you have done. I am certain Dr Barrenbridge has done everything possible, and we must also thank Henry, but without your prompt assistance all would've been lost...."

"Do not thank me," he snarled, "I chanced upon the scene and did what was necessary." His manner relaxed and he spoke softly as he continued. "Yes, thank Henry Jennings. But save your most grateful thanks for Judith Pearland. Barrenbridge and Parry-Barnard are away and it is she, helped by Grace Gandling, who have pulled Jed this far."

"I bore witness to her skill and I stand in awe. If he lives Jed will owe his life to the ability of that woman. Nobody could've done more. Now, go and see Jed. I will ride back to Downsland, but the coach will remain at your disposal and bring you back when you are ready. Stay as long as you wish, but my advice is do not tarry too long for this frightful weather will worsen. I will ensure you can return tomorrow. Now I must get word to Jed's parents." With that he turned before they could speak and was away.

Sarah led Agnes as they followed Grace to where Jed lay. Judith was standing sentinel close to him. She beckoned the two girls to move to his side and whispered her words.

"He is asleep, do not disturb him, not that you will. We did give something to ease the pain and it will now help him sleep. Sleep is the best medicine we can have. Which of you is Agnes? Well I can make no promises for his wounds are bad enough, but he lost blood and we will just have to see. But, like you, he is young. A strong man, otherwise healthy, and even in his dreams he will remember he has your love to look forward to, enough to speed his recovery I am sure."

Judith's words, kindly meant, brought little droplets of tears as Agnes's eyes surveyed her man, all her hopes for her future laid out before her. She leaned forward and spoke quietly.

"Dear Jed, beloved Jed. Come back to me and let us share love anew. Know that I love you and will be here for you. I will see you tomorrow my darling but my spirit will not leave your side for a second. I love you Jed, I love you." She looked up at Judith. "Will he be crippled ma'am?"

"His right foot is too badly hurt and may not heal properly. It may give him a slight limp but it should not impede him. I am concerned about the loss of blood, but we will watch over him and do all we can to see him make progress. I wish I could give you more comfort, but I must be truthful and say there is a chance he may not....." She said no more, conscious that Agnes had buried her face in Sarah's shoulder where the tears could flow unnoticed.

Cradling her friend as best she could Sarah spoke.

"Ma'am, thank you for everything. Mr Grayan believes you have saved Jed's life whatever happens now. He has a chance of recovery and he is in good hands here. Bless you for what you have done."

"Bless you ma'am," Agnes whimpered as she emerged from her hiding place and dabbed at her sore eyes with her handkerchief. "Thank you for his life. I can never thank you enough for that."

"Let us see what will be. Thank me on your wedding day. There is no need for it now."

The girls left shortly afterwards. Agnes said a silent prayer over her lover, and whispered her love several times over, and looked back over her shoulder continuously as she made her way slowly from the room.

**

"You will do as I say or taste the rod."

Clara was nearly twenty, wed, and yet had to submit to her father in all things, including a beating if he so desired. She would do as she was told.

"Meet this Sarah Brankly, find out all you can about Grayan. Who comes to Downsland, where he goes, what he does. I am keen to know all these things. It may be possible for Miss Brankly to arrange for you to speak with him. Find out if that may be so and do not let me down. I will not tolerate it and will deal with you as I have done since your birth."

Clara did not need reminding. The consequences of failure would be dire, unpleasant and painful. It never once occurred to her that her father's discipline was unusual when directed at a woman of her age. She simply acknowledged that until the age of one and twenty she was his to command.

Near Hawkhurst James Parry-Barnard was taking his leave of Lady Fitzgower after a prolonged visit, ostensibly a medical consultation, that had included a large amount of time spent at tea and therefore in agreeable conversation. He was in no doubt Harriet Fitzgower liked his company but did she prefer it enough for there to be an understanding in the offing? He would have to court her carefully and it might take time.

Perhaps she was just playing with him.

A woman of extreme wealth and social standing, an aristocratic lady, the child of parents with connections to the King himself; what would she want with a mere physician? And his mind dulled over like the skies over Kent this late November afternoon. But hadn't he spoken with relish about becoming a surgeon, knowing that fame would beckon? Hadn't he emphasised his own family connections, tolerably exaggerating some aspects in order to impress?

Would being the wife of a famous, successful and revered surgeon be adequate?

His heart was up and down. With every thought he both uplifted and destroyed his prospects. He was in turmoil and she had achieved that with so little effort.

Yes, perhaps she was playing with him.

She did, however, embody the perfect medium for advancing into the realms of private medicine at the highest level. Why, he would be sought out by the very best society could offer. He might yet be in a position of extraordinary privilege and mentioned widely throughout the land. Yes, Harriet Fitzgower was a prize worth fighting for.

Roger Culteney was also scheming.

He had indeed made his peace with his father and had returned home. He had condemned his wife out of hand saying he was seduced by a whore who saw only his money and position, and how much he regretted such a disastrous union with such a wretched person. She had then deserted him for a tailor, he explained. He prostrated himself before his father, full of apologies, swearing loyalty to his family, and saying what a reformed man he was.

But he was nothing of the sort.

He had betrayed David Grayan and absconded with all the money given him when some had been intended for Evershen. For the time being he was given very little by his father to whom he had lied about the funds he returned with. His father was left unaware of the financial loss his son had suffered.

Even now he was ingratiating himself with the wrong people, and placing himself in jeopardy by investing in wild schemes that had no chance of success. Small amounts yes, but the die was cast. In want of female company he had taken to visiting a courtesan whose services were not inexpensive, and so the money slipped away by degrees. And as his father's trust in him increased so did the income from that source.

He would've had no idea that a certain Lily Cowans had made her way from Dover to Downsland Hall, an event that might spell his undoing.

Chapter Six

"I am sorry to arrive unannounced and I thank you for seeing me."

David Grayan invited her to sit and remained standing, his face drawn and grey, his expression one of suppressed anger. Lily Cowans was guarded. She knew of him by reputation and everything she had heard was clear in the appearance and deportment of the man opposite. He looked every part the fiend he had been painted and she began to regret her journey.

"I will be brief. I believe you are a good friend of Mr Roger Culteney, an acquaintance of mine, and I am concerned for him as I have not seen him or heard from him, with all my efforts to find him proving fruitless.

"In my despair I wrote to his father and received a curt reply from his secretary, Mr Holbourne, with whom I am also acquainted. I am informed Roger left home a long time ago bent on adventure, so it would seem, and has only recently returned, but had not made his fortune as he had hoped.

"It was with some trepidation as you will imagine that I wrote to Roger but have not had the courtesy of a reply. I wondered, sir, if you had any further news. I am obviously reluctant to call upon him as I may not be welcome. I would be grateful for anything you can tell me sir, even if it is news not in my interests, for we had an arrangement. Our fathers are well known to each other and I believe they would've smiled upon an understanding.

"Indeed, it is through them that I was introduced to Roger."

Grayan studied her thoughtfully, but displayed a grimness that dismayed her.

"Miss Cowans, Mr Culteney spoke of you often and, if I may say so, I often encouraged him to make his intentions clear to you. However, I must urge you to abandon him as he has abandoned you. His adventure, as you call it, was marriage. He eloped with a young woman from Westlingstead and in due course deserted her. Sadly one of his unwise investments failed leaving him almost penniless. I suspect he has crawled back to his father.

"He cannot undo the marriage." Grayan lowered his eyes to his lap. "He tried to conceal his wrongdoings from me. He maligned his wife and blamed her for his downfall. I believe they eloped together willingly. She had her father's permission so I understand, a necessity being not yet of age." His voice sank to a near whisper. "He is no friend of mine. His behaviour has been despicable and is unforgiveable. That is all I have to say."

He did not look at Lily Cowans again. She was staring at him and there was the faintest glint of tears about her eyes although she was not sobbing. There was no movement at all, just a face of sorrow and disbelief. In time she spoke and as quietly as Grayan had done.

"Thank you sir. I will leave now...."

"The weather is too bad. You are welcome to stay the night...."

"Thank you but I am expected home in Dover and I must go now."

"I will send someone on horseback with a message from you. Stay and leave on the morrow. I insist."

"Very well sir, that is kindness indeed." Only now did he look up.

"Your coachmen and horses will be looked after and I will arrange a meal for you. Please excuse me, I have work to do. I will show you where you may write and I will arrange with my housekeeper, Mrs Forbes, to have it despatched, and accommodation will be prepared for you this instant."

A maid came into the room.

"Ask Mrs Forbes to join us at once," he ordered. He took Lily Cowans through to the next room where a large desk was situated and she wrote her letter, her hand still shaking with the shock. Once alone later she knew she would feel the full effects of the news and react accordingly, but for the present she must be controlled and stoical. Grayan gave his orders to Mrs Forbes and took his leave of his guest. She would not see him again until breakfast time.

A maid stood ready to take her letter as soon as it was complete. Mrs Forbes returned and offered to take her to her room advising that she would find all she needed there, for she had not arrived prepared to stay. Dinner would be in an hour.

68

Alone in her room at last she sat on the bed and contemplated all the intelligence she had come upon. Grayan was no monster. While waiting to see him she had been told about the young woodsman and the role Grayan had played, and now he had behaved with honesty and integrity addressing her, speaking words he knew she would not want to hear, speaking the truth and doing so in a strangely kind and sympathetic manner. He invited her to stay, sent a rider to Dover to advise her family. A gentleman surely?

Roger had told her about Marie and baby Charlotte and the awful sense of loss that had engulfed David Grayan since. Now she felt truly sorry for him, for he had today demonstrated what a fine gentleman he actually was, a fine caring and kind gentleman and a good master to those who worked for him, not a tyrannical beast at all.

Her thoughts fortified her and the expected tears did not come. She was more saddened for Grayan's loss and subsequent solemnity than for her own disappointment. She dined alone and retired, and only then did her heartache overtake her as she lay quietly abed.

**

Grace Gandling and Judith Pearland watched over Jed by turns, each resting when they could, but ensuring eyes were upon him at every second.

He suffered a fitful night as pain surged relentlessly through his damaged body. They mopped his brow, soaked with sweat, and did what they could to make him comfortable. They listened helplessly as his nightmares were made manifest in squeals and screams and yells. They saw him at peace, when he was breathing steadily, gave him water on the few occasions he seemed to be awake, and prayed for his survival.

And so the night passed and the coming day was heralded by birdsong, and with it came the moment they thought they had lost him. His breathing slowed to nothingness and as they prayed afresh for recovery he opened his eyes and winced with pain.

"Where am I?" he spluttered as the breath returned to him.

"You're in hospital Jed. Lie still. We will look after you. Agnes has been to see you and will be back this morning. For now remember she loves you and wishes you better. Recover for her Jed. Now lie still and we will tend you. Be still dear Jed. We are here." Judith's words pleased him and soothed him, as they were intended to do, and sleep overcame him again, precious sleep, free from bad dreams, free from pain.

He was still asleep when Agnes and Sarah arrived.

The new day was an unwanted intrusion into the life of Lily Cowans and she welcomed it not.

She washed and dressed and made her way downstairs for a breakfast she didn't want. She had picked at her meal the evening before but felt it best to eat what she could. Stunned, heartbroken and resigned she faced a different future now as she knew full well, and breakfast taken alone, she felt, might not be the perfect accompaniment to her unhappiness.

However, Grayan was there, although for all the conversation they had he might just as well have not been. He did not want to talk and she found herself longing for her departure.

"I shall leave after breakfast, sir, and I thank you again for your hospitality."

"I wish you a safe journey Miss Cowans, and I am sorry for the situation as you have found it. Now, if you will excuse me I must return to my work." Standing and executing the slightest bow in her direction he spun around and was gone. She left her food and went straight to her room to prepare for the journey home.

Perhaps she was wrong. Perhaps he was the very unpleasant person he was said to have become. Somehow she did not want to believe it, and hoped her earlier assessment was correct, that here was a man who simply could never come to terms with bereavement. Was he not to be pitied and helped? She would write when she was home and express her feelings, for he could ignore her letter or reply however he saw fit, and that was the most appropriate way she could disclose her thoughts.

He wouldn't welcome it, might not even read it through, might consider it a rudeness unbecoming a young woman, might condemn her for it, but she would do it. She had nothing to lose.

"Bless you, bless you," Agnes repeated yet again as she looked at Judith Pearland across the bed where Jed was asleep but breathing with a greater firmness and good regularity.

"Please Agnes, we must still see, must still pray. He is far from recovered. We have done what we could and done it as well we might, for that is our calling. It is why we are here. I hope that all will be well and that we have done our best, but it will take time until we know. And in the meantime Agnes, we must watch him, and you must be aware of the danger he is still in."

Sarah hugged her friend who was lost in silent prayer, both girls realising the significance of Pearland's words and knowing the poignant truth of the matter.

***

Charles Handlen preferred the company of any woman to that of his wife. He rarely came home and showed no interest in wife or children at this point. Hester could accomplish her pre-ordained function now she had given birth as required, and lead the twins through infancy and a time of their lives where there was no need for the presence of their father. That would come later, as would the governess, and Hester would then presumably be needed to carry further children within her, give birth, and see them safely through those first months.

She did not yet fully appreciate that. There was no realisation that her husband would deprive her of her boys or that her sole reason for existence was to produce more offspring. Hester longed to see her brother and show him Edward and George of whom she was so inordinately proud, but even with Charles's elongated absences she dare not invite David there.

There was the visit she had once paid to Downsland Hall, but of course she had been alone and the servants had not betrayed her. Now there was the boys' nanny to consider, and taking the twins out by coach might arouse gossip which could easily reach her husband's ears. There were more people to be trusted and there was no counting on that. Charles had personally appointed the nanny and Hester suspected she had a closer association with Charles than either cared to admit.

In a desperate quandary she struggled to find a solution and in the end wrote to David and explained the whole situation in the hope he might arrive at an answer that was practical. Grayan had continued to write to his sister at Margaret Cheney's address, and her friend would bring each letter as it was delivered and post any reply. On this occasion she hadn't seen Margaret for two weeks and so wrote to her in the first instance inviting her to call.

She did not realise that a senior footman, charged with taking out all the mail, was also charged with noting who Hester wrote to. Fortunately Charles did not attach any significance to correspondence with Margaret Cheney and it thus remained a safe route. He was more concerned that she might write to her brother.

But Charles did have a suspicious mind. He hated Grayan and was determined to prevent his wife having contact with him, and in due course he would come to have worries about the relationship with Mrs Cheney, about whom he actually knew so little. It would only need a moment's unintentional recklessness, a moment's thoughtlessness, a lack of concentration at a vital time and Hester would be undone. Both women knew this and guarded against it, but it was no defence for that act of carelessness that might spring from familiarity and destroy everything.

***

Sarah's mother was out in the farm and Edmund was pretending to be absorbed in the ledger resting on the table. Instead he was observing Clara Evershen who was on all fours with her back to him scrubbing the floor. A widower who had dearly loved his late wife, Edmund had never given any thought to other women but he had to admit there was something alluring about the young lady.

She was a beauty, that was true, and he wondered why she had never married. He was unaware of her past and that she was wed, but he was extremely aware that he was enjoying seeing her working hard on the floor with her rear raised in the air, her body swaying vigorously as she scrubbed, and he smiled with the pleasure it brought him. A beauty in all respects, he mused.

His pleasure was interrupted at once when Sarah walked through the door. She hugged her uncle in greeting despite not wishing to grant him any salutation of friendship and sat at the table to explain her presence. Edmund asked Clara to fetch his sister and Sarah waited until she came to the room and was herself seated, Clara discreetly going upstairs to carry out some task or other.

Sarah told them all about Jed and Agnes, and about how wonderful her master had been and how Judith Pearland had thus far saved Jed's life. She spoke at speed and gave no chance for them to question her! Jed's parents had now arrived from Lenham and were at the hospital with Agnes who was in good company, Sarah reasoned, so she thought she would return to the Hall, seeing her mother along the way.

Tea was made and Clara was bade to join them allowing her to renew her acquaintance with Sarah, and a date was set for them to enjoy some time together. Both girls had motives for such a meeting in addition to the friendship they hoped it would bring.

But it was soon time for Sarah to be on her way and with a heavy heart she hugged her mother once more and set off. At least the weather was kinder today, sunny but very cold, and she shivered as she dragged her cloak more firmly around her, trudging along the tracks to Downsland Hall and praying for Jed.

Her thoughts moved on to Clara. How she wished she had the girl's loveliness of face, then she might've attracted a husband of her own who would have loved her so much he would not have cared that she was barren. There was no sadness in these thoughts, just a dream that one day, come her day, a man might yet make her his and love her as she was. Poor Clara, for all the beauty she possessed she had been led astray by a scoundrel, so perhaps Sarah was better off as she was.

Better to be single than seduced and ruined by a man like Culteney, if that was what beauty brought you. But then she realised how unkind she was being to the girl, remembering her own recent memories of the rogue and the way he had spoken and behaved to Ginny. Perhaps the fates would be generous to Clara and enable her to love again, but in sincerity that was most improbable. What man would want a woman left wretched and sullied by an evil good-for-nothing? Did Sarah have more chance being unable to bear children?

Besides Clara could not be unmarried so maybe she would live as she could, a tainted woman nonetheless.

She was so immersed in her thoughts she didn't hear the voice behind her at first.

"Hello Sarah, hello there."

Turning, she saw Robert Broxford now just a few feet away.

"Hello Robert. An improvement in the weather thankfully." He was then by her side.

"Ah yes, it has been poor of late, but it is winter I suppose. Do you mind if I walk with you?"

"No, of course not. Be glad of the company. Are you going to Downsland?"

"Yes, I'm on duty anon. What news of Jed?"

"He's sleeping mainly, which is a good thing the doctor says, but they think he is making some progress."

"Was he very badly hurt? Many injuries?"

"Yes but most will heal with rest and in time. But we are praying for him as he not over the worst just yet Robert."

"Oh poor Jed. I will pray too. He is a good friend, a good man. I hope he recovers fully."

Sarah the maid and Robert the footman walked on, taking a short-cut on a path across a field. After a period of silence Robert spoke.

"Dr Barrenbridge is excellent I believe."

"Yes Robert, but Dr Barrenbridge wasn't there and Miss Pearland treated Jed. The master assisted where he could and said he was in awe of how well she worked."

"A woman? Oh sorry Sarah, it's just that I was surprised to hear you say that. I thought she was just a nurse..."

"For shame Robert. She wishes to be a doctor and I for one hope she succeeds. The master was impressed I can tell you, and if Jed survives he will owe his life to her. Nobody with her ability is *just* a nurse."

"Sarah, I meant no offence. I'm sorry. I know the master believes that women are the equal of men and says that one day we will have ladies in parliament, maybe a lady prime minister,

74

lady architects and engineers, lady surgeons, ladies who run businesses and banks and so on."

"And what pray do you believe Robert? Be truthful."

"I don't know, Sarah. It is not a concept that sits comfortably with me..."

"That's because you were brought up to believe that there is a role for men and another for women. We are supposed to be wives and mothers, aren't we? Subservient creatures not allowed to think for ourselves, just bear and raise children, that's the lot that's given us."

"Yes but I think the master is changing my feelings Sarah, so that is a good thing? Or he was, but he has changed himself so much since mistress died."

"But not lost his beliefs, surely? After all, does not Agnes Byrne work among the trees and plants on the estate, and was she not encouraged to do so?"

"Yes that's true, and she had to overcome opposition from the other woodsmen. Not Jed Maxton mind!"

"No, and Agnes is with Jed and I'm sure he senses she's there. Love can be such a strong force Robert. Have you ever loved, Robert?"

"Yes and I once had high hopes. I will tell you if you wish, but it is my secret and I ask you never to speak of it. Would you promise me please?"

They had left the footpath and joined the road that led past Downsland. The trees marking their route swayed slightly in the breeze, their leafless branches casting thin shadows hither and thither. They stood watch as the young couple passed, silent witnesses to their conversation.

"You have my word Robert, you may rely upon it."

"When I was young I loved a very beautiful girl in Westlingstead. She was so lovely but I knew I had no chance. She was my secret and hopeless love, too beautiful to ever look my way, and I was sure her father intended her to marry well and bring success to the family. My prospects remained poor and I am, even at this day, a simple footman.

"I know she is unwed but would have no time for me. I am nothing..."

"You fool Robert. A most handsome footman and I will say you look splendid in your uniform, enough to turn any girl's head. If you think you're unworthy you will be. You must strike out for a prize worth claiming. Anyway, not all girls are influenced by looks and wealth; some place true love, constancy and devotion above all else. Now Robert, who is she?"

"You promise you will say nothing?"

"Promise."

"She's Clara Evershen, the basket-weaver's daughter." Sarah stopped in her tracks and quickly regained her composure after the shock, as she knew she must, and fell in beside the footman immediately.

"I know Clara. She helps my mother and uncle three days a week, and I have just spoken with her when I called upon mama. She is a lucky woman to be loved by one such as you."

"I thought she must be wed soon. In truth, when she went to Ramsgate to look after an ailing relative I thought at the time she had married and was with her husband. Now I know that it is not the case. Do know if she has suitors, Sarah?" Sarah's thoughts were a dreadful tumble, a sorry tangle, but she knew what she could not say.

"I do not think so but I have little idea. However, I will be meeting her in a few days and will make discreet enquiries if you wish?"

"I do, but please do not mention me. Please do not."

"I have promised Robert and I keep my word. I will be very discreet; after all, you simply want to know if there is another. I will find out for you."

"Bless you Sarah. May I ask, do you think I might have any chance? She is such a beauty."

"Beauty isn't everything Robert. She may be unwed because she seeks a man who will love the person she is, not the face she shows the world."

They had reached the drive and begun the long walk to the main building.

Sarah was puzzling over Robert's revelation. Could he possibly be the man to lead Clara to salvation if the opportunity arose? Would he want anything to do with a fallen woman once he was aware of her past? He might well think it repulsive and utterly sickening. And she was married, like it or not.

"I haven't told you this, but when we were younger we often did meet up by that bent old tree just past the inn. You must know it?" She nodded, listening interestedly to this news.

"Well, we did, but we talked and talked and talked about so much. We shared so much common ground Sarah, and I found myself falling in love. We talked about village life, the Grayans and this mansion, about history, about all the things we liked and those we didn't.

"But I could not declare myself, for anyway I was no more than fifteen, and she showed no sign of any interest in me beyond our conversation. Her father saw her there with me once and ordered her home, telling me to leave her alone. He took her back to beat her, I am sure. I cried over that and resolved that I would do as instructed, and do so for her sake. And that was the last time I sat with her and talked with her."

"Robert, your secret is safe with me. I will make those discreet enquiries for you, rest assured. Thank you for sharing your story with me."

"Bless you for listening Sarah."

They concluded their walk in silence, pausing for a brief hug, the hug of two friends, before going their separate ways, Sarah hoping that Robert might yet find his beloved within grasp if he could come to terms with the horrors that had befallen her.

Chapter Seven

November rolled seamlessly into December with the weather doing much as it pleased, alternating betwixt cold, frosty periods, and warmer but wetter ones.

Two important clients of David Grayan came to stay at Downsland together with their wives and children, customers who needed to be impressed, and for a few days there was a degree of gaiety about the place. Meals were a grand affair and Grayan himself proved quite affable, much to the surprise of most of his staff. Sarah found useful employment assisting the childrens' nannies, in truth giving them a well deserved break from their charges, and discovered how dearly she loved being with young children. With it came sadness of course.

She organised games inside and out, partook of their own entertainments, and helped them devise a show in which all seven dressed in costumes either found within the Hall or hastily stitched together. The parents along with Grayan attended the brief presentation and appeared to thoroughly enjoy it, applauding and cheering with gusto at the end.

When they left there was an emptiness not just about the great house, but in the atmosphere too, and a darkness once more fell upon the scene, where considerable happiness had recently lit Downsland with its brightness.

Mrs Forbes subsequently reported to all staff that the master was happy, appreciated their hard work, and that the clients had been as impressed as they needed to be, Mr Grayan securing further business as a result and improving his reputation into the bargain.

Sarah had her long awaited meeting with Clara but it was an unexpected meeting that was to leave her shaken.

Jed improves with every day leaving Agnes with all the verve of a spring lamb. It is quite clear that Judith Pearland not only saved his life but ensured his injuries would heal properly, with the exception of the broken foot which might give him a small impediment. Henry Barrenbridge approved wholeheartedly of all she had achieved, saying he could've done no better himself, and she was duly found to be the toast of the village.

David Grayan retreated into his quiet, lonely world after his guests departed, and he has been fretting over two very long letters he has received, one from his sister and one from Lily Cowans, both of which have left him in some emotional pain.

Roger Culteney is promoting another potentially disastrous financial scheme with his new friends, and is having a liaison with Lady Matilda Haffley, wife of General Sir John Haffley. She is in her late fifties, and intimacy with her disgusts Culteney whereas she is overjoyed to be worshipped by a striking young man as she sees him. But she is very rich and her soldier husband is often away.

She has already parted with monies, ostensibly as an investment in Culteney's venture, but he has kept some for himself to maintain his standing amongst those he socialises with. However, General Haffley is unlikely to take sympathetically to being cuckolded and neither his wife nor her paramour are discreet or careful.

Hester Handlen awaits David's reply, still unaware Charles has frittered away most of their money and they will soon be in a difficult situation.

Thomas Evershen has set his daughter further tasks now that she is friendly with Sarah Brankly as he wants to know more about David Grayan. Meanwhile Clara has become aware that Sarah's uncle Edmund is taking notice of her in an indecorous manner and she is confused. He is widower but very much older, and she is a ruined woman, still married, although he does not know that.

She feels used, worthless and hates herself, and on the one hand she might entertain some time with him if he was prepared to pay, distasteful though the experience could be. But on the other she retains a little pride, despite all that has happened to her, and now dreams of finding true love, and does not wish for wealth or station. Nobody knows that she is not single. Of course, she accepts that true and enduring love is beyond her for she would simply be deceiving a loving man.

It is perplexing. She does not want to become a whore, but some money for herself (her father gives her very little) would be a refreshing opportunity. However, news would spread in a village like Westlingstead and any reputation she has left would be in absolute tatters, spoiling any chance, any *hope* of love. She knows what she shall do; meet Sarah again, as her father has decreed, and perhaps the issue of love could be brought gently into the conversation.

After all, her friend appears to be knowledgeable and sensible and capable of giving thought to baffling questions, arriving at reasonable answers.

***

Their first meeting had been a curious affair. Sarah had become wary when Clara asked so many questions about David Grayan. Several times when discussing other matters Clara abruptly changed the subject to return to the master of Downsland Hall.

But by-the-by they talked openly about their lives and circumstances although Clara naturally avoided any mention of Culteney and the marriage, and touched briefly on her time spent with the ailing relative in Ramsgate. Sarah knew something of the Kent town and decided Clara knew so little that it was obvious she had never been there. But of course Sarah knew the truth.

She wanted to know if Clara was happy working with her mother and uncle, and how family life was at home. There was something about her answers that suggested she was finding Edmund disagreeable, and clearly her father was a tartar, but she loved Sarah's mama and the work, that was true.

However, in the meantime Sarah had been startled to be ordered to attend upon Mr Grayan in his study, and she duly made her way there, worried but not afeared.

He did not look up at first, or speak to her. She glanced around, noticing the desk was much tidier but that various papers were located dotted about, in chairs, on the floor, on shelves, as if the mess she had seen before had merely been redistributed. When he did speak her took her by surprise, snapping out his words sharply.

"I showed you a letter when you first came here and asked your advice. I wish to do so again. It is related to the matter of the first letter, and from a different person, but it is an entirely separate issue as you will see. Miss Cowans was hoping she had an arrangement with Mr Culteney and was unaware, until she called upon me, that he had married, deserted his wife, and been temporarily inconvenienced by a substantial loss of money following an unwise investment. He is, I suspect, re-united with his family. Read this letter. And please sit." He waved at a chair in front of the desk and with some reluctance she took the proffered letter and sat as bade while Grayan's eyes returned to paperwork in front of him.

Lily's Letter

'I apologise for writing and beg your indulgence. I place no obligation upon you to read my letter and you may choose to read no further or abandon it later as you wish. I do not therefore expect a reply but would appreciate one if you desire to correspond.

May I please express my gratitude for your hospitality when I unforgivably arrived unannounced at Downsland, and say how indebted I am for your kindness particularly when you imparted the information relating to Mr Culteney as I expect you knew it would hurt me.

It is clear it may not have been a happy union had we wed, for his true character was unknown to me as presumably it was to you. I may have escaped with my reputation intact but that does not mean that I did not love him and I am not heartbroken. Indeed, I feel for reasons I cannot easily explain more sorrow for his loss than for knowing what a scoundrel he was.

You have suffered the saddest loss of all and I cannot imagine your pain, but perhaps you will in some way understand my hurt, for he was all my dreams, the stars in the sky, the warmth of the sun, my absolute everything, and I miss him for that. I love him sufficiently to say that I would forgive him the way in which he has deserted me.

Perhaps you cannot comprehend why I should say that, but I do believe Mr Grayan you know a great deal about deep, abiding love just as you know about the agony of loss. Mr Culteney spoke warmly of the love he knew you shared with your wife and I imagine you must still be feeling the tremendous devastation of bereavement in a way few could truly comprehend. The fact that Mr Culteney is still alive is no relief from my own sense of bereavement; in truth it makes the soreness of my anguish all the more unbearable.

It is most unlikely now that I will have the family I so wanted and it grieves me, yet it must be insufferable for you, although for both of us there is still a chance we may find enduring love with other people and we may even have the children we once so desired. I do not think either of us should readily abandon hope even at our lowest ebb, even when life itself is far from worth living, even when the pain burns fiercely in our hearts as it must do in yours every minute of every day.

I have no right to record my feelings about your situation and you will no doubt condemn my impudence and be offended that I have put pen to paper in such a manner, a manner unbecoming a lady, and you will think the worst of me for it.

But I honestly believe, and earnestly implore you to look for a light to lead you out of the darkness, for there is a light there somewhere to be found, and I will find such a light in my own terrible darkness.

Mr Culteney spoke often of your belief that woman should be the equal of man, and I have written on that basis, that as an acquaintance, as I hope you will see me, I should be able to express views that ladies should not be expounding in this fashion. I write as an acquaintance, not as a woman.

May good fortune attend you always. Mr Culteney praised your caring, kind attitude to nature and to those around you; please do not let such a remarkable character be submerged in endless grief.'

Sarah involuntarily sat back in the chair shocked as much by the letter itself as the fact the master was sharing it with her. It was a personal letter, a private document, and it concerned intimacy that should be confined solely to the writer and the intended recipient.

"I have read it sir." He did not take his eyes from his desk and once again he did not speak. Sarah sat and waited, studying his face. From what she could observe his expression was one of vexation and woe, of sadness and yes, perhaps a little anger. Had Miss Cowans's letter annoyed him and was Sarah the person to endorse this ire? To tell him simply that he was correct to be incensed? To agree that it was an extraordinary measure taken by someone who had no right to be considered an acquaintance? And so she waited.

When he looked across at her his expression had changed and there was an odd warmth that unsettled her. Gone was any anger, gone were the lines of aggravation and sorrow. She knew he wasn't smiling and yet for a fleeting moment that is what she saw, a barely discernible smile on a face that had long ago forsaken displaying such delights. And she knew she was shaking, and knew not why.

His voice was soft and quiet, his eyes glowing with a tender, questioning shimmer, as if all the answers lay before him waiting to be revealed.

"Do you believe a man may emerge from the darkness that has become his life, his world? That he may seek that light that leads him forth? Speak freely and without fear Sarah."

Perhaps he could sense she was frozen with fear, perhaps he could comprehend that he was asking too much of a servant, a fact she recognised easily. She had no place here. This was not where a maid belonged, even less to be confronted with questions such as these.

"If I frighten you then I apologise Sarah. I urge you to speak openly as you please, as you see fit. Answer honestly, I beg you." He looked as if he was pleading for her to ease his misery with her words and she knew she could not relieve such despair. "Please answer me Sarah. It is alright. Speak freely, you have nothing to fear."

In her wariness she weighed up all the circumstances surrounding this meeting, decided she must believe him and have no fear, yet was still curiously concerned about answering so openly. But it had to be done, it had to be, for he had asked her earnestly, and with that she took a very deep breath and spoke.

"Sir, any one of us may leave the darkness behind us. The darkness you speak of is a demon of our own making which will eat away at our very souls, devour us completely and destroy us if we let it." Still shaking, believing the wrong word in the wrong place might bring his wrath down upon her head, she uttered what she had to say with no lack of courage but in dread of what it could lead to.

Yet there was still a welcoming warmth to his face, impossible to explain or describe. She continued.

"Sir, a short while ago my beloved father died leaving my mother and me to run our small farm. Bleakness descended upon us as we grieved. There was no guiding light then, just the very darkness Miss Cowans writes about. He was so ill. Dr Parry-Barnard operated but could not save him. But we had to carry on our work, tend our animals and crops or they too would've died, and in time we found that light. We found it because we did not exclude our family and friends and neighbours.

"Because they cared they came to us and we welcomed them, and gradually the light led us forward into the very future my father would've wanted for us, a future of security, love and happiness. Yes, we found happiness again, despite our loss. And I have found happiness here working at Downsland, and I'm certain my father watches down and sees I am happy and is proud of me...... sir."

His expression did not change. There was silence. He stared at her as she shook. When he spoke his voice was again tender and mellow.

"You had told me about your father and I am very sorry. I was unaware he was attended by Parry-Barnard at the time, and that he was that sick. I am truly sorry. I did not know. I am pleased you are happy here. But do you not long for a husband? If I may ask, and I beg your pardon for doing so, is there a young man who holds your affections dear to him?"

"No sir. No man has come for me and none will. I am barren. I cannot bear children. What man would want a barren wife? I had a tumour cut from me when I was young and my hopes for a family were similarly cut from me." She had ceased shaking and was feeling stronger, braver. "But God spared my life when I might have died and God has spared me for other reasons I am sure." Grayan had sat up straight and placed his arms on the desk in front of him.

"Sarah, Sarah, I had no idea. I would not have shown you the letter .... please forgive me I beg you ... I had no knowledge of this and ... and ... and to think I have shown this missive with its references to children .... I cannot imagine I have been so unfeeling ....I ... I ... beg you to forgive me....."

"Sir, you did not know. You do not need my forgiveness. I am resigned to my lot. I have not forsaken my dreams, it is my hopes that have deserted me. Maybe one day a man will love me as I am but I do not expect that to be the situation. Presently I must do God's will for I know he has other courses for me to follow. Do not be dismayed sir. You did not know."

Grayan sat back slightly shaking his head.

"Sarah, you cannot know how I feel. It is a wicked thing I have done. I am so sorry. But please know this. I appreciate all you have said today. You have wisdom beyond your years. Perhaps it is through your words that I may yet find that light. I ask you this: I am of the mind to invite Miss Cowans to stay, would you be prepared to wait upon her as her maid during her stay? I know it is improper to invite a lady but as she herself points out I view men and women as equals, and she knows I am a gentleman. What say you Sarah? Should I do so, or not?"

Without hesitation Sarah responded, and with strength of purpose.

"Yes sir, on that basis you should. I too believe we are the equals of men. I will wait upon her if she will come...."

"Sarah, one other thing. I have sought my wife's spirit in the gardens she loved. Why cannot I find her there?"

She was taken aback but regained her composure with alacrity.

"You look too hard sir. She is there. She is by your side now. But in your grief you cannot see her because you have closed a cloak of darkness around you, the very darkness you and Miss Cowans speak of. Cast aside that cloak and your wife will be with you." She stood and awaited whatever might now befall her. "Just as I found my father, sir," she added hopefully.

"Bless you Sarah. Bless you. I am truly grateful. I will write to Miss Cowans, and I will tell her I have appointed you to serve her." Sarah handed the letter back. "Thank you. It was kind of you to come. Now, forgive me, I must return to my work. Bless you and good day to you." And he did indeed return to the host of documents in front of him. Sarah curtsied and departed.

On the way downstairs she contemplated the meeting. He was no ogre, just a very haunted, grief-stricken man who had allowed so much kindness to be buried along with his wife and child. Had she helped? Time would tell. But what an astonishing meeting! The master consulting her on something so private.

And then she considered Miss Cowans. That must be true love, she decided. To forgive a man who has turned his back on you for another woman. To forgive a man who has treated his wife so horribly. To forgive a man such awful sins because of love. How she must've loved Mr Culteney. This is love as I shall never know it, thought Sarah. And yet if I loved a man so strongly, with all my heart, would he love me just as much? She paused and looked back up the stairs. Yes, he's no monster, she reasoned, just a man engrossed in sadness and it is eating him away.

She recognised too that in all probability Lily Cowans had another objective in writing as she had done. Perhaps Miss Cowans wondered if she and Grayan could become rather more than friends in time, and Sarah chuckled with amusement as she carefully skipped down the remaining steps.

Grayan's meeting with Sarah had more benefit for him than she realised. It had taken Lily Cowans's letter and Sarah's comments to awaken him to the disaster ahead and hope was rapidly replacing despair. But there was a long way to go.

If his meeting with Sarah cheered him his next meeting provided a different effect.

***

"Do not think I am here for any other reason than confrontation sir."

The two men stood less than ten feet apart. Ralph Grayan was taller than his brother and possessed a naturally sinister appearance.

Here was the man who had taken David's place and was now head of family having inherited the home David grew up in when their father died, and inherited the family's wealth.

"You are not welcome brother. I care nothing for your purpose so state your business and go."

"My sister Hester. She is forbidden from contact with you. I ask you, and ask you as the gentleman you presume yourself to be, that you respect that arrangement. I have good reason to believe you and she have corresponded and it will not do sir, it will not do. It must cease forthwith. I will not tolerate it, I assure you."

"Damn you Ralph. Now get out of my house this instant. Go!"

"Heed my words sir. Do not persist in your correspondence or there will be the devil to pay."

"The devil is a better companion than you can ever hope to be, Ralph."

"You made your pact with the devil when you married that whore, and you killed my mother stone dead...."

Ralph's words were cut short as David advanced on him suddenly. Fearing he was to be attacked he raised his whip and brought it down across his brother's face. Unflinching as the stroke slashed into his flesh David caught Ralph's wrist and flung his arm aside with all the ease of a child casting a toy away in a juvenile rage. The punch that followed sent Ralph to the floor.

In a fury he tried to rise but his brother was upon him too quickly and he reeled backwards into a heap as David's right boot smashed into his chest.

"You are no brother of mine," he yelled at the forlorn figure whimpering by the door, a beaten man, with no courage to risk further injury in the pursuit of what he thought was a just cause. He muttered as he slowly got to his feet.

"Rot in hell David. Join that whore and your bastard daughter as soon as it pleases you. You will not be missed in this life."

David's eyes blazed, the livid scar on his left cheek now bleeding steadily, and as he took a step forward Ralph leaped through the door in his haste to avoid another blow. Brother chased brother from the building. A groom was holding Ralph's horse.

With a cry of "get out of my way, let go you fool, let go" he mounted the animal before David could catch him and galloped away swearing profane oaths over his shoulder.

That evening, unbeknown to David, his sister Hester was shown a letter she had written to him and sent to Margaret's as usual. Her husband Charles had indeed become suspicious and ordered letters despatched to Margaret Cheney be opened and brought to him.

Charles Handlen had first taken the letter to Ralph Grayan and then called upon Mrs Cheney. Now he confronted his wife having summoned her to their private quarters.

"Forthwith," he cried, "Edward and George will be kept in the charge of their nannies and you will not see them. Do you understand me? You will have very little contact. If I could have my way you'd have none at all. I have been to Mrs Cheney and made my position quite clear on the subject of your correspondence with your brother.

"Ralph has, I know, visited Downsland today and will have explained with great clarity, you may be sure of that, his desire to see communication between you and David brought to an end. Mrs Cheney stands admonished and will never help you again."

Hester had been white with fear when she first saw the letter but as she listened to Charles giving vent to his decrees and divulging his news with such violent unpleasantness her blood began to boil. How dare he order that their children should not see their mother? How dare he say that the nannies, unrelated women, should now look after the twins to her exclusion?

The fear had long passed. She was enraged, her face a picture of aggression and determination. She feared not what was to follow and was already thinking about how she might overcome this new situation and escape with the boys. David Grayan's injured face was of nought compared to the injuries Hester suffered when her husband had finished shouting at her. She made no sound, struggled successfully to avoid tears, and bore the pain with fortitude and without baulking or moving.

He left her there for her maid to attend her.

At Downsland it was Eleanor Forbes and Ginny Perkins who attended their master's wound. Ginny, like Hester, was fighting back tears for she knew shedding them was not how a maid should behave, and bravely tended the sore, her emotions buried behind the mask of a concerned but aloof servant.

The row had been heard by some, the flight of Ralph Grayan witnessed by many, and the anguish felt by most. Footmen, grooms, maids, gardeners, all knew that something terrible had happened and it had occurred between brothers. Most knew David Grayan's history and knew he had been disinherited. And they also knew that their master commanded their respect, even in the chill wind of bereavement and endless suffering which had changed the man, and they supported him regardless.

Now there was more sorrow to contemplate.

Chapter Eight

The day after Ralph's ill-fated visit David Grayan received a letter from Margaret Cheney requesting an urgent meeting and he replied he'd call on the morrow. Knowing he would be travelling to London he also sent a note to the Haskertons advising them that he'd like to see them but was unsure if he'd be welcome. They would have time to respond if they did not want him.

He knew only too well that his sister could be in trouble, for it was clear her husband had unearthed the route by which he and she communicated and had informed Ralph accordingly.

It was a fretful night. He was aware now that Charles was a violent man and was capable of inflicting a severe beating. The only thing that had prevented him going straight to his sister and confronting her husband was the twins, her sons, and how it might all fall out if he tried to interfere. Once he had heard from Margaret he knew he must see her first and gain whatever additional intelligence was available.

After breakfast, and having written and despatched his messages, he decided he would ride wherever the fancy took him, for it would surely calm him. It was a bright, cold December day but the wind was little more than a breeze and did not chill him as he rode.

His horse was strong and respondent, and took him willingly, sometimes at the gallop, sometimes at the trot. He skirted Westlingstead and headed through Kent's green pastures to the top of the Downs where he paused. The village of Lenham was away to his right as his gaze took in the wide panorama before him, where the Downs fell away into the valley below, the fields rising gently beyond on their way to the Weald.

It was indeed a fine day for it. He never once noticed the cold, enjoying instead the loveliness of this most Kentish of scenes, as he had loved the ride from Downsland through glorious rolling countryside filled with the fragrant freshness of the air. And in that moment Marie was by his side and he knew that she was. He called to her and received reply and was at peace at last.

They were re-united. The heavy burden upon his shoulders fell away from him, and as he looked at the sun, low in the winter's sky, he saw the light he had believed he would never see again. He felt Marie's embrace about him, and knew he had indeed shrouded himself in that cloak that had kept his beloved from reaching out to him. How he regretted it now.

Lily and Sarah were right. You cannot expect these things to find you, it is necessary to open your heart and invite them in.

The ride had largely diverted his mind from his brother and Charles Handlen, although his sister was rarely out of his thoughts this day, but now Marie was once again standing shoulder to shoulder with him and whatever action he took would be the right way to address the problem. And at once he thought that Hester and the boys could flee to the continent. He had business contacts in the Netherlands. He could arrange it. Would that be an agreeable course for her?

He would ensure they were well looked after and would have the money they required. And he could make the journey and visit her from time to time. This had to be the answer. He would return home and write to his friend Aldert Bakker and describe the situation and await the Dutchman's response.

He pulled the reins around and galloped back to Downsland. Marie rode with him and he knew he would never be alone again. Now he had another letter to write.

***

This was the very day Roger Culteney discovered his new scheme had feet of clay and was about to disintegrate into dust almost before his eyes. He needed to escape.

His first port of call was Lady Matilda Haffley but not with the intention of divulging the bad news, and certainly, on this occasion, not to provide entertainment and pleasure. His aim was to extract further monies and he explained, all rather excitedly, how well the investment was proving and that increased investment was heartily advised.

She listened intently, sitting on the edge of her seat and smiling broadly, and then nodding with agreement. He had won

91

her over. Now to collect what he hoped would be a sizeable contribution and make good his departure, and be gone forever.

Unfortunately Lady Matilda had other ideas.

She would arrange a draft he could take to the bank, and do so after they had repaired to her bedchamber. It was a delay he could well do without. But it was obviously the only way, a most disgusting way, a thoroughly distasteful way of gaining the funds, and he'd done it before so why not now, one last time?

He led her upstairs desperately trying to conceal his anxiety and haste. He little knew that making love to an unattractive old lady was to prove a fatal measure today.

Another man seeking funds was Thomas Evershen.

He too was anxious, and irked that Clara had not met Sarah Brankly again. More information was required. The previous evening he had waved his rod at Clara to emphasise both his impatience and the price of her failure, so today she had written to Sarah in the hope they could meet again anon.

Sarah was pausing from her labours and taking a brief walk around one of the gardens. Despite being devoid of flowering plants it had all the promise of a spring that seemed a long way off, but she knew how much attention the gardeners paid to preparing their charges for winter's onslaught and for success in the coming year.

It was not much different, she realised, from crop growing on her family's smallholding, or from protecting the livestock from the seasonal ravages, not that there was much risk on a lovely day such as this.

"Hello Sarah." She turned to see Robert Broxford advancing towards her.

"Hello Robert. Why are you here?"

"I am off duty and happened to see you and wondered if you had seen Clara at all?"

"No I haven't Robert, but be patient. I will write and we shall see what happens. Be patient."

And she smiled wickedly, and giggled with mischief. It was infectious. Robert laughed freely, and then they talked for a while before Sarah excused herself to return to work.

I don't know, she thought, I have a lovesick footman to contend with, and I shall be maid to a lovelorn lady shortly, assuming Miss Cowans comes, as I'm sure she will. This is a strange thing, this love. I do not properly understand it, but then I have loved my parents and my siblings, although for all that I do believe love has many shapes. My love for mama is not, I suspect, the love I would feel for a man. Love like that must feel different, indeed I am certain it must.

Miss Cowans can forgive a man she loved for terrible misdeeds. Master grieves for a love he can no longer enjoy. It is a strange thing, love. How will I know if ever it should strike me? If I am destined never to know will I go to my grave the poorer for it? Or will I be the better for it?

After all, I might be wooed by a man like Mr Culteney, whose love would be false. Oh! How would I know until it was too late? Clara utterly ruined by such a man, Miss Cowans left bereft by such a man. And yet the Master found the most beautiful and enduring love imaginable, so the Mistress must've known love in the very way I may not ever know. She must've felt that very love for him too.

Oh, hey-ho. Maybe it is better that I never know than be disappointed like Clara and Miss Cowans. But why am I so curious? Robert thinks he is in love, perhaps he isn't. But there's Agnes over there; now she knows what it is to love.

"Agnes, Agnes."

"Sarah, out in the garden I see. I fine day for it."

"Yes, but I shall be in trouble, for I should be back at work."

"Come, we'll go together for I am late and we can be admonished together."

"How is Jed, Agnes?"

"He is in good spirits. He can get up and walk a little and the doctor says he will be able to leave the hospital very soon. I can hardly wait and neither can he."

"I am so pleased for you both. Dr Pearland saved his life. You must be very grateful."

"I give thanks to God for that every day. Dr Barrenbridge believes she will be an excellent surgeon one day, but in my eyes she is already."

"Most certainly Agnes. But she has the misfortune in society to be a woman." Both girls laughed.

93

"No Sarah, she has the *good* fortune to be a woman, let us not forget that." And they continued on their way chatting quietly and with good humour and set about their various tasks with renewed vigour.

***

Sarah's uncle Edmund Forness was truly settled into Sarah's home, and was making himself disagreeable to Clara. Sarah's mother had gone to market and Edmund was taking advantage of her prolonged absence to allow unsubtle hints to float around the air and into Clara's ears where they were unwelcome and unwanted.

He sat at the table pretending to study the ledger, a book he had made a complete mess of thanks to his inability to understand both the figures and their meaning, and muttered under his breath loud enough for Clara to hear as she busied herself cleaning the fireplace. She was pleased all he had flung at her were words but she knew the dread day would come.

How would she react? She wanted to be able to repulse him, and she did not want to be labelled a whore, that much she had decided. She would not want his money, that too she had decided. But was she strong enough in mind? If she lost her post there her father would be angry and his wrath would not be confined to words. She found herself hoping Sarah would reply with urgency and that they could meet very soon. There might be the opportunity to speak privately to her about the situation but she would need to be tactful. There was always the chance Sarah might betray her and her troubles would become manifold, although she thought better of her friend.

But there was a lingering doubt.

Had not her husband betrayed her as he had betrayed her love? There was no trusting people and she concluded she needed to be wary with everyone forthwith. She shuddered as she heard the chair scrape and turned to see Edmund rise.

"Just going to the cows, m'dear," he announced and went out without a glance in her direction, leaving her to breathe a sigh of relief. "Please come home soon, Mrs Brankly, please come home soon," she whispered quietly to herself.

***

An enraged Ralph Grayan had returned home and made life a misery for everyone, especially his wife. Unable to get the better of his brother, and been badly beaten, he was aggressive and relieved his anger and frustration on those around him, especially the servants. One of his daughters paid for a few words of insolence with a fearsome beating.

He could control these people where he could not control David Grayan, for he was a ruthless bully who took on the weak in place of those stronger than him. It rankled that the only blow he had landed on his brother had been with his whip, whereas David had punched and kicked him to the ground and would've inflicted worse given the chance.

Now he poured drink after drink, a man with too many worries. He slumped in a chair in the room he occupied alone. Wife, daughters and servants wisely maintained a safe distance knowing his rages too well, and also understanding they would die out as the drink overtook him.

Yes, he had other worries too, some that he could not share with his wife.

Another man with undisclosed worries was Charles Handlen.

His prime concern was not his wife but his money. He was heavily in debt. Heavily. He had wasted far too much, spent lavishly when they was so little to spend, and continued a lifestyle that was beyond his pocket by some way. He was not unusual among his class but he knew ruination was not worth having about your neck in society.

How could he avoid it? That was the puzzle.

He had no money left to invest, and earlier ventures had failed him abominably. He had suffered ill-fortune at the gambling tables time and again, and had nothing left to play with. Nobody would accept his note. How dare they insult him so! And why were his mistresses so damn expensive?

Unable to go to his club in his present circumstances his choice of destinations for pleasure was cruelly limited.

Well, his wife could jolly well please him. That is what she was there for. So he went in search of Hester and having located

95

her dragged her to their bedchamber, his drunken lust defeating all sense of reason and propriety. He possessed no mercy, had no thought for her, and dealt with her as he often did.

***

David Grayan received three communications that pleased him.

Yes, he could call upon Margaret Cheney, he would be welcome at the Haskerton's, and Lily Cowans would be pleased to spend some days at Downsland.

He related the latter to Sarah in a very brief meeting. She was astonished by his warmth and friendliness but was out of his study before she realised it. Was he a changed man, she pondered? Did he perhaps harbour some interest in Miss Cowans? Now there was a thought!

She had herself received a message from Clara and done so before she could write to her friend. Now she could put pen to paper and agree to their meeting.

Earlier she had mentioned the vexed issue of love to Agnes, love in all its guises.

"Why Sarah, are you in love?"

"No Agnes, do not be so silly. There is no point as you know..."

"There is every point Sarah. You will find love, and possibly where and when you least expect it. Love is like that."

"I love my mama as you love yours, but your love for Jed is different?"

"Oh very, very different Sarah. But how to describe it? I have not the poet's skill, nor the ability of writers. I cannot paint a picture and wish I could. Jed is simply my whole reason for being alive. There is never a cloud in my sky when I think of my love for him. When I thought he was going to die I felt such an emptiness, such a dread, such real pain. I think that's when you know what real love truly is.

"He says such wonderful things to me, he praises me and ... well ... he make me feel so very happy. That's love Sarah. And you will know it one day!"

"I will not. Stop teasing...."

"I promise you here and now you will. There, that's an end to it." And both girls embraced as the laughter engulfed them.

Working just a short distance away Ginny Perkins had heard the conversation and watched the two girls dance down the hallway to their next tasks. The laughter died away as they vanished beyond doors and Ginny stood in the silence and allowed one small tear to escape and dampen her cheek. She wiped it away with her sleeve.

Love, she thought, is a fool's errand, and one I shall not indulge in for nobody would want one such as me. As she made her own weary way, dragging her feet into another room where polishing was required, she reflected on the way the young, like Sarah and Agnes, viewed love, as if it was some amazing object that might be purchased at the market, a magical object that could create dreams, and which was well worth having.

The master had known love and how he had suffered for it, and how she wished she could save him from his horrors. Was love really worth all that agony?

***

It was not love that was driving James Parry-Barnard forward in his pursuit of Lady Harriet Fitzgower, it was the social standing and financial rewards that drew him in. He had misgivings. Her father might reject the prospect out of hand. Although he came from a titled family he would not inherit the status, and for now he was little more than a lowly physician.

There was much against it and yet Harriet herself was appearing to encourage him.

Did she simply want him as a plaything? The likelihood of being used in such a fashion did not sit comfortably with either his conscience or his desire to marry into wealth and position.

She did not know he was not fully qualified, and did not therefore appreciate the danger into which she was placing herself.

He examined her, pronounced her to be in fine fettle, though not with those words, but took the precaution of prescribing a harmless remedy to ensure she did not relapse. Lady Fitzgower had no knowledge of the medicine and remained blissfully unaware she was being hoodwinked in the advancement of selfish gain.

As was their custom they took tea together, and where a blazing fire provided heat to dull the coldness of the day that had infiltrated the great house.

"I do hope you will continue to call upon me from time to time, I should so wish it doctor, as I am convinced you will keep me in good health, and indeed good spirits as you always do." They shared the mildest of smiles.

"Lady Fitzgower, it is my privilege to wait upon you, for I am in any case your family's physician as you know, and your health is of paramount importance to me. I shall of course come as I should come if you summoned me. I am at your service." They both bowed their heads very slightly in acknowledgement and continued to display their barely discernible smiles.

"You will unquestionably consider me impertinent, doctor, and I apologise for asking, but I am surprised such a highly respected and sought after physician is as yet unwed. May I be so impudent as to enquire if a particular lady has your attention?"

Parry-Barnard took a diplomatic sip of tea to give himself time to weigh up all the possibilities relating to this sudden and unexpected query.

"Lady Fitzgower, I could never consider you to be in any way impertinent," he began, still struggling for time to think, "so please do not consider your question to be improper. You will understand that I am a man of ambition, but my calling is driven by the desire to relieve suffering and I am in the fortunate position of being able to pursue that aim through my work.

"Nonetheless, I do believe there is no harm in being ambitious as it will ensure that I improve my medical knowledge and experience to the benefit of many people. However, it is also my belief that it would be wrong to devote myself to the many to the exclusion of those whose lives bring so very much to the lower orders. Your family, Lady Fitzgower, employ a large number of people who would otherwise be penniless and more prone to sickness.

"It seems to me I would be best employed being of service to your family, as I am now, and others in your situation, to the greater good of the people. It is important to me to marry well

98

and to marry a lady who shares my creed as I have explained it. Maintain the health of our class and we guarantee high standards for the ordinary people as a result.

"I am unwed as I have not found a lady I would be worthy of, but I humbly submit that my ambition would permit me to entertain a lady of standing in advancement of my work, that I be elevated to where I could do most good."

It was a hotchpotch of words, he knew, but they were the best he could muster in the time available and hopefully they expressed his views to her satisfaction. Her appreciative smile suggested they might be.

"Thank you doctor. I understand entirely and I cannot say how much I agree with you. My only regret is that more people do not openly support your views. It is to my greatest pleasure that you are my family's physician and I trust we shall not lose you should you be elevated, as you put it, beyond us." Her words, he felt, were designed to provide the opportunity he must now grasp.

"Lady Fitzgower, in my opinion your family holds the highest of positions aside from the King himself, and I would not imagine for one moment I will ever rise to royal circles." She smiled encouragingly and he felt obliged to continue. "I would be most happy to serve you all my days, my lady." He hoped that would suffice.

"Doctor, I am so relieved to hear it. But who knows? Through your association with us you may indeed rise to royal circles for we related to the royal family as you know." It was Parry-Barnard's turn to smile and bow his head in deference. "And who knows, perhaps your relationship with my family might improve in certain circumstances?"

Surely this was the intimation of her interest? His heart throbbed with anticipation, but he must tread with care. The wrong word, the wrong moment, and he could undo all he had achieved.

For Roger Culteney the wrong moment was nearly upon him.

Lady Matilda Haffley lay quietly in his arms. He had done all he possibly could to please her, an exceptional performance in his eyes, a valedictory performance, and he hoped he had done enough. Now she could please *him*.

She would not get the chance.

***

David Grayan wrote at length. He explained Hester's situation in depth, so that there might be no misunderstanding and so that his friend should be very clear on the circumstances. He'd known Bakker many years; the two had become friends through trade, the Dutch merchant once staying at Downsland when Marie had been alive. He was known to be honest and resourceful.

David had one real concern; the sea crossing.

The North Sea could be deadly and he had no wish to lose his precious sister and her babies. Therefore he wrote to William Scrans at Whitstable, describing his needs and stressing he would pay well for a crossing in a reliable, relatively safe vessel, in which good quality accommodation could be provided.

Scrans had known Grayan from childhood, and had over the years made his fortune legally and otherwise. They had shared their schooldays and their friendship developed apace once the two men, in their separate ways, were discarded by the families and left to their own devices.

Mostly Grayan's business involvement had confined itself to the legal side of Scrans's activities but he had, to his eternal discredit, taken part in the illegal work of owling, smuggling wool across to the Low Countries. Scrans was an able smuggler and managed to conceal his darker side behind his lawful operations, not that he felt the Excise men and the Riding Officers were in ignorance. Besides, he was a good companion to some and had, occasionally, provided money or welcome illicit goods so that a blind eye might be turned.

Grayan trusted him.

The next morning he was up at dawn, breakfasted, and ready to ride to Margaret Cheney's and thence the Haskertons.

Sarah did not even look up as he galloped past on the drive. She was absorbed in her own thoughts and her forthcoming meeting with Clara. The two met just outside Westlingstead and they walked across the fields deep in conversation unaware Clara had just become a widow.

100

General Sir John Haffley, a veteran of the Scottish campaigns and a hero of Culloden had, the previous evening, by virtue of returning home unexpectedly, caught his wife and Culteney together.

"I demand satisfaction," he had roared, having first bellowed his annoyance and anger at the pair and then sent Lady Haffley from the room. "Tomorrow at dawn."

Culteney had often shot fowl and deer but had rarely held a pistol and here he was, confronted by a decorated soldier who was fully acquainted with the firearm. But there was no escape. Not this time.

Two friends accompanied him to the chosen park. Facing death he became quite philosophical. If he killed or injured the General, a popular hero, he would have to flee the country in all probability and he had so little money to do so. But his friends might help, especially as they were not yet alert to the collapse of his investment venture. And if Haffley killed him he was free at last!

The outcome of the duel was inevitable, and Culteney died from his wounds shortly before his estranged wife met Sarah.

"Sarah, your uncle Edmund has been kindness itself, and I have been so grateful for employment there." Sarah sensed Clara wished to unburden herself of a particular concern and decided on a course she had planned during her walk from Downsland.

"Uncle Edmund, oh uncle Edmund. Listen Clara and I will tell you a secret. Do not speak of this I beg you. But I had good reason to leave home when the chance presented itself, for uncle Edmund unsettled me and made me feel uneasy, and I was not sure what was in his mind. It was when mama was not present I noticed he had a way of looking at me. I do hope he has not unsettled you the same way." Sarah's trap was laid and Clara was caught in it.

"Oh Sarah, Sarah," she exclaimed, taking her friend by the arm, "he does indeed. In truth, if I may speak of him this way, for I know he is your uncle, your family, I am worried he may see me as easy prey and I have no wish to be approached in such a manner. But Sarah, I must not lose my position with your mother for my father counts upon my wages and will beat me if I have to leave..... I mean ... I ..." Her voice trailed away as she realised she had inadvertently revealed too much. Sarah stopped and the two girls looked directly at each other.

"Your father beats you Clara? At your age?" Clara looked crestfallen and her eyes searched the ground as Sarah's hands gently grasped her shoulders in support.

"Not often, but it is painful and draws blood." Sarah clasped her friend to her bosom and heard the softest of sobs, realising that what Robert had told her must be true. A beast of a father she had.

"Come Clara, let us sit over here and you can tell whatever you wish. Tell me about Edmund."

The day was not matching the brightness and crispness of the previous day, but it was, if anything, marginally warmer if that was possible in December. Grey, overcast but no wind at all to speak of.

"Sarah, I know beyond doubt what Edmund wants of me, and if I do not surrender I will lose my position and my father will be very angry. Please tell me, what can I do, what can I do?"

"Bless you for telling me Clara. Together we are stronger, believe me, and we will assess this situation and come to an answer, we will. Now I have something to tell you and you must not be angry." Clara's tears ceased on the instant.

"Clara, the Master told me you are married and have been deserted. I am so sorry, but we are friends and I wish to help you, and I cannot do so knowing I am keeping a secret from you. Please do not be angry and leave me."

Clara looked at her for some moments and then reached out and threw her arms around Sarah and the tears fell anew.

"Bless you, bless you, bless you Sarah," she spluttered, her voice a mixture of anxiety and relief. "Yes, I am and my father knows and wishes to extract money from Mr Grayan. Oh Sarah, Sarah. My father wants me to engage with you and learn all manner of things about Mr Grayan and he will beat me if I fail. He wants to find a way to force Mr Grayan to give him money. I am in such a state and know not what to do."

"Clara, we will be together in this, I promise. I am so pleased you have told me for now we can be true friends."

"Sarah, bless you indeed, that is all I wish for."

They found they could talk openly and freely and Clara gradually revealed the story of Roger Culteney's wooing and their elopement, and how, when she had to return home, she had been given the worst thrashing of her life. It was Sarah's turn to weep.

"I once dreamed of marriage and status I could never hope for, but Roger promised me my dreams. Wealth, servants, position. I would give everything now for a husband with whom I could live in near poverty. What a fool I was. My dreams were never worth a penny."

"Clara, you have been cruelly treated by your father and husband. What poor girl deserves such a fate? I will protect you Clara. We will deal with this as one. Come let us walk some more and enjoy our time together, and talk as we wish. I have one other secret to reveal and I have decided I must tell you." Clara looked distraught.

"No, no, it is nothing bad. I will tell you no more than this as I will not betray a friend. You have an admirer, and a fine lad he is, but he knows nothing of your past. For now do not bury all your dreams Clara, for we do not know what lies ahead and what God intends for us."

Clara seemed pleasantly stunned.

"An admirer? But he will not want me when he learns my own secret."

"You cannot be sure of that. I am told love can overcome all obstacles."

"Love? Love! I loved Roger until he deserted me and then I hated him....."

"That is because you never truly loved him Clara. I am given to understand that when you love with all your heart you can forgive more easily, and you cannot."

"You know about these things Sarah?"

"My knowledge is not first hand, but I have come to learn something of this wonderful love that people speak of, and have applied my wisdom to it."

Here was the young woman, so worldly-wise and confident, speaking on a subject she had no real knowledge of, yet a subject that fascinated her and attracted her interest. And here she was propounding her wisdom in a way that demonstrated, had Clara realised it, that there was so little foundation behind it.

Sarah was always willing to learn and increased her knowledge daily, and like any self-assured young person presumed wisdom came with it. She was still a woman of business possessing the skills she had learned running the smallholding with her mother. The Master himself had sought her advice and put private matters before her for her consideration. Here she was assisting a friend as she had aided Agnes in her hour of need.

She had good reason to be confident. This must be the path, she resolved, that God had chosen for her when she lost her chance of husband and children. Sarah was, in her own eyes, no longer a girl. She had grown up and was ready to take her place in the adult world. Ideas relating to Clara's plight were already forming in her fertile mind.

The pair walked on and talked again. Friends. True friends. Stronger together.

And Sarah would settle Clara's problem, she was persuaded of that.

Chapter Nine

"I will not be dictated to, I assure you, and least of all by Mr Handlen, but I will not place your sister in jeopardy Mr Grayan." Margaret Cheney was sitting alongside her husband Albert who held her hand comfortingly. She looked concerned as well she might do.

"Mrs Cheney, I am grateful for all you have done and the risks you have taken, and I am also grateful that you will not place Mrs Handlen in further danger, for she is in peril, I know that as you do. However, I wish to speak with you about a plan I will devise, but I must stress that it will not involve you in any way. I merely ask your opinion."

"Mr Grayan, forgive me, but it is better that I have no knowledge of your plans, then if I am challenged by her husband I can speak with honesty and acquit myself." Albert nodded his agreement. "I am forbidden from writing to or visiting your sister. I have thought about writing to her maid, a loyal and faithful servant, but my letter is bound to be intercepted. I feel so helpless and so afraid for her. That dreadful man will do all in his power to separate her from her sons and I fear he may move them away at any time."

David was also afeared that separation was likely. Margaret, speaking slowly and quietly, added further words.

"Are you aware she is beaten, Mr Grayan?"

"Yes I am, but have learned that only recently. She has kept it from me believing I might take immediate action against her husband. As much as I might wish to do so, I have no intention of behaving in that manner, for Hester's sake."

"I am pleased to hear it. My husband would also like to take issue with him, but he knows the wisdom of refraining. Mr Handlen is a violent man. By the by, I do understand that he has been dismissing some of his servants of late, and that might suggest his money is dwindling."

"That is interesting Mrs Cheney. I know him by reputation to be a profligate man but had assumed his family enjoyed substantial wealth. It is something that may be of value to me or not, but I am grateful you have mentioned it. Very well, I shall speak no further of my plans, but please know my gratitude for all you have done, and for the friendship I know my sister has placed above all else. You have been a comfort to her, a rock upon which she has been able to stand strong and survive Handlen's worst excesses, and I am sad that neither of you can enjoy that friendship at this time."

"Thank you Mr Grayan. Please know that my friendship with your sister lives on in spirit. I will not be cowed by that awful man, but I will always do whatever I can for Hester, you may count on that."

He left soon after and rode towards the Haskertons', deep in thought, worried and vexed, and trying to decide how he could execute his plan if there was no means of communicating with his sister. He desperately needed help, needed to confide in someone, ask for further opinions and suggestions. And then he remembered Marie was at his side. Bringing the horse up to a stand he made a silent prayer. The answer was before him; talk at first to Henry Barrenbridge.

And with that he spurred his mount and galloped to his next destination.

***

Edmund Forness was alone with Clara.

Sarah's mother was feeding the pigs and would not be gone long. Clara felt better than she had felt for a long time. Sarah had eased her anxiety, but every moment she was alone with this man she fretted, and with good reason.

Today he had moved around to be behind her as she worked and she detested it. His eyes bore into her and she could not see what he was doing. She squealed as his hand touched her shoulder.

As quickly as he had made his move he took away his hand as Catherine Brankly came back into the room. It could not go on like this for much longer. She could not stand it. But she could not afford to lose the job. She was in turmoil and hoped and prayed Sarah would come to her rescue and soon, for Edmund would come again when chance presented itself.

Her friend was already giving the subject due attention, and feeling full of importance.

I shall consult the Master, she determined, as he has consulted me on this very matter. He will know what to do. Poor Clara, to be treated so. Taken for her beauty and abandoned by her husband, whipped by her father who forces her to do his unpleasant bidding, and afraid of my uncle Edmund, afraid of losing her position with mama.

Then qualms fell upon her.

I am a maid, and a new maid, and a very young maid. How dare I try to speak to the Master! It is not a maid's place. But then again he will not mind. He appointed me after I thrust my way to his desk, putting my friend Ginny's position at risk. That was a terrible thing to do; I would've felt such shame had he dismissed her, such sorrow for what I had caused. I could never have made it up to her.

But he was kind to both of us. He has always been a kind man, but it is sad that his loss has weighed him down so heavily and submerged that very great quality. No, he will not mind. I think he will not mind. I hope he will not mind. I will try anyway.

And I must find a discreet way to speak with mama. That will not be easy. Harder than speaking to the Master! I must at all costs protect Clara's post. At least I have handed her some intelligence to pass to her father that should please him and keep him occupied, and save her from more trouble.

Oh what a mess. At least I have saved myself such worries. It must be the purpose God set aside for me, it must be. To help others, particularly in matters of love and the problems it brings. Oh what folly is love. I shall be better off without it, indeed I will.

***

James Parry-Barnard was taking advantage of Henry Barrenbridge's temporary absence to instruct Judith Pearland on some medical matter or other, and was very much in his element and enjoying himself. Instructing the heroine of Westlingstead was a joy and a task he falsely assumed he had every right to do, he being a far better physician than she could hope to be.

107

She tolerated this knowing he would not remain at the hospital much longer, and good riddance. But she still needed more support from Barrenbridge and he was not of the mind to hand out any appreciable quantity. Parry-Barnard was away more than he was in attendance and he had hinted that his desire to make the most of private practice was about to be made flesh now he was on the cusp of qualification. She envied him qualification, but not the direction he wished his professional life to take.

"Miss, miss." One of the nurses had appeared in the doorway. "Mrs Brankly is here. Her brother has been taken ill." Parry-Barnard spoke before Judith could reply.

"I'll come at once Lizzie. Miss Pearland can look after things here."

Miss Pearland bristled. The assumption of authority! Surely they should discuss who should go and who should stay? She took a deep breath and allowed the fierce anger to subside as Parry-Barnard slipped through the door. The sooner he is gone, she supposed, the sooner I can qualify and be free of such wretches. And she shuddered with annoyance. Lizzie was still there, watching her.

"Lizzie, thank you for advising me about Mrs Brankly and I am sorry I was so rudely ignored before I could reply." The nurse smiled knowingly. "Right Lizzie, let us do good as only women can do." And the two returned to the ward and the next patient requiring their ministrations, smiling cheerfully as they went.

David Grayan had received a chilled but friendly welcome at the Haskertons'.

Gradually their obvious caution thawed. This was an altered character to the one they had grown to accept as the embodiment of unrelieved grief. He was still gruff and lacked conviviality but it was an improvement. But it was what he had to say later that surprised them.

"I had a letter from Miss Cowans in Dover. You may remember it was thought she might have become wed to my friend Culteney. Unfortunately he eloped with another young woman, a basket-weaver's daughter, married her, and deserted her when he was ruined by a financial disaster.

"Miss Cowans called upon me and I was able to reveal the sad truth. She learned of her loss and faced it with great fortitude. Later she wrote a letter that touched me considerably. I have taken to confiding with a young maid. This may shock you." They did indeed look shocked. "There is something about this girl, something I dare not try and decipher, something I dare not try to understand. But there is something. I showed her the letter and she was able to translate the simple message because she comprehended its meaning.

"I have been frustrated in my attempts to find your daughter's spirit about me. Such agony has driven me into a world that holds no future, no light, no happiness, and condemns me to search fruitlessly for something I will never find. I thought all I had to do was walk in the gardens Marie loved to find her there.

"Miss Cowans and Miss Brankly, the maid, told me I had wrapped myself in an impenetrable blanket of gloom through which Marie could not infiltrate, and that I had to open my soul to allow her in. When I discarded that blanket Marie came to me and has been by my side ever since."

The Haskertons were wide-eyed with astonishment, open-mouthed with amazement. It was Daniel Haskerton who spoke first.

"And this revelation has freed you?"

"It has sir. Marie will never leave my side now. We can be everything we were before her demise. I will make the most of this, I assure you. First I must seek your forgiveness for my appalling behaviour, but beg you understand I had been eaten away by some dreadful evil spirit. I have killed that evil being and it will occupy me no more." Georgina Haskerton, looking pale and almost horrified, came to life while her husband had relapsed into speechlessness.

"Mr Grayan, dear David, please tell me. You said you were touched by Miss Cowans's letter, but what part was played by this maid?"

"Sarah understood. Her father died tragically and she was left to tend their smallholding with her mother. Overcome by grief they nevertheless realised they had to maintain their farm, they accepted help and friendship from friends and neighbours, and gradually they emerged into the warmth of the sun. They opened their arms to the support of those that cared whereas I shut myself away."

"Oh David, if your transformation is thus achieved I am confident we will all be very grateful for whatever medium brought it about. You may count upon our close friendship."

"Mrs Haskerton, Mr Haskerton, I am equally grateful for your support, and I can only beg your forgiveness for the inexcusable behaviour you have experienced at my hands."

The Haskertons looked at each other with a pleasurable degree of acceptance and agreement. Daniel spoke.

"David, there is nothing to forgive if you are restored. But please tell us more these two ladies."

David related most of his knowledge and his relevant feelings while Georgina Haskerton looked positively spellbound. Her husband, sitting alongside her holding her hand as he had done throughout, was more relaxed now and following his son-in-law's words with interest.

Later, on the ride to Kent, David reflected with joyful feelings anew as the only gloom to be found, the closing of a dull, miserable day, descended on his journey. His first call was the hospital.

"I'm sorry sir. Dr Barrenbridge is away until later this evening, visiting an aunt in Rye. Is there anything I can do?"

"Thank you Dr Pearland, but it is a personal not medical matter. I will call in the morning if you think that will be convenient."

"I dare say it will be."

"Dr Parry-Barnard. Is he not here?"

"Calling upon a patient and will be back anon. Thank you for the title, sir, but I am not a doctor yet."

"In my eyes you are. When do you qualify?"

"Thank you again sir. But I need to consult Dr Barrenbridge about my progress. I do not foresee a university place as I am a woman, so I am unsure whether I shall ever have the opportunity to qualify by that or any other means."

"I see. I shall speak to him on the subject, if you have no objection."

"None whatsoever."

Judith had no objections but little hope. Grayan might support the progress of women but society did not. She had long held the view Barrenbridge had encouraged her for his own benefit when in truth she had so little chance of advancement in her profession.

Parry-Barnard had studied medicine at university, so she knew, and he was now presumably gaining experience under Barrenbridge. What she did not know was that he had not finished his course, probably due to excessive laziness, and had little chance of any qualification whatsoever.

But in these times people cared less about how their physicians and surgeons arrived at their posts and more about simply having medical help. It was not unusual for practitioners to have had very little training. It was an accepted way of life.

***

Thomas Evershen was delighted with two pieces of news.

With Sarah's uncle Edmund lying unwell in his bed Clara had been offered a few more hours employment in the coming days. Clara had also disclosed the information regarding David Grayan that Sarah had dreamed up, with Clara's consent, and was deliberating his next move. His daughter had done well on both counts and for once he displayed a small grin and a look of contentment, although somehow he managed to appear menacing and angry even at rest.

Despite an evil outlook the man basically lacked much intelligence, and therefore showed poor wisdom in the application of knowledge. He could scheme but he could rarely find flaws in his own calculations, whereas these machinations often possessed sufficient difficulties to undermine their success.

He decided he would write to Grayan again but choose his words carefully and with tact. In this he was handicapped from the outset owning very little diplomacy and a propensity to ignore care. Then he was struck by an idea. He would get Clara to write. She was educated. She would know how to best express what he had to say. And his sly grin disappeared as he erupted into a coarse laugh which had no humour and no jollity.

As yet Sarah did not know her uncle was ill. She busied herself with the work Mrs Forbes handed her, sometimes working with Esther, sometimes Ginny, and despite her concentration which ensured satisfactory completion of the tasks, her mind was constantly musing upon the various problems to be faced.

At this precise moment she was working with a new maid Emma, and showing her all that she needed to know, explaining the reasons why certain duties were necessary, rendering praise when the girl did well, but never admonishing. Sarah believed it was better to explain things further, demonstrating when she thought it essential, rather than tell someone off when they were making an honest effort.

She knew about Clara's paternal beatings, and she'd heard tales of maids being whipped at other great houses. Her own parents had treated her kindly, rectifying any shortcomings or acts of defiance with sharp words alone. Her father expected her to behave at school and so she did, never once requiring disciplinary measures be taken against her. The transgressions of some of those she went to school with were dealt with a strictness she didn't approve of.

I would never strike my own children, she declared, for there are better ways than the employment of pain. Sadly I shall never have children of my own so that I can prove my point.

Sarah had never heard stories of beatings at Downsland and had assumed they were not necessary, discipline being maintained by other means. Of course, that made the Master's rant at Ginny and the threat of a thrashing all the more inexplicable. She'd been told about the only maid who worked there who had been dismissed. Caught stealing the Master had given her a second chance, her sole punishment being the loss of twenty days wages. She repaid this act of compassion by stealing again two months later, and for no other reason than to buy a piece of jewellery for herself.

Apparently one of the grooms had similarly been caught stealing but the Master discovered he was being threatened to do so by a relative. Mr Grayan resolved the issue and the groom continued his employment under no further family threat. The Grayans, she understood, had always been like that. Indeed, the more she learned the more she realised how remarkable this man was, how capable, how caring, and it became easier to

112

comprehend why the loss of wife and child had affected him so badly.

***

The next morning Grayan called on Barrenbridge.

"Henry, will Miss Pearland qualify?" The doctor sighed, interlaced his fingers in front of his stomach, looked at Grayan, the floor and back at his visitor. And sighed again.

"David, she was an excellent nurse, and frankly that is all that is required of a woman. I trust my words will not be heard outside this room, but I have encouraged her in the hope the situation will change in time, and in the meantime she will be of benefit to the hospital. She has been more than that. I have shown her so much and her capability is beyond question. But she will go no further for all that you and I may wish it."

"Henry, Marie encouraged her, encouraged *both* of you, because she believed in her."

"I know, I know. But David, she is a country lass. She cannot hope to better herself in this field."

"Ye gods Henry. We have barbers carrying out operations. Butchers more like. And here is one able woman showing she is a physician and surgeon to match any I know. And I say that in deference to you as I believe you to be amongst the best."

"It is not up to me David, as well you know. You fight a lone battle against convention...."

"Henry, think back to what she achieved with Jed Maxton. Does that count for nothing?"

"David, let us not fall out over this. Frankly it does count for nothing. But I am happy to have her here to assist me, and will do so for as long as she wishes to stay, for I rely upon her and know she will not let me down. But I can offer her no qualification, and that's an end. Please do not reveal what I have told you....."

"Henry, you have my word. But I am shocked. By the by, what of James? Surely he is a qualified physician?"

Once again Barrenbridge sighed and looked hard at his friend before answering.

113

"I have not told you this, but do so now on the understanding it is a private matter. James did not complete his course at university. I took him on thinking that he must have some fine qualities to offer the practice, and I have always believed him to be very good. I will tell you this, but this is truly for the ears of nobody else.

"Not long ago, in my absence, he operated on a local man who died on the operating table. When I examined the body and spoke with James it became clear he had misdiagnosed and surgery was not necessary. Also, he made a fatal mistake during the operation and did not have the skill to either realise what was afoot or to correct it."

"Oh God Henry. The poor man. Do his family know?"

"No, for the good of the hospital I supported James. He'd told them that he'd tried everything to save him, that surgery had been essential. It would not have done to discredit him...."

"I am sad to hear you say that. Better surely to have dismissed him....."

"I do not think so. Whatever regrets I may have now it was the right decision. The man's family accepted the situation and thanked James wholeheartedly for all he had done. Far better to maintain the reputation of the hospital."

"Who was the man, Henry?"

"A village farmer, a Mr Brankly." Grayan's eyes widened and a look of shock spread swiftly across his face. He was clearly shaken.

"Did he have a daughter, Sarah, can you remember?"

"Yes I think that is so. Do you know of her?"

"She is one of my maids." He sat back in his chair the horror and sadness overwhelming him.

"David, David, what is the matter?"

"You have taken me by surprise, that is all. Still, there is nothing to be done now. But I suggest you rid yourself of James as soon as you can. I heartily recommend it."

"I believe he will go soon anyway. He has been busy acquiring posts as a private physician and will want to be away from all this."

"Then encourage him Henry. The sooner the better. Will he be well away from here?"

114

"Hawkhurst I understand. He wishes to settle there."

"And Henry. Tell Judith the truth."

With his mind in turmoil David had forgotten the purpose of his visit and departed without discourse on the subject. Although it returned to his thoughts as he rode away he made no attempt to retrace his steps. He was too disgusted, too angry.

Poor Sarah. How would he ever face her with such knowledge about her own loss? Her beloved father might've been alive now but for James Parry-Barnard. And his good friend Henry Barrenbridge had covered it all up, and was leading Judith Pearland along falsely as well.

He was beginning to see Barrenbridge in a very different light.

Chapter Ten

"Oh mama this is all such a mess."

Having learned that her uncle Edmund is taken to his bed, but thankfully not seriously ill, Sarah obtained permission from Mrs Forbes to attend her mother. She sits at the table with the ledger before her unable to comprehend the muddle her uncle has made of things.

"Uncle Edmund clearly has no idea what he is doing. This is all in such disarray."

"I'm sure Edmund knows exactly what he is doing Sarah, and I am confident there is no muddle."

"Mama, papa made sure I could do all this and he taught me well. He watched over me and checked everything I did and was happy it was work I could do."

"I don't think you, a young girl, should criticise Edmund. He believed you had not done it all so accurately and had to amend entries and calculations."

"I am sorry mama, but he is wrong and I only criticise because he has meddled and made a fine mess of it."

"Sarah, please leave the book alone. I will not have you speak of my brother so. He can attend to it when he recovers. Dr Parry-Barnard said it should only be three or four days. Edmund has been such a help to me. I won't have him maligned, and not by you."

Sarah knew when she was beaten, and knew her love for her mother was constant and never wavered. For that love she would argue no longer. She set aside the ledger and changed course.

"How is Clara mama? She is good here?"

"She is good company and a good worker. I am grateful for her and I can afford her with the money you give me, so now she will be here almost every day until Edmund is fit and able once more."

"You do not require me to return here for a while?"

"No my love. Your money is welcome. Go and earn it, we can manage." And she smiled with tender love and embraced her daughter.

Not very far away another resident of Westlingstead had received a surprise.

David Grayan had Thomas Evershen's letter to hand and had concluded the best action he could take was to visit the man.

"Get out!" Evershen bawled at his daughter Clara, who vanished as quickly as her legs could convey her. His voice softened and his furtive grin appeared.

"Please be seated sir." Grayan decided Evershen was like a spider trying to persuade a fly into its web. He sat without removing his eyes from the basket weaver who plumped down into another chair. "You have my letter sir. Have you come to settle with me?"

"I will tell you this Evershen. It had not been my intention to inform you but it is now necessary to do so. When you wrote at first I spoke with Culteney and ordered him to come and negotiate with you. He advised me of the agreed figure and I gave him that money for you. Do not dare to ask for more." Evershen's eyes were bulging and there was a look of genuine disbelief across his face, from which his rotten smile had disappeared.

"Evershen, the matter was closed then. There is no more."

"Sir, I swear to you he never came to me. I have had no money which is why I ask now."

"And you ask in the most evil manner imaginable. Your letter does all but actually accuse me of crime. And you expect me to believe what you say now? I would no more trust you than trust the devil."

Evershen was riled and looked it, but kept his voice under control.

"I have told you sir, and it is the truth. I have sworn to you that Mr Culteney never came. I have had no money and I would not ask now if I had."

They studied each other. Grayan sensed he had indeed heard the truth.

"Evershen, I will do this. I will ask Culteney for the truth of the matter. If indeed he defrauded both of us I will agree recompense with you. You have my word."

The basket-weaver's face screwed itself up and then relaxed so that a smile could decorate it.

"Sir, I am grateful indeed, as my poor ill-treated daughter will be. The money is for her future." Grayan knew that it wasn't.

The two parted company, Grayan ignoring the proffered handshake, and Evershen went in search of Clara to congratulate her. His visitor went home to write to Culteney's father.

***

She walked over fields and was not even aware of the drizzle gradually soaking her hair and clothes. She was beyond caring. Her tears occasionally dropped but mingled with the misty rain on her cheeks. Nobody would've known.

Every dream in her heart, every glorious hope, every eager anticipation, indeed the map of her whole future had been burned to a cinder before her eyes, and she was wretched. There had been so many golden moments passed, and so very many to look forward to. Moments of triumph and success, occasional failure, but above all else moments of real achievement.

Now Judith Pearland was as dead in spirit as she was dead on the path to happiness. She had guessed the unpalatable truth long ago, but had not dared to think that it might be so, and now Dr Barrenbridge had revealed it with words that cut her in two. Wanting to scream and shriek and barely able to control herself she had begged him excuse her so she could walk for a little.

She ran and ran, then walked when she tired, and eventually let out a piercing squeal when she was certain there was nobody to hear her, raising her face to the filthy grey sky as if to take issue with God himself. Now she crumpled into a bundle of sodden clothes as she fell beneath a tree, and as the drizzle became stronger rain driving against her head as she cowed against the bark.

Judith was oblivious to the fact she was no longer alone.

"Doctor, doctor. Are you unwell? Can I help you?" Startled, she glanced up at a man she didn't immediately recognise. "It's I. Abe Winchell. Blacksmith's son. You hurt miss?" She struggled to rise but had no strength left. "What's up miss? I'll take care of 'e."

"Abe, Abe. Yes I know. I'm sorry, sorry I didn't recognise you. Sorry." Her speech was slurred and lifeless.

"You're in a state miss, you really are. What's happened miss?"

"I ... I ... I ... I came out for a walk and the weather closed in. I've had news that shocked me, but I shall be fine." Her words were croaked as if it was too much to speak, and her eyes closed as her head rolled over on the bark. Abe stepped forward with haste.

"Here miss, I have my horse here. Let me help 'e up and we'll ride back to the hospital. Y'sit in the saddle and I'll lead. Let me help you." She surrendered and offered her arm but made no other movement lying helpless on the grass. Abe understood and suddenly she felt his arms around her and realised he was lifting her onto the horse. She collapsed forward and knew his arm was on her back to support her and she knew she would not fall.

With that Abe turned the horse and led it towards Westlingstead while the rider passed into unconsciousness.

Outside the hospital he cried out for help. Two people came to him and one ran and fetched Barrenbridge. Abe carried his charge inside at Barrenbridge's direction and offered to go to her parents' house on the edge of the village, and was despatched at once. He returned with them minutes later as the rain took hold and poured with great venom and pace saturating all who were abroad.

He explained about how he had found her and brought her back and asked to be informed of her progress. Only then did he return to the forge wondering as he went what awful news had been given the doctor. He found he was hoping for her swift recovery. But it was more than that; he was *longing* for her recovery.

***

Clara had made her way to the smallholding keen to impart her news to Sarah, and had been caught in a downpour. Sarah's mother insisted she take her dress off and dry herself and her clothes before the roaring fire. Once Mrs Brankly had gone to tend to Edmund Clara told her friend that the plan had worked and that her father had asked her to write the letter to Grayan.

119

"And then your Master arrives without warning to challenge papa. I was ordered from the room but my father, in a state if high excitement, later told me he had learned from Mr Grayan that Mr Culteney had been sent to negotiate a settlement which Mr Grayan himself would pay. Apparently he was not to disclose that the money was not his. But he never came. He must've defrauded his own friend and taken all the money for himself.

"I am not sure Mr Grayan believes my father but has promised to write to Mr Culteney's father to establish the truth and will recompense my papa if his story is correct. So he is happy for once and his rod remains untouched."

"I am so pleased for you Clara. But you will see no money."

"I know, but I would rather live as I do and live without fear than as things have been. At least your uncle's indisposition has given me some relief from my other problem."

"Yes I know, but do not worry, we will sort out your situation Clara, I promise you."

What bothered Sarah was that Mr Culteney might yet claim he came to an arrangement with Clara's father and duly paid him, and the Master would have to decide who was telling the truth. If it went in Mr Culteney's favour Clara might be in more trouble. She would need to see Mr Grayan as she had planned after all. Yes, that was the way to play it. In the meantime she had worries about uncle Edmund's book-keeping and his unwanted attentions directed at Clara.

Was life nothing but difficulties, she wondered? But surely problems were there to be solved and it had fallen to her, by God's will she presumed, to resolve these issues. And the thought gave her strength, indeed it did.

For one young man there was a pleasant enough problem to be overcome, one that would require all his tact and cunning but with a treasure worth collecting.

James Parry-Barnard was surprised to receive word that Lady Fitzgower had suffered the most minor of relapses and would he attend when he was able. She stressed it was not urgent, that she knew he was extremely busy, and he should only travel when work permitted.

He joyfully read into this that the lady had not relapsed and was merely keen to see him again, and had resorted to this ruse to attract him and to have a reasonable excuse for so doing lest her father should otherwise object. He laughed out loud.

My clever Lady Harriet, he mused as he shook his head in admiration, you are a delight and I love you all the more for it. Yes, my Lady Harriet, I love you. There, I have said it, if only to myself. I will be a most devoted husband and, I believe I am required to say, I will make you happy all the days of your life. You see, I am a romantic at heart. Shall I bring you gifts? Yes, of course I will, and lay them at your feet. Will I swear to worship you every day? I do so swear my beloved Lady Harriet.

And when I propose will I be upon one knee? Yes indeed. And when I have won your heart will I then become a wealthy and renowned physician with high status in society? Oh yes, M'lady, for that is the purpose of wooing you.

And he laughed again.

He would beg Barrenbridge's leave and depart on the morrow or the day after if more convenient. He had some patients to deal with including that rather objectionable fellow Forness and he would visit him later. Alone with the man the first time he had examined him Forness had shown himself not to be too ill to make a lascivious comment about the young woman who had shown him into the room.

Yes, she was a girl who would command attention, a beauty without mistake, but Forness must be three times her age. What a dreadful man. But perhaps he, James Parry-Barnard might see the girl again. And thoughts of benefitting from the pleasure of her company flooded his mind. Indeed, she was a beauty and he could pluck whatever ripe fruits he might before giving himself fully to Lady Fitzgower. Certainly a peasant girl would welcome the consideration of a handsome young gentleman!

Also giving thought to Clara Evershen was Robert Broxford. He was longing to see Sarah again in the hope she would have more news that might favour him. He had doubts. He could not possibly be worthy of a proud beauty and yet Sarah had given him hope. He did not see Clara the same way Edmund Forness and James Parry-Barnard did. He saw her as a young woman he could love and be devoted to, treating her with love and kindness, consideration and respect.

But could Clara Evershen love *him*?

121

He knew not, and dismissed the possibility too readily.

***

Jed had no doubt about love.

His love was beside him making him well again. Agnes Byrne's eyes glowed with love as she looked upon him. He was doing so very well, walking again with only the slightest limp, and he appeared so strong and, in her opinion, so handsome. Ye Gods, he was her everything and how she loved him! She crossed the floor and hugged him and he flung his arms around her and sought her lips, easily surrendered, and kissed her with great passion and feeling.

She responded with all her brave heart could give and hoped it would be enough.

It was, and their happiness was complete. Entwined and absorbed in each other neither noticed Grace Gandling enter the room and were shocked to discover their full-bloodied embrace had been overlooked.

"Oh don't worry about me. I just came to see Jed and I have learned all I needed to know! I think he is recovered sufficiently to go home."

"Please no," exclaimed Agnes, "not back to Lenham, please let it not be so." All three appreciated the humour and shared gentle laughter. Grace continued.

"It is not up to me, but Agnes you see he is well mended and we may send him on his way."

"He is indeed, and I am grateful to you and, of course, Dr Pearland." Gandling looked downcast.

"What is wrong Grace?"

"Agnes, Dr Pearland is here and very ill. Dr Barrenbridge is truly concerned for her I'm afraid."

"Whatever has happened Grace?"

"Abe Winchell found her collapsed in a field, soaked to the skin, and delirious and brought her here. I fear for her, I sorely do."

Both Agnes and Jed looked horrified, Agnes close to tears. Jed spoke.

"Is there anything we can do? I owe her my life, my well-being."

"Thank you Jed, but we must wait, it is all we can do, all any of us can do."

The three remained in respectful silence for several minutes. There were no more words to be spoken.

The December night took upon itself a gown of violence and mischief, the wind searching out every unprotected corner and thrusting cold, biting rain therein. The rain itself fell in mighty profusion, wave after wave borne upon the icy wind that now tore across Kent and slashed mercilessly against everything in its path.

Those indoors close to throbbing fires were safe, dry and warm. Animals sought what shelter they could, some brought into sheds for protection, others left to fend for themselves. It was not a night for man or beast to be abroad. For some folk the evening matched their dreary moods, for others they settled down to make the best of their homes and all their homes gave them, and praised God they had such sanctuary.

Chapter Eleven

It is nearly Christmas and there has been a transformation at Downsland. David Grayan has assumed an air of jollity which has bewildered most of his workers as they have grown used to his sombre moods and isolation and are not prepared for the change.

At his invitation Marie's brother and sister and their families came to stay for a few days and once again Sarah found herself an organiser of childrens' games and entertainments.

He received a letter from Culteney's father explaining about the death of his son. Thus unable to verify Evershen's version of events he went to the basket-weaver and agreed an arrangement which was paid there and then, and on the basis it was a full and final settlement. Clara is now a widow but free of the man who ruined her life, and works every day for Sarah's mother.

Edmund Forness was a great deal longer recovering from his illness and is now a largely subdued person, poor in spirit, who mainly sits around the house and gives Clara her orders, ignoring her otherwise, much to her satisfaction. He spends plenty of time immersed in the ledger which he does not truly understand.

James Parry-Barnard is leaving the practice and has moved into lodgings near Hawkhurst in order to be close to Lady Fitzgower, and is still unsure whether he has a chance of the lady. He is summoned often, usually on the pretence of a relapse, and he plays on this by administering harmless remedies for non-existent problems.

In time Judith Pearland recovered having been seriously ill and has resumed her position alongside Henry Barrenbridge. Their intercourse is confined solely to their work. She will not speak with him with friendship or about any matters not related to medicine. However, she has been seen quite frequently in the company of Abe Winchell who probably saved her life on the day of her collapse and he is helping to restore her spirits.

Another visitor to Downsland has been Lily Cowans. During her brief stay she was often observed walking in the grounds with Grayan and they appeared good company with each other during meals and in relaxation. One or two maids have speculated as to the future of this friendship.

From David Grayan's point of view the most important development had been the departure of his sister and the twins for the Netherlands, and receipt of news that they had arrived safely and been well looked after. His contacts arranged accommodation and transportation. He had put the difficulty of getting her away from her home to Sarah who suggested she go to the Handlens' pretending to be a friend of Hester's loyal maid.

Grayan organised the journey once the maid's name had been supplied by Margaret Cheney and Sarah worked a miracle, her first visit being to establish the line of communication. The maid was reluctant, afeared for her life, but having no family of her own finally agreed. Sarah was confident she could be trusted.

The second visit was to provide instructions.

One cold December evening, when Charles Handlen was with a mistress, and the boys were asleep and unattended by their nannies, the maid and Hester packed all they would need and made good their escape. Each carried an infant to the waiting coach standing some distance from the house, having first taken their bags. David and his housekeeper Eleanor Forbes had provided food and other clothing for them ready for their onward journey.

The meeting at Downsland had been limited due to the urgency, but David rode in the coach to Whitstable and handed his charges to William Scrans in good time for the sailing. It was vital they be away before their absence was discovered.

Charles Handlen was in an explosive mood, dismissing staff, handing out beatings to any who would submit, and issuing ugly oaths of revenge. He stormed to Margaret Cheney's where she denied any knowledge of what had happened and how, and made the mistake of punching her husband who fought back rather successfully.

He rode to Downsland sensing Hester might be there, tried to attack David and was given a savage beating for his trouble. He called upon the local Constable who went to Grayan and decided it would be prudent to accept David's word that he retaliated in self defence. With some degree of fear he related his findings to Handlen who rode away in a fearsome temper.

125

Nobody was aware that it was the very day that Charles Handlen also learned that he was facing financial ruin, his father refusing to bail him out further. Too much money, far too much money had been handed over father to son, the old man finally at the end of his tether with the wasteful child. Pleading proved pointless. The father was too resolved, too stubborn.

So Handlen resorted to crying on the shoulder of a mistress who sent him packing when she learned he had no money left to speak of, and he went away and drank himself into a stupor, this being the only course of action open to a man like that.

Grayan was well aware that Handlen would once more approach his own estranged brother, Ralph, and trouble could be brewing for the days ahead. But for now there was peace and happiness in this part of north Kent with the festive season close upon them. Two other visitors came and stayed, Margaret and Albert Cheney, both overjoyed with the news about Hester.

The place was alive as people came and went, and there was a constant hum of activity with so much work to be done. With this revival came renewed enthusiasm amongst the staff, and word swiftly spread to Westlingstead that the Master of Downsland was reborn. Such stories usually bore tittle-tattle about the possibility of a new amour in his life, a reference to Lily Cowans.

Jed Maxton has returned to work and he and Agnes Byrne have finally announced a date for their wedding next April.

Sarah Brankly smiles to herself. Some matters are resolved, some require no urgent attention, and some are currently puzzling her. Today she is considering Robert Broxford and his interest in Clara Evershen, for he knows nothing of her scandalous past, and Clara herself no longer expresses any attraction to finding a true love. On the contrary, she has determinedly refused to discuss the subject with Sarah who assumes her dreams have waned and died.

Robert and Sarah have met in the gardens.

"Sarah, please tell me, does Clara know anything of me?"

"Nothing at all Robert. I have told her she has an admirer but not revealed who, and now she does not ask. You may have to give her time. I will know when the time is right."

As usual, Sarah spoke with the authority of one of knowledge and wisdom and understanding. Such was the strength of her stance that Robert recognised immediately her superiority in this issue and bowed to her judiciousness. But it hurt him yet.

"Sarah, it has been many days long gone now, and I know I have pestered you for information, but you cannot imagine how much I think of Clara and do not wish to find I have been supplanted. There are many men better than I"

"Robert, you must never think like that. Remember what you will offer Clara and consider yourself to be the best prospect. You said her father was a beast and he may still object to you. She is not yet one and twenty and must obey him. I talk to her often. We are good friends and I will know when it is the moment.

"And in the meantime if anyone else approaches they will have me to deal with!" Both laughed, and then wandered on in silence as she decided how she would speak to Clara and encourage her to meet Robert. At least she was a widow and free to love. Robert broke into her reverie.

"The Master is happy again. You must be happy for him?"

"Oh yes, and there are these rumours about Miss Cowans."

"I know. Is there anything there, do you think?"

"I am not so easily convinced. Gossip does not appeal to me but everybody does it and loves it. And who knows Robert, one day the gossip may be about you and Clara."

He blushed a bright red and Sarah laughed at him. He smiled in return and gently pushed her shoulder which only made her laugh all the more. Then he put his arm around her but briefly and with that they said their goodbyes and went their separate ways. If Clara does not want him, Sarah thought, perhaps I should have him for myself. And the thought made her laugh out loud.

There was no arrogance about her. She might be self-assured, confident, but she respected the views of others and was willing to debate issues where there might be disagreement but not animosity. Sarah would always admit to being wrong. She was never afraid of that.

As she returned to her duties she mused on Robert and Clara, and on the Master and Miss Cowans. She had been maid to the latter on her recent visit and found her to be so pleasant and appreciative. They had enjoyed a number of brief conversations and it was clear Miss Cowans had taken to her. Yes, perhaps she might make a good wife for the Master.

Perhaps she might.

***

It was only a question of time before Ralph Grayan arrived at Downsland, doing so in the company of Charles Handlen.

"I demand to know where my sister is."

"I have no idea Ralph. Why ask me?"

"Do not try and make a fool of me. You arranged her flight. Now where is she?"

"You have irrefutable evidence to support your accusation?"

David was speaking quietly, his brother loudly and angrily. Charles stood back a little, and tapped his whip on his gloved palm. There was silence as the three looked to each other. Ralph thought he knew how to irk his brother and he tried to do so from a different course.

"You weak little man. Ran off with a whore. Was she good to you David? Did she perform as you might've wished? I've no doubt she did." He turned and exchanged malevolent grins with Handlen, no doubt believing his words had bitten deep. "You cannot behave as a gentleman because you are not one. So presumably arranging this dastardly deed and sending my sister away from her lawful husband was a wicked adventure and a jolly entertainment for you. Speak up David."

Glaring, David gave him his answer.

"I have finished with you as my brother, just as you once finished with me. I have nothing further to say. Since you both consider *yourselves* to be gentlemen I am sure you will do me the honour of leaving my house this instant. I have not heard from Hester, know nothing of her departure, and would not assist you if I could. You make alliance with this cowardly wretch," he pointed at Charles, "who has beaten your sister until the blood flowed freely so do not pretend Hester meant as much to you as you make out."

Ralph spun round. Handlen looked alarmed.

"Handlen, this must not be true. Tell me there is no truth in this accusation." His brother-in-law looked almost close to tears for two or three moments. "Is this true?" he yelled when no answer came. Handlen took a step backwards and tried to speak but words would not form on his lips. He was shaken to the core by this unexpected turn of events. Ralph was red in the face with anger and Handlen knew he had to respond.

"Grayan," stammered Handlen, "you do not believe this man, surely?"

"I am asking *you* Handlen."

"I ... I ... I ... have only exercised discipline as I thought was the right of any husband, yourself included......"

"Handlen, how badly did you beat my sister. Tell me," he screeched, his face screwed with the fury rising within him.

"Only ... only ... what ... what ... I thought was necessary. Her flesh was too soft Grayan, she bled too easily." Ralph could not contain himself.

He flew at Handlen who fell to the floor under the blows raining down upon him without making any attempt to defend himself. He cried out to David.

"David, David, save me." But David was laughing at the pair of them. He walked slowly to the fireplace and pulled the bell rope. The two were still rolling on the floor, neither having the qualities or ability to fight in such a manner, when a startled Ginny Perkins entered the room.

"Ginny, fetch some footman at once so we can break up this unseemly nonsense, and before I take on the pair of them and throw them out!" She fled and came first upon Robert Broxford. He stormed into the room pursued by two other footmen and between them they restrained the visitors.

"Right, gentlemen. Leave now or I will have you escorted out of my house. Do not return here. I have given you my answer and there is no more to be said."

Broxford let go of his grip on David's brother who swung a punch at him. It did not reach its intended target, the footman's face, for Robert threw his arm up in defence and punched Ralph in the midriff with his other hand. It was enough for David.

"That's enough. Have these foul men thrown out if you please." The footmen looked unsure. "Yes, yes, yes, I mean

129

throw them out, into the dust in front of their horses if necessary. That is an order. Broxford took the lead and grabbed Ralph again.

"Alright, alright," his victim shouted. "We'll go, but unattended by your thugs. Now leave us be."

At a nod from David the footmen released their charges and watched as they made their way out.

"Thank you all," David said in acknowledgement of the loyal efforts of his men, "and I am sorry you have borne witness to this. Truly sorry, but thank you once again." The footmen started to drift away and Grayan noticed Nancy, Sarah and Ginny cowering in a corner. He clapped his hands.

"Shoo, shoo, shoo, back to work," and laughed as they vanished from view with an alacrity that suggested they might not have been there at all. Mrs Forbes arrived somewhat breathless having been summoned by Esther Hammond.

"Sir, what has happened here? Whatever is the matter?"

"Mrs Forbes," he said as he gently clasped her shoulder, "a minor disagreement between two quite evil gentlemen, my brother and Hester's husband. They came to annoy me and I managed to create a division between them which I swear will never be healed. I do not think they will return, but we will see.

"Now, if I may, I would like to ask you to fetch help to restore my room, and ask you to accept my apologies for making such a dreadful mess."

Mrs Forbes understood, for she knew the history and had of course been part of the scheme to get Hester away and to the Netherlands.

"I hope this is, for your sake sir, the end of the issue, but I sense those two will not let it rest."

"Well Eleanor, we shall indeed see. I think they are too cowardly to act alone, or even simply together. That has been proved tonight! For now let us look forward to Christmas."

She smiled and set off to organise her maids and David went outside. There was no sign now of the departing visitors, but Marie was proudly at his side and he smiled again, contented by her presence, revelling in her support.

And all he had ever needed to do was to leave the door open to her, not draw a thick curtain she could not penetrate. "Bless you Lily and Sarah" he said to himself as he returned indoors.

***

In the ensuing days Sarah busied herself as a matchmaker and, having revealed the name of her admirer, managed to persuade Clara to see Robert and explain in full. Clara remembered happy times with Robert but knew he had no good position and no prospects and in those days she wanted to live in grandeur, with money, social status and servants to do her every bidding. How different she felt now! But surely he would not want her? He could not want such a despoiled woman.

"You must sit quietly with Robert and be prepared for his reaction. He is a thoughtful, sensitive fellow, and I am certain he is capable of great love, but he may be shocked and you must allow for it, Clara." Sarah was, as usual, speaking with the confidence of a much older woman who understood the ways of life and love, and could address her friend by calling on a fund of experience she didn't actually possess. Clara was impressed nonetheless. "If he is half the man I think he is he will be supportive and may swear undying love on the spot, anxious to relieve you of your burden. Just be ready lest he should be unable to tolerate this new knowledge."

Robert's reputation had been greatly enhanced at Downsland and in Westlingstead by the way in which he went to his Master's aid. Each person telling the story had added their own elements to make his efforts all the more heroic and brave. The footman was self-effacing and extremely shy, saying that he did as was bid and held the warring men apart, and that was all.

Legend suggested he may have saved David Grayan, taking on two brutes at the same time and, according to one account, laying them both out. Robert knew the truth and related it to anyone who asked, and was rarely believed. Clara thought it now put him so far beyond her reach that any progress in her interest was unlikely.

"Give him the chance Clara. He is worth having and you must try. I will talk to Robert and prepare him in some way. Please trust me. He will not desert you, I am sure." Sarah was far from sure and rather worried for both of them, but pressed on and found Robert later.

"Clara wishes to meet you Robert, but I must warn you, she has a tale to tell and it may not be much to your liking......"

"Sarah, Sarah, what tale, what story?"

"Clara must tell you herself. But let me say this. I think she will welcome your love and the girl you dream of can be yours. But she also needs you in other ways Robert. Love is not always about the feelings we have, it is about being caring and tolerant, devoted no matter what may occur, and being there for someone in times of despair."

"Oh Sarah, you alarm me. Has she committed some crime? Is she in trouble?"

"Listen Robert, her tale is as hard in the telling as it will be in the receiving. Give her patience, allow her to speak in her own time, and do not think just of yourself, think of her. Now will you do this for me, and for her Robert?"

His face had paled and lines of concern ran across his forehead.

"Now I am sore worried Sarah, but I will do as you ask and remember what you have said."

Sarah realised he would now expect the worst, but whether he would abide it remained to be learned. If he wanted her it would be of no value to either of them if he resented her in any way, looked down upon her, and felt her used and dirty. What would a marriage make of that?

But they were old enough to at least talk as old friends and to extend to each other courtesy and, hopefully, generosity of mind. If he rejected her then, painful as it might be to both, it would be for the best.

South from the Downs, across the Weald to the west, another man was assessing his chances of advancement with a lady.

James Parry-Barnard had convinced himself Lady Fitzgower was within his grasp and that any opposition from her father, the Duke, could be overcome. She had such an array of symptoms of medical problems that Parry-Barnard was sure she was studying a book on the subject. Every visit, new symptoms. Every examination, new medicine. Most of it as useless as it was pointless.

Her suffering was conceived simply to summon him so that they could be together.

On this occasion she was able to assure him she had recovered from her previous complaint thanks to his ministrations, but now had other complications. He summised there now could be no part of her anatomy that had not developed some disease or irritation, and he had cured them all.

He was encouraged by the knowledge the most frequent difficulties required examinations of a more intimate nature to which she showed no obvious signs of embarrassment or discomfort. On the contrary, they appeared to be appreciated rather than endured. Her mother rejoiced that he was doing so much to help her poor daughter.

And now he was taking tea with his patient as was usual after a consultation. It was time to make his move.

"M'lady," he began, placing his cup carefully upon the table, "I have given a matter very considerable thought and wish to put before you my feelings for your perusal. However, if you have guessed what I wish to say, and prefer me to desist, please tell me and I shall not speak another word."

Harriet Fitzgower slowly placed her own cup on the table next to her, leaned demurely back in her chair, put her hands together in her lap, smiled sweetly and bowed her head very slightly.

"Doctor, please speak freely. I would not presume to guess what you have to say to me, but let me express the view that there are topics which may be of more interest than others, and I do so hope your theme will appeal to me." Her words left him throbbing with fear and anticipation in equal quantities.

"It has been my honour and privilege to attend you, and your family, and trust my skills have enabled you to enjoy the very best of health." Knowing how often he had been sent for and the number of her ailments he had treated, he doubted 'the very best of health' was truly applicable.

"It occurs to me m'lady, that we have become more than physician and patient, for I have enjoyed your convivial company away from the rigors of my calling. We have talked about so many things and, if I may be so forward, we seem to share a love of discussion whether we debate in agreement or from opposing views.

"I humbly beg your indulgence. I am strongly persuaded that we may share the conviction that we can both do so much good, for it is with great humility that we, as privileged people, can ensure that the population is well employed, in good health and contentedness. By maintaining our position, our healthiness and wealth, by allowing our enterprises in commerce to flourish, we are able to provide sustenance for the many poor people we see around us.

"Only through our magnanimity and devotion, thanks to the blessing of rank the good Lord has seen fit to bestow upon us, can we truly help the less fortunate. We owe it to them to retain our wellbeing, success and status, even though we must keep them at an appreciable distance and under our control, to guarantee their survival. That you and I, m'lady, have been endowed with the ability to contribute to that accomplishment is a burden we carry with modesty and meekness."

Harriet Fitzgower looked ready to applaud. Parry-Barnard continued.

"It would be most improper for me to speak with you on a certain matter before consulting your father, but equally I have no desire to impose upon him and waste his time if the issue does not have favour with you m'lady. If I may speak openly, I wish to say that uniting our families should provide the medium by which we could both do so much virtuous work for the ultimate benefit of the common people.

"Together we would be such a force m'lady, and we would be ideally situated to uphold and promote our eminence in society to the greater good of the country. So with your father's kind permission I would like to approach you for your hand."

She looked as if she could leap at him ready to be engulfed in his arms, only propriety keeping her sitting demurely where she had listened to his discourse, and retaining silence for good measure. Now she must speak, but not make her excitement manifest.

"Doctor, thank you for your words with which I wholeheartedly agree. I am flattered that a man of your standing should wish to ask my father's permission and, should he grant it, I will quite willingly listen to what you then have to say to me. Quite willingly." She glanced up and smiled, her eyes reaching into his as she spoke those two words, and he knew he had won her.

***

Henry Barrenbridge was quenching his thirst at the inn and pondering life.

Not so long ago he stood at the head of a renowned medical practice, believed he was shortly to see his investment produce a large sum of money, and was on the verge of proposing marriage to his landlady.

His world had become seriously damaged.

There was no fortune and he had lost the money he gave Roger Culteney. Parry-Barnard was about to leave for good taking at least one guilty secret with him. Judith Pearland was distant, confined herself to business where he was concerned, and was unforgiving. He thought about approaching the landlady but as yet had so little to offer, and his own future was far from secure.

He wasn't assured of his continued friendship with David Grayan, but had accepted an invitation to spend Christmas at Downsland so perhaps the bonds could be strengthened after all. He did not want to lose Judith but he sensed she would be away if the opportunity presented itself.

It wasn't a pretty picture he was studying.

His ruminations were at odds with those of David Grayan who was relaxed and, wrapped up against the cold, partaking wine on the terrace overlooking the gardens. The gardeners were keeping a watchful eye of their charges anxious that a bad winter should not ruin their preparations for spring.

Grayan was thinking of Sarah Brankly.

It was by the merest chance that he consulted her over Hester's flight. He had been in good humour despite being sickened by his sister's problems and fretting lest the escape should go awry. In a moment of reflection he summoned Sarah and presented her with the difficulty. How could he get details of the arrangements to Hester?

He had taken Sarah into his confidence and told her all, and she had sat controlling tears that might otherwise have fallen freely, dazed by what she was hearing. But in an instant she had made her suggestion and offered to play her part in spite of the

135

obvious dangers. Hester's maid might have given the game away at any point, if only to save her own skin.

Grayan did not want the risk at first, but gradually relented realising it might be the only way and now time was of the essence.

She wrote pretending to be an old friend who had long lost touch and stating how dearly she would love to see the girl, Annie, again. The response lacked no caution for at that point Annie had no conception of the real purpose, and said that she would be pleased to meet her although she could not recall her.

David Grayan knew full well what a magnificent role Sarah had enacted, for the scheme worked. Initially Annie was concerned but was enthralled by the plan and the freedom it would bring her and her mistress. A new life. A new beginning. Freedom. She would be free of Charles Handlen and would no longer need to bathe Hester's wounds, the most heart-rending work she had ever undertaken.

Handlen had once beaten Annie but not in the ferocious fashion used on his wife, and Annie had no wish to repeat the episode. She would've left his employ but she had no family and nowhere to go, and would not have carried a reference with her to find work elsewhere.

Sarah had performed a miracle, of that David was sure. The escape went well and Hester, the boys and Annie were away from England's shores before Charles woke up to what had happened.

And it was thanks to Sarah.

The longer David sat there, the more he thought about Sarah's arrival at Downsland and all she had achieved since coming there, the more he knew he was thinking of her with ever deepening affection. He did not believe in God but if he did he knew he would consider Sarah had been sent by the Almighty. She had helped lift him up to the light where he found Marie's spirit waiting for him. She had, with extraordinary bravery, sorted out the medium by which he could communicate arrangements with his sister.

A remarkable young woman.

And she had proved herself to be a blessing with young children that had stayed at Downsland.

Truly, a remarkable young woman. And how easily he might've flung her out when she had the tenacity and courage to come to his study with Ginny that time! She must've been afraid, yet she won him over. Remarkable indeed. He felt that he owed her so much.

So he resolved that she should not remain a mere maid for much longer. Perhaps an improved position could be made available? Yes, that might be the solution.

Chapter Twelve

It is the new year. Mid-January and there is a blanket of snow across Kent. The hurrying white-grey clouds are thrusting their way past on a chill north-easterly and more snow is falling, and everywhere is bitterly cold.

Marie's sister Mary and her family returned to Downsland for Christmas where they were joined by Henry Barrenbridge and a business associate of David Grayan, Frederick Ullness and his wife.

All the staff at the Hall seemed happy enough having plenty to do and delighted to see the house become a place of good cheer and bonhomie once more.

Shortly before Christmas Day Clara and Robert had met and her story was told.

At first Robert felt revulsion as he listened, but then he remembered Sarah's words about love and tried to feel sorrow and tolerance and found that he could. Having overcome a hurdle he discovered how much he wanted to hug her, tell her he loved her, and that he was ready to be by her side to help her and support her, but the words would not come. He was still marooned by his inbred thoughts which he longed to despatch to free himself.

Yes, he loved her. Yes, he could come to terms with her sad tale, her miserable past. Yes, he wanted to take her away from her foul father, and he wanted to remove her from all the evil that had gone before. She was young. He could understand why Culteney appealed to a young woman who sought to better herself, and why she was swept away on the romantic tide of elopement.

It wasn't about forgiveness. It was about acceptance. It should be about love.

Finally he took her hand, held it tight, and swore he would love her with all his heart forever, and that the past need never come between them. Presently they embraced and their lips met for the first time. With that kiss they both knew that they had found true love.

Now to find Sarah and ask her to help defeat opposition from Thomas Evershen!

James Parry-Barnard had a depressing Christmas thanks to opposition from a father, and he spent the period alone in his new lodgings drinking far more than was seemly.

The Duke had all but thrown him out on his ear for his impudence in asking permission to offer marriage to Lady Fitzgower. His position as family physician was terminated. His subsequent letter to Harriet was returned unopened.

He could not return to Westlingstead. He would have to start afresh. He had other private patients and his mind turned to Dorothea Landspur, a woman not yet in middle age who had been widowed early in life and must surely be in need of a gentleman. She had the right social standing despite being nowhere near the level of Lady Fitzgower, so she might be a good starting point.

Perhaps he had aimed too high, too quickly.

The difference between Harriet Fitzgower and Dorothea Landspur was that the latter was in exceedingly good health and proud of the fact. But James had been recommended by one of Dorothea's acquaintances when she had been taken ill not long ago and had no doctor of her own.

He had cured her ailment much to her pleasure and she had been extremely grateful and companionable on his last visit. In mid January he was due to make a final call and he knew he must make the most of the occasion. Thus he plotted a devious plan.

Medicine, that was the answer. He would prescribe some medicine that would, in time, actually produce unwellness, and he was sure to be summoned. Every visit had to count. When he had remedied her health things should be sufficiently advanced for a proposal. Yes, that is how it was to be, and he set about finding a concoction that would meet his requirements.

Henry Barrenbridge felt that his friendship with David Grayan had been rekindled especially since Parry-Barnard had left and Judith Pearland was now fully conversant with her situation. He managed to make himself feel justly rotten for his behaviour, which he acknowledged was wrong, and suffered accordingly. At least Grayan had entertained him well over Christmas and appeared to be on good terms with him, but he was pondering his own future and that of the practice.

Should he move on? He couldn't let his friend down so, no, he would not leave. He might need another assistant and not every physician would be keen to work for David Grayan! His unconventional views were not agreeable to all by any means. There were those who feared that such beliefs could bring down the country by encouraging rebellion. The lower orders must be kept under foot.

Judith Pearland had been little more than a village peasant girl when Marie Grayan persuaded her to take up nursing and although, Barrenbridge admitted to himself, she showed enormous potential in medicine she stood no chance of undertaking any sort of course and qualifying as either surgeon or physician. Damn Grayan and his wife, he concluded. To promote women in any field was a serious mistake, let alone any woman from a very modest background as Pearland was. With any luck, he reasoned, she would marry the blacksmith's boy and settle down to motherhood like any good woman and be away from him.

David Grayan was presently in Dover, the guest of Mr and Mrs Cowans, Lily's parents, an occasion that increased gossip at Downsland many times over and which spread into Westlingstead with undue haste.

Before departure he had summoned Sarah to his study.

"Sit down," he ordered from the other side of the desk. "Add up the columns in this ledger and write and answers on this paper." Unsure of the true reasons for this command she carefully worked her way through the mass of figures and wrote the answers, as requested, on a piece of paper and handed ledger and paper back to the Master.

"Excellent. Everything is correct. Sarah, I do not wish you to work here solely as a maid. You have been very helpful to me in a number of affairs and I would like to offer you another position. Yes, you can continue to assist as a maid but I would like you to work for me in other directions, bookkeeping, correspondence, and as my personal adviser in business and in private matters."

The faintest of mocking smiles appeared as he spoke the last line. She appreciated the humour and accepted it as wit that was neither malicious or hurtful and intended solely to amuse.

"I hope you will accept this new post. It will bring increased remuneration, of course, and I will give you money to buy clothes as you will not always be dressed as a maid. How does that sound?" He waited for no answer, for there was none forthcoming from a startled Miss Brankly, and continued.

"I beg you to accept." He looked straight at her with eyes that challenged her to object.

"Sir, I wish only to be of service to you, and will do as you require of me. But I am not worthy of your considerations....."

"You are, and that is all that matters. So, yes or no?" After the briefest of pauses she replied.

"Yes sir, if it is your wish, and I hope I shall not let you down. It is a great burden you place upon me and I shall worry."

"You will not worry Sarah, for I have given this much thought, and I will ensure that you make a success of this as you do everything."

"Thank you sir. Now may I please consult you on a subject that bothers me?"

"Yes of course."

She sat back, determined to call upon his services since he wanted her to advise him, and he had given her the ideal opportunity to speak.

"Clara Evershen and Robert Broxford, a footman, are in love and wish to marry but Clara's father will object. How can we overcome his opposition sir?"

He studied her and tapped his finger-tips together in contemplation.

"Yes, I am aware of their relationship and have pondered this problem myself."

"Oh ..... you know sir?"

"Yes Sarah, I know."

"But ... but how sir?"

"I am master of Downsland and know more than you might imagine." Her eyes bulged with surprise. His mouth moulded into a faint smile.

"Let me think on this. I have it in mind to promote master Broxford in some way and I can always call on Clara's father to, as it were, persuade him. Leave this with me Sarah, and I will solve this one for you."

As once before she found herself outside the study without realising she had departed. Yet she admired him for it, and she clung to respect for a man she knew was wise and clever.

Grayan's visit to Dover was not entirely for leisure as Mr Cowans had invited him to make one subject abundantly clear.

"I do not approve of you entertaining my daughter without an escort or chaperone. It's a disgrace sir. My daughter is no hussy but your actions could render her liable to accusations of being one such. I will not have it sir. Heaven forbid that we should ever reach the time when such occasions are not frowned upon and come to be considered quite normal. God please forbid it should happen.

"I hope it never will, so would you please respect her, and for that matter respect my feelings and those of my wife, and do not place dear Lily in an impossible position."

"My apologies for the offence caused, and I assure you there will be no recurrence. You have my word sir." It was a promise Grayan would find easy to keep, even if he vehemently disagreed with Cowans, for it was unlikely he would invite Lily again without her parents. And her father's diatribe overlooked the fact she had called upon David in the first place, doing so unattended.

So he took the opportunity to ask if all three might wish to come and stay and Downsland and was assured that yes, they would. With that he assumed the difficulty Mr Cowans could not meet with equanimity was confined to history.

During his time at Dover the four of them had taken a walk right up and across the cliffs that dominate the English Channel, and on to St Margaret's Bay. The snow had not been so bad around the east Kent coasts and their journey had not been troublesome. David and Lily spent much of the walk side by side in discussion, the conversation and company being utterly agreeable to both, but with the weather closing in, the wind strengthening and sleet beginning to fall, they made a hurried descent to Dover and the end of their perambulation.

David realised he was looking forward to entertaining them at Downsland, but with Kent in the grip of a vile winter it was unlikely to be in the foreseeable future.

***

142

Westlingstead was, in contrast to the Kent port, covered in snow, and more was promised by the filthy clouds driving past, caught on the relentless wind and threatening to deposit their loads wherever they could cause most disruption to man and beast.

The wind had pushed the snow into drifts against the buildings and the village inn was no exception. The landlord had engaged eager assistance to ensure the door was accessible.

A log fire blazed in the hearth throwing light and heat around and about, rather more light than the dismal candles could manage this icy January evening. Abraham Winchell sat in a corner nursing a tankard of his favourite brew, and beside him sat Judith Pearland.

She had no qualms about being seen in the hostelry or with Abe Winchell, despite the knowledge that tongues wagged on both counts. Not proper for a lady, let alone a nurse. Most still referred to her as a nurse, even those that worshipped her for Jed Maxton's life, and there was always somebody ready to buy their heroine a drink in the Green Man. Many villagers felt an uneasiness about their esteem for this woman as they tried to balance her successes against the fact she was female.

The older villagers in particular found it an enigma they could not comfortably resolve.

Even Abe Winchell's mind suffered restless periods when wrestling with the puzzle, but tonight his mind was at ease. He enjoyed her company and the atmosphere was conducive to their friendship and conversation. She was, after all, a village girl and an ambitious one, but she wanted to rise above her station and he knew she could not.

He also knew Dr Barrenbridge had recently let her down having, in an ungentlemanly manner, encouraged her in medicine and then taken the floor from under her. He often privately recalled that day she had been taken ill and he had brought her back, perhaps saving her life. It was the day Barrenbridge had broken the bad news. He also remembered lifting her from the ground to horseback. As light as a feather, she was.

143

Judith had little recollection past a vague idea that a very strong person had seized her where she lay prostrate and placed her in the saddle. At the time she wanted to die. Now such masculine action seemed a rather curious and romantic gesture, not that she was ever bothered by romantic thoughts. Her work, her calling was her priority in life.

At first her parents had not smiled upon her desire to be a physician, but in time they mellowed. They would far rather she marry a local lad and settle down to be wife and mother, and now she was being courted by just such a man and one they knew to be hard-working, loyal and honest, with a good future ahead of him. So maybe she would abandon nursing and take up her role as the blacksmith's bride.

Had they but known it they would've been horrified to learn that their daughter did not think she was being courted and would rebuff any attempt by Abe Winchell to improve their relationship. Marriage and children were not for her. Abe was her saviour and a friend, and a good neighbour, and that was all.

The blacksmith's son was also of the opinion there was no hope for him there, and never considered that his friendship might be construed as wooing. But he knew he did indeed have a secure future with his father likely to hand over the reins very soon. Business was excellent and his father was happy to retire into the background, assist when he was needed, and leave the running of the smithy to a very able lad.

Mr and Mrs Winchell secretly hoped that their son would marry Miss Pearland and soon, perhaps this summer, and waited patiently for good news of that order.

***

Clara and Robert met when they could and treasured every second of their precious time together. Only now did Clara come to grasp the true meaning of love and to realise how blessed she was to hold Robert's heart in hers. But they had to avoid detection and keep their love from her father.

She was bringing him money from her work for Mrs Brankly, more than he'd hoped for at first, and he was wallowing in the gratification of the money Grayan had brought him. For the time being she was his angel and could do no wrong.

However, Clara was seeing an earlier problem rearing its head again. Edmund was improving in health and mood and appearing far too often where she was working, his presence carrying with it a degree of threat that left her feeling intimidated. There was no mistaking the look in his eyes and she became convinced he would make a move anon.

Every night she cried herself to sleep only to awake suddenly amidst a most dreadful nightmare.

It could not go on like this. She would need to leave Mrs Brankly's and her father would be most unforgiving. In her desperation she wrote to Sarah pleading for help.

As she was writing her father came from nowhere, taking her by surprise, demanding to know who she was corresponding with. She was so engrossed that she hadn't heard his approach, and he was always the stealthy one. He grabbed the letter and made the best of reading it. Not an educated man he could nonetheless gather together the important issues.

"So my daughter, this Edmund wants his pleasure with you, does he? Have you encouraged him? Is he a young man perchance?"

"No ... no ... no papa. He is old and a widower, and I have not encouraged him, truly I have not, and I wish to leave there and return home but must obey you. Please help me papa." She shuddered, her face drawn and pale, the beads of sweat forming on her brow. She was afraid.

"You ask me for help Clara? You do not, do you? You are writing to this Sarah for help. You do not seek help from your father. You seek help to save you *from* your father." His anger was rising, the fury leaving him red in the face, and he was shaking with rage keeping his voice barely under control.

"You will indeed obey me. You stay in your work girl, and if he wants you let him pay and pay well. You are a filthy used wretch so it makes no odds, but make him pay and then make him happy so he pays again." A disgusting laugh erupted from his throat. "Come here, my sweet, and let me remind you of the need to obey me." He grabbed her wrist and dragged her to his own room where he flung her on the floor and took the rod from the cupboard.

His voice was now soft, redness was fading from his face, and there was a repellent smile of delight replacing the raw ferocity that had been there before. There was no escape and she submitted as she knew she must.

Two violent strokes had been administered when she became aware of a frightful and alarming squeal from behind her. Turning she saw her father clutching his chest, eyes bulging, and falling to his knees, once again red in the face. He appeared to be struggling for breath.

Adjusting her clothing she screamed for her mother and said she would fetch the doctor. Her mother arrived as she was heading downstairs.

"Papa is having a fit. I am going to the doctor," she yelled as she bounded through the door and down the street to the hospital.

***

January made its weary way towards February, dragging its heels and hurling foul weather in any direction that pleased it. Even when the wind swung to the south-east it brought snow, sleet and rain and a coldness that could freeze the blood.

David Grayan returned home and found an eager Sarah Brankly ready to apprise him of both fact and fiction, although she did clarify exactly which pieces of news were unsubstantiated gossip. It was a matter of fact that Clara's father had died, but a matter of tittle-tattle that Abe Winchell was wooing Dr Pearland.

He listened attentively aware that he had created something that might run amok in his life and prove most unsatisfactory. Sarah had presumed her new post entitled her to arrive without notice and discuss any issue that he might find interesting. But for the moment he found it amusing.

The time spent with Lily Cowans had been very enjoyable and he liked her, but he was certainly not going to reveal his thoughts to his new assistant! He was in a good humour and found he could easily tolerate the earnest endeavours of Miss Brankly.

146

Later he talked to his housekeeper, the redoubtable Mrs Forbes, running through a number of routine issues and making decisions on a variety of matters. Business concluded he sat back in his chair as Eleanor Forbes relaxed in hers the other side of the desk.

"Is Sarah Brankly getting above herself Eleanor?"

"No, not at all sir. She is quietly delighted with the position you have given her, and the increased pay, and she has been teased by others but always gently so, but no, she is just Sarah as we have grown to know her. Confident as ever but never forceful."

"Do you think she feels it has given her additional privileges?"

"In what way sir?"

"To come and see me without my summons, for example?"

"Ah I see. Yes, perhaps she does. Would you like me to speak to her?"

"If you would please. Make it clear it is not an admonishment, simply information. If she wants to see me she only needs to speak to you first and you can arrange it."

"Yes sir, I'll deal with that."

"The other maids Eleanor, what of them? Anything I need to know about?"

"No sir, there is no discord and plenty of happiness from what I hear. All is proceeding as should be. I have no problems with any of them."

"Good. And the others?"

"Cook grumbles, but then Cook grumbles when there has been little to busy herself with, and now she grumbles because there is too much! But she gets all the help she needs as she has assured me herself. You know Cook sir. The men are busy and there is nothing untoward there, especially as one or two are, as usual sir, paying too much attention to the younger maids!" They both laughed.

"And your husband?"

"Very well, thank you sir. We are both in contentment with each other and our lot in life."

The meeting ended as cordially as it had been conducted and Mrs Forbes made her way downstairs while David Grayan returned to his correspondence. Life at Downsland was more or less back to normal, at least for the time being.

***

Dorothea Landspur was only too happy to swallow the measure of tonic just as she had unfortunately swallowed James Parry-Barnard's explanation, delivered, as would be expected, with notable verbosity.

She hoped it would be a long time before she needed a doctor again. He hoped he would be summoned back urgently. He could not have imagined how quickly that summons would come.

Henry Barrenbridge had received something purporting to be good news from an unexpected source. A young, newly qualified physician had written to him from Leicestershire enquiring about coming to work at Westlingstead. He had heard so much about David Grayan and his philosophies, together with his renowned philanthropy, that he would consider being employed there to be an honour indeed.

Barrenbridge was dismayed by Philip Jaunton's enthusiasm for his friend's unconventional approach, much of which he disliked intensely, but was conscious that Jaunton might be manna from heaven in the existing circumstances. After all, here was a man who actually wanted to come and work at the practice, a gift most definitely.

So he wrote inviting Jaunton to visit saying he would book a room at the inn when he knew he was coming, but that any offer of a position would depend on the outcome of their meeting. Then he wrote to Grayan with the news, who replied warmly and suggested Dr Jaunton could stay at Downsland, as could Henry, so they could all meet.

In the meantime Parry-Barnard received an urgent summons from Biddenden where Dorothea Landspur had been taken very ill. Concerned he rushed to her bedside and administered the antidote taking care to collect up the original mixture he'd left as a tonic. He thought everything was going to plan and said he would call the next day convinced she would be much better and that he could forge ahead with improvements to their friendship.

He had no idea she had decanted some of the tonic separately which her maid kept for her.

Clara had been busy at Mrs Brankly's both before and after her father's funeral. Her mother was surprisingly supportive suggesting to Clara she'd been as afraid of Thomas Evershen as she had been. Neither seemed to be truly mourning.

It was a Thursday morning when trouble arose.

It was still cold but much of the snow had gone leaving heaps of slush in far too many places, and there was little sunlight to try and warm the soil. Clara had wanted to leave Mrs Brankly and her father's death gave her a clear path away from her torment, but she stayed for the time being in order to provide money for her mother. This, despite the large amount of money Evershen had tucked away when he died. Mrs Evershen knew where to lay her hands on it and did so freely, taking over her late husband's mantle and denying Clara any income.

Now this lovely young woman, beloved of Robert Broxford, was baking bread and dreaming of her love and hoping any barrier to their marriage had been removed, when Edmund walked in and silently sat at the table to open the ledger. He appeared to be ignoring her. Catherine Brankly was tending to the chickens.

Clara looked round and saw he was no longer at the table and assumed he had left the room as quietly as he'd entered. Suddenly his hand was clasped across her mouth as he used his other hand to grab her waist. A strong man, he swung her round with ease and kissed her without passion or tenderness, his spittle splattering her face as she struggled.

Then he used one hand to grapple with her dress but as he lifted the garment he was caught temporarily off guard and she broke free and screamed.

"Hush yer mouth my pretty one. Be silent, I tell 'e." And he hit her full in the face splitting her lip. He threw her to the ground but she rolled over and avoided his attempt to seize her. With that she attacked him, clawing at his face, kicking him, and at the very moment Mrs Brankly, having heard the scream, came flying into the room. Edmund took his opportunity.

"Get 'er off me, sister, get 'er off. Gone mad she 'as. Attacked me for no reason."

"He grabbed me, kissed me, and wanted more, then smacked my lip. Look at the blood."

"Don't you go believing 'er lies Catherine. See 'er off, go on, see 'er off."

Mrs Brankly ordered her out telling her to never return, and she was gone. At home her mother helped bathe her wound but gave no sympathy being more interested in the loss of money. Mrs Evershen made it clear she did not believe Clara's story and insisted she'd attacked Mr Forness in order to be dismissed.

Clara could not believe her ears. She took hold of the cloth held to her lip and went to her room where she hurled herself on the bed and cried amidst a terrible wailing of anguish.

***

In Biddenden Mrs Landspur was becoming a great deal worse, but sent for a reputable doctor who had attended her some while ago. An old man, now retired, he came as swiftly as he could and conducted a full examination, asking questions as he went. He asked to see the tonic and the medicine Parry-Barnard had brought the previous day.

He wrote a note to the apothecary and a rider was arranged to gallop at full speed to Tenterden to obtain the appropriate medicine. By now the doctor had his suspicions but could not imagine a fellow physician might poison a patient, even by accident. It was a strange affair, but he kept his feelings to himself, for he had no evidence, just a nagging doubt that all was not as it should be.

The doctor took away the two medicines intending to go himself to Tenterden and ask the apothecary's advice. The new medicine having been given Mrs Landspur was sleeping soundly so he took his leave saying he should be summoned if required, otherwise he would return on the morrow. He also left clear instructions with the maid that Parry-Barnard was not to be admitted to the house under any circumstances.

Returning home after calling at Tenterden he sat down and wrote a letter to a learned gentleman he knew in London asking if information about Parry-Barnard could be obtained, and urgently so.

The following morning Mrs Landspur was much recovered and the doctor was in attendance when Parry-Barnard called. He was abruptly informed the lady had her former physician with her and had no need of his services. There was no need to call again.

Unable to obtain any explanation he left and resolved to write to Mrs Landspur. What strange matter did he see before him? How could it be so? He'd said he would come back if summoned and she had called in another doctor instead. How strange indeed.

This was an unwanted intrusion into his plans and it did not make sense.

So he wrote and sent his letter and made his way to a local hostelry for refreshments, convinced he faced only a temporary difficulty, one he could talk his way out of given the chance.

At Downsland David Grayan received a letter from his brother that demonstrated that the feud was far from over and was not showing any signs of abating. But the letter did reveal one piece of information of interest to the reader. Charles Handlen was ruined and was obliged to sell his house and this was, apparently, because of his wife's behaviour. Grayan managed a wry grin.

He penned a pithy and blunt reply.

Another man in receipt of a letter was Henry Barrenbridge. Philip Jaunton would be travelling south within a day or two. His visit could not come at a better time. Judith Pearland was as efficient as ever and becoming unbearable having no words to say to Henry beyond those concerning the medical work they were undertaking at the time. She never smiled, barely looked at him and avoided him if she could, but it did not affect her professional and competent approach to her employment and she was still loved by the villagers and many others who came in contact with her.

Henry detested it, and hoped Jaunton would be suitable for appointment. Since James Parry-Barnard had departed he'd not only missed male companionship but been saddled with a morose and cold assistant who happened to be a woman. If only he'd been honest at the outset, but then it was Marie who had encouraged her and persuaded him and he didn't have the strength of character to stand up to David's wife.

Elsewhere Clara's life was being made a misery as she discovered her mother could be as dictatorial as her late father. There was no violence it was true, but it was obvious she would have to find work that brought money in, and in her new despair she turned to Sarah.

Sarah had sought leave from Mrs Forbes to answer her mother's summons and had learned about Clara's wicked behaviour although she guessed what had really occurred. She looked at Edmunds scratched face and felt a glow of satisfaction that her friend had fought back, and it cheered her.

"Sarah," her mother announced, "your uncle and I wish you to stay briefly. My brother is sore wounded as you can see, and he is unable to make out the figures in the ledger and deal with any such business matters. We would be grateful if you would deal with the ledger while your uncle recovers, and also help me here now Clara has been dismissed. Dreadful girl. What could have so taken her, I do not know." Sarah knew, just as Edmund knew.

"Yes mama, the housekeeper is understanding but I will need to send a note. I'll write it now."

That task dealt with she sat at the table, breathed in deeply and reached over for the ledger and the many pieces of paper that appertained to the smallholding's business in recent time. Edmund discreetly took his leave and went into the farm.

Withholding various sighs, lest her mother should comprehend their meaning, she set about the enormous task of correcting Edmund's dire efforts. It took the rest of the day but eventually, and much to her pride, she completed the process and all was once again in order.

"Mama, if Uncle Edmund is not able to see to this due to his injuries, would you like me to deal with them for the time being?"

"Why yes Sarah, that would be a good idea. I do not want my brother upset any more than he is, and I know that, in the circumstances, he would appreciate being relieved of a difficult chore."

Yes, thought Sarah, I'm sure he would! For the present she was only too pleased to have the accounts back in her hands and would not give them up lightly next time.

Chapter Thirteen

"I understand sir, that you do not believe in God."

David Grayan lowered his cutlery onto his plate where he left them while he studied his guest, doing so with a thunderous look. Philip Jaunton, seeing this, acquired the appearance of a man afeared.

"Dr Jaunton, I do not discuss my religious beliefs."

"No ... no ... no ... no, of course not, no. I meant no offence sir. My apologies." These were clearly accepted as Grayan then smiled at him and started to eat again. The man from Leicester tried to pursue a different line.

"I am a great admirer sir, and share your interests in equality......"

"Thank you Dr Jaunton," he interrupted, "so are you aware that Dr Barrenbridge has a woman assistant who is good enough to be a doctor yet is barred from qualifying because of her sex?"

Jaunton looked perplexed and unsure of himself, the first time he had done so since arriving at Downsland and going out of his way to prostrate himself at Grayan's feet, acts that he did not comprehend annoyed his host beyond reason.

"I ... I ... I ... I was not aware sir. Does she ... she ... she practice medicine here?" were all the words he could manage. Grayan's face showed he had gained the upper hand, was pleased with himself, and he once more sat back to answer.

"Yes, and surgery, and successfully so as Dr Barrenbridge will testify." Barrenbridge looked as if he was willing to do nothing of the sort. "Yet she is not a barber, nor a physician, but as things are in this country, Dr Jaunton, she is permitted to work as a doctor without actually being one. That being accepted amongst men, of course, although both you and Dr Barrenbridge are members of the Royal College and therefore have qualifications to your credit.

"Our local blacksmith has been known to pull a tooth or two, and engage in blood-letting, but I would not trust him to set a broken bone or prescribe something for a fever. However, I would trust Judith Pearland with my life. What say you Dr

153

Barrenbridge?" This took Henry by surprise but he quickly recovered his senses and decided on diplomacy rather than truth.

"I agree wholeheartedly. She has established a high reputation in north Kent and is sought after."

"So Dr Jaunton, if Dr Barrenbridge appoints you would you be prepared to work as his second assistant, in truth beneath Dr Pearland, as I have no hesitation in calling her?"

Both doctors looked dumbstruck. Grayan looked at them contentedly. He had hit home hard and ensnared them, and a smile of grim satisfaction was upon him.

"Come come, Doctor, you said you share my views on equality. Surely you have the answer to my question ready on your lips?" Philip Jaunton had a simple choice. He had spent every moment in Grayan's company trying to impress him with his worship for his unconventional views, and with his desire to work for this extraordinary man, and now he could lose his opportunity at a stroke, or accept the conditions attached and hope to advance himself in time.

"It would be my greatest honour to accept such a standing, and to be second to a doctor you would trust your life to sir. I too would be proud to call her Doctor and accept her instructions sir."

His host did not doubt that he hardly meant a word. Barrenbridge took a gulp of wine to prevent himself choking.

"Good. An appointment is in Dr Barrenbridge's gift and I will not interfere in any way whatsoever. But I will say this. You are entitled to your own opinions Dr Jaunton. Never be afraid to express them, especially before me. I prefer the truth to all else. So gentlemen, let us drink a toast to the truth."

In another part of the county another doctor was about to get a shock, and the truth was at the heart of it. Dorothea Landspur's former physician paid a call on Parry-Barnard at his Hawkhurst accommodation.

"Mr Parry-Barnard, I believe you have lied about your qualifications to gain access to Mrs Landspur and to administer medicine accordingly. I have received a letter from a friend in London confirming the position regarding your medical training. I have asked an apothecary to look into the medicine you supplied Mrs Landspur before she was taken ill.

"His opinion suggests the concoction may have been quite poisonous to her system and that your remedy made the situation worse. She is grossly unwell but I have every good reason to think she will now recover.

"I have not come here to accuse you, to make any allegations at this stage. Providing Mrs Landspur recovers I propose to take no further action. You may be fully justified in your diagnosis and treatment and be able to prove it, or at least disprove what I have told you. But if her condition worsens or she is taken from us, then I will set about you Mr Parry-Barnard. Fortunately the good lady has not been made cognisant of your apparent misdemeanours, and I prefer that to remain the case, for her sake.

"Quite what you hoped to gain I have no idea. You are a despicable individual. I strongly recommend you leave Kent at once before you are exposed as the scoundrel you are. Now, I will hear nothing from you today, so be silent. If you do not leave I will take you to task, I truly will."

And he turned and let himself out leaving Parry-Barnard sickened to the core. Exposed! Yes he was undone. His mind was awry and he slumped into a chair without knowing he had done so. But he reached a conclusion quickly enough and jumped to his feet. There was only one possible course of action, and he might yet redeem himself with Dorothea and save himself as well, especially as she did not know about these allegations.

***

Agnes Byrne and Jed Maxton were enjoying a winter's walk now the snow had cleared for the most part and were so engrossed in each other neither noticed the icy air. The sky might not have been clear but the clouds were white and puffy and a low sun managed an occasional appearance.

Love was the mainstay of their conversation but there were intervals when they discussed other topics.

"Tell me Agnes, what of the Master and Miss Cowans?"

"Well Jed, methinks they must be a match. Master's been to stay with her in Dover and they will be coming to Downsland soon, the family, y'know, her mama and papa. Perhaps Master will speak with Mr Cowans. Sarah says she's a lovely lady and she should know. Master chose her to wait on her when she first stayed here and she says she is so elegant, but not aloof. She talked a great deal to Sarah, so hear tell, and they enjoyed each others' company. I believe she will make a perfect match for Master."

"And what of Sarah? Will she be wed?"

"I hope so, but she cannot offer a man children, so that is against her. But I hope there is a man who will love her for all that."

They walked on in silence, arm in arm, individually contemplating the issues of David Grayan and Lily Cowans, and marriage for Sarah. Then Jed spoke again.

"What is Sarah making of her new position Agnes?"

"She is happy and I am happy for her. Although she might seem self important there is not a shred of arrogance about her. She is never aloof or unfriendly and is always willing to learn. That is what I like about her Jed. She will listen, debate but without forcing her opinion, and speaks only of the knowledge she has. Unlike some!"

"Ah yes Agnes. Some can talk for hours and merely show they know nothing!"

They laughed and walked on and returned to their own love and their forthcoming wedding.

"Will I make you a bride you'll be proud of Jed?"

"Why yes, and will I be a groom you be proud of?"

"All I have dreamed of Jed. You are the finest of men."

"And you the loveliest of women."

"Oh get on with you Jed. I am plain and ordinary and you only love me because I can swing an axe to match you men."

"Nay, I love you because you're you Agnes. But I also love you because you've shown us men you can be our equals, and some don't like it, I know."

"Yes, and let us not forget Dr Pearland, saved your life Jed, and they won't let her be a real physician cos she's a woman."

There was time for thought. They climbed over a stile and Jed helped her down into the next field.

"Reckon its true Agnes. If Mistress was still alive she'd be qualified now."

"I am told that would not be the case Jed. Mistress encouraged her but must've known there were limits."

"Aye Agnes, limits set by men."

"Well said my beloved! Well, let us hope the new Mistress is just as supportive. From what Sarah says there is good reason to believe she will be."

"But sad if Dr Pearland cannot advance."

"Sad, but we cannot change the world, and we can remember she gave you your life, and me my husband."

And they embraced and dissolved into a most wondrous kiss, here in the cold, uninviting but extremely striking Kent countryside, surrounded by views that matched the exquisiteness of their love.

***

Sarah had wasted no time seeking employment for Clara at Downsland. Mrs Forbes was pleased to take her on as Sarah herself was often at Grayan's beck and call and she was thus a maid short at certain times. Robert Broxford was delighted as was the widowed Mrs Evershen. Sarah revelled in the happiness she thought she had brought to everyone concerned. An accomplishment to sate the appetite of Miss Brankly.

She was also happy because she was able to visit her mother and carry out the book-keeping and correspondence without interference from Edmund. Her uncle had an excuse that he could not see well after Clara's attack, an excuse Sarah knew to be false, but it enabled him to leave the ledger alone by justifiable pretext. He concentrated on the practical aspects of running the smallholding while Mrs Brankly now had the occasional assistance of another young lass from the village.

Once again Sarah had been asked to be the personal maid to Miss Cowans during the forthcoming visit and she was overjoyed. She loved Miss Cowans and shared the opinion of gossip that she would make a fine bride for the Master. She so wanted him to be happy and to be in love again, and Lily Cowans had given her the impression that she acquiesced with the Master's beliefs in all things, so would surely be the ideal complement to an unconventional man just as Marie had been.

Perhaps during the stay she could entice Miss Cowans to reveal more of her interest!

Perhaps.

Abraham Winchell was shodding a horse and thinking about Judith Pearland. A good woman but one he could not aspire to. How he wished he could provide the means for her qualification but he had no idea how he might go about it, realising a considerable amount of money would be needed. Maybe you could buy a qualification, he wondered, and dismissed the idea.

After all, hadn't he had to train at his father's knee and hadn't it taken many years to call himself a blacksmith? And that was nothing compared to becoming a physician. The village barber had carried out some small surgery until the hospital was set up, and his own father had been known to pull teeth in days gone by, but that was nothing to what Judith had achieved. She'd saved Jed Maxton's life, that was certain, and had performed other miracles if all the tales were to be believed.

But she was beyond him.

Unless, of course, he could find some way to please her. Some way to helping her achieve what most saw as the impossible task. He needed to think. He needed help in that and did not know which way to turn.

***

The body was found on the road near Biddenden.

The old doctor had been stabbed clean through the heart. He was discovered by a shepherd who observed a saddled horse without a rider just off the main track.

Not far away Dorothea Landspur was now recovering from her enforced illness and the shock of learning of the murder, both of which had left her swooned on a chaise-longue where a maid was fanning her. Rousing slightly she spoke to the maid.

"Elspeth, have Dr Parry-Barnard fetched for I am sure to need him and he will be a comfort for me." The maid looked on nervously for she had to speak and knew it was not her place, but realised she must take the risk.

"Ma'am, it is not for me to say so but Dr Williams did not agree with Dr Parry-Barnard, did he? He was very concerned about your treatment......" Mrs Landspur was glaring at her.

"Elspeth, just have him fetched if you please and do not question my orders." With that she closed her eyes and leaned back leaving the maid to dash away to execute those orders.

At Downsland the young maids had decided Ginny Perkins's head had been turned and teased her with little mercy until Sarah asked them to desist.

She had made some chance remarks after seeing Philip Jaunton that led the girls to believe she was so smitten she must be hopelessly in love, and they could understand why.

Jaunton was youthful with a flash of golden blond hair. Tall, slender, well-groomed and very well dressed he had made an impression on all the maids. Courteous to them, gently spoken, gracious with impeccable manners, so they thought, he looked the handsomest man in Kent as far as they were concerned.

He had an athletic appearance and walked with calm assurance, very upright and exuding physical strength. He had deep blue eyes which Ginny said almost mesmerised her. But more than that his face had an appealing warmth to it in which the eyes radiated friendship and compassion, and his neatly formed mouth often fell into a disarming smile. Ginny loved his smile which she had seen frequently aimed at her, and happened to pronounce her rather hopeless desire to be kissed by those lips.

Consequently conversation at the Hall often revolved around rumour and gossip at Ginny's expense when she herself had announced that, as a mere servant, she would never have the opportunity to experience any friendship with the man. Nevertheless, it was widely agreed that it was to be hoped he would be appointed Dr Barrenbridge's assistant, with one or two suggesting they might not mind suffering an ailment if he was to treat them.

In Biddenden Parry-Barnard was escorted to Mrs Landspur by a maid who was openly cold and distant.

Dorothea in contrast welcomed him saying she was so pleased to see him. Now did James know that his mission was reinstated. He received even more encouragement.

159

"Mrs Landspur, I have heard the dreadful news about Dr Williams......."

"Dr Parry-Barnard, would you please do me the honour of calling me Dorothea, for I feel we are more than acquaintances, more than doctor and patient, and yes, it is a tragedy about Dr Williams but it may be he was old and set in his ways and you have the benefit of more recent experience in medicine. I am sure you were doing your best for me and I apologise for summoning him."

"Mrs Landspur, Dorothea, please call me James, and I'm sure you acted in your best interests as you saw the situation so no apology is necessary."

They took tea and revelled in pleasant talk very much at ease together. It was most unusual for a woman to offer her Christian name at such a time in the relationship and James was positively excited by the gesture, conscious that he had moved into another stage of his masterplan. Here was a desperate widow who must surely see the attractions of the younger man before her! But he was overlooking one important issue that Dr Williams had mentioned and had clearly forgotten its relevance.

***

David's sister Hester was enjoying life abroad where her brother had provided the funds for a reasonable house, arranged by Aldert Bakker, and was increasing her circle of friends, learning Dutch as she went. Her twin boys, still little more than infants, seemed happy enough, but she had started to long to see David and wrote to ask him to come when convenient. She was, as yet, unaware that her estranged husband was ruined.

In her missive she asked if the maid Sarah could accompany him as, apart from being able to serve him, she would be welcome as the heroine who made everything possible and besides, Annie would like to meet her again. She gave due praise to David for devising the scheme and making it work but it was Sarah and Annie who were the vital elements, the conduits of information without which it would never have happened.

She wrote at length about her happiness in being free and asking if Charles had even the remotest idea where she was, for there was always at the back of her mind the dread notion that he might pursue her if only to fetch the children home.

There was a further concern. There was mounting hostility between her own country and the one she now called home. The Dutch were feeling oppressed by the overall rise in the supremacy of the British and resentful that the uniting of the two countries in the previous century had not developed to their benefit. Mr Bakker was increasingly perturbed by the situation and was hoping that further war between the two could be avoided as, in his view, there could be only one winner.

Anything that further weakened the Dutch republic, as war with England might do, could provide the impetus for other countries, such as France, to seek to overrun the Netherlands, and such opinions brought pain to Bakker's heart. He had willingly helped his friend and business associate arrange the flight of Hester Handlen but he knew it could be a brief respite. He was pleased she had invited him as the occasion would allow him to privately explain his fears to Grayan.

David Grayan was well aware of troubles brewing across the seas but had no immediate fear for his sister. Charles Handlen was ruined but Ralph Grayan was a serious threat and possessed all the determination necessary to pursue Hester and deal with David, and in his anger and bitterness he was losing all sense of reason, ready to spend large amounts of money to obtain information and take revenge on his brother.

Handlen was no value to him in any respect. Edward was now heir to nothing at all, but this did not bother Ralph. The boy had to be brought to his home and reared there with his own four children. He would disown Hester and cast her out and David could do what he wished for her, and be damned for it.

But those boys had to be brought back. It was a matter of honour and in his deranged state he believed there was nothing more important. He even persuaded his other sister to write to David but she did not send the letter, concealing the fact from Ralph and her own husband.

***

The man looked puzzled as well he might.

Dr Williams had been slain with one blow, a knife through his heart. There was no sign of the weapon but the assailant knew exactly what he was doing, exactly where and how to strike. Nothing had been stolen from the old man, a fact confirmed by his grieving widow, and his horse had been left at the scene. This wasn't about theft. It was murder and for murder there must be a motive.

Surely Dr Williams could have no enemies? So just why was he killed?

It was the man's job to find out why and bring the murderer to justice. Yes, today it was a puzzle but he'd solved other riddles successfully apprehending the criminals responsible and he didn't doubt he'd work this one out to a similar satisfactory end.

Chapter Fourteen

There was no sign that spring might be coming.

On the contrary, winter continued to spread its ugly tentacles throughout north Kent as February approached the end of its course.

David Grayan has entertained Lily Cowans and her parents at Downsland and has arranged passage to the Netherlands for him and Sarah for a brief stay with his sister. He has advised Robert Broxford that he wants to make him responsible for special duties aside from his employment as a footman and has assigned him tasks of a varied but simple nature.

This has enabled him to pay Broxford more without upsetting the footmen who believed they enjoyed greater call on seniority amongst their own ranks, and also enabled him to visit Mrs Evershen where he assured her that Robert and Clara would provide for her once they were married.

It was a surprise visit but Grayan wanted it to be so in order to mitigate any resistance to the betrothed couple's plans. He explained that Robert had been promoted, was now a man of means, and he and Clara would rent a small cottage on the estate. Mrs Evershen was so shocked that the Master of Downsland should pay her a call in person, and about so lowly a matter, that she agreed the match providing she was indeed to be suitably maintained. He found it unnecessary to mention the money he'd given her late husband.

Following his appointment Dr Philip Jaunton has taken up his post with Henry Barrenbridge and has moved into lodgings in Westlingstead. His presence has caused many a heart to flutter.

Grayan may not be a God fearing man but has the utmost respect for the beliefs of others, whereas there are a few who despise him for his attitude to the Almighty, not least the Reverend Farhoe who is openly aggressive towards someone who should be setting a better example. Farhoe is able to ignore the good the Master of Downsland has done for this part of north Kent and the village of Westlingstead in particular, instead upbraiding Grayan for his ungodliness.

Judith Pearland finds Jaunton contemptuous if unintentionally so and is aware he detests the concept of being under the command of a woman. For a man who professes to admire Grayan so very much she finds it hard to reconcile his hostility to his position with his respect for the Master's teachings as he calls them. There is now a degree of tension at the hospital with Henry Barrenbridge only too aware that he cannot help himself feeling for Jaunton in the situation Grayan has placed him in. In its turn this adds to the tension and uneasiness.

Sarah has busied herself with the work of her own new post and is often found buried in figures and correspondence at Downsland, and then again at her mother's. But she loves it and tackles it with enthusiasm. Sadly her world is about to suffer a serious disturbance that will have far reaching consequences. She enjoyed waiting upon Lily Cowans once more and is firmly of the opinion Lily will make a good Mistress for Downsland when she and the Master are wed.

To the south-west a man has been making enquiries.

Jack Robins is a parish constable, an unpaid part-time volunteer post but one eminently suited to a man with his background. Now retired he is a former soldier who became a Bow Street Runner in London where he was notably successful in his work. Tall, powerfully built, strong and with a deep booming voice, he is nonetheless often found to be in good cheer and is believed to be tireless in any engagement he undertakes.

The murder of Dr Williams is his current interest.

***

The troubles began when Mrs Evershen was taken ill and attended by Dr Jaunton. Clara had been summoned from Downsland to care for her mother and was much taken by the handsome new doctor, who in his turn clearly appreciated the exquisite beauty of the daughter. Despite her ailment Mrs Evershen noticed that he was admiring Clara and immediately thought him a better prospect than Robert Broxford.

Not far from where widow Evershen lay recovering and plotting Sarah Brankly was busy with some documents relating

164

to the smallholding and was dealing with matters that required her full attention. Her mother was on the farm. She did not see her uncle Edmund staring at her for had she done so she might've realised his intentions were far from honourable, a fact manifest in his facial expression.

Thwarted in his pursuit of Clara he was pondering a quest for some amusement with Sarah. Unlikely to be wed, unlikely to know the pleasures to be thus enjoyed with a man, unable to bear children .... why, he thought, she might welcome his interest if she believed it her only opportunity. And there would be no chance of leaving her with child!

In the morning her mother would be taking some food to another daughter in Harrietsham. Sarah was staying the night to help on the farm before returning to Downsland around noon. He would act then.

Abed that evening Sarah was looking back over the stay of Lily Cowans. Thinking of her with the Master brought strange and unusual feelings that rendered her almost in pain, an unpleasant sensation rising in the pit of her stomach that she might have been inclined to associate with illness. Yet she knew she was well. Lily was a lovely woman, not with outstanding beauty but attractive enough, not buxom, Sarah considered, but not slender by any means, with a round, jolly face unscarred by her experiences with Mr Culteney. Short, light hair daintily dressed completed the picture of graceful elegance, especially as she was always clothed so well in attire that suited her entirely.

Yes, she would be a good match, and the Master seemed smitten. Sarah giggled to herself but felt the strange sensitivity hurt her inside. Whatever could it be, she wondered? She hoped she was not actually sickening but, hey ho, if it was to be the case it would have to be endured.

She'd been the centre of attention amongst the gossip-mongers at Downsland, the young maids being particularly excited to hear news of Miss Cowans. Sarah had kept her own counsel as far as possible but given out small, tantalising snippets upon which those who revelled in chitchat could place their own interpretations, adding embellishments as they always did. There had been one lengthy conversation with the lady when she had been invited to sit and share the tea she had brought the guest.

It had not been possible to lead the talk around to issues that Sarah would've liked to discuss, and as she was conscious of not overstepping and saying something she should not she let Miss Cowans dictate the topics of conversation. She was praised for her part in Mrs Handlen's flight and for helping the Master to come out of his self-imposed darkness.

"Mrs Grayan is with him now," she told Sarah, the kindness in her voice settling comfortingly about the maid, "and he is happy, for she is always by his side and for that we should be grateful. It is my greatest sadness now that there is a rift between him and his brother that has already brought violence and which cannot be mended. Mrs Handlen's flight has worsened a desperate situation and I fear Mr Grayan loses no sleep over the loss of his brother. It is sad, but we must be pleased the Master we knew has been restored to us, and must accept that we cannot change what must be.

"I discuss these things with you Sarah, as I know you have the confidence of Mr Grayan and that you are aware of what is going on from his own lips, and I trust you will respect my own words as part of a private conversation between us, not to be spoken of elsewhere."

"Yes Ma'am, as I respect such private matters between the Master and myself." Lily Cowans nodded in satisfaction as Sarah spoke.

Lily had proceeded to ask after Sarah's family, showing interest in how her siblings were progressing and concern for her mother having to run the smallholding.

"My uncle Edmund is a great help, my mother says, and she has a girl from the village come in to assist at certain times, and as I do the book-keeping and all correspondence I believe my mother is coping very well, thank you ma'am." Lily did not doubt that this young lady was capable of making such an assessment so full of confidence was she, and the thought nearly brought a knowing smile to her lips. So young but so assured!

It was while Sarah was musing on her time with Miss Cowans that she drifted into peaceful, undisturbed sleep.

***

Jack Robins was not at peace and was restless.

He had taken to visiting friends, relatives and now former patients of Dr Williams. This was no chance slaughter, no highwayman stealing and killing, no ruffian bent on theft. The more he tossed around his thoughts the more Jack Robins knew that Dr Williams was the chosen victim of a ruthless murderer. The doctor's clothing was untouched apart from where the weapon had pierced cloth and flesh alike. There was nothing to suggest a struggle. So perhaps the doctor knew his assailant and was simply taken by surprise. That was the direction Jack Robins knew he should take.

And that course had presently brought him to where Mrs Dorothea Landspur resided.

Unlike many parish constables Robins had no qualms about approaching his betters, as he termed them, but was pleasantly surprised to find Mrs Landspur welcoming especially when she learned he was pursuing Dr Williams's killer.

Showing due deference and remembering his manners he sat on the edge of a chair in her withdrawing room when requested to do so rather than recline in at as he would do at home.

"I am so sorry to trouble you, ma'am, but I am told Dr Williams was your physician until recent years and that he attended upon you lately. God rest the poor gentleman ma'am," he crossed himself, "that he should meet so untimely an end, but if there is anything at all you can tell me I would be so very grateful as it may give me some clue as to the motive for such a crime."

Dorothea clutched her bosom as he spoke and he saw the colour drain from her face as if she had just been confronted with some unpalatable event, which in a way she had.

"Constable Robins, I cannot imagine that you believe I would know anything about such a heinous crime, or that it would have any connection to me, and I am most disturbed at the suggestion."

"Ma'am, I did not intend to imply any sort of connection whatsoever, and apologise for any offence given knowing it was unintentional on my part. But I must have this murderer and I am simply tracing the victim's recent activities and speaking to everyone I can find who had contact with him for any reason."

"No offence was taken Constable Robins, but please understand the atrocious shock I have suffered. He was an excellent physician and although I was sad when he retired I have had no need for medical assistance until now."

"I do not ask for details Mrs Landspur, please rest assured I do not, that would be most improper, but would you in your goodness please tell me something of the doctor's need to call upon you, bearing in mind he had retired and you said, or rather suggested, he was no longer practicing?"

"Constable Robins, I do not believe I said or implied anything of the sort. When I was ailing a new doctor was recommended to me and I naturally summoned him first.

"Dr Parry-Barnard proved to be ideal and offered me remedies that were most efficacious in restoring me to health. Unfortunately I had a worrying relapse and decided to ask Dr Williams to call as he lives close by whereas my new doctor lives in Hawkhurst. I was prescribed medication which was prepared, so I understand, by the apothecary in Tenterden, and again it proved successful although I was particularly unwell for a day or two.

"Learning of Dr Williams's demise I once again asked Dr Parry-Barnard to call, which he has done, and I am in the best of health as you can no doubt see."

"Ma'am, I am so very pleased you are, just as I am sorry you were taken ill in the first place. I thank you for your help and for taking the time to see me. I need keep you no longer."

She rang the bell and the maid appeared, ready to escort Robins out. Away from Mrs Landspur and at the front door he turned to the young girl.

"Tell me miss, did Dr Williams and Dr Parry-Barnard ever meet here? I completely forgot to ask your Mistress and do not wish to disturb her again over something so trivial."

"No sir, they never did, but when Mistress was very bad and Dr Williams came he told me not to allow Dr Parry-Barnard in, and I did as I was bid sir, for he came again and went away. But he came again when Mistress sent for him after ... after ... after the murder." And she collapsed into floods of tears while the Constable took it upon himself to take her in his arms and offer comfort.

168

Ah now, he thought to himself as the maid recovered herself, there's some news, some news indeed. Now why would Dr Williams bar Parry-Barnard I wonder? Mrs Landspur gave me no indication and did not seem to know he had been refused entry. Interesting. He released the maid who was fully comforted and restored and grateful for his kindness, and he bade her farewell thinking that perhaps, and at long last, he had his hands on something important.

***

At Westlingstead's hospital relations between the doctors were deteriorating rapidly.

Judith Pearland was thriving in her role as Barrenbridge's assistant and enjoying giving Philip Jaunton his orders which he was obliged to take and did so begrudgingly. He complained to Henry who sympathised but had to pretend he didn't. Both men were fully qualified and it rankled with the pair of them that they had no choice but to follow the edicts of Grayan who was their patron and therefore their paymaster.

The one task he did not mind being given was another visit to Mrs Evershen where it was reported the daughter was showing minor symptoms of the same problem.

Mrs Evershen was improving thanks to Jaunton's care but Clara had a slight fever and might easily have caught the complaint from her mother. There was little Jaunton could do other than provide some medicine for relief rather than cure, for the problem would have to take its course. He promised to call every day until both ladies were better, an arrangement that appealed to all three quite handsomely with the mother noting the way Clara and the doctor looked at each other.

Sarah Brankly had fed the chickens and returned with some eggs while Edmund carried out some pointless task elsewhere. Her mother was long gone and would not be back until mid-afternoon, sometime after Sarah had departed. Apart from offering the necessary courtesies in deference to her uncle she was learning how to avoid him where possible and ignore him when the circumstances were in her favour.

169

Neither appeared to take any notice of each other when he entered the room, but he suddenly turned and made straight for her, grabbing her around the waist and slapping his lips against hers. In that moment of shock she instinctively broke free and before he could grasp her again she gave him a mighty kick that saw him collapse to his knees, bright red in the face, gasping and making a noise like a stuck pig.

Recoiling, faced screwed up by rage, she yelled at him.

"Never do that again. Never come near me. Never. That's what you did to poor Clara isn't it? And my mother believed you against her. You dreadful, wicked man."

Somehow he managed to climb back to his feet, eyes flaming, and staggered across the room. Sarah quickly gathered her things and flew through the door and in her haste ran into Robert Broxford who had no time to move from her way.

"Whoa Sarah, why the rush?"

"My uncle Edmund has caught hold of me and kissed me and I have escaped," she furiously spat out the words as Edmund came in pursuit.

"Hold on missy, you have no reason to attack me like that," he bellowed seeing Robert.

"Every reason. And what pray will you tell mama? That I attacked you as Clara did? Even my mother would begin to doubt you, you wicked man."

Robert decided to step in.

"Stay sir, advance no further. Stay. Leave Sarah be or you'll have me to deal with."

"Aye, and I'm not afraid of you, lad. Come here if you're man enough." A small crowd was gathering.

"Right sir, I shall have you now."

"Stop it, stop it," cried Sarah, "No more violence."

But Edmund took advantage of Robert lowering his fists in response to Sarah's appeal and lunged at the footman landing the first blow, the only blow that did so, for Robert was too speedy, too agile and it was but a few brief seconds before his opponent was flat on his back, moaning, finished.

Slowly getting to his feet he aimed his last remarks at Sarah.

"You're finished here Sarah. Your mother will believe me. You'll have to come crawling back here and face your reckoning, so you will. You'll answer to your mother. But I'll never let you back in this house, so help me God." With that he slunk back into the house while Sarah fell into Robert's arms sobbing her heart out. The crowd dispersed seemingly disappointed Edmund had made such a poor fight of it.

Chancing upon the scene had been the Reverend Farhoe who now made his way after Edmund determined the console the older man who had been so viciously set about by a much younger person. Robert held on to Sarah as they set off along the road, past Farhoe who studiously ignored them and their greeting, and on towards Clara's.

Knowing her to be unwell Robert had decided to call to ask after her and her mother and, with his permission, a distraught Sarah felt she would like to come too as she had nothing else to attend to now, and sadly shared an affinity with the girl relating to Edmund Forness and his appalling behaviour. It was not to be any sort of pleasurable visit.

***

Another visit that was anything but pleasurable took place near Hawkhurst where Parry-Barnard had a call from Jack Robins.

Pleasant enough Robins nonetheless exuded an air of suspicion that made his host nervous.

"Please tell me what you can about your visits to Mrs Landspur, sir. I obviously do not expect you to disclose any medical matters or comment upon your professional involvement. I'll tell you this sir: I've been told you attended the lady but on one occasion you were prevented from doing so on the instructions of Dr Williams. Is that so, sir? And if so, why would that be please?"

Parry-Barnard was feeling the beads of sweat forming and desperately trying to keep them in check.

"I ... I ... I ... well ... Constable ... I ... I was, I mean I am Mrs Landspur's physician and when she was taken bad she called in Dr Williams, as I understand the situation to be, as he was nearer than I. I do believe there may have been some sort of misunderstanding between the doctor, Mrs Landspur and her

171

maid, although I cannot imagine why, and I was indeed asked to leave at that time, perhaps to avoid me catching Mrs Landspur's complaint. But I departed without question and, as you now know, I am attending her once more.

"You will understand Constable," he was gaining in confidence, "there is a professional code of ethics amongst doctors and as Dr Williams had been summoned he had no need to consult me and would not expect me to interfere. Not unless Mrs Landspur specifically asked for me."

"I see sir. Are you aware Dr Williams took samples of the medication you prescribed to an apothecary in Tenterden for identification? Now why would he do that do you suppose?" All the new found confidence Parry-Barnard had amassed vanished and was replaced by feelings of near terror and doom which magnified themselves when he started to recall Dr Williams's words. He needed to think quickly.

"Well, Constable .... returning to the issue of professional ethics it is not at all unusual for a second doctor to do this if he was unsure what was before him. It is all too easy to prescribe something that might act badly with the initial medicine, so it is a practice to be certain rather than guess."

"I see sir. But he could've consulted you as you would know what you had given Mrs Landspur."

"I expect he thought he could use the services of the apothecary rather more swiftly than finding me. I have other patients and might not have been so readily located. I'm sure that would be his line of reasoning."

"Thank you sir. That's most helpful. I apologise for taking up your time but you really have been extremely helpful."

Parry-Barnard relaxed at last and smiled. It was a short-lived freedom.

"The apothecary was of the opinion that the two medications you prescribed Mrs Landspur might, as you suggested sir, have worked against each other. Is that possible?"

"N-n-n-n-no, not at all. I have the details here if you would like to see them and any good apothecary or doctor will confirm that they could not have acted against each other."

"Thank you sir, that won't be necessary now, but I'll bear in mind you have information."

The information Parry-Barnard had was at variance with what he'd prescribed and deliberately so. That had all been part of his plot. Keep evidence that he supplied the correct medicine in such a manner it would cast doubt on the work of an apothecary in analysing it.

Robins left soon after and Parry-Barnard hoped he'd seen the last of him. It was to be a forlorn hope.

***

It was a cold, deserted place to be, a place where the wind can penetrate the thickest clothing and freeze the flesh, but she was used to it. She had grown up here and had learned to live with all that nature could inflict upon humans and animals alike, and enjoyed her walks regardless of the weather. Today she was enjoying it even more for her mind was at rest and there was warmth in her soul with much in her life to give her pleasure.

Climbing out of Dover to the south Lily Cowans rested once on her way to Capel and that was on the first peak of the cliffs to look back across the town and up to the castle beyond set, as it was, on the cliffs to the north, the very place she and David Grayan had walked not so very long ago.

Since then she had stayed at Downsland again, this time with her parents, and had many happy memories to look back on, some to truly cherish. Grayan had been such an attentive host and she'd loved the walks they had shared, finding him exceptionally good company, and pleased that he was the man he had once been now he had found the spirit of his wife.

In a strange but pleasing way she'd felt that Marie had walked with them and neither lady objected to the presence of the other. She experienced an inner calmness suggesting Marie had accepted her and that she was welcome where Marie had strolled with her husband. Lily had been almost gleeful believing that the three of them walked together in harmony because Marie wanted her there.

Roger Culteney was still in her thoughts and still in her heart but she had overcome her loss and his memory lay peacefully within her, quiet and dormant. She knew she was free to love again, just as she knew Grayan was liberated from his grief and could give his heart with Marie's blessing, not that his wife would settle her blessing on an unworthy woman.

Lily had to consider her position. No longer youthful but young enough to be wife and mother and therefore an attractive proposition.

She had found much common ground with the views and opinions of David Grayan whereas her parents had not. There had been no heated arguments, just well-reasoned debate in which agreement to differ had been reached with ease on most topics. Lily had mostly held her tongue when her father was taking issue with Grayan as she was more often than not inclined to disagree with Mr Cowans. But these were not insurmountable difficulties.

The young maid Sarah appeared to like her. The girl had done so much for her Master. Taking Lily's own letter as her guide she'd provided the impetus for Grayan to rediscover his life as it once was, and then she'd been asked about Mrs Handlen's need to remove herself and her twins from her husband. She'd had the answer and had executed the plan to perfection working well with the other maid Annie who went in fear for her life. Grayan was relying on Sarah and perhaps that was a good thing.

Lily could not see her own father asking a servant for advice, never mind showing them private correspondence! It wasn't the right thing, but Lily had accepted it in Grayan just as she realised she would do so herself. If only she had a maid like Sarah! You didn't mix with servants. Good heavens above, what was the world coming to? But it had been the Grayan's way and it had left them ostracised by most of society, yet Lily discerned it was her way too given the chance.

Maybe times were changing. Probably not in the future Lily saw in front of her, but perhaps in years and years to come. Grayan was trying to start a revolution the world was not ready for and was more likely to start a rebellion that could lead to the overthrow of governance, possibly the monarchy and leave the country open to invasion. She shuddered but not from the cold.

She'd learned many of the things those in high places had to say about the Master of Downsland, the reasons why they condemned him out of hand, and about their fears that might be well founded. Just over the Channel where she was gazing now there was a feeling of unrest in France so it was possible some of the concerns about Grayan's attitude were right to be aired.

As she turned for home she decided some matters might be better left alone. The man was happy in the north of the county where presumably he could do little harm to the nation as a whole, yet could do so much good as he had already evidenced since his arrival.

A wry smile lit her face. Sarah would understand she thought. Sarah would understand!

***

Sarah was presently most unhappy and distressed. Added to her own woes she and Robert received a cold reception at the Evershen household where Clara seemed to make it clear by her expressions and empty conversation that they were unwelcome. When they left Mrs Evershen could not help herself saying she was pleased to see them go, and remarking Clara would be better off without him.

"Now that nice young doctor, Clara..."

"Mama, pray do not match-make. He is handsome but he has position and I do not."

"He sees your beauty my precious one. He will love you regardless. Better be wed to a man of status than a jumped-up footman."

"It is not the time to think of being wed. I am betrothed to Robert and for now that is quite sufficient."

"Dr Jaunton will come again on the morrow. Make the most of it my proud beauty. He likes you. Make him know that you return his feelings."

"Oh mama, that is no good."

"Listen to me my girl. You could turn any head. Even win the heart of that David Grayan if you had the mind to. You can win Dr Jaunton's heart and be better for it."

Along the road Sarah and Robert sat together sadness filling their eyes. There were no words. Both were lost in their dire thoughts.

Sarah was wondering about her dear mother and how this latest episode might damage the abiding and secure relationship twixt mother and daughter, the love that had brought her to where she was today. Edmund stood poised to wreck her life. Oh, how could she overcome this?

Robert was sensing that Clara was indifferent to him and that there might be sound reason. It could be Mrs Evershen of course, that would be understandable, but what if there was something else? Was he to wait until Clara told him in her own time? And would it break his heart?

They had been staring at the ground in front of them and suddenly the view was interrupted by a pair of feet. It was Reverend Farhoe.

"Sarah, the Good Lord will forgive if you prostrate yourself before him and pray for absolution for your sins, but forgiveness here on Earth will be harder to come by, very much harder I assure you. Mr Forness will expect retribution for your lies and will expect your mother to deal with you as she sees best.

"And as for you Robert Broxford, shame upon you attacking an old helpless man so mercilessly and all because you believed the untruths this wanton girl told you. There can be no forgiveness here. Mr Forness has sworn to refuse you clemency and I have failed to persuade him otherwise. Go to the church Robert, and pray for your salvation from the Almighty or you will be forever damned."

Robert was too stunned to speak. Not so Sarah.

"Father, my uncle grabbed me, forced a kiss upon me, and would've made his sinful behaviour worse had I not broken free. He punched Robert first and Robert retaliated. He desisted the moment my uncle fell to the ground. It was in defence. I have not lied and Robert has done no wrong."

Paul Farhoe, sounding like a demented preacher, bellowed at them.

"You evil child. You blaspheme before God girl. You will suffer eternal damnation if you do not repent. Your mother will punish you and drive Satan from your body with her blows. Then you must come to church to pray for your redemption. Go there now Robert or the wrath of the Almighty will be upon your head...."

"I am going to work Father. Sarah is right. I have done nothing wrong and neither has Sarah. You are mistaken. Good day to you." And they both rose and marched off while the priest shouted his condemnation after them, much to the entertainment of those passing by.

"Robert, I must wait and see my mother on her return. Please seek out Mrs Forbes and tell her what has happened and that I shall be there as soon as I can."

"Sarah, what about the retribution the Father spoke of? I am worried for you." She giggled.

"Do not worry for me Robert. I will be fine. There will be no retribution of the sort. My mother cannot possibly believe two girls, one her own daughter, wilfully attacked Edmund for no reason. Doubt will be cast. I will be fine. Go now, and go with my thanks for your kindness, chivalry and company."

Robert was touched. Chivalry? He'd never been praised for that before!

He reluctantly set off, casting a doleful look at Sarah who was trying to appear unafraid. She'd decided to go to the edge of the village in the hopes of meeting her mother there but as she trudged down the footpath she learned Edmund had the same idea and had already found Mrs Brankly.

There was no greeting for the daughter. Catherine Brankly strode purposefully towards her home, Edmund by her side, Sarah in the rear and no words passed between them at all. Once indoors the discussion that followed threw a cloud of horror over Sarah for her mother not only believed her brother but claimed it had been a plot by the girls to help exonerate Clara at Edmund's expense.

Worse was to follow.

Retribution, as visualised by the clergyman, was promised much to Sarah's chagrin. And there was the prospect of Edmund witnessing her punishment. That was too much. Sarah made to leave but her mother caught her arm.

"Leave here daughter, and you never return. There will be no welcome. You will not set foot in this home again." Clearly Mrs Brankly thought the threat would deter Sarah from departing without her punishment but alas it had the opposite effect. She pulled herself away and, turning at the door, called back.

"I love you mama. I would never turn my back on you in that way. I pray you will not exercise your threat for I cannot live without you. But I will not be punished for something I haven't done. Uncle Edmund knows the truth about me and Clara. One day soon I pray he will confess. I love you mama, but now I must return to the Hall." And she was gone.

Chapter Fifteen

March that year began with a roar as strong winds swept across Kent, sometimes bringing rain but more often sunshine as the days lengthened, and gradually those winds eased and the people began to feel the first warmth to suggest spring was making its way to the county.

David Grayan is preparing for his voyage to the Continent knowing the storms across the North Sea can be vicious and hoping William Scrans has secured a strong, well-manned vessel. Not long ago his companion for the journey, Sarah Brankly, had sought an audience with him.

"Sir you have been gracious in asking my humble advice on certain matters and now I need yours." He sat up attentively. "My uncle Edmund made forceful advances and I was obliged to push him away and dash into the street. My mother was in Harrietsham at the time. I ran directly into Robert Broxford who was passing and told him what had happened whereupon he punched Edmund, who was pursuing me, to the ground. My uncle landed the first blow sir.

"Edmund told my mother I had attacked him and she believed him and I when I refused to be punished for something I had not done she banished me. My own mother whom I love so dearly. I cannot comprehend how she could banish her own daughter, but Edmund is her brother and she felt she must support him against me.

"I am struggling to cope with the pain of separation, so much so that I yearn to return and take my beating so that I might hug mama and be welcome at home again. But it is a point of principle sir. Yet I miss mama so very much."

He studied her from across his desk. How forthright was she! Poised and strong in purpose. A mere maid, not yet of age, speaking to her Master with flowing confidence, and all because he had asked her opinion about Evershen's letter when she came seeking a post! Since then she had lit up his world, not least helping him to find Marie's guiding spirit, without which he might have been lost forever and died an old curmudgeon in purgatory.

In what other great house would a maid have the nerve to approach the Master thus? He admired her and knew he had been in danger of being condescending towards her, at times wanting to metaphorically pat her head as you might do a small well-behaved child who had achieved something creditable. Now he was a better man, and treated her with well deserved respect.

"I have a suggestion Sarah. Let me write to your mother and tell her you came to me with your story, and as I have punished you myself I trust she will accept the matter is closed and will invite you back." Sarah's face told a story. She did not think he was being serious and thought he was merely playing with her, and he knew he had failed in this assignment.

"Or .... perhaps we could visit your mother together. She is hardly likely to refuse to see me and it may be that we can resolve the problem by discussion. If I could persuade your uncle to abandon his quest for retribution your mother may well relent." He looked at her again and her expression had barely changed. He sighed heavily and awaited her reply.

"It is still a matter that requires my wholehearted apology and I will not seek forgiveness for a wrong I have not done. Both your suggestions sir would need me to apologise. That means that I would have to accept my uncle's version of events." They looked directly at each other. He knew he was letting her down and it sore worried him.

"Leave me to think on it Sarah. I will find a solution."

There being no possibility of further progress there and then Sarah rose, curtsied, thanked him and left the room downhearted and disappointed. Grayan had not treated the dispute with any importance or seriousness, but it was to be hoped he could produce the answer and she had a degree of belief in that.

The idea of his letter was preposterous. It would mean both him and Sarah being untruthful about her punishment and she wouldn't countenance that, for this was an issue about the truth itself.

***

The truth was beckoning elsewhere in Kent, and retribution was also planned.

Jack Robins had been going backwards and forwards betwixt Biddenden, Tenterden and Hawkhurst and getting everywhere and nowhere.

In Tenterden the apothecary was certain foul play had been at work, but lost his faith in his analysis faced with the prospect of appearing in court as a witness. Robins went to Parry-Barnard and asked for the notes relating to the medication he'd administered to Mrs Landspur and took these back to Tenterden.

The apothecary's uncertainty gained momentum and Robins realised he was chasing a lost cause.

But he received a long letter from London regarding the doctor and the fact he had recently been at Westlingstead under the renowned Henry Barrenbridge, so decided that was his next port of call.

Barrenbridge listened, studied the notes and the information the apothecary had provided, reminded himself that Parry-Barnard was not qualified and had brought about the unnecessary death of a village man, and elected to go with caution and tact.

"Constable Robins, Dr Parry-Barnard in my opinion provided the correct medicine, much as I would've done I expect. I say that without having examined the patient or seen my colleague's diagnosis. The apothecary is perhaps a little confused. In truth I think he may have thought something was amiss and drawn it to Dr Williams's attention and it could well be the case that Williams assessed the overall picture and found nothing wrong."

"Are you aware Doctor, that Parry-Barnard had no qualifications of note?" This startled Henry. The Constable had obviously made enquiries.

"He studied at university and I gave him the opportunity to complete his training here where he had practical work and made an outstanding success of it. Has the patient in this case cause for complaint?"

"No sir. I am investigating the murder of a doctor, Williams by name sir, and merely trying to piece together what the good doctor was about in the days prior to his untimely death."

The words hit Barrenbridge a hammer blow.

"Constable, are you suggesting Dr Parry-Barnard had something to do with this?"

"I beg your pardon, no sir. Most definitely not, but Parry-Barnard was attending a patient in Biddenden who later called in her old and retired doctor, Williams, after she was taken proper poorly sir, and it was Dr Williams who took her medicine to the apothecary for his opinion. As you have advised me sir, that you, as an experienced and noted physician, believe there to be nothing amiss with the prescribed remedies I am quite happy with that, and bow to your knowledge in these matters. I apologise if you think I am suggesting Parry-Barnard made a deliberate error. Even then there is no evidence to connect him to the murder."

"I am pleased to hear it Constable."

"Yes sir. Do you know by-the-by, if your colleague ever met Dr Williams?"

"I've no idea. Sorry."

"Thank you sir, I shall detain you no longer."

Robins made his way home, full weary and still trying to paint a complete picture when there was so much missing, but convinced he was closer than was immediately palpable.

At Westlingstead Henry Barrenbridge was perplexed and flustered.

Philip Jaunton had been moaning to him as usual about being under Judith Pearland's command, a villager had been brought in having suffered a serious injury in a riding accident, and now Robins had turned up with bad news that had left him vexed. Jaunton had gone to the Evershen's so he required Pearland's assistance with the patient and she seemed to be able to manage demonstrating yet again her excellent skills.

His mind wasn't on what he was doing. With a timely intervention Pearland prevented him making a bad mistake and then annoyed him by offering a suggestion he wasn't sure about. In a fit of scarcely controlled temper he said she could get out if she didn't want to follow his own methods.

"I will not leave this man to die sir. You cannot manage alone and I do not agree with what you are doing. He will be maimed if you proceed as you are, and I believe we have every chance to avoid that." This was too much for Barrenbridge.

182

"Get out now. Send Miss Gandling in and get someone to fetch Jaunton at once. At once, do you hear!"

"I'll go for Philip myself." And she was gone, nurse Gandling entering instantly.

Along the road Jaunton was taking time with his patient. Mrs Evershen was recovering well, but still in her bed. After a brief examination he returned to the main room where Clara was. Happily she was no worse, if anything much improved and clearly delighted to see the doctor who, in his turn, made his delight equally obvious.

So he was quite perturbed when Pearland arrived. She explained with brevity what had happened, how Barrenbridge intended to deal with it, and that she'd been sent away after arguing.

"Ye gods," he exclaimed, "I think you're right. I'll go at once. Ye gods!" He made apology to Clara for his hasty departure, who showed her immense disappointment, thanked Pearland and raced to the hospital.

There he found himself in a difficult situation. Pearland was absolutely right and Barrenbridge was about to condemn the patient to permanent disability. He tried to argue his case but was rebuffed by a furious Barrenbridge who ordered him to assist and consider his position when surgery was completed. Jaunton complied with reluctance. He knew the man could be restored to full fitness but there was nothing he could do about the proposed treatment, so entrenched in his beliefs was Barrenbridge.

Grace Gandling had watched this with growing unease. The senior doctor would do it his way and was in a such a rage that could not benefit the patient's surgery, and so it proved. With increased concern Gandling played her part until it became evident that it was not going well with Barrenbridge's anger spilling over into his attempts to cope.

Finally he made a fatal mistake and all their attempts to stem the bleeding failed and they were forced to watch the man's life slip away until all they were left with was his corpse.

It was Gandling who spoke.

"I'll go and tell his wife. She's outside." Neither man spoke. Jaunton was looking contemptuously at Barrenbridge and feeling his own fury rise within him. The nurse slipped quietly away on her sad mission and Jaunton started to clear up as the other doctor departed without words.

Left to me, Jaunton thought, this man would not only be alive but his injuries would've healed almost perfectly. And, he agreed with himself, Judith was right too. Well, Barrenbridge wants me to consider my position and I think I have already made my decision.

***

"I am so sorry to be a nuisance sir. Just one question if you don't mind."

Parry-Barnard had greeted Jack Robins at the door and not admitted him. The Constable was taking on the form of the devil as if determined to haunt him and make him feel guilt.

"Did you ever meet Dr Williams sir?"

"No. Never."

"So you wouldn't know what he looked like?"

"No, of course not. Now if you will excuse me I have to go to a patient."

"Yes sir, I will not detain you and apologise again for bothering you."

I am annoying him, Robins concluded as he walked away. That is good. I have often found that the guilty do not like being questioned continually and I am beginning to think that this person may be the murderer. I know a guilty man when I see him and Mr Parry-Barnard has the look of culpability about him.

I think him a fraudster. And it must surely be dangerous to pretend to be a physician and administer all kinds of medicine to the sick. Poor Mrs Landspur. If Dr Williams was correct she might have been poisoned to death by this quack. Now, let me see. Mrs Landspur is a wealthy widow and not of any great age. Did he hope to ingratiate himself and do well out of it?

Make her ill, cure her and pocket the money. But being a quack doctor he nearly finishes her off. But wait. Was there another explanation? A wealthy widow of good appearance and still of an age to please a man. Was that the attraction? Let us look further. She commands high social status beyond his lowly means. Might he want to marry her for position and the riches that might bring?

Yes, perhaps that. You do not poison someone who could be of value to you either way, so is the truth that he intended to make the dear lady unwell and then restored her to health in order to visit her as often as was necessary? Did Dr Williams arrive at this truth and confront him? Even a quack would know how to kill with a knife to the heart. A deadly enemy indeed.

***

Sarah cut a sad figure as she prepared for the voyage. She'd never seen the sea let alone set foot on a ship. Yes, she'd seen paintings but suddenly the spectre of actually taking this adventure was troubling her, and to this was added the anguish of not being able to say goodbye to her mother.

If only Miss Cowans was here, she reflected. Miss Cowans would help me. All the Master could do was mock me but then I am being unfair. There was nothing wrong with his suggestions, it was just that they mocked the truth rather than me, and it is a stand of principle. I know, I think Miss Cowans would say write a letter, and that is what I shall do.

The missive was short but full of the tender love of a daughter for her mother, and explained that she was to leave anon for the Netherlands as she had told Mrs Brankly and wished she could say goodbye in person.

It worked and in her reply her mother said they could meet at the churchyard.

There they embraced and wept and spoke so few words, for few were necessary. Her mother was afeared for Sarah given that she faced a long, uncertain voyage, and a notably dangerous one, but knew her daughter would go. Ever adventurous Sarah would attempt almost anything just as she had when going directly to Mr Grayan for employment. She never contemplated failure and it was rarely her companion.

At the hospital failure was all they had.

The junior doctors were faced with a nasty dilemma. Both were aware Barrenbridge had made a critical error that had cost a man his life, and the reputation of the establishment and their

185

careers as medical people could be left in tatters. The wife had been informed that tragically there had been nothing they could do and she had accepted the situation as grief overtook her.

Henry Barrenbridge wanted the incident covered up for the sake of the hospital and for all their own sakes. Judith Pearland knew that if she spoke out she would be ridiculed simply because she was a woman unless, of course, she had Jaunton's support. Barrenbridge knew her predicament and elected to undermine her at every turn by the straightforward expedient of buying Jaunton off.

He was promoted to senior assistant on the understanding that the true cause of the disaster was never revealed, and that marooned Judith high and dry, ruined whichever way she went unless she accepted the new state of affairs. Unable to do so she left the hospital for good. That night she returned home a woman worn out by circumstances beyond her control, her vocation devastated and shattered.

She had wanted to help the sick, that was all, and had been so proud to be called a doctor, but now there was nothing remaining and it was not possible to explain to her parents. Naturally they now thought she had abandoned her efforts and might settle down with the blacksmith's son, but Judith's mind was not balanced as she had been torn asunder by all that had occurred. It felt like the end of the world, the end of all she'd believed in. Her life was finished.

***

At last she had been able to retire to the room where she longed to be, and ran her fingertips slowly and softly along the top of the counterpane, looking at the pillow where his head had so surely laid.

The letter had arrived while she was preparing for dinner and had no time to read it then or since, especially as they were entertaining friends from Canterbury and it was a private document. Now, when they were all readying themselves for the night, she had been able to slip into the bedchamber he had occupied during his stay, place the candle on the table and use its light to illuminate his writings.

186

She treasured every word and read the letter thrice over despite its length.

She clutched the papers to her bosom and stared out of the window at the moon rising in the sky beyond as a multitude of thoughts ran amok through her mind. Pleasant thoughts, tantalising thoughts, intriguing thoughts, beautiful thoughts; they were all there to be revelled in.

But there were also thoughts of fear. Disturbing thoughts.

David Grayan wrote about his forthcoming visit to his sister and Lily wished she was going with him. But at least he would have good company in Sarah Brankly, and it was that thought that created a pang of jealousy in her heart.

Envy that she could not go was to be understood, and it wasn't unusual for a man of high standing to travel with a servant although normally a male one. It was envy that Lily knew Sarah would keep him company where a servant would usually be in the background. And there was the voyage itself, dangerous and prolonged, across treacherous seas for hours on end.

Lily Cowans began to wonder if she would see David again.

She wondered if she was in love but dismissed the notion. Then she wondered if he had fallen in love with her and decided probably not. But had he not written yet another letter full of news and good tidings to cheer her? How she loved receiving his letters. They did indeed cheer her.

Surely he would not write so if he had no feelings for her? Perhaps he was in love after all. Maybe she could return his feelings. It was all so confusing but quite delightful.

So she read the communication again and considered if there were any clues in the way he wrote, but could not immediately find any, concluding the whole was the largest clue of all. Here was a man who was writing in a familiar way to a woman he had taken to. If not, why write in such a way?

Warmed by these thoughts she took up her candle and walked along the quiet passageways to her own room, disrobed and climbed into bed where blissful sleep came swiftly amidst her happy waking dreams.

***

187

Another young lady experiencing the pangs of love was Ginny Perkins.

Over time she had formed an attachment with one of the stable hands, Mark Grenchen.

They had often met in the grounds at Downsland and thought nothing of their developing friendship, but as the weeks and months drifted by they realised that there was a bond between them and there was more to it than affection.

Eventually Mark, shy by nature, and never presuming to be worthy of any maiden, declared his love and to his surprise saw Ginny leap into his arms and devour his lips with hers as he clung to the girl who had made him more happy than he could ever have imagined it was possible to be.

They were a lovely couple, their joy radiating about them wherever they went and it was Sarah who felt stirred by it most. She was so pleased for Ginny as it was through her that she was able to boldly approach Grayan for work, and she believed her debt had been repaid now her friend had found the deepest and most enduring love.

Everything will be complete, she deliberated, when the Master marries Miss Cowans. Oh how happy I shall be. What perfection! Jed and Agnes, Ginny and Mark, Clara and Robert ... a very complete picture. It is a shame I shall never know the love that passes between man and woman but, hey ho, I have been chosen for other things.

I wish I could find a loving husband for Mrs Handlen but she remains married to that monster so such a task must forever be unfulfilled. However, I will enjoy seeing her and Annie again.

Most importantly I have made my peace with mama, whom I love so dearly. She told me she was obliged to uncle Edmund and was relieved I had not accepted my punishment, even though she was still inclined to believe her brother. I asked her if I had ever lied to her, and if she thought I ever would, and she just hugged me, kissed me, and blessed me. I think it was her tactful way of saying that she knew I was speaking the truth but without evidence to the contrary she had to accept Edmund's word.

I understood that. It must be difficult being a parent in such circumstances. Perhaps it is no bad thing I shall not be a parent for I would detest having to choose between child and sibling if the truth was in question. At least I have said farewell and we know we still love each other. I shall be all the better for that in the days ahead.

I wonder what it is like going to sea? Will I be seasick? It's an adventure, that it is, but I am growing in fear as the day approaches. It is all so new. But it is my purpose to serve my Master and I am so looking forward to seeing his sister and Annie. I have read books in the library about the Netherlands and I am excited to see the country.

Very flat, but it appears they have tamed the country so the flow of the rivers is controlled by dams and sluices to avoid flooding, and to provide irrigation. It all sounds so very advanced, I am not sure I shall ever comprehend it, but perhaps I will get to see some of it.

Yes, in truth I am excited. A little afeared, but excited, and that is the way it should be. And now I suppose I should start packing.

Hey ho.

Chapter Sixteen

Philip Jaunton found rest problematic after the uproar at the hospital and discovered a novel way of consoling himself and easing his conscience.

Once Clara Evershen had recovered he booked a room at a Faversham inn, took her there and seduced her. Although her mother was horrified at first she reluctantly approved in retrospect given that Clara was, by definition, a fallen woman, and the doctor was a good catch.

Mrs Evershen took great satisfaction in informing Robert that Clara had a new lover.

Sadly for Clara the doctor had no intention of proceeding further. He had taken the Westlingstead Beauty and was satisfied. A village washer-woman, as he termed her, was not for him. She was a passing fancy, a conquest, and nothing more.

Judith Pearland had lost everything and was in despair.

Henry Barrenbridge was restored to his former self, content the true story of the injured man would never be revealed, and with Dr Jaunton proving a popular success at the hospital life had returned to normal.

David Grayan and Sarah Brankly had embarked for the Netherlands unaware they had been followed to Whitstable. Ralph Grayan had his brother tailed every time he set forth from Downsland and, having seen the pair board a ship at the harbour, it was not difficult for money to buy details of the destination. Ralph was pleased.

"The Netherlands. So that's where my sister resides is it? You've done well master Crombie. Here's your money for you are worth every penny." The agent bowed in deference, took the purse, and left the room. "Now my brother I will pursue you and bring Hester's children home, you may be sure of that." He spoke to emptiness as there was nobody to hear his words, his vow.

***

A sea voyage was a novelty to Sarah. The ship had appeared enormous with its masts reaching right up to the sky, even more impressive when the sails were unfurled. The sea itself was more captivating than in any of the paintings she'd seen. Grayan had explained a great deal to her and the ship's master, at his request, described how the ship sailed, how it was steered and how they worked with the wind as well as the tides, currents and waves. Sarah was enthralled.

Wide-eyed she loved being on deck when the weather permitted and looked in awe as the sailors went about their business, often scaling the ropes and the masts, often dashing around for no obvious purpose although she knew everything they did was vital. She was amazed, and could not take it all in.

But above all else she was happy.

It was as if by leaving England they were leaving life's problems behind. As the Kent coast vanished it felt as if she was starting a completely new life, and puzzled such feelings.

She waited on her Master, and after dinner he invited her to sit with him for conversation, and she related the sad tale of Robert Broxford's lost love.

"It may be for the best Sarah. I know Clara is your friend but after her dreadful treatment with Culteney I would've thought better of her than to cast aside a good man like Robert. She may still believe she is worthless, or she may simply be the kind of woman who enjoys such fickle attentions. I know it pains you Sarah, but she has chosen her way and Robert might have saved himself trouble, for she might have wandered after marriage."

Sarah knew he was right, but was still full of sorrow. Robert had accepted all that had passed and had taken Clara to his heart to love her forever, and now she had scorned him.

"You do not know who the lover is Sir?"

"No, I don't. I pride myself in knowing a great deal but that intelligence has not reached my ears yet."

Then they talked about the Netherlands and the trade Grayan had conducted there, and then spoke warmly of his sister and her new life.

"It will be special for me Sarah, for I had but a fleeting glimpse of the boys and too little time with Hester, so I must make the most of this visit. Bless you again for your idea and for

191

executing it well, and I do not forget the role Annie played. Without her the scheme would not have worked."

"Do you know of Mr Handlen sir?"

"He is a ruined man, all his money has gone and he has sold the house and vanished I hear."

"May I ask about your brother sir?"

Grayan looked straight ahead for a moment, lost in thought. His expression was one of resignation when he finally spoke.

"Yes, he will not let it rest. He wants to bring the boys back to his house and rear them alongside his own. As far as Hester is concerned she can rot in the same hell he wishes me to. What a sad family eh, Sarah? I am pleased you have made some degree of peace with your mother but how your business will all resolve itself I do not know."

"No sir, neither do I. It is most unpleasant. Uncle Edmund sold his own property to come and live with us and although I suspect he still has much of the money he may no longer have enough to find somewhere to live. I imagine sir that you do not know where the matter of your sister and your brother's animosity may end."

He simply nodded and produced a small smile as he gazed at her.

"Come Sarah, it is a clear night. Let us go on deck and look at the stars."

***

Jack Robins was in a quandary.

He had to try Mrs Landspur again and was not looking forward to the prospect of such an encounter, particularly as he was now convinced Parry-Barnard was hiding something and he had to try and encourage the truth from someone, even if he could persuade the truth to be revealed unwittingly.

Dorothea Landspur was not welcoming and made her irritation known to him. He knew he wouldn't have long and could ill afford to waste time.

"Mrs Landspur, Dr Parry-Barnard is attending you now once more I understand." She just glared at him. "Do you know why

Dr Williams ordered that he be refused admittance?" Surprise decorated her face, a genuine reaction Robins deduced.

"I know nothing of that, I assure you. How did you hear of it pray?"

"From Dr Parry-Barnard himself ma'am."

"Oh. I see. Well, I have no idea."

"Are you aware Parry-Barnard has no qualifications? He did study medicine at university but failed to finish the course." Surprise was replaced by shock on her face, and she gripped the arms of her chair to steady herself.

"I ... I ... I was not aware, but he is an excellent physician who also studied under Dr Barrenbridge at Westlingstead where he enjoyed a reputation of the highest order, I assure you. I am quite happy for him to treat me."

It was time for Robins to play the ace of trumps.

"And are you aware Dr Williams took a sample of Parry-Barnard's prescribed medicine from here to an apothecary who pronounced it suspicious in content?"

The colour drained from her face and Robins was afraid she might swoon and collapse. Fortunately she gradually regained her composure, with one hand still clutching the chair arm and the other drawn across her breast in a gesture of horror matched by the look on her face.

"I know nothing of this," she stammered, "but I wish to know what is meant by suspicious."

"The concoction may, in the apothecary's opinion, have actually made you unwell, and the remedy could've reacted against it, worsening the symptoms. Parry-Barnard freely gave me his notes showing exactly what was prescribed and I asked Dr Barrenbridge himself to check them and he found nothing amiss, even adding that, subject to an examination, he might've prescribed them himself.

"The apothecary, on the other hand, did not believe the notes matched the composition of the liquids he tested......"

"So Constable, who do you believe?" She was gaining in strength and confidence. "An eminent physician like Dr Barrenbridge or some apothecary with no medical training whatsoever?"

193

"Ma'am, it is not a question of belief or otherwise, it is an issue of conflicting information and it is one I have to look into, and I beg your pardon if you think ......"

"Constable, I have nothing further to say and wish you to leave now." She rang the bell.

"I have had enough of this. Go now, go now." And without ado he rose, bowed and followed the maid from the room.

Jack Robins was not a man to give up once he had his teeth into something, and he was confounded if he was letting this go. He would find the merciless killer and bring him to justice and the more he thought about it the more he knew it was Parry-Barnard he had to net.

***

Dr Philip Jaunton was beset by a problem he could well do without.

Clara Evershen pursued him and was making life very awkward. Prompted by her mother she would call at the hospital at most inopportune moments, occasionally waiting for him to leave the premises so she could walk with him. There was too much gossip in Westlingstead relating to the pair of them and he loathed it. There was jealousy amongst the younger single women who envied Clara's involvement with the handsome new doctor, and as a result she was ostracised by many of her friends.

This didn't bother her providing she could secure him for herself. He had sworn undying love in that room at the Faversham inn. Surely she must mean something to him? Surely she would get to wed this man and be elevated in society?

Nothing could've been further from Jaunton's mind. He knew nothing of her past, any more than any of the villagers did, but she was a passing dream, a night spent in paradise, a pleasure enjoyed and never forgotten but not to be benefited from again. She meant no more than a brief fancy, a dalliance with a beauty, and she could be easily discarded.

Achieving the latter was proving difficult to say the least.

In Leicester you took a girl and nobody really noticed. In a small community like Westlingstead everybody was awake to the chance of tittle-tattle. Here it was widely viewed that the new doctor had partaken of a clandestine arrangement with Clara Evershen and should be ashamed of himself. Clara was seen as little more than the whore she'd tried to avoid being labelled as when Edmund Forness wished for her in his obnoxious way.

There were girls who privately dreamed that it could've been them and men who were privately sorry they had not sampled the Westlingstead Beauty.

Another man wrestling with an enigma was Abe Winchell.

He was trying to puzzle how he could help Judith Pearland and perhaps win her heart at the same time. Neither aspect looked promising.

Abe was due to take over the village forge from his father so moving away was out of the question. Judith could never be anything more than a much revered nurse in the locality but departing for elsewhere would be pointless anyway. The simple deduction he had arrived at after eliminating every other possibility was that he had to reach an answer right there in Westlingstead, and frustratingly he was right back where he started.

Now wait a moment, he exclaimed to himself, I've heard tell that Sarah Brankly is a good adviser in these situations and, if stories are to be believed, she has helped the Master of Downsland!

That is who I must speak to, indeed it is. She will help me and I am sure she will want to assist Dr Pearland, as I shall always call her. With a broad grin he returned to his work with greater enthusiasm, realising he had all but solved the problem in his own eyes, a satisfied man.

Wearing a similar smile was James Parry-Barnard as he took Dorothea's hand and led her to her favourite armchair. He poured their tea, took his own place opposite her, and returned her slight nod of pleasure and contentment.

"That wretched Constable Robins has been here again. I sent him on his way. What a dreadful man. He sees evil in everyone. In his position he deems to condemn all he meets assuming them to be up to no good and he angered me."

"More questions Dorothea?"

"Yes James, more questions, and nearly all about you." He gulped without realising he had done so.

"I was so dismayed. He tried to make a big thing of the fact you are not qualified and I put him in his place James. I consider you to be as qualified as anyone and happily put my life in your hands. He'd even been to see Dr Barrenbridge at Westlingstead, one of the most widely respected physicians in the country, the doctor you served under with credit, and Barrenbridge confirmed your diagnosis and choice of medicines.

"Robins implied you might have unintentionally poisoned me! The very thought." James was trying to take diplomatic mouthfuls of tea as a means of disguising his unrest but was undone when he eventually spluttered and spilled his drink in his lap. It took his hostess by surprise.

"James, are you in difficulty? Are you choking?"

"No, no Dorothea, just a tickle in the throat. I am in no trouble I assure you and apologise for my accidental behaviour, absolutely unforgiveable....."

"James do not apologise, it was not your fault, and I am concerned for you."

He needed to take the conversation away from this course and, once more relaxing in his chair having replaced his cup on the table, sought to pursue his primary interest namely gaining the hand of the widow. This was comfortable ground for such a man and his poise improved as he tactfully found ways of praising her non-existent loveliness (much to her obvious gladness) and her grace and elegance which was rather more accurate but nonetheless over complimentary in the way such praise was delivered.

It was now or never.

He rose and with his customary verbosity spoke eloquently about his regard for her, his respect and admiration for the finest of true ladies, how unworthy he felt in her presence, and finally how he had come to love her. She did not look in the least surprised and even managed a wan smile.

Then, with romantic drama in mind, he took two steps forward and went down on one knee and proposed marriage whereupon Dorothea burst into spontaneous laughter, having the good grace to cover her mouth in mock embarrassment. James did not know if he had won or lost.

Minutes later he knew beyond any doubt he had lost.

"Me, marry someone in your position? Oh James, you have misread me badly." She was struggling to control her mirth. He felt belittled and angry.

Rising to his feet and preparing to depart he spoke through gritted teeth.

"Mrs Landspur, speak of this and I will deny it, but I will acquaint you with the truth. Yes, I gave you medicine that would've affected you adversely, and did so with the intention of administering the remedy. That way I was guaranteeing you would need frequent visits from me, so that I might woo you. You laugh at me but know now I am laughing at you, you despicable old woman. All was proceeding well until you invited Dr Williams instead of me.

"Dorothea, your laughter has died. How strange. Yes, it is I who am laughing now. Remember my words, old woman, speak of my confession and I will simply deny it."

And he marched from her house leaving her gasping for breath and in a state of collapse.

***

The weather was kind when Grayan made landfall in the early morning, a gentle breeze disturbing flags and a chill biting uncovered flesh. Sarah noticed it as she stepped ashore and instinctively pulled her scarf around her face as she was led to the waiting coach. Aldert Bakker had his fine and stately mansion by the river Vecht in Breukelen, not far from Utrecht, and there was quite a journey ahead of the pair. Bakker had sent his coach and would escort them from his home to Hester's residence just a few miles away.

Sarah was absorbed by the countryside, much of it flat as she expected it to be, yet there was something enticing and picturesque about it. Grayan related what knowledge he had particularly about the history and commerce of the area, and explained that a number of wealthy Amsterdam merchants had built riverside mansions in Breukelen in days gone by and Bakker had bought one of these.

Slowly the morning evolved into a day less settled as clouds reared up from the north and began to blot out the blue skies, and as the sun disappeared behind those clouds so Sarah saw the landscape rather differently. No less interesting to her, but now seemingly flatter and unchanging.

They had over a hundred miles to travel and it would take much of the day. There was a halt made for a meal and it was after her refreshments that Sarah drifted into a deep sleep, unaware she had come to rest on Grayan's shoulder. At first he had smiled pleasantly and then he had adjusted his position so that the sleeping maid might be more comfortable and so that she was firmly nestled against him. He watched through the window but his mind was on Sarah and not the passing countryside.

How lovely this was to have the young girl this close to him. He smiled again as he considered that it was most improper for a maid to fall asleep against her master! Each time he smiled it was with affection for this extraordinary girl, and his mind wandered back through her times at Downsland starting that day when Ginny unexpectedly brought her to see him.

Irked by the intrusion and the over-confident self-promotion she had indulged in, he'd handed her Evershen's letter more in jest than seriousness, a mocking gesture. But for some reason she'd impressed him with her response, being not at all obviously overawed by meeting him in such circumstances. Yet she must've been nervous! Yes, she'd been impressive, even offering to work without pay while she was assessed.

Here was a young lady who knew her mind and knew how to succeed. And he smiled again and looked down at her sleeping form and allowed her to slip closer still, where he could feel her warmth penetrate his cloak, and it pleased him. So much had happened since that first day, not least that she helped him find the spirit of his dear wife Marie and might thus have been saved from eternal suffering and an early death.

Suddenly life was worth living, and he smiled once more and again diverted his gaze from the land to the girl snuggled up beside him. And the coach rattled and thumped its way along the road, swaying around corners, bumping and juddering, Sarah sleeping peacefully as both occupants were tossed about by the motion.

He was sure she was smiling contentedly.

***

Robert Broxford was anything but contented.

He had talked widely about his attachment with Clara Evershen and was now being ridiculed in the village although not to his face. Here was the man who thought he had won the loveliest girl to be found and had lost her in one night of folly. How could she go away with the doctor? Only a harlot would do such a thing and the woman who had pledged herself to him had turned her back and rejected his love and was now nothing more than a trollop.

He wanted to attack Jaunton but what good would that do?

Deep inside he knew he loved her still and would forgive her transgression if she would have him back. His love was strong enough to overcome the chitchat to be located in the village. He had written to her expressing his desire that they be reunited but he'd had no reply. No doubt Mrs Evershen had ensured her daughter did not correspond with him. There was a bigger fish to be landed.

However, Clara was about to learn that she had been nothing but a conquest, a tale for a man to boast about in his cups, a used creature easily abandoned. Philip Jaunton came and made it quite clear to her, doing so in front of her formidable but shocked mother.

"It meant nothing Clara. Surely it was nothing to you? But there is no future in it. I will not return here and I will not entertain you at the hospital. You will leave me alone or pay the price, I promise you. I have no fears here; people talk freely about you Clara, doing so in a most derogatory fashion, but my reputation remains intact. It was not I who spread the rumours and it was not I who confirmed them.

"You could not wait to publicise an event you should've been utterly ashamed of. You're a peasant girl. Be grateful that I took you at all. You were most fortunate and owe your success to your good looks. I had everything I wanted from you and want no more."

He spun on his heels and departed with Clara open-mouthed but speechless falling into her wailing mother's arms.

Back at the hospital he and Barrenbridge attended to what patients they had and for once there were no local villagers. Two minor operations had been carried out, one on a young girl from Barham whose father had carried her in his arms from their home, and one on a man from Chatham. Both were there because of the reputation of the establishment.

A woman who had walked from Charing was treated for a petty ailment, and a young man who had ridden over from Canterbury with an arm injury was also dealt with and sent on his way knowing his injury would heal anon. These visits were not unusual although most patients were either from the village or places not too far away.

Grace Gandling was busy. She was now in charge of the nurses of which there were five local girls, none truly experienced, but all keen and capable. They rarely worked together at the same time and it was left to Grace to ensure sufficient were on hand at any time. She enjoyed her work seeing it as a vocation, and enjoyed her elevated position where she could pass on her skills and knowledge to others, training them correctly.

But she detested what had happened to Judith and hated both doctors for it. Judith was in a terrible state and had sunk into a soulless existence of moroseness from which even Abraham Winchell's humour and good cheer could not lift her.

Knowing Sarah was away he went across to the hospital and sought out Grace. She led him outside to a quiet spot where they could talk in private.

Whatever her feelings for Judith Pearland, however contemptuous she might have felt for Barrenbridge and Jaunton, Grace was loyal to those who employed her and made no statements or comments in support or condemnation either way. Quite accidently she let slip a piece of intelligence that Abe noted and was pleased with, and which made the conversation worthwhile.

"I expect Mr Grayan will be sad Dr Pearland has left us. His late wife was so very supportive and I understand he was delighted when Dr Barrenbridge appointed Dr Pearland as his assistant when Dr Parry-Barnard went, just as I believe he was pleased Dr Jaunton was able to join us in a junior capacity."

"Does that mean that Dr Jaunton was junior to Dr Pearland?"

"Yes, that's right Abe. But he is now Dr Barrenbridge's only assistant and is, as you say, making a name for himself and doing very well. Popular with the younger woman in the village I hear tell!"

"I imagine so Grace, I imagine so."

Their brief time together over Abe returned to work believing he had one additional piece of information to tell Sarah, and that the Master might be interested to learn of Judith's treatment. Could it be that the Master was as supportive as his wife and prompted Barrenbridge to make her his assistant? Yes, he had a little extra piece of news, and Sarah had Grayan's ear did she not?

Yes, that was the way to approach this.

Chapter Seventeen

Aldert Bakker welcomed his guests and introduced Grayan to his wife Lotte who joined them in the coach as they drove to Hester's rather more modest accommodation. Sarah had been impressed with Bakker's mansion and its riverside setting but felt it far inferior to Downsland Hall in size and location, and indeed in grandeur.

Arriving at the house Sarah diplomatically climbed down after Grayan and the Bakkers and circled around towards what she assumed was the rear entrance, observing Hester dashing down the steps to embrace David as she went.

"Sarah, Sarah," a voice cried. It was Annie running across the track to greet her friend. The girls hugged and Annie shed a few tears of happiness. "Oh Sarah, Sarah, I am so pleased to see you. How was the voyage? How was the journey here?"

"Everything went well Annie, thank you, and if you will kindly lead me to your quarters I am sure we can talk at great length."

"I think we will both have some work to do first!"

"Yes, I am forgetting we are both maids and have duties to perform. But take me anyway."

And they skipped off to the rear of the house where Sarah was introduced to the cook and another young maid, a local girl called Mila. Almost immediately the bell rang and Annie sped away leaving Sarah to converse with the two in the kitchen and finding that both spoke perfect English.

Mila took Sarah to her room and showed her where her Master would be accommodated.

Sarah and Annie weren't required at dinner and took their meal in the kitchen talking excitedly and asking each other a host of questions. After their own meal David Grayan and Aldert Bakker retired to partake of Mrs Handlen's best cognac and cigars which she had arranged specially, and Bakker took the opportunity to express his fears.

"Grayan, there is war in the air." Then he shook his head as if to refute what he had just said. "No, I do not expect war as we might think it. Any war between our countries will be at sea and about supremacy of the seas. That is where Britain's strength lies, as you know full well. It is simply that there is resentment here that we have not been an equal partner, if I may use the word, in the relationship between our lands. What concerns me is that we may expend too much fighting a lost cause and leave ourselves open to invasion. I particularly fear the French.

"Well Bakker I think both countries have too much to lose and little to gain. Trade is going well, as you and I can testify, so why rock a safe ship?"

"My point in saying this my friend is that I am worried for your sister. She has been welcomed here and is well liked but I cannot foretell what the future holds, especially if there is an invasion and we are overrun."

"I understand your view. I imagine you are worried that if Britain and the Dutch engage in more war, and as you rightly surmise it will be at sea, travel to and from here would be difficult if not impossible."

"Precisely, an added problem if your sister had to flee again. Is there no chance of her returning to England, perhaps to Downsland?"

"I will always accept her at my home, but her husband and my brother will find her there, and may take the support of the law to extract the twins. Her husband has certain legal rights whether we like it or not."

Both men sat in silence for a few moments contemplating all that had been said as they sipped their drinks and occasionally drew on their cigars.

"Well, please be assured I will think carefully on your warning Bakker. I realise you feel it is serious and since you live and work here you must have your ear to such intelligence. I will give it thought."

"Good man. I will look after your sister all the time she is here, you have my word, but look to the future. Make your own enquiries. See if anything else can be planned."

The conversation between Lotte and Hester in an adjacent room had been light and gay by comparison.

Lotte had talked at length about their own children, now all adults and far from home, and Hester spoke with a warm heart about her hopes for her boys.

"If we remain here do they have a good chance in life Lotte?"

"Oh my dear, there will be much opportunity. And they will speak Dutch from an early age which will help them through their education and beyond into the world of commerce. And what will you tell them of their father Hester?"

"That he has gone away and may not return. Perhaps I will say more when they are much older, but we shall see."

"And you will tell them they are English?"

"Yes certainly, and tell them much of where they come from. But I do not want them to yearn to visit the land of their birth."

"Quite so Hester, quite so."

In time the ladies joined the gentlemen. Tomorrow they would dine at the Bakker's leaving David and Hester the day together with the twins. Annie and Sarah would be going to Mila's home for that evening and since it was just a few minutes walk away would present no problems with travel. Edward and George would be left in the care of their Dutch nanny.

The night proved a restless one for Grayan who was sufficiently disturbed by Bakker's warning to be giving the matter every attention. As yet he'd said nothing to Hester.

***

Edmund Forness did not see how fortunate he had been to have escaped justice having assaulted two women, and was already looking lasciviously at the girl who now came to help his sister about the house.

Why should he worry? Catherine had believed him, even when one of the women had been her own daughter. The new girl, Lydia Grant, always smiled sweetly at him, spoke kindly and seemed interested in him. Surely she would enjoy a hug and smile upon him some more.

He had taken to teasing her and she laughed as she told him how wicked he was.

Then there was the day he chased her around the room offering her a kiss. Lydia, who was not above mischief and cheekiness, took it in good part as she kept a safe distance and laughed louder than ever. The scene was set for events the next day.

It had been a long time since Ralph Grayan had laughed about anything and his wife avoided him whenever possible.

He was drinking too much, was in a state of permanent anger, wore a scowl on his face that frightened the children, and sought no pleasure from any activity in his life. His sole concern had been the revenge he was plotting for his brother. Defeat David and he'd get Hester's boys and then she could go to hell.

In his rage he occasionally smashed things, once sweeping plates, glasses, cutlery and food off one end of the dining table before storming away leaving his bemused wife at her seat. She wasn't frightened of him but was afeared for what he might do in one of his terrible tempers. She was aware he was spending a great deal of money trying to find out exactly where Hester was, and driving himself into a fury when he found he had paid for useless information, sometimes given by unscrupulous people in order to defraud him.

It was happening all too often and his wife was wondering if they might be facing financial difficulties soon if he could not be persuaded to desist. She knew he had taken to gambling and visiting courtesans and was not giving due time to his business interests. It was a bad mix.

He was determined to go to the Netherlands despite his wife's warnings that Hester might not be in the country and could've travelled further into Europe. Ralph was of the opinion money could buy whatever you needed to know, that it could unlock impenetrable doors, that it could clear away fogs and mists that obscured the truth, and that it could persuade people to discard loyalty and reveal what you wanted.

But his quest was not simply to retrieve the twins, he had sworn to deal with his estranged brother.

Edmund Forness was approaching the end of his own quest.

Mrs Brankly had set off down the road for the far end of the village with some eggs for a friend and Edmund decided to take advantage of her absence. Lydia had often mentioned how much she would like to see the pigs and today he offered to take her down the farm for that purpose.

Eagerly she followed him, full of youthful excitement, little realising what he was truly about. When they were a notable distance from village habitation, and where there were bushes and undergrowth, he grabbed hold of her, forced a kiss upon her and flung her to the ground throwing himself on top of her. He put one hand over her mouth and reached down with the other.

The startled and frightened girl gathered her scattered wits swiftly and with a mighty effort bit firmly into his hand. He released it with a cry whereupon she screamed with every breath in her body. Help was but a few feet away.

Edmund felt the raw pain in his back as the plank of wood was smashed against it. Looking up in dread surprise he saw his sister with the remains of the splintered plank in her hand and a look of horror and wrath on her face.

"Get away from her, get away now," she screamed. He meekly rose and tried bluff.

"She attacked me sister. Just like the others. It was self-defence. Look how my hand bleeds."

"I saw what you were doing." she cried, "By what good fortune did I return and finding you out did I walk down here. You've lied to me, nearly cost me my daughter. I am going to send for the Constable."

"Sister, sister, do I mean no more to you than that?"

"Nothing. Nothing at all. You can rot in some God-forsaken filthy prison for all I care. Come here Lydia, let me help you."

Shaking and crying the poor girl grabbed hold of Mrs Brankly, squealing for a release from her torrid nightmare. She was led to the house while Edmund quickly assessed his situation and decided to make a run for it. He was off across the fields in no time.

It was only the fact Catherine Brankly needed to attend the bewildered and terrified girl that prevented her from bursting into tears herself. To think she had believed Edmund, her own brother, against her Sarah. To think he had tried this with her own daughter. Unbelievable.

Her agony was complete as she remembered dear Sarah was in the Netherlands and she would have to wait to make her peace.

Later, when the Constable had been sent for and Lydia had been reunited with her family, Catherine came home and threw herself to the floor begging forgiveness from her God and from Sarah as she wept and rolled about on the floor in anguish. Nothing she did could appease the pain that throbbed through her body, and she cried out and implored Sarah to come home knowing it was a vain plea.

Edmund had vanished and the Constable agreed it was pointless looking for him as he could've gone in any direction. Lydia's family was just too pleased she was safe and had not suffered worse at the man's hands, but the girl herself was still distraught, sobbing continually, and they were aware it was a lifetime sentence she faced, an encounter never to be forgotten, its memory embedded in her mind forever.

In her own distress Lydia's mother sent for Judith Pearland in the hope of providing medicinal comfort to her daughter. Judith came at once having heard the story and sat with Lydia for several hours, sharing her horror, listening, hugging when necessary, speaking soft and kind words, the most appropriate words and the words Lydia most needed to hear.

That night she slept in Lydia's room, there to be by her side with each passing nightmare. And in the morning the storm had passed, even if only temporarily, and the two were together in a remarkable friendship forged from adversity. It was the tonic Lydia needed more than any medicine, and it was a tonic for Judith.

For both girls it heralded a new beginning.

***

The rain fell unceasingly nearly all day but they cared not one jot.

David and Hester had a most wonderful day in each others' company and saw much of the boys as well as sharing some time together with Sarah and Annie, who were very appreciative of being wanted thus. Sarah was conscious that she had rarely felt as happy as she was now and was so pleased to see the Master equally exultant. In truth she knew she was ecstatic partly because Mr Grayan was so genuinely cheerful, and she was delighted for that.

What a shame that he fell into such darkness when his wife died, for he is such a great man, so clever, so kind and generous, so strong and able, so successful. And as she pondered these epithets she found herself thinking, nay, *hoping* Miss Cowans would make him happier still. But it was then that the inexplicable aches returned to the pit of her stomach and induced a feeling of sadness to mar this happiest of times.

It was a strange puzzle, but once thoughts of Lily Cowans slipped from her mind so the feelings of unbridled gladness enveloped her again.

Lily Cowans had taken another walk on her beloved cliffs, this time to the north, and had reached Walmer and its castle forgetting she had come a long way and faced a torturous journey back, much of it being uphill. So she turned at once and started the trek home, flat shoreline at first and then a gentle climb towards St Margarets and then a tougher ascent to the top. From there it was relatively easy going before a welcome dip down into Dover itself.

She had much to think on.

What were her real feelings for David Grayan? She mulled this over dozens of times and arrived at various inconclusive answers. Was she bothered about him being abroad? Again there was no one response that was in any way apt. Yes, she was worried for him, but no, he was where he was needed and where he wanted to be and he could take care of himself. Was she worried about this feud with Ralph and how it might end? Of course, and yet she was powerless to play any part.

David was sensible enough not to be drawn into violence for the sake of violence, but he would defend his sister to the very end. Yes she was worried.

At least he had the faithful Sarah to wait on him while in the Netherlands. Faithful Sarah. The innocent maiden, yet brimming with confidence and having demonstrated wisdom beyond her tender years. He liked Sarah. Liked her very much.

And Lily experienced the same feelings Sarah suffered but could not explain.

But Lily knew what they were.

***

Jack Robins ignored the protocol he had employed previously and relaxed back in his chair and crossed his legs nonchalantly, tapping his fingertips together in front of him, as he listened to Dorothea Landspur pouring out her tale of woe.

She dabbed at her eyes with her kerchief but there were no tears to dry. Robins decided this was part of an act. Her maid, Elspeth, stood at her side looking horribly nervous, her hands clasped low in front of her apron while she stared at the floor.

Mrs Landspur had summoned him stressing the urgency and was relating what James Parry-Barnard had told her having informed him of his closing words.

"Repeat any of this and I will deny it."

Robins twisted his mouth into a peculiar shape suggesting he was either not sure he was hearing the truth or was unsure what to make of it. She continued.

"My maid misbehaved but on this occasion I am grateful. Elspeth heard a disturbance and, concerned lest I be in trouble, crept along the hall and listened outside. Normally unforgiveable behaviour, worthy of dismissal, but on this occasion I have overlooked her transgression."

Robins did not know whether to laugh or cry and tactfully did neither.

"Elspeth heard all that Parry-Barnard had to say about ... about ... well, about poisoning me, or at least administering medicine to make me ill. She heard it clearly as she will testify." Elspeth looked most unwilling to do anything of the sort. Robins deduced this was a pre-arranged venture between the two, almost coercion on Mrs Landspur's part. Poor Elspeth. Do what you're told or lose your post.

"Thank you Mrs Landspur. I will just make some notes and let me say I am grateful you have sent for me. Now, why do you think he might want to confess?" This took the woman by surprise. Over the years Robins had honed his skills at taking people by surprise as it often procured the truth even if not in words, and Mrs Landspur's face alone spoke volumes.

"This ... this ... this is a private matter and must go no further Constable. It will sound every bit as ridiculous as it was, but the confounded man had the nerve to propose to me and I laughed out loud. I fancy he did not take kindly to my humour, and most certainly not to my outright rejection, and he retaliated as best he could by shouting his confession.

"My interpretation was that he could be utterly mad. Mad I tell you! He should be locked up. To imagine he might be suitable for my hand is preposterous, but to try to obtain any degree of intimacy by ... by ... by poisoning me, well that is a madman at work." Elspeth had looked up as her Mistress spoke, eyes bulging, mouth open with shock, her face draining of colour.

Robins carefully observed both women.

"Mad or not Mrs Landspur I will have him behind bars, you may count upon it. Your assistance in this cannot be overstated. You have been a great help to me. Now if you will excuse me I must make haste as I wish to find Mr Parry-Barnard at once. Should he call here please do not admit him.

"I believe, as you do, that we have a dangerous individual at large, and we cannot under-estimate what actions he may take." This had the desired effect as both Mrs Landspur and Elspeth took on a look of trepidation and dread. "I intend to run him to ground as quickly as I can. I will catch him out in some way, but if he should elude me or escape he may seek revenge."

Both women clutched their throats. Good, thought Robins, they are mine to command now. No more acting, no more Mrs High-and-Mighty. I can only catch this villain with their help which must be given fully and freely. And with that he departed and rode off to Hawkhurst at speed.

***

Sarah learned a few Dutch words and expressions during her visit to Mila's with Annie.

There wasn't much the English girls could teach Mila as far as their language was concerned, for her English was excellent. It was a joyous evening decorated with copious quantities of laughter. Mila's parents joined in the fun and there were visits from her sister Sophie and brother Arend and their young families.

210

Sarah proved popular with the six young children who came first with Sophie and later with Arend and once more demonstrated her ability to entertain and organise appealing games for the small ones.

All too soon it was time to depart and Mila's father insisted on walking them back to Hester's.

They bade him farewell at the rear entrance and made their way to their rooms still laughing as they recalled the evening's fun. They stopped in their tracks when suddenly confronted by David Grayan.

"No, no, no, do not let me interrupt your pleasure ladies. Mrs Handlen and I have only returned ourselves this last half hour and we heard you coming in, and we would like to invite all three of you to join us for some refreshments so that you can relate some of your tales about tonight."

Mila looked astounded, Annie looked startled, but Sarah looked as she'd half-expected such an invitation, and she spoke at once.

"Thank you sir. We would like that very much, but may we just take our cloaks to our rooms....."

"Of course Sarah, of course. Come to the withdrawing room whenever you are ready."

David and Hester had also experienced a most pleasant evening in the company of the Bakkers, enjoying an excellent repast and delightful conversation, the emphasis here also on humour and the good things in their lives.

After dinner David and Aldert discussed more serious issues but did so briefly for it was not a night to be marred by unease and qualms. Aldert was satisfied David had accepted his opinion and would act upon it as he saw necessary, and the matter was left at that.

For Hester it was time to revel in this most glorious of events and she did so with enthusiasm knowing only too well it was a brief interlude, and that soon her brother would leave for England. If only she could return there. During their time together she realised she was somewhat homesick and longed for David's company rather than any short snatched meetings as this was proving to be.

In a quiet moment alone with David she related her sadness knowing it would make him sorrowful too, but he squeezed her hand and told her softly he would give it all substantial consideration as he felt the present situation was unsatisfactory for everyone. The fact he had already realised the position was not very acceptable warmed her and she recognized he would find a solution.

Back at Hester's the five drank each others' health and talked endlessly until their eyes were barely open, and finally retired well into the small hours. Sarah and Annie shared a hug outside Annie's room and nearly fell asleep in their arms.

The next day there was an air of gloom as if all of them acknowledged that the gaiety of the previous day was a facade of sorts, a shell that provided safety and comfort, and that things were not at all satisfactory in their present state. Their happiness was temporary and it couldn't continue, and they knew it. Sarah wondered how it would all work out in the times ahead and fretted it would make the Master retreat into the sombre being he was when she walked into his study that first occasion.

In a short space of time so much had happened and she mused on the changing circumstances since she started at Downsland, like the changing seasons she thought, with good times and bad times, successes and failures. And she thought of her mother and that monster Edmund, hoping it could all be resolved well, little knowing that the truth had been revealed and Edmund was gone.

Unfortunately Sarah's mother was now being ostracised in Westlingstead having harboured such an evil man, and supported him against her own daughter as well as Clara. She had been spat on, abused in the street, and the chickens had been stolen. What utter misery she felt, and Sarah so far away.

She was afraid Sarah might reject her.

The Rev Paul Farhoe tried to pour oil on troubled waters and only made matters worse. He too had supported Edmund and was not easily forgiven, Robert Broxford telling him that he should go to the church and pray to God, comments that caused much mirth amongst villagers present.

But Mrs Brankly had an unexpected visitor.

Judith Pearland came to see her and sat and talked and proved a great comfort. Afterwards she went with Catherine into the farm and worked tirelessly with whatever tasks needed doing, and the two of them brought the whole into shape and order in no time. She promised to return the next day to help and came with Abe Winchell whom she had persuaded to assist.

Most of the villagers having respect for Judith and Abe gradually took pity on Catherine and her troubles eased accordingly.

Then Judith came with Lydia Grant and the three of them cleaned the house, baked food and saw to the animals. It was a tremendous healing of an open wound and earned an unwanted blessing from Father Farhoe who was trying to restore his own standing in the village.

Alone that night Catherine Brankly wept for their kindness and for the miracle Judith had achieved.

It was a time of beauty and wonder, and she hoped Sarah would come home safely and make the story complete.

Chapter Eighteen

During the voyage back to Kent Grayan spoke to Sarah about his dilemma.

Her suggestion was that he should bring his sister back to live at Downsland and invite her husband and Ralph to meet there and all of them discuss the issue once and for good.

He smiled inwardly. She spoke as an adult, a woman of wisdom and experience, and yet there was a child, a child who could see an answer in simple terms however impractical they might be. If only it was that simple indeed.

"Your sister sir, she cannot keep running. In your place I would bring this to a head for that is the only way you can all live in peace."

If only it was that simple. If only.

"And you have no idea where her husband might be sir?"

"None at all."

"I would try and find out sir. Enquiries need to be made."

This time he smiled openly but kept his head turned to avoid her gaze. Self-assured, she possessed confidence beyond her immature years but seemed to lack a clear view of reality in matters like these.

"I shall make enquiries Sarah, and I shall of course let you know." He did not want to sound patronising or mocking but he could not avoid it and was fortunate she did not notice.

The parting had been sad and harrowing for brother and sister and he assured himself that the whole business must be sorted out by one means or another. Hester living in the Netherlands was not a suitable answer, he knew that now, but what else could possibly be done? For the moment it was the safest choice but it could not last.

Sarah and Annie had shed a few tears as they hugged in farewell. Sarah did not yet know what had occurred in Westlingstead and the effect on her mother, so for the instant she was happy in herself but upset to leave her friend behind.

She had grown used to the Master talking to her about his private affairs, an unusual situation between Master and servant, but not so rare where David Grayan was concerned, and less rare in her new and elevated position under him. There was no surprise when he asked her to join him after dinner as the vessel made its way across relatively calm waters, and they engaged in a convivial evening, talking until late.

They took a final turn around the deck but although she was well wrapped she felt the cold. He instinctively put his arm around her shoulder and with equivalent instinct she nestled up close to benefit from the extra warmth. Presently their short walk ended and they made their way to their cabins, pausing outside her own. For a second or two they were gazing into each others' eyes and exchanging glowing looks, but then Sarah was gone and Grayan walked to his quarters without any further thought on the subject.

For Sarah it was time to undress and snuggle under the covers but she never stopped thinking about their walk and the way he had held her to him to protect her from the cold, and then the way he had glanced at her by her cabin door. His eyes had penetrated her but far from perturbing her she welcomed his glance as it had filled her with a feelings of tenderness, comfort, security and care, and they were feelings she enjoyed. The memory filled her mind wondrously as she fell asleep.

***

In the morning with the Kent coast in sight the North Sea delivered one of its worst storms and the ship was tossed carelessly about. A sailor was lost overboard and there was nothing to be done about it. Sarah remained in her tiny cabin and fell victim to seasickness in a wholehearted manner. It bothered her she could not attend her Master but since she assumed she would be quite happy to die and was about to expire anyway perhaps it didn't matter.

There was a knock at the door but she had no strength or inclination to respond.

Then there was a stronger hammering and she was sick as she opened her mouth to call out. Grayan let himself in, closed the door and went straight to her aid. Although pleased to see him she could not ignore the torture her body was putting her through

215

and promptly heaved a horrible mixture down his chest as he sought to help her.

She was horrified but he made it clear it did not matter in the least. He stayed with her, cradling her in his arms as a father might hold a new born baby, taking no notice of her vomit as all too often it fell in his lap and over his front.

In time the storm eased and Sarah passed into sleep, the deep sleep of the exhausted.

When she woke she saw strange surroundings and then saw Grayan sitting close by. She became conscious she was in a bed and then the memories flooded back. Her head hurt, her mouth was dry, and he was suddenly by her side with water for her to drink.

"Take it slowly, just sip it Sarah."

"W-w-w-w-where am I?

"My cabin. I carried you here to recover. One of the crew has cleaned and tidied your quarters and packed your things ready, for Whitstable is not far away."

"I must be filthy ... I was sick ... I ... I ..."

"I have attended to you Sarah and all is well." He saw the look of horror on her face.

"Sarah forgive me. I did not intend to convey the wrong impression. I have merely cleaned your face, hair and your night attire. Pray do not think I have disrobed you in any way. I would do nothing so improper I beseech you to believe that."

"Sir I am pleased to hear it, but I would never think you improper, and I am grateful beyond words for your kindness."

"Thank you Sarah. Now when you feel able I will escort you back and you can dress and collect your things. Rest for a while. Sip the water and go along when you are ready."

"But I should be serving you sir."

He burst into laughter.

"No Sarah, it is my privilege to wait upon *you*. Do not worry yourself, and do not move until you are sure you are better. The Captain says we can stay on board for a while after docking and that is what we shall do."

"Oh sir, I am so sorry ...."

"There is nothing to apologise for. You cannot help sickness. Now recover in your own time and we'll depart when you are ready. No more words now." And he was gone.

***

He sat very comfortably in his chair looking relaxed and untroubled, a man without cares, a man without worries, a man unafraid. He had not invited his visitor to sit as he intended to keep the upper hand with this upstart.

James Parry-Barnard oozed contemptuousness as he eyed Jack Robins up and down.

Robins, quite deliberately, had not mentioned his call on Mrs Landspur or her revelations, and was concentrating on engaging his foe in general conversation about the case rather than ask direct questions. All part of his strategy.

"Dr Williams, so I am given to understand sir, was well liked and had proved a successful physician in his time. Many were sorry to see him retire. Had you heard of him sir, before you moved here?"

"No I hadn't actually."

"So you didn't know him by reputation although he can hardly have been held in the same regard as Dr Barrenbridge who is, I believe, quite exceptional."

"Dr Barrenbridge is, and I would expect him to be better known than Dr Williams. Now is there any point to this discussion Constable, as I am busy?"

Robins smiled almost ruefully. He had learned how to adjust his expression to create whatever impression he wished to make. As usual his tactic was working.

"Well sir, I am grateful for your time. As you can imagine I am talking to many people trying to build a picture of the man himself and his movements on that fateful day, and I am certain, as a fellow physician, you must want his murderer caught. He was, by all accounts, a fine gentleman, and his loss is all the greater for that. He seems to have been very approachable. Did you find him that way sir?"

"He was simply a fellow doctor. Our discussion was purely professional."

217

"I see sir. And when did you have a discussion with a man you said you'd never met?"

Parry-Barnard stiffened. Before he could concoct an answer Robins spoke again.

"According to the apothecary Dr Williams was coming here to confront you. Now Mrs Landspur tells me you confessed to administering medicine to intentionally make her unwell. Her maid was alerted by the noise and came and listened at the door and also heard your confession. Williams came here and confronted you, didn't he, and you went after him to kill him."

"This is nonsense. I will hear no more...."

"I assume you have destroyed the shirt you were wearing. Dr Williams was clutching a piece of the material when his body was found, a piece presumably torn from you in the struggle. I don't suppose he stood much chance against a younger, stronger man. He must've known he was fighting for his life and struggled as best he could."

"What on earth are you talking about man? Get out of my house."

"I have enough to take you with me Mr Parry-Barnard. Mrs Landspur's testimony, supported by that of her maid, will do for now. If you will be so good as to come with me now sir."

Parry-Barnard leaped to his feet, anger etched in every feature of his face.

"How dare you. Dr Barrenbridge confirmed I had given the right medicine...."

"According to your notes, yes sir. But your notes are at odds with the apothecary's findings."

"And you believe an unqualified man?"

"Yes, just as I disbelieve an unqualified man, which is what you are."

"You fool. You cannot begin to understand. You'd be laughed out of court."

"I certainly wouldn't be if I could find your torn shirt sir."

"You *are* a fool. There was no struggle, no piece of cloth in his hand..."

"How would you know that sir?"

Robins had finally stunned his opponent into silence. He spoke quietly.

"You are correct, there was no struggle, no piece of cloth. Now if you please, prepare to come with me sir. There is the attempted murder of Mrs Landspur for you to answer to...."

But he was cut short as Parry-Barnard threw himself at the Constable and pushed him over. In an instant he had grabbed his walking cane. Robins was quickly on his feet and in time to see the man rip away part of the casing to reveal a sword-stick, the sharp end aimed directly at him.

Robins tried to make a lunge at the killer but misjudged Parry-Barnard's athleticism. Nimbly jumping aside the doctor thrust his sword into Robins's chest and then was through the door and away down the road.

Fortunately for the Constable he sustained little more than a flesh wound and within seconds he was after the murderer.

Parry-Barnard had turned as he dashed away and was astonished to see Robins hard on his tail, and decided it was better to turn and slay his nemesis. As Robins closed him he took a well aimed stab at the Constable who was expecting the attempt and ducked under the blow, taking James's legs from under him. Quick as thought Robins kicked the sword away and the two men grappled on the ground beating each other with their fists.

But Robins was too big and too strong and eventually punched the other man into semi-consciousness and left him lying there groaning. A coach drew up alongside. Robins had hired one for the purpose convinced he would be taking a murderer away. Between him and the two coachmen they lifted Parry-Barnard inside and the Constable went to fetch his horse which he secured to the back of the vehicle.

As they pulled away Robins looked at his blood stained uniform and remembered he'd been stabbed. Nothing too serious, he told himself as he held a kerchief over the wound and allowed a broad grin of satisfaction to adorn his face.

***

Clara Evershen was beginning to regret losing Robert Broxford and realising her pursuit of personal improvement above her station had been doomed from the outset. She wanted the status without regard for love, which was of mere secondary importance, and had made too many sacrifices as a result.

Now she had nothing and it was her own fault. She was indeed worthless, little more than a whore, and had given herself freely to the most undeserving of men who had taken their pleasure and thrown her aside with ease. She had nothing and she *was* nothing. And she had rejected the one kind man who had truly loved her. Life was unbearable, made worse by a mother who cursed her and Philip Jaunton by turns whilst spending the money her late father had acquired from David Grayan and did so without giving Clara a penny.

But money no longer mattered to her. Nor did life. She wandered around the village, a lost soul, and on this occasion ambled into the churchyard where she fell down upon a gravestone and wished herself buried beneath it.

Gazing at the morose grey clouds overhead she was suddenly aware of a face looking down at her.

"Miss Evershen, are you unwell?"

"Dr Pearland ... I ... yes ... I am well thank you." She sat up and was surprised when the doctor sat down next to her.

"It is most unusual, you will own, for someone to lie down on a grave. Some would call it desecration though I do not. You must have your reasons."

"I have but they are mine alone."

"You called me doctor. You are aware I am not qualified and no longer at the hospital?"

"Yes, but you are more of a doctor than Dr Jaunton can ever hope to be, at least to me you are."

"Is Dr Jaunton part of the reason you were lying here?"

"Yes, and I think everyone in Westlingstead knows how I was treated and condemns me as they freely talk about me."

"I do not condemn you and have never talked of your misfortune. I think we are both victims in a world where women count very little."

Clara rallied and sat up straighter, fascinated by Pearland's comments. They spoke at length and gradually Clara told her whole story and found a supportive spirit in the doctor.

"Let me call you Clara if you will allow me, and you must call me Judith if you please."

A new friendship was thus formed above the place where the bones of Alfred Maunden had laid for over a hundred years, and where those of his widow had laid for eighty eight.

In time the women rose and strolled around the churchyard and then down into the fields beyond, engrossed in pleasing conversation, oblivious to the wintry weather now upon them, with Judith listening to her friend's words of despair then suggesting how Clara might overcome her problems even to the point of winning Robert back.

It was a very different Clara Evershen who returned home later, a very determined, relieved and happy Clara Evershen. It was only much later that evening that she recognised how well spent her time with Judith had been, and how the former doctor had helped her and encouraged her and made her see things in another light.

That same evening Judith was drinking in the Green Man with Abe Winchell by her side, a companion and nothing more, when he spoke words of high praise.

"Know you won't be talking about it, but you know how people talk about all that's going on around, and there's much talk about you and what you done for Lydia Grant and Mrs Brankly an' all. See you walking with Clara today. You helping her too?"

Judith looked at him quizzically.

"Helping her? What would I be helping her with?"

"Well, I suppose she's not herself what with that Dr Jaunton treating her badly and blackening her name, and as you been so helpful with Lydia and Mrs Brankly I thought maybe you was making everything better for her. You're good at that, right good I reckon."

Judith laughed a little and then stared at her drink, deep in thought. Had Abe sown a small seed?

"Is that what people say, that I've helped someone?"

"Yes they do. That you saved Lydia from her nightmares and I been there when you've talked to Mrs Brankly and I been impressed by the way you treated her, and people reckon you made it alright for her and she's accepted by folk again, just like she was before. So I wondered if you helped Clara."

"Not your business Abe, but I thank you for your own kind words and you may rest assured if by talking to anyone I can make them feel better, well, that's what a doctor is for. Now get me another drink, I'm thirsty." And they both laughed.

***

Henry Barrenbridge was rather distressed by what he'd just been told.

He sat quietly in his room, alone with his thoughts after Constable Robins departed, and felt strangely nervous without knowing why.

Robins had imparted the news about Parry-Barnard and the fact Barrenbridge might be required to give evidence, and now the doctor was sore troubled. Fate had caught up with James, the physician who had killed Mr Brankly with his incompetence, but what of himself? He was culpable only insofar as he'd covered the tragedy up to protect the hospital as well as himself so he had nothing to fear surely?

James might go to the gallows but there was no reason to believe he might divest himself of the guilt of Mr Brankly's death. In any event Barrenbridge was innocent of the killing. But his disturbed mind relentlessly prodded him and he was reminded of the recent case in which he brought about another man's demise on the operating table. Once again he had installed a cloak of secrecy to hide the terrible truth, in this situation his own incompetence, and had embroiled Philip and Judith in the deliberate shrouding.

It had forced Judith out. No, she would be ignored and mocked if she spoke out. But Philip? He had the power to ruin Barrenbridge and the thought made him shake with fear. Fate had caught up with James; could it stalk Henry?

***

Lily Cowans had decided to write a letter to David Grayan so that it should be ready for his return.

It became a particularly long letter and she began to wonder if he would be bothered to read it all. But then she felt he would do her the honour of reading it properly and might enjoy doing so if he entertained feelings of affection for her, and she hoped that was the case. She would know soon enough if he replied in kind. Maybe he would even make his feelings clearer to her. Maybe he would.

Roger Culteney still loomed large in her thoughts but was no longer fully embedded in her heart. On the contrary, she had grieved and was now recovered and had another interest which was occupying a heart so torn and damaged by one man's despicable behaviour.

She concluded her letter by writing that he would be welcome to stay with them in Dover in the spring and her father had extended such an invitation through her. He would surely accept. There was no chance of refusal.

Another lady writing a lengthy epistle was Clara, widow of Roger Culteney. Her missive was to Robert Broxford and she had taken Judith's advice in the wording and composition, not begging his forgiveness or for his return, but explaining her ill-considered affairs in the hunger for position and wealth, and expressing her sorrow at losing the one lovely man who really mattered to her.

Judith had said not to ask for him back but to mention that she would always welcome any communication from him, and that she was remorseful, accepted she had been wrong and was sad for him that she had turned out to be such a ghastly person. She added that, sadly, she had not been worthy of such a fine man.

The letter was sent to Downsland Hall in hope but also in heart-rending resignation that he was a lost cause. What a fool she'd been. Like Lily she wished the man she was writing to would at least read her letter, but now she must rebuild her life as Judith had proposed. It seemed strange to write a letter at Downsland and then post it back there but she could not countenance handing it to him.

Besides, she kept well out of his way, and on the odd occasion they passed or saw each other he had looked away and ignored her.

Judith Pearland had gone to Sarah's mother to do some more work and then on to Mrs Vernon's for a similar purpose when she came upon Philip Jaunton. He raised his hat and smiled and she returned his nod of acknowledgement, but he surprised her by speaking.

"Miss Pearland, I know you wish to ignore me, but whether you believe me or no I do care for your welfare and health and am truly sorry for the present circumstances...."

"Dr Jaunton, please do not speak to me so. I have no time for your nonsense. You know what happened to that poor man and chose to hide it to further your career. I have nothing whatsoever to speak to you about other than to implore you to reveal the truth. My knowledge of the incident is of no value by itself as I am lowly woman, but it would have value in support of the truth if you spoke it. Now good day to you."

And she was gone leaving him standing in the road, vexed and uncomfortable. He ambled slowly on his way, head down, chastised and recognising that the truth would haunt him forever. Not just the truth of the dead man, but the truth that he had acquiesced in the deception and for his own benefit. Yes, Judith Pearland had been forced out and he was as guilty of that as Barrenbridge.

Suddenly Judith's comments had struck a raw nerve and he ceased to be at peace with himself.

Chapter Nineteen

Love appeared to be blossoming well before spring blooms were ready to dazzle the countryside with their splendid colours and profuse spectacles. The remains of an unloved winter dawdled about, unwilling to surrender and leave the scene, determined to hurl the final miseries of combined coldness and wetness upon mankind for as long as possible.

The weather and the passing seasons played no part in the romances that were leading lovers towards the altar.

Ginny and Mark were envious of Agnes and Jed who were to be wed in April, with Ginny in particular hoping she and Mark might name their own day soon. Agnes had never felt so happy and was excited about their forthcoming nuptials, just as Jed was excited about the small home they had secured on the Downsland estate, courtesy of the Master. Both had been working on the derelict property to make it fit to live in.

Mark never lost an opportunity to remind Ginny of his love for her, and did so in many varied ways, on one occasion leaving a brief but delightfully sweet poem pinned to her door overnight so that she found it in the morning. It was his own verse, beautifully stated, and the work was decorated with drawings of spring flowers. It reduced his beloved to tears of joy.

If there was romance abounding in certain places it was decidedly absent elsewhere.

David Grayan hardly had time to settle in at Downsland on his return from the continent than Ralph arrived and in the company of three large ruffians.

It did not take long for David to realise the men were there in a defensive capacity rather than an aggressive one and he felt able to relax.

"Are these creatures to carry you out Ralph? Or to protect you from your own kinsman?"

"Do not mock me. They are here should you set your thugs on me."

"Thugs? Are you that afraid of me? My footmen, if you recall correctly, separated you from Charles Handlen, not from me. But no matter. Why are you here?"

"You have secreted Hester in the Netherlands I understand. Not far enough away from me. I shall have those babes from her."

"Ah, so you have me followed do you? And presumably your spies were able to tell you I was home again, which is why you have rushed here now. What news of Handlen, Ralph?"

"He has sailed to Jamaica on business....."

"I understood he had no money and no business..."

"He is of no concern to me. His boys are my business...."

"You shall have them over my dead body Ralph."

The two men, less than four feet apart, glared at each other. Ralph was shaking with rage, David looked calm but entrenched.

"Over my dead body. That is what it will take. Are you prepared to go to such lengths?" His words were quietly spoken but expressed a firmness that unsettled his brother.

"Damn you. Damn you. I will have them and you will not stand in my way. The law is on my side and you may have to contend with that. Now will you tell me where I may find Hester?"

"Use your money and your spies Ralph. You are wasting your time here."

Ralph was sufficiently enraged to want to attack David but knew it was futile and he could not contemplate employing his three men in such an assault. In fury he stormed out followed by his escort while his brother laughed out loud. But in the silence that followed David was serious. Now he had to do something. There was no longer any choice.

***

Sarah had been astonished to learn what had happened with Edmund and had hurried to her mother's to be smothered in love and hugs and tears and frenzied caresses. They were united and that was all that mattered.

She'd been surprised to find Judith Pearland there but Judith swiftly and discreetly slipped out taking Lydia with her leaving Sarah alone with her mother. Catherine Brankly was overwhelmed to see and to hold her daughter again, and to be forgiven so easily and so freely for her transgression. Sarah was just pleased they could be together again. Eventually the early excitement faded and the pair settled down to pleasing conversation, with Mrs Brankly keen to hear about the visit abroad. For her part Catherine related the story of Edmund and Lydia and all that had happened since.

"I had forgotten something and returned and I thank the Lord I did. I could not find Lydia, who should've been indoors, and went into the farmyard. Edmund had just seized her and kissed her, then he threw her to the ground. I do not know what came over me Sarah. I grabbed an old rotten plank of wood and smashed it over his back.

"Even then he wanted me to believe Lydia attacked him, but I sent him away. He has since vanished, nobody seems to know where. Oh Sarah, you cannot begin to understand how I felt. I was in such pain about the way I had treated you, and to think my own brother had set about you the same way. It is unbearably awful..."

"Oh mama, dear mama, do not upset yourself. The truth is out and we are a family again. I love you and always knew the truth would come and we would be reunited."

They hugged again.

"I took Lydia home where her mother sent for Dr Pearland. She was wonderful with poor Lydia who was so very distraught and even stayed the night with her, and she has worked some magic there for the poor girl is much improved and, as you can see, has returned to help here. At first I was despised and ignored by my neighbours, and our chickens were taken. One was killed and nailed to our front door. Oh it was awful.

"But dear Judith came to me, talked to me, and then helped me here, and then came with Abe Winchell to help on the farm and gradually it won the villagers over and I am accepted and forgiven. It is thanks to Judith, it truly is. I am so grateful...." And her words became tears as the shocking memories flooded her mind, Sarah reaching over to take her in her arms.

"Most important is your forgiveness Sarah...."

"Mama, mama, there is nothing to forgive. As long as I still have your love..."

"Always, always my darling. Always. And I hope I have yours."

"Of course you do mama. Love everlasting."

***

Robert Broxford read Clara's letter and was much touched by the contents.

When he'd seen who it was from he'd assumed it would be full of self pity, but the only pity she expressed was her sorrow for the pain she had caused him. She explained her pathetic reasons for eloping with Culteney and for being seduced by Jaunton, wrote that there were no excuses, she only had herself to blame, her silly girlish ideas of advancement worth nothing at all.

Expecting a plea for his love and forgiveness he found instead a simple concluding remark that she would welcome any communication from him at any time.

He would show the letter to Sarah and ask her advice.

Also in need of advice was Dr Philip Jaunton. He was wrestling with his conscience and finding it hard to live with the irresponsible way he'd behaved. Judith had caught him off guard and her words had stung, and that was without her commenting on his treatment of Clara, hurtful remarks he knew she would be able to make.

He was working with a man who had not come up to expectations as far as reputation was concerned, had played a part in Judith's departure and subsequent breakdown, and was discovering that his admiration for David Grayan, well deserved it had to be said, was tinged by the fact he could not accept a woman as his equal or better, whereas Grayan could.

Yes, he'd taken the Westlingstead Beauty for his pleasure but what an easy success that had been. He'd only achieved it because she wanted to wed him for status and he had misled her until he got what he wanted. Only now did he see himself as the wicked man he was.

Being deeply religious, despite his un-Christian behaviour, he elected to seek out Father Farhoe for guidance believing the priest would offer some solace and suggest a path to righteousness and forgiveness. An unprincipled man and a fire-and-brimstone man of God was not a good combination and unsurprisingly the two did not get on well together, Farhoe seemingly over-zealous in seeking eternal damnation and shame and the most fearsome retribution for Jaunton's sins.

This wasn't what the physician wanted. He sought advice and to be blessed with God's forgiveness and left the church without either. This tugged at his soul. He was a tormented man thinking God had abandoned him in his hour of need, and that it was impossible to find peace, let alone an answer to his predicament.

In this intolerable quandary, and eager to relieve his suffering, he made a decision based on emotional distortion rather than logic or sense and ran to the Evershen's to make apology and to offer Clara his hand. Clara was reluctant but her mother treated her to such a look of disdain and threat that she chose to accept. And after he had left she found she could rekindle her dreams of social standing and took to them greatly.

For now he had resolved one part of the difficulty he found himself in.

She was a lovely young woman and in truth he would be fortunate indeed to find anything comparable. In atoning for his appalling behaviour towards her Jaunton felt that God was smiling upon him and agreeing with his proceedings, but he still had to overcome the issue of Henry Barrenbridge.

But perhaps he could use that to his advantage. Perhaps he could become a partner at the practice and, as Barrenbridge's protégé, be placed in a position to take over when the older man retired or decided to take a lesser and more relaxed role. He knew the man controlled the purse strings and there were funds available now Judith had gone; it was not something that Grayan had much of a say in especially if Henry recommended it.

All that was required was a little blackmail. Not a very Christian solution to a dilemma, but a positive result would further improve his standing with Clara and make the match more worthwhile in her eyes, and her forgiveness all the more assured.

And the extra money would enable him and Clara to set up home in reasonable accommodation to Clara's complete satisfaction. She would leave Downsland and have a maid of her own. That should please her.

***

Finally Robert had a chance to show Sarah the letter from Clara. The news was all around Westlingstead and she was surprised Robert hadn't heard.

"Robert, this letter was written before there was a change in Clara's circumstances. I am sorry to have to tell you this but Dr Jaunton has paid his respects and apologised to Clara, and asked her to marry him. I am so sorry Robert, but I imagined you must know...." And her voice trailed into nothingness as she stared at his forlorn face.

"You mean everybody in Westlingstead knows except me?"

"I am so sorry, but yes."

"Thank you for telling me Sarah." And he screwed up the letter and threw it down.

"You could always write if you felt so inclined Robert. Just to thank her for her letter."

"All I want to do Sarah is to write and say I am always here for her and will always love her and no other."

"Well, do it Robert. Write and say that, but be sure you mean it."

"I do Sarah, with all my heart." And he picked up Clara's letter and straightened it out.

"May I ask a favour of you Sarah?"

"Yes, of course."

"Will you read my reply before I send it? And what should I do when I encounter her about our business here at Downsland?"

"I will read your reply, of course I will. When you meet her here remember you are both on duty and smile as you would smile at anyone else we work with. That is all you need to do. If she chooses to speak listen to what she has to say. She may simply say 'good morning' or 'fine day' and you need only respond in the same way."

"Thank you Sarah. I understand. I have no idea what I would do without you."

"Don't be silly. Look to yourself. Be yourself and the answers will always come."

They shared a sad smile, with Robert nodding in acknowledgement.

The news of Clara's betrothal also came as a shock to Judith Pearland who took the opportunity to call upon the Evershens' where she was met with blunt rudeness by the mother and disinterest by the daughter.

Dismayed she returned home to find a letter from David Grayan asking her to visit him as soon as she wished, so she set off immediately for Downsland where she was escorted at once to his study. He rose from his desk to greet her and led her to some seats by the window having ascertained she wanted no refreshments.

"Miss Pearland, it has come to my notice that you have left the hospital and abandoned your career and wondered if you would like to tell me why. My late wife was a great champion of your work; you were highly regarded by Dr Barrenbridge and indeed by people throughout the district. Jed Maxton owes you his life."

She was stone-faced and sat looking at him unblinkingly, gathering her thoughts. Decision made she spoke and did so quietly but with firmness and authority.

"I think you are aware sir, that Dr Barrenbridge misled me as to my future and prospects. It was thanks to your own kindness that I was placed as his assistant when Dr Parry-Barnard left, with the new doctor under me. Dr Barrenbridge is your friend sir, but I will tell you this and you may regard it as nothing more than opinion or even dismiss it as a malicious act of vengeance. That is your right sir.

"A man was recently brought to us following a serious riding accident and he was in a bad condition sir. I knew what had to be done to allow him to heal properly but Dr Barrenbridge disagreed and sent me to find Dr Jaunton. Even he agreed with me but was unable to change Dr Barrenbridge's mind. He was given the wrong treatment and incorrect surgery and died from blood loss on the table where he had been operated on.

"Had I spoken out alone my testimony would've been laughed at as I am a woman. Had Dr Jaunton spoken my voice would've added credence to his claim, but he chose not to. I suffered badly and was eventually found collapsed and brought to the hospital by Abraham Winchell, the blacksmith's son as I believe you would know sir. I recovered but did not feel the situation could continue. My departure allowed Dr Barrenbridge to make Dr Jaunton his assistant which I believe to be the price to be paid for the young doctor's silence.

"That is all I have to say sir."

He had studied her face and manner throughout her discourse and her expression had not changed anymore than her demeanour had. He knew she was telling the truth and his memory reminded him that Barrenbridge covered up the death of Mr Brankly, even though he himself had not killed Sarah's father, in order to preserve the good name of the practice, as well as his own.

It had happened again and this time it was Henry who had made the mistake.

"Thank you Miss Pearland. You have been through a torrid time and I am sorry it made you unwell, just as I am sorry for the way you have been treated. I will not repeat what you have told me unless you give me your permission to do so." She shook her head. "But I will investigate in my own discreet way. And in the meantime you may count on my support in any venture you wish to undertake. I owe that to you as I owe it to my wife and I will do whatever I can for you.

"We both believed in equality in all things, but perhaps this is further proof that the world is not ready for such philosophies, especially when it threatens the good order that society has established for its own benefit, convention being dictated largely by men. Thank you again. You are welcome here at any time Miss Pearland, and in my absence you may wish to talk with Miss Sarah Brankly, whom I believe you know. She now assists me in certain matters.

"She is young but capable and I wish to encourage her. Let me say this; I have not lost faith in you as a person or as a doctor, and as I told Dr Barrenbridge I would willingly put my life in your hands as a physician and surgeon. You will make your mark Miss Pearland, you will."

There were no further words and the two stood up, Grayan ringing the bell and Judith donning her gloves, then shared nods of mutual respect and acknowledgment were exchanged as Ginny emerged to lead Grayan's guest away.

There was much for both to think on.

***

Later in the day Sarah was also in Grayan's study, but alone and dealing with some minor correspondence. She felt important but not in an arrogant way. It was simply her way and she was always self-effacing and modest in most matters. The young assistant rose smartly when her Master entered and sat again when he did as he took his place behind his desk.

"I've been invited to Dover, to the Cowans, and will go during April for a few days, but not until I have seen Agnes and Jed married of course."

His announcement went through her like a knife and she felt the same troublesome sensations in her stomach yet again, and still was she unable to explain them. Why should such news hurt her so? If only she understood.

"Yes sir," she replied at last, "and I am pleased you will be here to see them wed. They are much in love." She pondered the thought but alas had no knowledge of that type of love to call upon. She loved her mother dearly but presumably love for a man was different.

"Yes, and I do not believe they may be alone this year. Ginny Perkins and Mark Grenchen appear to be sharing love. It is certainly the subject of much gossip here." He laughed lightly.

"Sir, you are well informed, but are you also aware that Clara Culteney, as I shall call her, has accepted a proposal from Dr Jaunton and they are to be wed."

"Goodness me, no I wasn't. Well now, love is all around us, and love will be blessed by the coming spring I daresay, the season for young love to blossom. What of you Sarah? Is there love in your heart? Oh please forgive my impertinence Sarah. That is a private matter I should not enquire after."

"There is love in my heart for so many things and I do not consider your question impertinent. I love mama, I love

233

Downsland, I love my work here, I love my time spent at home, love our beautiful countryside, my love is boundless sir. But no, there is no love in my heart for a gentleman. God has found me other work to do for his greater good rather than be a dutiful wife and mother, and I am happy."

"Bless you Sarah. You have used words in a way an artist paints a picture. It is a glorious talent. And you have other gifts too, no doubt inspired by your devotion to God's calling. I would like to ask your thoughts on two matters if I may. Shall we take tea and talk in more comfortable surroundings?"

"Why yes sir, if it pleases you."

"Good. I will ring and we shall retire to the room next door where we may relax in peace and take our refreshments."

She was still slightly stunned by his approach to a young servant, someone who was little more than an inexperienced maid, and was often nervous in his presence as she was now. For all her confidence she was acutely aware that she was just a maid who had been helpful to her Master and was being rewarded with a position she felt she deserved but shouldn't have. It was a confusing issue!

Grayan began by revealing all that Bakker had told him, and that Ralph might well discover where Hester was.

"Would your sister settle here at Downsland sir?"

"Yes, most certainly and my brother would take her and the children from here given half a chance. He seems to think the law is on his side."

"Have you consulted a man of law about that sir?"

"No I haven't. A good point Sarah and I shall do so urgently. I have learned that my sister's husband has gone to Jamaica supposedly on business, but I need to make more enquiries. He may well stay out there especially if he has creditors after him in England. I do not know what capacity he has out there. He may have no substance to him or he could be involved in a business scheme of some sort which he hopes will reap rich dividends."

"Is war really likely sir?"

"Possibly but where and between whom is in the lap of the gods. Our colonies in the Americas are restless, the Dutch may be resentful of our domination of the seas, and the French are a threat. The safest place in all these circumstances would be England for my sister."

They sat and discussed all these details like old friends, firm acquaintances and Grayan found he was enjoying the occurrence and was completely relaxed in her company, a tranquillity surrounding their presence together which left him at ease.

"I think sir, if I may say so, I would want to bring you and your brother and sister together to discuss this business quite openly, as I suggested before. But you should wait until you know the legal position."

He smiled averting his face from her gaze. He did not want to appear condescending.

"I will think on that once I have sought legal advice. Changing the subject I asked Dr Pearland to attend me and I found her news most disturbing. Sadly Sarah, much was of a confidential nature which I cannot reveal to you, but you may in any case know of her situation. Do you know why she left the hospital?" Sarah shook her head. "Well, it is a private affair and something I cannot consult you on, but I am concerned for her as I have the greatest respect for her medical ability and know she would've made an excellent physician and an equally good surgeon. Ye gods she proved that enough with Jed Maxton.

"If you are conscious of anything that I should need to know please tell me for I wish to help her."

After a few seconds of contemplation Sarah responded.

"Sir she helped my mother as I have told you, just as she helped poor Lydia after my uncle's attack, and I believe she was of assistance to Clara although such help appears to have gone to waste. Could it be sir that her vocation lies away from medicine itself yet remains medical in essence?"

"You mean healing the mind?"

"Yes sir, that is I suppose exactly what I thought now you have expressed it so well."

"Be careful with your flattery Sarah." She saw him smiling and returned the gesture with a short laugh, understanding his humour and finding it agreeable.

"Judith is often at my mother's and I will find a way to talk to her and will let you know if I feel there is any way you can help." He looked serious.

"Why thank you Sarah." And they both laughed, she realising she had stepped a little too far, not that he seemed to mind.

"By the by Sarah, if you have not heard already, Dr Parry-Barnard has confessed to the murder of a Dr Williams of Biddenden and will be tried accordingly. We are well rid of him here. I do not approve of the death penalty but he will probably go to the gallows. If I remember correctly he attended your dear father."

"Yes sir, and we were grateful for all he did and know he could not do more. For that alone I shall be sorry to hear of his hanging, but if he has killed someone then justice must be done."

"Indeed it must Sarah."

They returned to the study and to their work soon after, Sarah experiencing a strange intuition that Grayan had been trying to tell her something but with no idea what it might be.

Chapter Twenty

April brought Easter with it giving the Rev Paul Farhoe plenty to keep him busy as he fussed around his flock, held services, and used the opportunity to denounce the ungodly of which there were a few in his parish, not least David Grayan.

Since then he has married Agnes and Jed with the wedding party being held at Downsland Hall on Grayan's instructions (he also provided food and drink) and the whole event proved quite a jolly and frivolous affair with much merry-making well into the night. It was attended by almost everyone from Westlingstead as well as staff from the Hall, notable absentees being Clara Evershen and Philip Jaunton.

Apart from the bride and groom Judith Pearland was also toasted, much to her embarrassment.

Farhoe did not tarry long at the celebrations and, having quaffed a sizeable quantity of ale, condemned what he saw as an act of debauchery and marched off back to the village in a state of drunkenness and did so by a meandering route, singing an unknown hymn.

David will soon be leaving for his brief stay at Dover and has been pondering what he can do for his sister Hester.

He has taken legal advice and has nothing to fear. Despite his bluster Ralph cannot lay claim to the twins without their mother and as David is actually the older brother, despite being disinherited, the law should support him if Hester lived at Downsland.

Ginny and Mark will be wed in July, their home nearly ready. Clara and Philip will have a quiet ceremony in May when the doctor hopes to obtain suitable accommodation in Charing. They have a pleasant looking property in mind and are assured of finding local staff without difficulty.

Jaunton has carried out his plan ruthlessly, but although reluctant at first Henry Barrenbridge decided it was all for the best as perhaps he was beginning to tire, and being able to take on a lesser role had an appeal. The younger man is regarded as

Barrenbridge's partner and is paid accordingly, more than enough to acquire the house and the servants to go with it.

Living away from hospital and Westlingstead is an attractive solution for a couple who have earned the contempt of local people.

There has been plenty for Sarah to do at home and at Downsland and she has been extremely busy, but has worked, as ever, without complaint and without tiring, happy in all she applies herself to.

Clara discarded Robert's letter and ignored him completely, and cannot wait to leave the Hall and be away from the gossips who are making her life a misery. Robert seems resigned to his loss and goes about his duties in a solemn mood, devoid of all humour, and has told Sarah he will never love another for his heart forever belongs to Clara.

Judith has found ample employment in various capacities around the village, happy to turn her hand to anything that needs doing and has even helped Abe in the forge. They are still often found drinking ale together in the Green Man and rumours run amok but do so without any foundation. She has no interest in marriage as she has made clear to Abe and he accepts that he will not be successful in changing her mind, whereas both families cling to the belief they will be wed eventually.

***

"How did you find out about Mr Handlen sir?"

Easter and wedding over David Grayan is preparing his plans for bringing Hester home and is putting his design to Sarah in case he has overlooked something or she should produce an improvement in the detail.

"I asked my brother. He would have no reason to be untruthful. He cares not for Mr Handlen or even his sister but for some purpose wants her children in his care. I cannot imagine why Sarah, but if you can please tell me. He came to blows with my brother when my brother attacked him having learned how he beat my sister. Yet he pretends he cares nothing for her.

"If that be truly the case why worry about the boys? It makes no sense."

238

Sarah moved her lips around in the manner of one in contemplation and looked out of the window as if seeking guidance from the estate beyond.

"I do not say this lightly sir, and do so with due deference to you as my Master, but could it be your brother is not in his right mind, perhaps driven to the brink of madness? I hope I have not offended you sir?" He did not look offended, just very serious.

"I am not offended Sarah." He sighed deeply and stared through the same window she had gazed at. "My own thoughts had travelled by the same route. I would write to his wife but dare not for I might make trouble for her rather than me. My feelings are that he may have reached that brink Sarah, and be beyond it.

"For all that I could not see him sent away. I said I had disowned him but regret doing so, for in truth he is still my brother with the same blood flowing through our veins."

Sarah, still possessing an innocence that marked her as a girl not yet an adult, had a suggestion that brought a smile to Grayan's lips, although once more he turned his head away so she should not see it.

"Sir, Dr Pearland is very good talking to people. She has helped my mother so very much as she helped Lydia Grant after my uncle attacked her. She helped Clara too but the foolish woman has had her head turned and deserted poor Robert Broxford. Dr Pearland would be the best person to talk with your brother sir."

He slowly turned towards her and showed her the kindest of faces.

"Thank you Sarah. I will think about that. I have much faith in Dr Pearland and may speak with her on this vexed subject. Thank you again." He didn't really mean it and Sarah knew it.

"Now, I have decided my sister can live at Downsland and I am making arrangements for her to return here. As you know I have learned I have nothing to fear from the law so I will have to decide how to deal with my brother when the occasion arises. I will be back from Dover before the matters are finalised but I have, as you are aware, instructed Mrs Forbes to prepare a suite of rooms and I have organised workmen to provide separate access. That should afford my sister a degree of independence which I think is essential."

"I am pleased to hear it sir, and I know it is not my place to say so but I do think it an excellent arrangement. I hope your visit to Dover is enjoyable sir.

"Thank you for allowing me to wait upon Miss Cowans sir, she is such a lovely lady and if you would be so kind do please give her my regards. I think she will make someone a fine wife if I may say so sir." Sarah was fishing and Grayan realised it and did not take the bait.

"I will pass on your regards Sarah, you may be assured of that. You have the address and I ask you to write at once if a matter of urgency arises. Despatch any letter with Robert Broxford. Mrs Forbes has the same instructions but it may fall upon you to carry out the writing."

"Yes sir, and I will be delighted to do so if circumstances dictate."

"Good. I am looking forward to seeing Miss Cowans again but cannot afford to be away long at the present time. When I return my sister's plight moves to the fore, but there is nothing more to be done for now. However, I will come straight back if a problem occurs. Now, if you will excuse me I have other business affairs to attend to."

Sarah rose and curtsied, gathered her papers, of which there were many, and left the study without further words, wondering if he might propose to Miss Cowans while away. She had not been able to draw him on the closeness of his relationship with the lady but Sarah felt he had displayed a diplomatic aloofness by ignoring her comments, and she giggled to herself. One day, she admitted, I will go too far but hey ho, he will not be angry with me. I hope he proposes to Miss Cowans for her acceptance would be the most wonderful news when there has been so much love to be found this spring!

And the pangs of pain appeared in her stomach once again. What on earth could it be?

Lily Cowans was to be found on her beloved cliffs where she was sitting on a favourite tree stump looking across the Channel, and revelling in the comparative warmth of the April sunshine. It was too good a day to stay at home. Life felt good as well. She was happy and was smiling without noticing it.

David Grayan would be there soon and they would walk these cliffs to the north of the town as they had done before, and they would talk and be absorbed in each others' company, and she would feel happier than ever. As such thoughts drifted through her mind she was conscious of the same feelings that plagued Sarah and they made her unhappy for she knew full well what they were.

In a moment of untypical cruelty she reminded herself she was a lady and of course David would seek her hand soon. Why, he might approach her father during his forthcoming stay! Surely he could have no designs on a young serving girl? No, surely he couldn't. Lily had nothing to fear. David had some station in life. Marie might've been a merchant's daughter, but they were a wealthy family in their own right, and Marie was truly a lady for all that.

A serving girl? A village peasant? No, he could have no designs on the faithful Sarah, and she could obviously have no ambitions there, and that was all there was to it. She realised she was being cruel and admonished herself, but still suffered the pangs of pain and the pangs of doubt, managing to recall she was, in her opinion, the better capture.

Surely she was?

***

Judith Pearland was discovering a new interest and Abe Winchell was at the centre of it.

She had very successfully shod a horse under his guidance and was looking particularly pleased with herself as well she might. Her face, so sad of late, gleamed with pleasure and shone with a light Abe hadn't seen before, a face full of pride and radiating achievement.

He had been mocked for suggesting it, but her attitude had changed as she had learned more and more, and done so first hand. It had been first light when she arrived and she had been persuaded into helping him with the fire while he explained the tools and the way in which they were used, pointing out the importance of heating some of the ones to be employed.

She loved it and by late morning was shodding Davey Mickton's mare. Abe stood back and applauded. It had been an excellent piece of work.

"Y'know what Judith? I can see why you're a good physician. You listen well, learn well and then apply your new learnings well." He saw her face drop and sought to restore her. "And you'll be good at whatever you do, just like you bin with the 'orse. And like you bin with Lydia and Mrs Brankly. Perhaps you can't be a full doctor Judith, but you can be a success in some other ways, and maybe you should be looking. I'm proud of you today, just as I'm proud to call you a doctor, but I'm proud of what you did for Lydia and Mrs Brankly too, and you're right good at it."

He felt horribly inadequate and knew his futile words would not save the day, but she surprised him with an impish grin.

"Abe, you're a wonderful man, and you say the loveliest things for which I thank you. So now I'm going to put my arms around you while nobody's looking and kiss you, unless you'd rather me not."

It was the one response he could never have dreamed of and it left him flabbergasted. She saw his discomposure and laughed in a sweet way.

"Oh come here Abe and let's kiss, you silly boy."

"Y-y-y-y-y-yes .... J-J-Judith, er ...... doctor, I ... I ... I ..."

"You're not used to the idea of a woman asking a man, are you Abe? Well, if it helps, I've not done this before and I'll tell you this. I've never kissed a man. You'll be my first."

"J-J-J-J-Judith, I not kissed a girl neither, that's why I'm taken aback."

"Good. Then we'll learn together. Now have you tethered that mare well? Because we don't want to be interrupted do we?"

The well-tethered mare became the sole witness to a moment of ecstatic glory as the blacksmith and the doctor melted into each others' arms and shared the most passionate of kisses.

It was thus the second new interest Judith Pearland developed that morning.

***

For Henry Barrenbridge it was a sobering time.

He regarded David Grayan as a good friend and had been proud to set up the medical facilities in Westlingstead, but had kept recent news from him. Obviously Grayan knew about Judith but was in ignorance of the fact Philip Jaunton had effectively become a partner on a much increased income, and that Henry was trying to reduce the time he spent at work.

Both doctors were extremely busy so Barrenbridge had little chance to decrease his occupation at the hospital. The arrangement had been that he would run the place with two assistants and some nurses as well as a cook to work when required and an odd-job man. There was no spare money now to pay for another assistant doctor, and surely only a question of time before Grayan learned the truth.

Jaunton had openly blackmailed him, but it was easy to surrender and allow life to flow at its usual rate rather than cause a hiccough from which there might be no escape and a horrible day of reckoning. He had already made Grayan aware that Parry-Barnard had cost Mr Brankly his life and that the truth had been conveniently buried.

The senior nurse Grace Gandling worked tirelessly at everything that fell within her compass and much else besides, but was awake to the problems at the hospital. It was not her way to complain or speak out, and definitely not to take any action that might imperil the practice, yet she knew so much, so very much was wrong but felt helpless to correct it.

She met Judith often but was always loyal. A local girl, like Judith herself, she'd been elevated largely by Marie Grayan's involvement but was otherwise content in her post tending the sick. She never discussed with anyone the difficulties at the hospital and never aired any opinions or criticism of the doctors. They were private matters and her loyalty was her unshakeable rock. Being loyal was right and proper.

However, that loyalty was shortly to be put to the test.

Dr Jaunton carried on with great efficiency and enjoyed marked success with the patients even though many despised him. How he longed to be wed and away to live in Charing. At least then he would not be among these people when he was not at work and not have to see their glowering looks and hear their sneering remarks muttered loudly behind his back.

Clara fared no better and also yearned for the day. Not long now, of course, and her nightmare would be over and she would have her status, her dream home and servants to wait on her. She would choose them and make sure none had the beauty to tempt her new husband!

But one element of her nightmare was determined not to go away.

Mrs Evershen harboured hopes of joining Philip and Clara in their new home and neither the physician nor her daughter wanted her but had found no way of avoiding it yet. Unbeknown to all three fate was about to play a hand.

***

Ralph Grayan had sailed for the continent in the company of one of his heavily-built brutes and the man who had David successfully followed. Aloysius Crombie was a dark character who looked sinister and threatening despite his small stature, and who had the habit of wringing his hands together as if expecting a treat at any moment. Ralph had paid him well for his information and was offering him a small fortune if he could now locate Hester.

Crombie had the advantage of having been to the Netherlands several times and had easily convinced Grayan there was every chance of success. Besides the prize was one worth winning. Once ashore he knew who to contact. He'd arranged for a coach to meet them and had suggested moving northwards in the direction of Amsterdam.

Ralph was so absorbed in his search for his sister, so engulfed by hatred, so angry and bitter, that he was indeed losing all sense of reason. Even with Crombie by his side he should've realised he had no idea where they would start, how they might come about clues, or could be sure Hester was actually in the Netherlands.

If they found her might she be well protected? It could take more than the villain he brought along to prise her away, let alone take the infants while their mother stood by. He'd already decided kidnapping was a possible answer, but by heavens he'd have those children whatever it took.

His brother had travelled to Dover and was being entertained by Lily Cowans, neither realising that her father was expecting David to seek permission to ask for her hand.

David and Lily walked arm in arm, as did Mr and Mrs Cowans a few steps behind, as they ascended the cliffs away from the town. Lily had decided that it was a time for frank talking. She had waited patiently for such a long time hoping Roger Culteney would propose and he never did, so she did not want this situation to get out of hand and follow her previous and disastrous wooing with nothing to show at the end.

"David, I must speak to you about a serious matter, and I apologise for doing so as it is not a woman's place. However, I am certain you of all people will allow this deviation and, in any case, you are already aware that I am my own person and act regardless of my sex."

"Lily, you have my ear, and rightly so, whatever you have to say, for you know my thoughts on the subject of womens' so-called roles. Speak freely."

"I will be blunt then. My friendship with you has grown to the point where I have felt deep affection for you, and now that affection has deepened still. I wish to know if my feelings are returned and if there may be hope for me should we find we love each other. I waited long enough for Roger so I am sure you will understand my concern. Please speak just as openly. If there is little hope you will not hurt me and our friendship can continue every part as good as it is now. I trust I am assured of that."

"I do not know the answer and that is the truth. I adore being with you and share a strong affection for you but cannot say that love will grow. However, many people marry for far less and love does indeed develop. I appreciate your candour especially on matters where we also share a common desire and belief, and the equality of man and woman is one of my basic creeds as I believe it is for you.

"May I beg your indulgence Lily and ask you for a brief period to consider my feelings. I will tell you before I depart I promise. And if we are not to be wed then please let us remain the very best of friends as you suggest." She hugged his arm closer, looked up into his face and smiled. It was all she could hope for, but she felt the tide had turned in the wrong direction and she was lost.

She knew then she loved him dearly and ached for him, just as she knew he did not quite share the same feelings of love for her. Yes, it could grow. Yes, they could wed and be so very happy together, two like minded people on life's highway, and might yet experience the enchanting beauty of true love for years to come. Why couldn't he see that and take the chance?

Lily thought she knew the answer.

***

Clara dashed along the road to the hospital.

Her mother had been poorly all night and now she was in fever and tossing and turning and making no sense. Philip Jaunton was busy with an injured boy so Henry Barrenbridge returned with Clara and examined her mother. His diagnosis was instant. He explained the situation to Clara, said that Mrs Evershen needed immediate surgery and that he would arrange to have her brought to the hospital.

Once there Barrenbridge prepared to operate with the help of Jaunton who was now free. Grace was present. It started well. The patient had to be cut open to deal with the problem and that part proceeded as well as could be expected. Jaunton started work on the offending organ and was stopped by Barrenbridge who told him he was not handling it correctly. The young doctor was amazed, for he knew what had to be done and could effect the surgery efficiently, but his partner would have none of it, ordering a different treatment which Jaunton realised could be fatal.

The two argued heatedly, Grace tending Mrs Evershen with growing concern and with bewilderment at their behaviour. There was a terrible row and all Grace could do was try and stem the bleeding as she recalled she had done once before. Finally she could take no more and yelled at them.

"Doctors, the patient is dying. Stop arguing. Finish the operation."

246

No more words were spoken, with Henry taking control and completing surgery in a most savage way. It was left to the horrified Philip Jaunton and Grace Gandling to make the best of it afterwards and Mrs Evershen was eventually taken to a bed in the next room.

She lived about two hours and died without regaining consciousness. The two doctors had continued their argument in a furious exchange of words before Jaunton had been ordered out. Grace could make no sense of it, but with one of the young nurses attended to Clara's mother until they needed to do no more, at which point both shed tears for the failure.

Grace did not have the knowledge to question either doctor but had sufficient experience to know Jaunton was absolutely right and that Barrenbridge's surgery was hazardous in the extreme. Her mind returned to the other patient who had died in almost similar circumstances. The senior physician was given to outbreaks of temper but his rage as he tore at Mrs Evershen's entrails was dreadful beyond description, and the poor woman was so obviously doomed.

Clara had heard the row but had no idea what it was about, assuming they were simply trying their best to save her mother, and had then sat by the bedside while the two nurses went about their ceaseless but hopeless work looking after the stricken patient. She had no tears to shed and after a few minutes rose and departed for home, sad at her loss but hardly heartbroken.

Philip was not far behind and sat with her for a while once indoors.

"Philip, I cannot wait to be away from this wretched place. I want to be with you in our new home and I am sad we cannot go there now far from these awful people."

"Let me say this my love. Our reputation counts for nothing here anyway, so if you are in agreement there is nothing to lose if I move in with you now until the wedding. We might upset Father Farhoe but what might that matter?"

"It cannot be right Philip. But I would love you to be here. I would be so lonely now without mama and as for the priest, well we can be two more wicked people for him to revile. I will agree as long as you are as discreet as can be allowed in the circumstances."

"Thank you my beloved. I shall come here tonight. I must return to work but will be here later." He wrapped his arms around her and held her tight to him.

"Philip, what was the shocking argument about?" He'd been expecting this and had not yet devised an answer.

"Dr Barrenbridge is the senior partner and I should not have taken issue with him, but you will understand we were fighting for your mother's life and sometimes such emergencies lead to heated discussion such is the urgency involved. But there was nothing wrong. We did our best my beloved."

"I know you did Philip, and now we can at least move to Charing when wed and go without mama, so perhaps her death is a poignant blessing."

Clara's grief was without sincerity, her sorrowfulness false, her conduct as heartless as her words bore witness and Philip, even more determined to enjoy her fruits straight away, abetted this humbling of her mother knowing full well the extra burden of damnation the village would then heap on her. He was a doctor, a successful doctor, a man, and he would survive their ridicule, but Clara's reputation, already in tatters, would be soiled past recognition. And she would have to endure their scything comments for days and days to come.

At Downsland Robert Broxford was inconsolable as he went quietly about his business and kept his own grief to himself. Even now he would take Clara back, marry her and never mention the past. He loved her that much.

His devotion was almost an inspiration for Sarah. She had done so much to ensure he should accept Clara as she was, recognising his love for what it was, strong and deep and eternal, and in time he had overcome his disgust for her realising that was what love was truly about. And it was all thanks to Sarah's teachings!

She might've been proud of it too, but for the latest episode which had seen poor Robert spurned. Sarah did not believe her friend, as Clara had become, could be so fickle, but perhaps she had never really known her. Perhaps you never really knew anyone, she wondered, and maybe everyone could surprise you, shock you, and do so either in an appalling manner or in a pleasing way.

248

Esther Hammond broke into her reverie.

"Sarah, there you are. Oh dear Robert, how he pines for love lost."

"Esther, where did you come from?"

"I have a message from Mrs Forbes. She wishes to see you, but not urgently."

"Thank you Esther. Yes, poor Robert, but I think he has gained by not engaging with such a woman as Clara has turned out to be. It would not have been a happy match."

"Do you think he could love me instead Sarah? Such a handsome man."

"Ah that is the way of it Esther. Thank God I shall never know this love between man and woman. How delicate and brittle it is, how painful it can become. Esther, he will love Clara until death, and he will never love you the same way. His love for Clara is so deep his heart will never be free. Give your love to someone else Esther, someone who will return it as it should be."

"How can you say these things without knowing such love yourself?"

"I observe things Esther, that is how I know. And such observations lead me to believe the Master will soon by wed, but I will speak no further on the subject. Now I must go to Mrs Forbes."

"Why bless you Sarah. So the Master is in love? Miss Cowans I'll be bound."

"Wait and see, dear Esther, wait and see."

***

By good fortune rather than successful enterprise Aloysius Crombie had heard of an Englishwoman recently arrived in Breukelen. Unfortunately, from his point of view, the informant decided more money was to be made from this intelligence and went to Aldert Bakker and sold the story of Crombie's arrival and quest to the merchant.

This enabled Bakker to move Hester and the boys to his own home and mount a guard which in turn frustrated Ralph Grayan.

Crombie purchased the details of Bakker's address, much to Ralph's delight.

Refused entry Grayan elected to head back to England realising he was powerless as the situation stood, and resolving to tackle his brother at the earliest opportunity now he was armed with the knowledge of Hester's whereabouts.

Crombie had done well for his paymaster and looked forward to his earnings.

Back in Westlingstead Grace Gandling sought out Judith Pearland and poured out her story unable to come to terms with what had happened before her very eyes.

Judith asked for precise details and knew Jaunton was right and Barrenbridge was wrong. He'd killed another villager. She explained all she needed to and asked Grace what was to be done.

At last, her loyalty tested beyond endurance, Grace opened her heart to Judith.

"The one thing we cannot do, Judith, is rely on Dr Jaunton. He is, in my opinion, the better doctor, but Dr Barrenbridge is in such a state, so easily enraged, that he is a danger to patients. Oh Judith, I know not what to do, I truly do not. But I cannot allow the matter to rest and I will not do so."

"Grace, you know as I do that another man died when Barrenbridge misjudged the surgery, and now he has taken the life of Mrs Evershen. There may be others Grace. We must act, we must do something or more may perish."

"What can we do? Mere womenfolk! We cannot obtain Dr Jaunton's support for he is now a partner in the practice and he is culpable in the shield that had been placed around these deaths. He will cover for Barrenbridge and for the sake of the hospital and his own post."

"Nonetheless, we must speak with him Grace. Will you attend with me?"

After a few moments contemplation Grace answered.

"Yes, I will."

Chapter Twenty One

She lifted her head and looked at the massive castle rising up to the sky just as she had done so many times before. It dominated the town and represented security and power and she worshipped it as she loved the mighty hills and white cliffs beyond.

Lily Cowans had never felt happier.

It was quite the best day of her life. Now she had the answer and her future was as secure as Dover castle, and at last she was at peace.

***

David Grayan was back at Downsland and preparing for the next stage in the plan to bring Hester home. He was not yet aware his brother had been to the Netherlands and located her.

Judith Pearland and Grace Gandling had sought an audience with Philip Jaunton and found nothing but animosity and opposition. Jaunton is now living with Clara and both are attracting abuse, although people are not so openly attacking the doctor, conscious that they may need his help if they are ill or injured.

Judith has decided to seek a meeting with Grayan and knows she is risking a great deal, but her conscience will not let her rest, the issue being far too serious. He may mock her, rant at her, throw her out, but she will try.

Abe Winchell is coming to terms with a serious disappointment of a different kind.

He has learned that his cherished kiss with Judith was not a precursor to a more lasting intimacy and an attachment. It was an adventure, some harmless fun, and of no particular value beyond being a brief diversion and pleasant baptism for both of them. She explained it all to him when he declared his feelings and found them as unwanted and unreturned as they had always been.

His father had once told him that it was a mistake to ever try and understand a woman.

"Abe, I have never understood your mother but it has not prevented us having a wonderful life together, full of love and happiness, a marriage blessed with four of the best children a couple could hope for. She understands me too well, but it doesn't work the other way! But do not think I am unhappy for I am not. I love your mother and will to my dying day. We are contented. But there are things she says and things she does beyond my comprehension."

His light-hearted words brought broad smiles to their faces, and Abe tried to smile recalling them now, but no smile would come. The pain was too raw, too recent. Judith's kiss had lit a fire to match anything in the forge. How sweet that kiss was, how soft and tender, yet passionate and full-hearted, and it was over as if it had never existed, and Abe wanted to taste those lips again.

His confusion was complete.

At Downsland work on the suite for Hester has proceeded a-pace and Sarah has been especially busy being left to handle the invoices, correspondence and day-to-day paperwork arising from the project, including the purchase of materials. More than one supplier has been surprised, first to find a young girl in charge of that aspect of the work and secondly to discover she is a canny negotiator, not easily fleeced. Grayan smiles inwardly at her achievements, for she is as much his own success as hers.

"Thank you for keeping a watchful eye on her, Eleanor."

"Most of the time there really is no need sir, for her father must've trained her well, and she learned even more after his death."

The Housekeeper's comment brought a wave of sadness to David's mind for he knew the truth about the unnecessary demise. Eleanor Forbes continued:

"Sometimes I cannot explain her. She appears so confident to the point of being arrogant and yet she is not. She seems self-important but she is nothing of the sort. She is not afraid to ask and is ready to learn, but carries out her duties as if she had been carrying out these tasks for years."

"Do not try to understand Eleanor," he laughed, "for our Sarah is Sarah and I believe her to be very happy here."

"Indeed she is sir. Mind you, she has mentioned pains in her stomach over the last few days although she dismisses them easily. She did wonder if it was related to the surgery she had as a child, and has thought about seeing a doctor just in case."

"Yes ... right ... well, Dr Pearland is coming to see me. I'll ask her to meet Sarah and perhaps she could examine her."

"Yes sir. I'll tell Sarah .... but .... I do wonder if it is a different kind of problem sir."

"What do you mean?"

"Well .... I'm not sure .... I cannot imagine it to be the case, but as she described it to me I could've been listening to someone with a broken heart. Perhaps it is all to do with all the problems at home, what with Mrs Brankly and that awful business with Edmund Forness. Perhaps she misses her father, I just don't know."

"Well, Dr Pearland will find out I am certain."

***

Sarah was fully occupied with her work but still found time to visit her mother from time to time. The two had developed a bond since the Forness affair that went deeper than that betwixt mother and daughter, a bond that made them stronger and reliant on each other.

"It's very sad mama that Clara has deserted Robert and worse now she has invited that man into her parents' home. She deserves to be ignored but I cannot agree with the unpleasant things that are said within her hearing. Why do people have to be like that?"

"Well Sarah, people are like that because we are all raised to be God-fearing and to live by the standards of civilised folk, standards that leave us in good stead, standards that have stood the test of time my dear."

"But those very standards should prevent us saying nasty things about people when we know they can hear."

"Oh Sarah, if it was that simple. You must remember that some folk round here cannot come to countenance what Clara has done with her life. It is against all their teachings, it is against

God's will, and they feel they must make their feelings known. For an unmarried woman to go away and spend a night with a man is beyond their belief and understanding, and against all that God tells them is right. You must try and understand how deep those beliefs go Sarah."

"I know mama. I try to be Godly in all I do, for God has told us how to live, hasn't he? And I think God chose a path for me which I must follow. I cannot bear children but I earnestly believe God wants me for other reasons and will guide me on that path, to his greater glory."

Her mother hugged her.

"Mama, when I was operated on, well, I mention it because of some feelings I've been having in my stomach, and I just wondered if it was starting afresh, and wondered if it could. Do you think it could happen again?"

"What feelings are these Sarah? The tumour was removed and shouldn't come back, but only a physician would know. You must go and be examined my love."

Sarah described her feelings. Her mother's expression changed from concerned to knowing.

"Why Sarah, I do believe you may be in love! Who is the lucky man, pray tell?"

"Mama, do not mock. How could I be in love.....?"

"You cannot help love Sarah. If you love a man it is because love has grown in your heart even if it has grown unbid. We cannot always choose where the heart finds a safe haven for our regards. You cannot always say – well, I will love this person, and expect love to blossom. It may not happen. But affection will bloom in your heart and grow into boundless love without your agreement! It was like that for me and your papa.

"We met by chance and had no thoughts of love. I thought your papa an unpleasant man. I have never told you this so do not be angry. He thought me a conceited woman. We angered each other easily and you would not consider a relationship possible. We avoided each other but found it a difficult arrangement as he was a farmer's son and I a milkmaid employed on that farm.

"Eventually we were working together more often and how we abided each other I do not know. But one day we had a row and suddenly, as we hurled insults at each other, we realised how ridiculous our argument was and started laughing. We collapsed into each others' arms weeping tears from the laughter. And then he kissed me.

"Somehow, do not ask me how, we had fallen in love without realising it, without wanting it. And Sarah, how I yearned to be kissed by your papa again! The next kiss was past description, I can tell you! And we were married three months later."

"Oh mama, that is a lovely story. I never really knew how you met...."

"Well, you could've asked..."

The tears were rolling down Sarah's cheeks, tears of happiness, and her mother smothered her with an enormous cuddle.

"So you see Sarah, you could be in love, not from choice, but in love for all that. Now, who is it? Tell your mama." And she chuckled lightly.

"If I am in love I have no idea with whom!"

"I would think you have, but there is no need to tell me. I just hope he is worthy of your love my darling, and will return your feelings...."

"That can never happen. No man wants a barren wife...."

"None of that nonsense now."

"Besides, there is the path God has chosen..."

"And God may want you to have this man because much good will come from it. Think of that. Maybe you can wed him and still pursue God's path but in a better way."

"Oh mama, you say such lovely things, but it is something I cannot dream of."

"Well, ask the doctor about your feelings just in case it is a medical matter."

Sarah agreed on that course of action, but privately railed against being seen by either Barrenbridge or Jaunton. But there was Judith Pearland, so yes, she would seek her out first.

In love? It could not be so. Who could she possibly love? She was close to nobody, was she? And it was that thought that brought her to an astonishing possibility. Did she love the Master? Of course not, whoever heard of a maid loving her

Master? But didn't mama say you couldn't always control your feelings? Surely that was not what God intended? What a hopeless love that would be anyway! And so pointless for I imagine he is to marry Miss Cowans, and besides I am a young maid and that must be all he sees. No, it cannot be love, it must be something for Judith to attend to.

***

In due course Judith Pearland arrived at Downsland where Grayan insisted she see Sarah first.

A short while later Ralph Grayan arrived with his two travelling companions, neither of whom was introduced to David.

Ralph was red in the face, given to frequent hearty coughing and spluttering his venomous greetings while his brother stood smiling benignly at him. Eventually he gave up the struggle and instructed Crombie to explain while he collapsed uninvited into a chair.

Crombie told David his sister had been located but she had been moved to the home of a merchant, Aldert Bakker, who must be an associate of David's, and they had been refused admission. At this point the Master of Downsland burst into spontaneous laughter, an action that set his brother into another fearsome coughing fit.

"Ralph," cried David, "this mission will be the death of you, you fool. Hester and the boys are going to live here and that is an end to it. I have made legal consultations and there is nothing you can do about it in law. I think that is the end of the matter."

"Mr Grayan," Aloysius Crombie began, "I do not think you understand my client's position..."

But his words died in his throat as Ralph, with a final choke, tried to rise and fell forward and thence right out of the chair, silent and motionless.

Ginny Perkins answered Grayan's summons and was sent for Judith who arrived within moments and swiftly examined the prostrate and unconscious Ralph.

"He has fever. I cannot see to him here. Can he be taken to a bed, and urgently?" Without words David and his brother's strong henchman were instantly with Ralph whom they gently lifted from the floor.

"There is a bedchamber on the first floor, close at hand," advised his brother, "and we can carry him there. Ginny, tell Mrs Forbes to come there at once, together with Robert Broxford and yourself as well please."

The two men made light work of moving Ralph and within minutes had the stricken man on the bed where Judith set about an immediate examination with the staff ready to run whatever errands might be necessary. David and Robert helped undress Ralph as Judith continued her work.

"He is very, very ill. I will do what I can but I am not a doctor and not at the practice as you know. You may wish to send for Dr Barrenbridge and urgently."

"You are a doctor. I said I would place my life in your hands without hesitation and my brother could have no better physician. My staff will get what you need from the hospital and I will write a note to Dr Barrenbridge at once. My instructions will be carried out without question and you may have a free hand here doctor. Do whatever is necessary. Is he in danger?"

"I am sorry, but in serious danger. And the fewer people here the better. We do not know how contagious this may be. Please leave it to me. Would one of your staff be willing to work with me?"

"Yes, I would."

They looked round to see Sarah standing in the doorway. She continued:

"I'll do it if Ginny will wait outside to take any messages." Ginny nodded.

"Thank you Sarah. I'll tell you what I'll need if you can write it down and if you sir can have the note taken to the hospital."

"Most certainly. I'll write as well and Robert can take both. I'll get you pen and paper Sarah. Robert, get a horse ready. Mrs Forbes, please make whatever arrangements are required here, and please ensure our other two guests, as I suppose I must call them, are looked after. Their coach, horses and coachmen too, if you please." With that he was through the doorway.

He returned almost at once with the pen, paper and ink for Sarah to take down Judith's instructions, and he repaired to his study to write the brief letter to Barrenbridge.

Minutes later Robert was galloping towards Westlingstead as Judith and Sarah settled down to caring for their patient.

"He's very ill Sarah. We can treat him but he is also in God's hands and we must pray the Almighty smiles upon his recovery. I think he has been ill for some time and has become steadily worse without realising it. His collapse was inevitable." She told Sarah about the problem and how she intended to deal with it, while secretly hoping Barrenbridge would stay away. She had, after all, come to inform Grayan of her concerns about the doctor.

At the hospital Henry read the letter and with some reluctance ordered the medicine and other requirements despatched immediately. He would rather go to Downsland himself but Grayan had asked him not to. Shortly Robert was on his way back carrying what was needed and a verbal response from Barrenbridge.

"Tell Mr Grayan I will attend at once if summoned." It was all he could say. He deeply resented Pearland's involvement but was powerless, and was far from happy that she was at the Hall. What could she be doing there in the first place?

***

David Grayan wrote a letter to Ralph's wife and said she would be welcome at Downsland, sending it later by Ralph's coach which returned home with Crombie and his companion.

A day later Theodora Grayan arrived alone unannounced.

Clearly upset and worried she was nonetheless calm and accepted David's assurances that her husband was in exceptionally good hands and that everything possible was being done for him. David escorted her to Ralph's bedchamber where she stood close by and made a silent prayer, and then they returned downstairs. He had not yet mentioned that Ralph's physician was not a man.

Judith and Sarah had watched over him ever since he had been brought there, taking it in turns to sleep but never leaving him

258

without someone alert to his condition. One or other was always at the bedside.

"David, what does the doctor say? Do I need to send for our own physician?" Theodora asked when they were seated, David choosing this moment to tell her about Judith.

"Theodora, the physician is one whose hands I would want my life in if I was ever taken ill. I have to tell you the doctor is a woman of outstanding medical skill and has saved lives here in north Kent, and probably many times over. Bluntly, because of her sex, she cannot yet qualify but she has worked under Henry Barrenbridge who you must remember, and he has been rightly impressed. You and Ralph have nothing to fear in that respect, and I would say it is unnecessary to send for your own doctor at this stage.

"Ralph is approaching the crisis and Dr Pearland has prepared for that, and has used all her ability to ensure that there is no more that could possibly be done. If he survives it will be down to Dr Pearland." He saw Theodora's look of horror and the hand that went to her throat in shock.

"I am afraid he is seriously ill and needs your prayers."

"May I attend him David?"

"Dr Pearland suggests not. Keeping us away is vital. He is in good hands. In addition to Judith one of my maids, Sarah Brankly, attends him and that is all that is necessary. I have the greatest faith in both these ladies Theodora."

"Thank you David, and bless you." She slowly rested her hands back in her lap and took a deep breath.

"I know he has this dreadful obsession with Hester's children, and I have been very concerned about him of late. He gets in such an uncontrollable rage, and I cannot imagine why he wants those boys anyway. I dare not ask him David, I dare not. He loathes you, blames you for the death of his parents and detests the way you live. He does not forgive you for marrying Marie as you are probably aware.

"Whatever he has wrong with him now may have been brought on or exacerbated by that hatred. I wish I could understand him. I love him you know, love him dearly, but I cannot understand this desire, this furious desire, to have you undone at every turn. I wish I could do something to ease this burden, but he is not a man to be spoken to, least of all by any woman, and I fear him, I truly do."

"Well Theodora let us see what will be. Let us hope and pray for his salvation from this terrible illness and then perhaps we can start to relieve other pains."

She shook her head in response and sighed.

"I was so shocked when he left so suddenly for the Netherlands. And that man Crombie, he makes me shudder, but is in my husband's confidence, more so than I can ever hope to be, and Ralph relies on him in so many ways. I am certain Crombie has encouraged him, possibly for personal gain as Ralph pays him extremely well, but it annoys me and sickens me."

"Yes, he has the look of the devil about him I'll grant you. An obsession can drive a man to extraordinary measures and if Crombie has done well for him Ralph may have found him useful in unintentionally feeding that obsession. Ralph may be sick in other ways Theodora and we must be prepared for that. I apologise for mentioning it, but I must speak my thoughts. Your husband may be sick in the mind and we may have problems yet to come assuming he recovers from his present indisposition."

"Oh David, I could not have him taken from me either by this illness or because his mind is unwell."

"No, we both wish to avoid that, and we will strive for that I promise you. It is another good reason to let Dr Pearland attend him for she may be able to help him in other ways later. I believe her to have remarkable skills with people and their problems, so let us wait and see."

Theodora nodded and then asked if she could take a turn alone in the gardens in the spring sunshine, and David bade her go wherever she wished in both house and grounds, and he would appoint a maid to wait upon her. She thanked him and went out and David went in search of Esther Hammond.

***

An otherwise less cool and sunny April day gradually slipped into a deep red sunset and the approach of eventide, and with it came the coldness of the night and Ralph's darkest hour.

Both Judith and Sarah were by his side, sometimes simply watching and praying, sometimes wiping his fevered brow, sometimes saddened by his unknown struggles as he writhed and moaned and groaned, sometimes offering all the comfort they had which, in truth, was precious little. They whispered softly to him, encouraging him to overcome this scourge. They willed him forwards. They held his hands. Sarah sang a sweet little song she'd learned in childhood and the music drifted across the bed and around the room and off into the night air.

Past midnight and his condition was worse than ever.

David and Theodora sat together downstairs, both awake but exhausted. Ginny was asleep in her chair just outside the bedchamber.

Gone two in the morning and Ralph roused, gave a pained cry and collapsed back on the bed. Sarah was holding his hand as Judith bathed him and slowly his breathing weakened and stuttered until there was little left of it. For a moment they thought they had lost him and then his breathing became stronger and their ministrations increased in fervour in response.

Judith forced some medicine into his mouth. He spluttered slightly and she shed a tear.

"That is a good sign Sarah. Pray now more than ever. Live Mr Grayan live." Almost in reply he murmered quietly and as his head settled more comfortably on the pillow his breathing became regular and firm. "Pray for him Sarah. We cannot lose him now."

And at three in the morning Judith went to the door. Ginny was awake.

"Ginny, go to them. Tell them he lives. The worst is over. But please ask them not to come yet. We will let them know."

At eight that morning Ralph opened his eyes and saw two smiling faces looking down at him.

"Who are you?" he gasped and croaked. Sarah replied before Judith could speak.

"This is Dr Pearland who has saved your life sir." Judith looked aghast.

"Dr Pearland?" Ralph squeaked as he struggled to understand.

"Yes sir." Replied Sarah. "A lady doctor. Now do as she tells you sir and you will get better."

Both Ralph and Judith wore the same expression of astonishment, but Ralph drifted back into sleep before further words were exchanged. Judith laughed and took hold of Sarah hugging her to her bosom, and cried tears if joy.

"Oh you angel Sarah. Bless you my love, bless you. Now go and find them and tell them if they wish to come and stand by the door they may. And have some food and drink sent here to us."

Theodora eventually retired but David was too awake to contemplate sleep and set off for a lengthy walk around his estate where he often stopped to talk to those he employed there, including Jed and Agnes who were busy amongst their beloved trees.

After taking just a little food Judith fell asleep in an armchair, a deep contented sleep, while Sarah watched over both patient and physician and tried to puzzle why it was so wrong for this woman to be called a doctor. And then she too fell asleep.

By mid afternoon Ralph was awake but still very weak. He had taken drink, medicine but no food, and Sarah and Robert had helped him change into fresh clothes to replace the ones that become filthy with his night-time tussles with the fever. Then Judith and Theodora returned and sat by the bed and they talked about simple matters when Ralph wished to speak and remained silent when he did not.

David came in and stood close by.

"So brother, you are recovering." They looked at each other then Ralph spoke.

"Come here brother. Let us embrace and thank the Lord I am still here. Bless you for all you have done and bless Dr Pearland." Slowly David walked around the bed and then gently seized his brother in a moment of sublime sibling tenderness. Theodora looked on, surprised but happy and allowed the tears to well up but not to fall. It was not the place for them.

Later Judith told David about Sarah's involvement and about her words to Ralph when he first awoke.

"Goodness me Dr Pearland, did she say that indeed?"

"Yes, and she is a very special woman, and I can see why you value her so. But she is so much more than that. Perhaps it is because she is yet so young, but I know I have been with a quite astonishing woman sir, and you will treasure her I am certain."

Grayan looked into her eyes and nodded once.

"Yes I do treasure her, probably more than you can realise. I will go to her to thank her but I understand from Esther, her friend, she is in a very deep and well-deserved sleep." They smiled at each other, knowing smiles, smiles of acknowledgment.

"Ginny worked hard too sir."

"Yes I know and I have thanked her. But my most grateful thanks are for you Dr Pearland. It seems my brother may have expunged the demon that was devouring him and possibly it took this vile fever to free him, but thanks to you he lives and may fully recover."

"Thank you sir. I will continue to nurse your brother for the time being if I may....."

"Please stay as long as you wish. And please attend to my brother. Please."

Judith nodded in reply. He spoke again.

"By the by, you came here for a different reason. When you wish I will be pleased to speak with you."

Chapter Twenty Two

'The month of May has seen many happenings, some good some bad, but the best occurred at the end.'

Sarah was to write these words in her diary many weeks later as she reflected on events in her life both at home and at work as spring moved inexorably towards summer. At the end of April she noted:

'Esther has been a good comfort to Robert and is often seen with him. She has consoled him well but he still grieves for Clara believing his love for her cannot wither and die. In this he is not dissimilar to the Master when he lost his beloved, retreating into a shell of apparent misery seemingly for eternity. Such a waste in a fine young man. Esther is the only person he will talk to and I have spoken with her privately as she is such a good friend to me, and I know she would like Robert for herself. It will take much time.'

Gradually Ralph Grayan recovered sufficiently for him to return home with his wife, and he went a transformed man with all the wickedness and hatred gone from him.

With his departure the Haskerton's came for a brief stay and they were followed by the arrival of Hester and the boys, accompanied by Aldert Bakker and some men who had travelled from Breukelen to take care of the luggage. All were made welcome, as was Annie the maid whose reunion with Sarah was particularly poignant. The travel arrangements had proceeded well and the voyage itself had been on surprisingly calm seas. Coaches David had made available brought the party and the baggage to Downsland.

The Rev Paul Farhoe is not overjoyed at the prospect of marrying Clara and Philip and he has worked hard on their redemption, a process in which the couple displayed an appreciable lack of devotion and commitment. Seeking forgiveness for something they would continue to do, right up to the wedding day, did not sit comfortably with the priest's views of righteousness, and Farhoe prayed constantly for their salvation.

That he was marrying them at all was simply down to the fact Jaunton was a revered physician and that Farhoe might need his professional services at some time. There was also the matter of Clara's sizeable donation to church funds from her late mother's estate, and that helped ease the priest's conscience. So Clara and Philip continued to live together prior to the wedding and did so, not with God's blessing, they were told, but in the hope they would repent afterwards.

She had given the rest of her money to her grateful betrothed. Their new home in Charing was ready and she had selected those she wished to work for them. They would not make much money from the sale of Clara's house which was little more than a cramped tumbledown premises, and the proceeds would have to be divided between siblings. This did not apply to the money Mr Evershen had obtained from Grayan as that was hidden away, its existence known only to Clara.

It was widely expected, and by a larger audience than just the parish priest, that the wrath of God would be hurled down on the pair in time.

Earlier, while his brother recovered upstairs at Downsland, David met with Judith Pearland. She had come to the Hall to reveal her concerns about Henry Barrenbridge knowing she would be discrediting a renowned physician and a close personal friend of the Master.

First she had seen Sarah and examined her fully concluding there were no health problems.

"I think Sarah that your pains may stem from recent events in your life. They are the sort of pains we all get when faced with unpleasant situations, and the feelings can be worse when it is our family involved, just as it would be with anyone you loved."

"I have been told I may be in love with a man, I know not who, and that I am hurting for him in some way."

Judith suppressed a grin that was in danger of escaping.

"Sarah, I would be more inclined to think about what has occurred in your family unless, of course, you have a secret love, a man you have never spoken of." She sounded mischievous, something not lost on Sarah who blushed a deep crimson.

"I have no secret love......."

"Oh dear Sarah, your face gives you away my dearest one. You *are* in love!"

"I have no idea who it can be."

"Methinks you have a very good idea, but keep your secret, I shall delve no further."

She smiled in such a delightfully warm manner that Sarah embraced her and laughed with the joy of it all.

Judith's next meeting was more serious in nature. Fortunately David Grayan was in good humour for three reasons. Firstly his brother had recovered, secondly Dr Pearland had been largely responsible and thirdly Ralph had emerged a changed man, and it was the latter he was most interested in to begin with.

"Sir he was often in fevered delirium, making terrible sounds, but he also mumbled and cried out about various matters while he was in that poor state. When he had recovered he was quite embarrassed that I had listened to his ramblings. He was already shocked that he'd been attended by a woman, as he'd been bluntly informed by Miss Brankly," Grayan smiled at the thought, "and now I was able to tell him what he'd said while seriously ill.

"I encouraged him to speak and gradually the whole story emerged and we were able to talk together and try and overcome his loathing. He blamed you for hastening your mother's death, as you know, and then for your father's demise. I reminded him that, as you were disowned, he inherited a great deal including status, enormous wealth, the family seat and much else besides.

"If you hadn't been disinherited he would've seen a fraction. I think that proved a sobering consideration sir, one he'd managed to overlook in his developing hatred for you. He loves Hester and was violently jealous of the relationship between you two. In truth he had no intention of depriving the boys of their mother. On the contrary he wanted them all to live with his family simply because he loves them so. I understand sir that Mr Handlen beat your sister viciously and that when your brother learned that he wanted to kill him.

"Love for his sister sir. And finally I discovered that it was jealousy of another kind that drove him into blind rages. He envies all you have achieved sir. He wishes he could be more like you, be more successful in business and be respected by all

266

around him. And I say this with some caution sir, but I think he envied you marrying for love, even at so great a cost, and he was jealous of the marriage you had.

"We talked about all these things sir, and I will only repeat them to you, never anywhere else. And slowly he came to acknowledge the folly of all this envy, especially when he recalled that he has shared a loving marriage with his own wife. He did not want to marry her, anymore than you wanted to marry Lady Fitzgower he told me it was. But he did as he was told and after they were wed love grew and now he is ashamed about the way he has treated Mrs Grayan in the meantime.

"I assured him that he and his family would always be welcome here with you and Mrs Handlen. I am sorry I took that upon myself for it was not my place to do so."

Grayan laughed out loud.

"Excellent Dr Pearland. And of course you are right. No, I am pleased you have extended such an invitation of my behalf."

"One other matter sir. I learned that he sent Mr Handlen abroad and advised him he would have him killed if he set foot in England again. I do not believe he meant it sir, but I am not sure."

This time they both laughed.

"Thank you for what you have done Dr Pearland. I can never thank you enough. Never. But you will always have my gratitude for returning Ralph to good health and to me as my true brother. Now, do please tell me about the issue that brought you here."

Judith seized the moment and felt strong enough to do it. She explained fearlessly about the two surgeries that had gone wrong, about Henry Barrenbridge's errors and his rages, and how the two patients died. She told him about her position and how Dr Jaunton had used that and his knowledge of Barrenbridge's failings to obtain what was effectively a partnership in the practice that also meant there was no spare money for another doctor to be appointed when she left.

She sat back to await her fate. It was several minutes before David spoke. He was busy recalling the unnecessary loss of Sarah's father and Henry's complicity in the cover-up that followed.

"Thank you for telling me all this. I obviously had no idea. I know what it must mean to you coming here to speak thus, an act of some bravery, but bravery of the heart, bravery of the soul, bravery of the conscience, and I applaud you for it. As you are aware your sex is irrelevant to me in this respect. You sit before me as a physician and one placed in a most astonishing and frustrating position.

"I will speak with Dr Barrenbridge urgently. We are old friends as you know and he will tell me the truth which I do not doubt will not be at odds with what you have said to me. Thank you again. You have done the right thing, be assured of that. I owe you a great deal already Dr Pearland and I will give you whatever support you need in life, be certain of that."

"I ask for nothing sir. I do not know where life may take me now and until I know that I have no need of support."

"I understand, but please acknowledge that you realise my offer has a practical value and is not alone a reward. My late wife thought highly of you and so do I. I want to see you make a great success of your life, not let so much talent slip through your fingers to be lost forever. By God I will not let it happen, d'you hear?"

She took the comment in the light-hearted way in which it was delivered.

"Thank you sir, that is most reassuring. I have never sought reward, never sought riches or status, and possess a simple desire to help people. I found a haven for my beliefs in nursing and then, thanks to your wife, as a doctor. Perhaps now my desire can locate another course to pursue with the same outcome, helping people."

"From what I hear you have made a good start, not just with my brother but with Mrs Brankly and the girl she employed, as well as with Clara Evershen. It is not your fault Clara fell away from a brighter future. She abandoned a good man in Robert Broxford and may live to regret her choice. But *you* do have a future and you *can* help people."

It was something for her to think on, something for her to grasp.

***

Barrenbridge confessed at once. The whole story.

"Henry, how good is Dr Jaunton?"

"Excellent. Better than me at that age. And better than me now it would seem."

"Henry, you have done many great works in your life and I will be forever grateful for what you have done for me here in Kent. But perhaps it is time for you to retire."

The physician had been looking down as if in shame and now his head sunk further.

"You are still revered here and I will not damage your reputation. There is no reason why you could not lend a hand from time to time, but I think it has become far too much of a burden running the hospital. You will be loved by the people as much in retirement as in your work, especially if you are to be occasionally found treating the sick, just as now.

"I will give you a handsome pension, a property of your own, and I insist upon doing it Henry. You are a very dear friend and I will not turn my back on you. I will appoint Dr Jaunton to run the hospital and he can in turn appoint two new physicians and I will personally oversee the operation, at least for the time being. I want Dr Pearland, as I shall always call her, to have a role in this and be based at the practice, but will tell you more at a later time. It is not for now.

"Rest assured Dr Jaunton will understand me very clearly, very clearly indeed, and he can jolly well work with Dr Pearland or be gone. I do not expect her to work as a doctor although her assistance is, I believe, to be valued in that respect. Philip Jaunton can live with his hussy in Charing where she will be out of harm's way, and he can work here, an excellent arrangement, don't you agree?" Henry nodded once.

"And you my dear friend can live in peace and security and find contentment, still forever Westlingstead's wonderful doctor. Do not refuse me, man. Besides, I believe there is a lady you admire." Henry appeared shocked. "Now you will have the means to offer your hand."

"H-h-h-h-how do you know that David?"

"I am the Master of Downsland. I know more than most people realise. Now, what say you?"

David urged his friend with a cheerful glance that reflected the humour in his remark about his knowledge of Henry's attachment.

"Yes. It has to be yes. Of course it must be. But can you tame Philip?"

"It will be take my offer or leave. In the case of the latter I will attempt to buy his silence, but I do not think an ambitious young man like that will lose the chance of a great opportunity, do you?"

Henry concurred and at last managed a wan smile.

"Come, let us drink my dear friend. This is not the end. Let us drink to a future full of promise and enjoyment."

In another part of the Hall Sarah, Esther and Annie were discussing other issues relating to the future. Sarah was constantly consulted about the Master's matrimonial plans but he certainly had not mentioned them to her! Even Sarah was not brave enough to ask him. She did wonder why he had said nothing.

He had returned from Dover full of happiness, so it seemed at the time, but perhaps the business with his brother and his sister's arrival had pushed Lily Cowans out of immediate consideration.

"When he is ready he will tell us." Sarah declared.

"Yes, but it will be Miss Cowans, won't it?" asked an eager Esther.

"Miss Cowans will make him a good wife and we will all benefit, but it is not for us to speculate. It is always possible she rejected him."

"Oh you tease us Sarah! They were made for each other, and you think her a very special lady."

"Indeed I do, but for the Master, as we all know, love is all important and he will not marry for convenience or simply to please us maids."

They giggled and then Annie set off on some task she was due to complete.

"Talking of love Esther, how are things with you and Robert?"

"I console him, but all he wishes to speak about is his love for Clara. It leaves me with an ache in my stomach, it really does."

"My advice is to talk of love in a general fashion Esther. Relate it to the beauty of the countryside, of which we are blessed with fine examples here in Kent. Relate it to the sunshine and the spring and the flowers, all the nice things that we enjoy."

"Sarah, you are so clever and say such marvellous things. I only wish I could think like that, but I will try with Robert. I love him so much."

"Good, let that love fill your words and you will find it easy. I suggest this. I will find a brief poem in the library which you can learn by heart. Recite it when you have a moment with him, but do not look directly at him, speak the words into the air."

Esther was agog with awe.

"Oh Sarah, would you really? What an idea. Yes, I shall do it."

The two parted to set about their duties, Sarah pondering Esther's aching stomach.

"If love is so painful," she queried aloud as she walked along a corridor, "why do people bother with it?"

**

David did not waste time with Philip Jaunton. Rather than reveal Judith Pearland's submission he simply referred to Henry Barrenbridge's confession and put his new scheme to the young doctor.

"You can live in Charing in your fine house with a wife to show to the cream of society, an arrangement that will bring countless invitations you may be sure. You will receive remuneration well in excess of your present income that will enable you to live to the standards you both aspire to. You will become part of a fawning society that I am certain you yearn to join.

"Your professional future will be secured. It will be your practice. However, I will watch over you with the eyes of a hawk for some time to come. You may appoint assistant physicians but you will consult with me and I will have the final word.

"Dr Pearland will be attached to the hospital where she will be allowed to practice. But do not fret doctor, she will not interfere with your work, nor will you with hers. I will explain at

271

a later time should Dr Pearland wish to take advantage of my offer, but for now no more need be said.

"You professed to admire me and my beliefs and you have demonstrated that not all my values are to your liking. You will change your attitude to women whether you like it or not, and you will afford Dr Pearland due respect in all matters at all times. Women are our equals doctor, and if you have a high regard for my philosophies you will adopt that vision was well as any others you do not agree with.

"Dr Barrenbridge will be treated with the utmost respect. You will keep me informed of all that is going on at the hospital, and I will have Miss Brankly check your accounts." Jaunton's eyebrows rose to an alarming level at the prospect of a young maid being thus employed.

"The world is yours to seize with both hands. You can make your name, and your path in society is assured. However, there is no negotiation to be had in this venture. You have my conditions and must accept them. Please be certain I will offer you the very deference and esteem I wish you to give to others as I already accept you, on Dr Barrenbridge's recommendation, as a very fine physician and surgeon.

"Finally, as you will now be treating your nurses as your equals and not as servants, please grant Miss Gandling an increased income and a title befitting her role. She will wish for neither, but I wish it for her, and you may tell her that."

Philip Jaunton had the appearance of a man who had just been ruined, not elevated to a higher station, and he remained speechless for two or three minutes.

"Aye or nay sir?" enquired Grayan.

"Y-y-y-y-yes. Yes sir," came the faltering reply.

Within seconds David had left the hospital where the two had met leaving Dr Jaunton in a bewildered and shaken state, but awake enough to realise he could not refuse such a generous offer. He would have to live with Grayan's teachings, as he had always referred to them.

Grayan rode back to Downsland, saddened by his own hypocrisy yet believing he had done the right thing for the practice and helped his friend into the bargain. He had made an important decision about Sarah, one that must ease his aching conscience.

**

May came with its share of rain but this particular evening the weather improved as the day faded.

Judith had spent the entire day working at the forge with both father and son, but now, with business concluded, Mr Winchell retired to his cottage and the comfort of his favourite chair and the company of his wife. Abe and Judith, tired but contented with their labours, made their way to the Green Man and relaxed in a corner away from the few other drinkers.

"It has taken you a long time Abe to learn your skills and I am in wonderment thinking about that and how well you apply them....."

"That makes two of us then Judith. I am awestruck thinking how you use the skills you have, and that's not just medicine is it? Now you're good talking and can make people better just by talking with them. Look what you done. There's Mrs Brankly, Lydia and now I hear tell the Master's brother. You have God-given powers. It's like the laying on of hands, y'make people well again with words."

"That's almost blasphemy Abe. Laying on of hands, God-given powers? Not me."

"Mebbe not, but you's very good with words, allow me that. And them words got healing powers."

"Words? I just talk with my heart and maybe others should try that more often."

"Them words Judith, them words has the power of medicine, don't y'see what I'm saying. You don't always need medicine or surgery or anything like. When it's right to do so you give your patients words instead, and it works."

"Didn't work for Clara did it?"

"It worked all the time she needed help but when she stopped needing it she became rotten again. It's like someone who stops taking medicine and then feels ill."

"I think it's you who has a way with words Abe."

"Well, I wish I had the words to say I love you Judith. Cos then I'd say will you marry me too."

He drank off his ale, wiped his mouth with his sleeve, and stared around aimlessly awaiting whatever remark she might launch at him, and knowing he would not like it.

"Let me settle to something Abe and then we'll see. I am a ship without a harbour and when I am safely moored I will know where I stand with you."

"There you are, words agin. Well, I'm a safe harbour and I'm waiting with a spare mooring just for the finest vessel that ever sailed, the Judith Pearland."

"Abe! You have words too! And they are just the loveliest words, believe me. And you have strengthened my resolve to settle my life. I must answer my calling in one way or another and then I shall seek the shelter of your anchorage you may be sure. I am summoned to Downsland in the morning and it may lead to the very solution I yearn for. So we shall see."

And they refilled their tankards and drank each others' health and happiness and revelled in the merriment that was overtaking them.

Afterwards, as he walked her home, she pushed him into the shadows and kissed him before he knew what was upon him. He felt his heart explode with love, just like before. If this was paradise it was all he could wish for.

And he found he did not mind Judith taking control of their pleasures one little bit.

Women, he decided as he lay his weary head down to sleep that night, are truly our equals and she can lead me wherever she wants and I will meekly follow! Just remember this Abraham Winchell; don't try and understand her!

***

They sat quietly together as David Grayan spoke.

He'd explained about the changes at the hospital, what was to be expected of her there, and also the role he hoped Judith would take up if she felt she could adapt it to suit herself.

Then he came to the matter he'd least looked forward to.

"Sarah, I am very sorry but I now have something to say which may distress you, and may leave you thinking the worst of me.

"As you know Dr Barrenbridge was here and we discussed a number of issues arriving at the scheme I have elucidated. He related to me an incident that concerns you and your family and which has sore troubled him." He saw Sarah stiffen and her face become serious.

"Dr Barrenbridge was not available when your father was taken ill. Dr Parry-Barnard carried out surgery but could not save your father. When he spoke to Parry-Barnard afterwards Dr Barrenbridge was not convinced he had acted correctly and had he operated in a different way your father might, *might* have been saved. There is no guarantee and Barrenbridge was not there, so it may be that the other doctor was right in his diagnosis and treatment, we will never know.

"I have given this great thought and understand the pain it will bring but I did not feel it was right to have this intelligence and not speak of it. I would not want there to be any secrets between us. I am so sorry if I have done wrong here."

She answered at once, but without changing her expression, although he could see tears in her doleful eyes.

"Thank you sir. It was the right thing to do, to speak thus, and I am grateful. We believed at the time Dr Parry-Barnard did all he could and we had the utmost faith in him, having found him to be an excellent physician. In the circumstances I think it would be foolhardy to imagine it could have been different. Dr Parry-Barnard worked furiously to save my father and I do not want to believe he acted incorrectly. He kept my mother informed, either in person or through a nurse, about everything he did. I am happy he did his best, but I thank you for sharing your knowledge as it cannot have been easy for you sir."

Her head bowed and her shoulders shook and he knew the tears were falling. Instinctively he moved to her side and put an arm around her whereupon she wept bitterly and turned into him to nestle her face to his bosom. He placed his other arm around her and hugged her.

Gradually the tempest eased and she collected herself, moved from his embrace and wiped away her tears and dried her face. He went to the table and poured some wine.

"Here, take this Sarah." She drank without hesitation.

"Thank you sir. It is alright now. I cried for my father, not for what you told me. I will be fine now, thank you sir."

In a little she left the room and as she did so she noticed the smallest tear on his own cheek. The Master was crying. Slowly she closed the door behind her and left him, wishing she could stay and hug him as he had cradled her, but it was not her place.

***

May came with a variety of news and events.

People in north Kent learned that James Parry-Barnard had gone to the gallows for the murder of a fellow doctor, and they were shocked and dismayed, many believing they owed their lives or at least their good health to the physician. It stunned those at the hospital.

Philip Jaunton and Clara Evershen were married and went to live in Charing where the new Mrs Jaunton lost no time in upsetting her staff with her attitude and strictness; but villagers in Westlingstead soon forgot about her, and decided they wanted the service of the hospital's new head rather more than they wanted to condemn him.

The wedding was attended by his parents and two friends from Leicester, and by Judith and Sarah, both feeling it was right and proper to be there in support of the bride as a friend. Clara repaid this kindness by largely ignoring them.

Esther Hammond has learned a short poem Sarah found for her, and recites it privately as often as possible lest she should forget any part of it, but has yet to find a suitable opportunity to use it with Robert.

Lily Cowans walks her beloved cliffs and has more than once visited neighbouring Folkestone where she joins two friends for the pleasure of their company. It is her world and she is at ease in it. How she enjoyed David's visit and she reflects upon it with much happiness, for at its close he spoke with her on the subject closest to her heart, spoke with honesty and openness, and gave her the future she yearned for.

She had been pleased she had pressed him for at long last the position was clear and she was not to be left high and dry, hoping, dreaming, wanting. Roger Culteney had kept her at armslength. By contrast David Grayan had proved himself a man of honour and commitment who would keep his word. He had just needed a gentle prod!

Ginny and Mark go riding around the estate together, with Grayan's permission, but it has taken her some while to learn how to stay in the saddle! On one occasion she became entangled in an overhanging branch and was deposited seat first on the ground.

Mark dismounted and rushed to her aid.

"Are you hurt my love?" he asked the grinning Ginny.

"A little sore I dare say Mark."

"Here, let me rub it better."

"Not where I am hurt!"

"Nobody would mind and nobody would see."

"I would see and I might mind."

"Wager you wouldn't!"

Philip Jaunton has approached other young physicians he knows with a view to appointing assistants but with one exception they have no desire to be part of the David Grayan revolution. David Gordon studied with Jaunton and he is reluctant at first but at least willing to visit Westlingstead.

A tall Scotsman from Annan in the south-west of the country, a redhead with a matching fiery beard, he has an athletic build and is a renowned sportsman. He owns a monstrous laugh which has quite frightened some ladies until they become accustomed to it.

Hester has settled in most comfortably and been overjoyed with a visit from her other sister and her family. The Grayan family is at last reunited. David wept private tears during the visit, tears of ecstasy. He has exchanged a number of letters with Lily Cowans, a fact noted by Sarah and other staff who eagerly await notice of his betrothal.

Judith spent an afternoon walking the estate with Sarah, two kindred spirits, discussing the opportunity David had placed before her before deciding, with her friend's agreement, she should accept and set to at once.

Grace Gandling has been embarrassed to be appointed Manager of Nursing at the hospital, accepted the title with great reluctance and rejecting the increased income offered. She hated her title and took it simply because Grayan insisted, nevertheless making her feelings known to him and rather bluntly so. He did not mind. He was annoyed she would accept no further money but conceded that point.

He stressed to her that his primary desire was to keep Jaunton in his place and to ensure she had a proper say in the running of the practice. She understood that and appreciated it. Soon the new Manager of Nursing was going to have a different matter to contend with, and one that might change her life.

Chapter Twenty Three

Words alone cannot heal.

But Judith Pearland had learned that words can provide a medium for healing where medicine has no place. Words can help heal a mind that is ravaged or troubled, words can bring people together, words can end animosity, anger and bitterness.

Not words alone. Judith had a natural proficiency for using the right words in the right way, and for using the skills of listening and analysing to great effect, and David Grayan wanted her to put these gifts to good employment. She was caring by nature and had all the time in the world for someone in distress.

She could debate matters in a clear and well-reasoned way that enabled the person to understand their problem better, and by talking lead them to their own decision and to overcome their troubles. It was a talent that could be used to great effect as Grayan knew full well, and it would fulfil her desire, her calling, to help others.

So without further ado Judith accepted his offer of a paid position based at the hospital, but was not yet sure how she could develop this new idea, this new fantasy as she described it. But she was willing to try. It would be up to her to work as she saw fit.

News spread with alacrity in north Kent. Her achievements were almost legendary and although her success had been confined to the village and Downsland knowledge of these deeds soaked into the surrounding countryside and towns where it was greeted with immense interest.

By chance it took only two days before a man and a woman arrived at the hospital asking for her.

The wife had strayed and the husband had beaten her, whereupon they had found life together difficult to sustain and yet they both yearned for the gratification of their marriage that had existed prior to her dalliance. There was aggression on both sides: the husband was unforgiving, his wife had been ungodly and broken her marriage vows, and for her part she accepted her sin but believed she would be punished by the Almighty, not beaten to the ground by the man.

By the end of their time with Judith the pair were hugging and weeping and ready to repair their damaged marriage. The husband openly forgave his wife and apologised for the beating. The wife was more circumspect and successfully begged his forgiveness without offering any herself for his act of retribution.

"Then I suggest," said Judith, "your husband allows you to beat him, without resistance, and that should settle the score."

After a moment's silence the couple fell into each others' arms amidst great mirth, and Judith knew she had won. It wasn't quite the sort of problem she'd wanted to have to attend to but she was pleased she'd been able to help.

In close-knit communities news of this particular success spread swiftly and then engulfed the land beyond, and Judith's new calling was established. The couple hadn't been quite what she envisaged but they were a start.

And she became known as the woman who can heal with words.

As Sarah was to write in her diary a few weeks later:

'People have been coming from near and far seeking the woman with almost mystical powers. Sadly Judith cannot help them all but as she can use her medicinal knowledge as well she seems to be often curing the sick in body and mind alike, much I might say to Dr Jaunton's chagrin! But I know he now admires her and has a better understanding of what she is doing. In truth, he is much in awe. It is probably something akin to a miracle but he even accepts that the work does have a role to play in medicine, so that is an achievement in itself.'

At the hospital Grace Gandling was in for a shock.

In fact she screamed. She had never seen a man in a kilt before and the sight of David Gordon before her nearly produced a swoon. Regaining her senses she escorted the amused visitor to Dr Jaunton and retired to the ward bemused, baffled and full of disbelief.

"The man's wearing a skirt, did you ever!" she exclaimed to one of the nurses.

Jaunton welcomed his friend and explained that Grayan would want to meet him.

"I canna understand a man who thinks a woman his equal," Gordon admitted, "but I would be proud to work with you Philip and I would not be here if I did not. How do I influence this weird man?"

"Only with the truth David. Tell him you do not agree with his vision. He will question you but will accept your right to your opinion."

"But how will he see my opinion?"

"As different to his, that is all. But he may try to persuade you...."

"He will not succeed."

"No, but you will have a better understanding of each other. Mutual respect David, that's all important as I have learned from David Grayan. I would not be in this position without that."

"Hmmm. Very well, let's see this man of revolution. Hmmm ... only a mad Englishman could think as he does. By the by, I hope I have not distressed that nurse."

"Manager of Nursing, David." There was no disguising his contempt and sarcasm.

"Och, the woman needs a man Philip, not a fancy title."

"No, she needs your respect. I could not manage without her, and her title is bestowed by Grayan himself, so exercise care there my friend."

"Hmph. I hae ne'er heard such nonsense Philip and I think you have taken leave of y'senses!"

In truth, Grayan delighted in the man's forthright honesty. Gordon had no qualms about saying his piece, and displayed no apparent deference to the Master of Downsland beyond affording him basic courtesy. There was no pretence. Respect, yes, but that was as far as it went. Forewarned by Jaunton the Scotsman behaved and spoke in a manner Grayan appreciated, and debated the issues freely and fearlessly.

"I hae to say sir, that I seemed to have frightened that lassie at the hospital by arriving in ma kilt. I think she is called a manager of nurses, aye? A peculiar title and one I have not come across yet." Jaunton lowered his face to hide his smile.

"Dr Gordon, that is what Grace Gandling is and you will call her that if you are appointed. You will find yourself very grateful for her as she is a very experienced and capable medical woman whom you may rely on. Isn't that right Dr Jaunton?"

"Oh yes sir, very much so sir."

"You may not agree with my philosophies Dr Gordon, but if you work here you will abide by them and not show any contempt for them."

"Aye, of course sir. I understand that."

"And you will work with and respect Dr Pearland. I am certain Dr Jaunton has explained her role in my hospital and in the wider community."

"Aye he has sir. She heals with words I understand, heals matters that medicine cannot."

"That is about it doctor. But she has extensive powers and has proved a notable success. She is a pioneer of a different type of medicine and you may find her invaluable, apart from the fact she is, in my eyes, a physician who saved my brother's life and the lives of others. Dr Pearland will answer your call for help at any time I assure you, and not let you down."

Gordon pondered this. A woman called a manager of nurses and an unqualified female quack with strange abilities that might be said to border on witchcraft. He wasn't sure he wanted the post.

But later, back at the hospital, he decided that spending time at Westlingstead could be an interesting, varied and revealing affair, well worth his while. Certainly amusing, and what tales he would have to tell wherever he went from there!

***

"Just some money and some food sister. All I ask."

Catherine Brankly had an unexpected and unwelcome visitor. Her brother Edmund Forness, unshaven, unkempt, his clothes reeking and covered with all manner of muck and filth, looked as desperate as he appeared.

"You brute," she cried, "you set my own daughter against me having tried to have your way with her, your own sister's girl. You are evil. Now be gone and never return. I disown you. Get you hence, do you hear me?"

"Give me what I want or I'll take it."

282

"Get out now or I'll shout for help."

He started towards her and went to place his hand over her mouth but she moved away sharply and let out a piercing scream. Wary, he turned and fled leaving Catherine to fall into a heap on the floor, overcome with the terror she had just faced. So he was back. Perhaps he'd never gone far, so would he now be close by ready to haunt her or, worse still, to steal from her. And he'd shown he was prepared to attack her. She shook with such thoughts.

She needed someone's help but who to call upon? She must tell Sarah, maybe Dr Pearland also. They would have the answer.

Mrs Brankly did not mention him to Lydia who came later to assist her, or to another daughter who called upon her that morning. But when she had the chance she walked over to the hospital and found Judith and gave her the account of Edmund's visit.

"Unfortunately Catherine our village Constable appears to be an excellent cobbler but a less effective upholder of the law. But with your permission I will ask Abe Winchell's opinion as he has many friends around these parts and it may be possible for your brother to be well advised to stay away. We could do with someone like Dr Jaunton's new assistant as our Constable."

"Oh has one been appointed?"

"Indeed. A Scotsman who towers above us and possesses a shock of red hair and would put the fear of God into Edmund!"

"A man from Scotland? Well, well, well. Does he speak English?" Judith laughed.

"Yes he does and very well too. He made Grace scream when he first arrived for she had never seen a man in a kilt before."

"Goodness me. A kilt you say? And does he meet with Mr Grayan's approval?"

"Very much so, I am told. He oversaw the appointment."

During the day Judith put the problem of Edmund Forness to Abe and he promised to keep an eye out, suggesting that Catherine speak with John Willows who lives nearly opposite as he was certain the man would be pleased to watch for her. Willows knew Forness and, so Abe said, did not like him. Judith decided she would pay John a call first, to test the lie of the land, rather than subject Catherine to a possible rejection.

She needn't have worried. John was delighted at the prospect and said he'd be available day and night. After passing on the good news to Catherine she returned to the hospital to find Grace with a most wicked look of amusement on her face, a very rare sighting indeed for the woman was usually serious and often unhappy with the doctors.

"I have to tell you Judith I am quite taken by Dr Gordon. He has praised me for my work today, and remarked on the high standards of the practice, which he presumes are due to my guiding hand, which they are of course, and he has been impressed, so he says, with my knowledge.

And then he said, if I have this correctly, that I am a very bonny wee lass."

"Grace, you have an admirer...."

"Only with regard to my work ...."

"Not so my dear. I have seen the gleam in his eyes when he watches you....."

"Well, that's enough of that! Did you ever. He can take his gleam right away from me."

They shared laughter. Judith had never seen Grace so gay and carefree, so it had to be assumed Dr Gordon was at the root of it, and that deep inside Grace had actually welcomed his attentions!

Catherine Brankly went over to ask John Willows for his help and stayed nearly an hour. They talked continuously and easily, finding much common ground, plenty to amuse them, and enjoying the chance to discuss each others' lives. He had been reluctant to call upon her lest tongues should wag but had always wanted to offer his services in whatever capacity they might be required.

The upshot of this meeting was that John returned with Catherine to the farm and spent much of the remainder of the day working there. She learned that he had worked for a Faversham brewer, and otherwise carried out various odd-jobs around the village for whoever might require them. It was obvious he had no great wealth but then neither did she.

He'd never married but she discovered he had been let down, almost at the altar, by a girl he'd known from childhood. She was amazed that they had lived opposite each other all these years and never really been friends, being no more than passing acquaintances, neighbours who would pass the time of day with you in general matters and nothing more.

However, discord was about to appear in Westlingstead and with it peaceable friendships were to be tested.

***

The Rev Paul Farhoe had been considering Judith Pearland's rise to prominence and declared her to be a blasphemous person as she was pretending to be able to perform miracles, and that the concept of healing with words alone was an affront to God and to the saints who had possessed such powers. Miracles were acts of the Good Lord, he proclaimed, and to try and claim to be the medium by which they might be brought about was heresy.

He stopped just short of calling her a witch, leaving it to like-minded people to draw such conclusions without openly suggesting it himself.

One sermon was all it required to rouse the bigots and those with deeply entrenched views and within days there had been arguments in the street, heated debate within households, and a brawl outside the Green Man, although that may have been due the quantity of ale consumed rather than a deterioration of serious discussion.

Suddenly Judith's new found life was in danger of being extinguished just as it was about to blossom. Something had to be done and the situation was largely resolved by intervention from an unlikely source.

Sarah had sat open-mouthed listening to the sermon and at one point had taken Judith's hand to offer support and strength, a gesture much appreciated but little needed as the doctor's reaction was more one of disbelief and scorn. At the first opportunity Sarah garrulously reported the issue to Grayan who sat calmly taking it all in while she gabbled away. He knew it would be futile for him to take any action as Farhoe had denounced him as being in league with the devil and intervention would only add weight to the priest's skewed opinions.

Grayan, with the calmness he had displayed throughout, quietly advised Sarah he had no hold over Farhoe but that we would make it clear to the villagers that he did not agree with the implied condemnation, and that they should all remember all the good things Judith had achieved, not least in saving Jed's life and restoring his injured body to full health. She knew it would have to do but it was far from adequate.

The following Sunday the packed church waited as Farhoe made his way to the pulpit but he had barely reached it before Dr Gordon rose to his feet. Gordon, a devout Christian, took Farhoe to task in a brief diatribe that left the priest speechless. Using quotations from the bible Gordon issued forth a well-researched and well-presented monologue in defence of his colleague, appending a list of names of villagers, most there in the church, who had good reason to thank Dr Pearland for her efforts.

At the end, as he sat down, Grace Gandling leaped to her feet applauding and was quickly followed by Jed and Agnes and then most of the congregation. Nearly all walked out of the church at that point, leaving a fuming Farhoe to damn them all with only a few of his own supporters left to hear his response.

Those few thought the priest was right but were still uneasy about his condemnation of Judith, most recalling that she had indeed been of great benefit to their health.

Dr Gordon was suddenly the hero. Of course his actions had been driven in part by his desire in ingratiate himself with Grayan and he knew the Master would be made aware of his stand. Judith did not attend the service, for although God-fearing herself she had found her faith sore tried by Farhoe's outburst a week earlier.

Sarah was looking forward to her next meeting with Grayan, and in her joy had made an important decision. His happiness was so vital to her. All she wanted was his happiness and she knew he would find it with Miss Cowans, and she would be pleased to serve them both.

Disappointed he had not yet made an announcement she thought she would raise it with him. It wasn't her place, but she would take the chance. In the event she found it far from easy.

Chapter Twenty Four

Esther Hammond had taken to pining.

She longed for a love she couldn't have, just as the object of her affections yearned for one *he* couldn't have. Unfortunately it was starting to affect her work and she not on her best behaviour either, so it was only a question of time before Mrs Forbes was forced to issue a stern reprimand and a warning. That night poor Esther cried herself to sleep. The following day she resolved she would recite her poem to Robert come what may.

In the event her memory failed her and in her nervous state she muddled the words, and finally gave up the struggle and sat looking across the rolling fields of the estate where she had pinned her gaze, on Sarah's advice, from the outset.

Suddenly she was aware of laughter and turned to Robert who was perched on a log just feet away. He was guffawing fit to burst and she felt so wretched, so lost, so humiliated.

Finding his breath and the power of speech Robert spoke.

"Esther, Esther, did you learn that poem just for me? Esther, that is so romantic and I am so deeply touched, I truly am. But it was such a tonic. I haven't laughed so much in weeks."

Hurt and embarrassed she jumped up and ran back to the Hall in tears and ran straight into the arms of a startled Mrs Forbes.

"Goodness me Esther, whatever is wrong?"

"He laughed at me, laughed at my love, mocked my stupidity and I hate him," she squealed at the top of her voice before pulling away and dashing to her room.

Ah, thought Eleanor Forbes, young love come to grief, yet I doubt that is the case. Sarah is alone in the Master's study and I will send her along. The sooner this is sorted out the better. I have never dismissed anyone and do not intend to start now. That girl must pull herself together. First I shall find Sarah and then I shall find Robert Broxford, and he will know I have found him!

While the Housekeeper went with determination and purpose in pursuit of Sarah and Robert there had been a development of a rather different kind elsewhere.

In the village there came about an occurrence that some described as an act of God, but no doubt they were being facetious and revelling in the humour the matter brought them. Paul Farhoe was climbing out of the bath-tub when a bee landed on his rear and stung him.

He could do little about it, not being able to see the wound except in the looking glass, and was unable to locate the sting itself. In some agony he knew his only possible course of action was to visit the hospital and hope someone other than Jaunton, Gordon and Pearland was free to attend him, but it was a vain hope. Apart from anything else Grace deliberately fetched David Gordon determined to add to the priest's discomfort.

Farhoe found himself faced by his immediate nemesis who ordered him to lie on the bed so the wound could be seen. Gordon asked Grace to bring in two of the young nurses on the premise that it was part of their training but primarily to add to Farhoe's embarrassment. He made a long job of the examination and treatment, tutting and repeating 'Oh dear' several times to add to the drama, then applying a lotion that he knew would sting a hundred times worse than the bee's incision. Farhoe yelped. Everyone else was suppressing laughter.

"It's a gid job Father your profession requires more kneeling than sitting!"

In time the patient was permitted to dress and leave and at long last laughter echoed throughout the hospital. Now alone with Grace, who was weeping tears of happiness, David Gordon went to her and bodily lifted her onto a footstool so that their faces were the same height and inches apart. She showed no signs of distress, just surprise.

"I wan' tae kiss ye lass. Do ye wan' tae be kissing the man from Annan, I ask meself?" There was no holding Grace back.

"Yes doctor, or as I believe you would say .... Aye!"

Grace had never kissed anyone, never mind one with a full beard, and after the initial passion they dissolved into fits of giggles as she found herself with a mouth full of hair. It was only a matter of minutes before they perfected the art and this time their lips met in a sustained and intoxicating kiss that left them both gasping for breath.

"Right, Manager of Nursing, back to work," he commanded in humorous vein as they regained their senses.

"Aye doctor, aye." She replied in a mischievous lilt, imitating his Scottish pronunciation precisely, and taking his hand as he helped her down to the floor. Matters were rather more serious back at the Hall where Robert Broxford faced an irate Eleanor Forbes.

"For heaven's sake man. You've lost Clara. Take Esther to one side and tell her the truth either way, and then we can all get some work done. Love is interfering with the efficient running of this house and I will not have it. You suffer perpetual sadness Robert Broxford, but you're a young man and you're not the first to be disappointed by a girl, so decide what you want and deal with it.

"You can't have Clara, she's married to someone else. For pities sake stop wallowing in the loss many a boy has had to come to terms with and become a man, and do the decent thing and let Esther know where she stands. I cannot abide all this nonsense in this house, do you hear me Robert Broxford?"

He heard and understood, and returned to his duties chastened but quite prepared for what he had to do next.

In Westlingstead the story of Father Farhoe's plight spread at a pace producing much merriment and absolutely no sympathy whatsoever, save from a handful of devout souls who would support their parish priest through thick and thin, and had done so in the case of Dr Pearland's denunciation.

At the Green Man a would-be poet devised a simple poem in which the name Farhoe was rhymed with a similar word in an ode that was as disgusting as it was funny.

And in the church, in a most un-Christian way, Paul Farhoe was plotting revenge, and doing so while kneeling of course.

Sarah placated Esther but her mind was elsewhere. She had her meeting David Grayan anon and was now feeling a little more afraid of asking him about Miss Cowans. But it had to be done.

"Esther, you will be dismissed if you are not careful." She tried to sound reasonable and firm but realised her friend was becoming a lost cause.

"I do not care. He laughed at me Sarah ....."

"Yes I know, but perhaps if he so rarely laughs he will have appreciated your efforts, for surely you must've made him happy in that moment. And I will not let you be dismissed. Stop being foolish. Robert is not lost and you may win him yet, and you may have taken a large step in that direction.

"He is so morose, does not laugh, and is so wrapped up in his misfortune I suspect he cannot see the wood for trees. When he ceases to feel sorry for himself he will start to notice you more, and I cannot stress enough if you made him laugh, even if unintentionally, he will thank you for it. As far as I am aware nobody else has achieved that."

Esther calmed, dried her eyes and spoke in a whisper.

"Yes you are right Sarah. And I must not be dismissed."

"You have become part of his sorrow with your sympathy Esther. Cease listening just to his woes and spread some good cheer before him. Cease being miserable with him and be warm and humorous."

Sarah heard the clock chime and realised she was late, so gave Esther a kiss and a hug and dashed to the Master's study, hoping her friend would recover swiftly and not annoy Mrs Forbes any more.

Standing outside the door, she took a very deep breath, knocked and went in to face whatever fate might provide for her, and hoped it wouldn't be her who was dismissed. But she would ask him and trust that he would forgive her and not mind too much.

***

As always they sat opposite sides of the desk.

Sarah apprised him of all relevant business matters insofar as they concerned her duties, developments in Westlingstead and around and about, and also about gossip where it was not malicious or unpleasant and where it might be of interest to him.

He duly gave her thanks and presented her with the additional work he required of her, then sat back as was his habit at the end of these meetings. Looking across the desk he saw a face he had seen a number of times, the face of seriousness and purpose, and he knew Sarah had something of great importance on her mind, a matter she was about to share.

David Grayan had learned so much about Sarah and her expressions over the months that he knew this particular appearance was full of foreboding. She would either inform him about an issue of enormous disquiet or ask him a question that he might have trouble answering.

"Sir ...." He looked into her eyes, bold and deep, and knew it would be the latter.

"Yes Sarah?"

"I wish to ask you a question. I do not wish to make you angry and I do not wish to be dismissed. If you would rather me not ask I shall desist. It is a question no servant should ask her Master for it is a matter no maid should worry herself with."

She hadn't blinked. He realised he was seeing a glorious beauty in that simple face, a beauty that came from within, a beauty he'd acknowledged privately to himself so often before, a beauty he'd come to yearn for. But never before had it shone with such radiance. Never before had it pleaded so desperately for attention yet it did now. He spoke almost in a whisper as he returned her gaze with all the earnestness he could muster.

"You are no servant Sarah, you are a vitally important senior member of my staff. But even if you were not I would want to hear your question. I cannot imagine you ever making me angry and I would never dismiss you for I could not bear to consider a day might dawn when I would never see you again. Speak freely, speak without fear, speak as you wish."

There was a silence broken only by birdsong slipping softly in through the open window. Her face hadn't changed, she still had not blinked, yet he was aware that caution was present, as if she had doubts about proceeding, despite his assurances. Her voice was as quiet as his had been.

"Sir .... it is not my place for all that .... "

"Please ask me your question Sarah, I insist."

Now she looked glum and curled her bottom lip inwards as if trying to silence her mouth. He saw this, widened his eyes and smiled in such a tender manner that she was encouraged.

"Sir .... it has been such a joy for me to serve you, and to serve Miss Cowans during her time here. Bless you sir for appointing me as her maid, she is, if you will permit me to say, a very wonderful lady whom I admire greatly."

The pains were in her stomach and now, in this terrible moment, the moment she must learn the truth, she accepted their meaning and dreaded them worsening.

"Sir .... sir ......" She paused and moistened her lips with the tip of her tongue. "Sir ... are you to be wed to Miss Cowans?"

As she went to speak her question he suddenly knew what it would be, and also knew the real reason she was asking, and it shook him a little. Both were talking in soft whispers.

"Sarah ....." He took a deep breath and saw her face sink in anticipation. "Sarah, no I am not to wed Miss Cowans. I could not take her away from her beloved coast. She adores the hills and cliffs and shore around Dover and would never settle here." Sarah relaxed and the pains lessened and the briefest of smiles of relief appeared.

"But that is not the main reason I am not to marry her Sarah." She immediately looked concerned again. "The truth is that I love another. My heart belongs elsewhere and I must go with my heart. I love the lady beyond words Sarah and she is the only lady I would ever wish to wed."

Sarah's pains intensified to the point where she clutched at her stomach to try and ease them. Without hesitation she blurted out her next question.

"May I know who she is sir?" He saw the pain now etched in her face and answered swiftly.

"Yes Sarah. It is you. I love you with all my heart Sarah. It is you I love, love so deeply and so fully."

Her hand now involuntarily rose to her open mouth and her eyes widened in awe and fear, as if she failed to comprehend what he was saying and was afraid of the true meaning.

"Sir .... you tease me .... pray do not, I beg you."

"I do not tease you over something so serious. Over the months my affection for you has deepened into enduring love, a love so precious I could not lose it. I have hesitated to declare my feelings Sarah for fear of driving you away, but you have presented me with the opportunity to tell you.

"I thought if I declared myself you might leave and I would've ruined your life, a life I know you love here, and I could not do it. But now I am faced with a situation where I must be truthful and open up to you and take the consequences. I do not feel I am worthy of you Sarah, but I offer you all my love and if you can return my feelings it would be with great pride that I would offer you my hand in marriage, and consider it the greatest honour should you accept.

"Stand with me, stand shoulder to shoulder with me, as my wife and as the Mistress of Downsland, for I cannot live without you." His eyes pleaded insatiably, eyes full of hope. She was staring at him in the manner of one who has just seen a ghastly spectre. She was pale, her hands were to her face, and she shook slightly.

"Sir .... I beg you ..... I cannot bear you children. You ask too much of me ...."

"There are my sister's children as you know, and you love them almost as your own Sarah. If you desired to have a family we could take in orphans. What an opportunity that would be for them! To live in a home filled with love, indeed a place to call home, the chance to learn so many things, the chance to have a real future."

She was weeping tears that fell unchecked over her hands and into her lap. Anxiety or joy he didn't know.

"Sir .... sir ...... I must think. You startled me."

"Sarah, I am so sorry. This was what I feared and believe me I had no intention to upset you like this. Please forgive me, I have been so inconsiderate and hurtful..."

"No you have not sir. I love you as you love me but you have been my secret love, my impossible love, my love without a future, my love that must never be spoken of. You have surprised me, that is all and I feel shocked."

He crossed the room and poured a drink which he offered to her.

"Do you require assistance Sarah? I feel as if I have behaved dreadfully and dishonourably..."

"Oh no sir, no sir. No you have not. I am just overcome, that is all." She sipped her drink and then allowed him to escort her to a more comfortable chair.

"I am a servant sir ...."

"No, you are the lady I love and wish to marry. Pray do not reject me out of hand. At least do me the honour to think on my proposal ....."

"Sir I love you greatly, but please allow me to regain my composure. It has been an unexpected shock, that is all."

He sat in another armchair close by and partook of wine as Sarah slowly drank hers. After a few minutes she looked up and saw his enquiring face.

"Sir, it is I who am unworthy. Whoever heard of a maid marrying her Master?"

"Then let us start a new movement, a revolution. People expect it of me! And you must now call me David if you please." A wide grin spread across his face and she knew she loved him and would be his.

"Sir ...... David ..... I don't know, I am so confused, truly I am. Sir, I mean David, I know that I love you but marriage, it would be such a step. Please give me time to reflect on your proposal and what it would mean to me." He nodded.

"I would like to go to my room if you please sir .... David."

"Of course, but come to me at any time if you wish to talk further."

He held out his hand to help her from the chair and as she rose she was seized by her feelings and she almost threw herself at him. He embraced her at once and they kissed furiously, feverishly and with immense passion. As the fire subsided and their lips parted she leaned back slightly.

"Yes David, I love you with all my heart and I will marry you," she whispered, and then their lips met again in delirious ardour.

***

Lily Cowans had wandered across to the Alkham valley, meeting an old friend on the way. This was her life, the life she loved. She didn't need it to be any other way. She didn't need to be married and would not have taken to living away from this most stunning and scenic of countryside, and of course away from her friends.

She was free and that was really the most important thing.

The freedom to come and go as she pleased and to always enjoy her hills and cliffs, her spectacular coast and her wild, wicked dreams of being seduced by a famous smuggler. Of course she knew the harsh realities of smuggling and wanted no part in it, and had no romantic notions allied to those that carried it out, famous or not. She knew Grayan had dabbled although not directly and her own father had benefitted from some excellent brandy in days gone past.

No, she was pleased with her freedom.

David had been the perfect gentleman and yes, she'd have married him if asked, but she might've come to regret it for two reasons, her own desire to remain in Dover with all it meant to her and, of course, his love for Sarah which he simply could not get away from. He went to her with Lily's blessing.

There was no sadness, or if there was Lily was suppressing it. No, in truth she did not need a man, and she would always be a friend for David whose company had been excellent, and that was all there needed to be between them; friendship. She'd waited for the letter that informed her that Sarah has accepted his hand, and had received two prior missives that failed to mention it. Was he having doubts? Finally the letter came and Lily rejoiced for both of them and wrote and told him so. He wrote saying he had gone to Mrs Brankly's to ask her permission and the poor woman was so shocked that she nearly fainted. Lily believed that yes, she would be shocked!

The betrothal was generally received well at Downsland and Westlingstead as well as most of north Kent. There were mumbles of resentment at the Hall and one or two people here and there in the village who were quite bitter about Sarah's success, but on the whole it was welcomed.

Grayan's household was lifted by the news despite half a dozen of the staff being indignant about Sarah's rise to power and resolving to ignore her. But Sarah carried on being Sarah and gradually won them over, especially as the weight of support amongst those employed in the Hall and on the estate was positively in favour. The dissenters risked being ostracised and gave in quite easily.

Paul Farhoe was beside himself with anger and annoyance but had to accept the situation. Grayan was a major benefactor because most of the local people were God-fearing and David wished to be seen to be supporting their beliefs, even though he was a disbeliever himself. So it was in the priest's interests to treat the Master with deference and bow to his desires.

At the hospital Henry Barrenbridge roared with laughter.

"Well, the old devil," he exclaimed as Philip Jaunton revealed his information, "he's going to marry his maid is he? Well, well, well. The rascal, but I dare say she's worth it, young miss. Probably do him good." Jaunton had also advised Clara who privately went into a state of shock and unbridled jealousy.

"It could've been me. I'm the beauty," she said quietly to herself when alone. "Why didn't I stay at the Hall and work my magic on him? I'd be the Mistress of Downsland and the envy of them all.

Why did I let that chance slip through my fingers? I had no idea he might marry *that* far beneath himself. Sarah Brankly, the little minx! You're no friend of mine Sarah. Tried to marry me to that Robert Broxford you did. What a match that would've been, with no servants, hardly any money and a hovel to live in. At least I have married well and have a good home and people to wait upon me. I will be more than your equal one day Sarah, for you're nobody, marrying nobody, just a man who is shunned by those that really matter, an outcast of society, reviled for his evil unconventional ideals.

"Perhaps I am better off with Philip. At least we can now rise through the ranks and be seen as people of class and breeding, and we will be the better for it. He wants to go to London and that is the place to be. Society as it was ever meant to be, and I shall be part of it with wealthy influential friends. My goodness, we shall be invited to balls and banquets, and when Philip makes his name people will want us to be there, and want us to invite them to our own events.

"Yes, that is a much improved prospect. And little barren Sarah Brankly can be a country girl seduced by a fool and laughed at and mocked forever."

Judith Pearland, Grace Gandling, David Gordon and Abe Winchell went to the Green Man to celebrate and the landlord had the devil's own job removing them in the early hours when he wanted his bed and needed to close up. Judith and Abe went in a drunken meander to the forge, arm in arm enjoying vast quantities of mirth, and collapsed in the hay to sleep off their inebriated state. This action resulted in both being severely reprimanded by their respective parents for their unseemly behaviour and told they would have to be married.

As it happened this suited everyone.

Grace might've been the worst for wear but retained her sense of propriety and waddled home, leaving her escort, Dr Gordon, at the front door. Somehow he managed to get to his own home and his own bed.

Dr Barrenbridge had been left to run the hospital that evening and it's probably just as well nothing very serious occurred.

A most pleasing upshot of all this celebratory bonhomie was that Esther and Robert walked out into the estate chatting cheerfully about Sarah's good fortune and came upon a rock where they had often sat, rarely admiring the view across the Swale beyond Faversham. Usually they slumped into a shared chasm of grief at Robert's loss, but today they marvelled at the scenery and partook of laughter which Esther, on Sarah's instructions, encouraged.

They returned to the house arm in arm, still happy, grinning and enjoying moments of humour as they went, and by the side of the walled garden they kissed.

Catherine Brankly's senses were completely overcome by her daughter's news, and she did not know which way to turn, running the farm more on instinct than anything else for a couple of days. But she had able assistance from Lydia in the house and John on the farm, and it may be that the presence of the latter discouraged Edmund from approaching, for he was seen near the place.

The following night, in the early hours, he broke into the house but Catherine was disturbed by the noise and crept downstairs to find him searching for food and money. Standing on the stairs, bedpan in hand for protection, she screamed. He gathered up what he could, actually precious little, and dashed through the door whereupon he was set about by John Willows, responding to the scream.

Edmund limped away and was never seen in Westlingstead again, his encounter with Willows proving a decisive factor in his expulsion. Following that, John and Catherine became closer friends as might be expected.

Judith and Sarah had spent a cordial afternoon together after the announcement was made. Their friendship was assured and entwined in their love for each other, a different kind of love, a vital and blissful love for all that, the love of two kindred spirits, recognised by David Grayan and accepted as such. He had that understanding and blessed their friendship.

Chapter Twenty Five

The wedding was a grand affair and Downsland Hall was alive with a throng of hundreds of people from far and wide who came to witness the extraordinary spectacle and partake of David Grayan's hospitality. The Reverend Paul Farhoe had conducted the ceremony in a packed church with many folk outside unable to gain entry. He might have been reluctant but he was left with no choice.

Sarah Brankly, now Mrs David Grayan, was Mistress of Downsland and happiness was everywhere. Eleanor Forbes welcomed her with open arms and a tear in her eye. She would forever be the loyal servant to the maid who had won the Master's heart. Sarah would never be above herself, Eleanor knew that. Sarah would always be the Sarah they had grown to love. And the Master had once again found true love, and that was all that mattered.

Mrs Brankly had pride of place as the bride's mother but was embarrassed by it all. John Willows accompanied her and was a great comfort to her, but David was always close by, as was Sarah, to ensure she was not overwhelmed. Catherine could still not believe it. Her daughter, married to the Master of Downsland!

Once again Paul Farhoe partook of the celebrations, and partook of rather too much ale, and was escorted home by one the villagers, the young and flirty Caroline Battey, whom he took to his bed that night. He might have damned David Grayan but was easily undone by a cunning Miss Battey.

The Haskerton's came as did Marie's siblings and their families. The Bakker's arrived from the Netherlands to add an international flavour to proceedings. William Scrans was there and he cut an extraordinary figure by managing to look like everyones' image of a smuggler, but fortunately few knew the truth and he otherwise explained his profession as a trader which went part way to being accurate.

David's brother and sister were present with their families which gave rise to much rejoicing. The Cowans came, and once again Downsland Hall was host to many visitors staying for three or four nights making the old place ring with the splendour of it all. Mrs Forbes had her work cut out for it had been some while since the Hall had so many guests staying, but she managed, just as she always did, ably supported by keen staff, and so her success was created.

Hester was a good host taking David's role as he was otherwise engaged, and she helped Mrs Forbes work her magic to ensure all the guests were well catered for and enjoyed their time there.

She made a special welcome for Margaret Cheney and her husband, true friends in times of trial, loyal and faithful throughout.

The wedding day itself was shunned by society in the main, despite invitations being made, and of Kent's aristocracy was there no sign. There was a strong belief that Grayan's unconventional views, manifest in so much that he had done and achieved, was a gamble with the firmly established good order which maintained the country. Having such a close relationship with the people was frowned upon and it was widely thought his attitude might encourage those people to get above themselves, possibly even to rebel and that had to be controlled and eliminated.

It could've have been that they were looking across the Channel to developments in France and starting to fear a serious uprising, a full rebellion that would bring down the King, the government and their status, threatening their lives into the bargain.

Eventually the newlywed couple left the gathering for their lovers' cot, but the party roared on well into the night. However, by daybreak all was quiet apart from the sound of a light drizzle on the windows, the only sound Sarah heard as she awoke.

***

She looked at the man next to her. Her husband was sleeping, his gentle breathing barely audible. How she loved him! And she'd loved him all the time, knowing she had been denying it to her friends as a way of trying to ignore it, believing it harboured an impossible dream.

Yet here was the dream come true. Hadn't her mother said that one day a man would come for her? Never would she have expected it to be this man! A wonderful, remarkable man. She'd known for weeks she'd lost him to Lily Cowans little knowing that he did not truly love Lily and longed for his Sarah instead.

And as they lay quietly abed last night he'd told her that she herself was the wonderful and remarkable person, not he, that she was the woman who had led him out of his self-imposed misery and made such a glorious difference to his life. He'd thanked her for saving him and blessed her for her love before once more taking her tenderly in his arms and sharing that most beauteous and enchanting of kisses.

Oh to be held in that loving embrace! What joy. What wonder. To feel his lips on hers and to be taken on a fabulous journey of ecstasy and bliss. Paradise indeed. Lost in soft white clouds of love, devoured by sensations so new, so resplendent, so meaningful. This precious man, this precious love. And he had praised everything about her to illustrate what an astonishing woman he truly thought she was. That was kindness, but it was also love, and it meant so much to her.

It made her feel special, that she was loved for many good reasons, not for fickle adoration alone. She felt important and vital to him and that made her heart swim in happiness and contentment. He had called her a heroine but she doubted she deserved that particular soubriquet!

But she was his, his wife, his lover and was Mistress of Downsland, and she would be a credit to him.

He had gazed into her eyes and she knew he was awakening her very soul. In musical tones that sung like a choir his sweet compassionate voice had spoken such magnificent words of love. In a quiet moment of reflection as they lay between the sheets he suddenly sat up and looked at her again.

"Sarah, you have the face of an angel and the lips of a goddess." She'd giggled.

"No David I do not..." she'd protested. But he'd arrested her remonstration with his own lips.

And when their passion was spent he had one further thing to add.

"Marie has blessed you too, my darling," he'd whispered in her ear, and that had made her wedding day complete.

Epilogue

Dr Jaunton made a name for himself by running the hospital at Westlingstead and eventually moved to London and greater things, taking the grateful Clara with him on his rise through society. They had seven children, although three died in infancy, and Philip then died from an infection caught from a patient. Clara married twice more, having three more children, and died a widow at the good age of seventy eight having outlived four husbands.

Dr Gordon became the head of Westlingstead's hospital and married Grace, but sadly they were not to be blessed with the children they yearned for.

Henry Barrenbridge did marry his landlady but eschewed the idea of a house provided by David Grayan, he and his wife preferring to live in her abode, which was comfortable enough, and which had been their home together since his arrival in the village some years before.

Edmund Forness remained an outcast turned aside by his own children who loathed him for his past misdemeanours, and thus left destitute had to steal to live. He joined a gang of smugglers which proved his undoing. He went to the gallows having shot and killed an Excise man off the coast near Folkestone, and was mourned by nobody, no family shedding any tears.

In time John Willows offered his hand to Catherine Brankly but she rejected him with great kindness and affection, and they stayed the closest of friends maintaining their interest in the farm. Lydia still worked for Catherine, and Sarah often joined them all on the smallholding for whatever work was necessary. Grayan himself worked there occasionally and took a particular delight in attending to the pigs much to Sarah's amusement.

Catherine was happy where she was but overjoyed with Sarah's marriage for she could see, as only a mother could, that true love abounded. Unsurprisingly Sarah and David wanted Catherine to enjoy a better life but it was not for her. She had all she wanted.

She preferred to have her own home, the one she knew, rather than move into a larger house, perhaps on the Downsland estate, and give up the smallholding, which was Sarah's suggestion. In truth, Sarah knew the answer, but felt duty bound to offer. Mother and daughter still retained that precious bond that was made more secure and stronger by events.

Judith married Abe and while he took over the forge she developed a branch of medicine that remained, to some, in the realms of witchcraft, but at the same time helped save many lives. Although viewed as heresy, especially by Paul Farhoe, Judith treated problems of the mind and did so successfully. In due course she became quite renowned for what, for the age, was pioneering work.

Sadly she died before any recognition could be placed upon her, and left a grieving husband and three young sons to mourn her passing. Her funeral was attended by dozens of people from all parts of Kent who appreciated the help she had given them and those they loved. Sarah was overcome with grief for the woman who had been more than a sister to her, and whose work she admired so greatly.

It was not the end of the story for gradually the acceptance of illness of the mind was given the credence it deserved, but it would be many, many years yet before her kind of counselling would be brought to prominence and provided with the credit it deserved. Even in Victorian times those thought to be mad were simply locked away.

In time news arrived that Hester's husband had died of disease in the West Indies and so she was released at last.

Sarah had helped her raise her boys in addition to the three orphans she and David saved from a terrible life of misery and despair, so often the lot of orphaned children at the time, and all five of the young found security and love as they grew up at Downsland.

The new Mrs Grayan's only real sadness was her dear friend Esther.

No progress had been made with the mournful Robert Broxford so, at Sarah's suggestion, Esther proposed to him. Shocked by her forwardness he took some time to recover but then disappointed her, not because women should not make proposals, but because he'd sworn to be faithful to Clara. They saw very little of each other after that and Esther was a long time returning to her former self.

In truth she never really recovered and died in the hospital at the tender age of twenty-seven having contracted a fever the physicians could do nothing about. Grace told Sarah she believed Esther had no wish to live and it hastened her end. Every week Sarah made the pilgrimage to her grave to lay flowers and tears, kneeling and saying silent prayers and remembering happier times, and hoping Esther had found peace at last.

Ginny left Downsland when she and Mark started their own family but she returned as Housekeeper when Mrs Forbes retired. Jed Maxton became estate manager in due time, Agnes being particularly proud of his achievements and elevation.

David Grayan died at the age of eighty-eight having outlived Sarah by six years. He also outlived his siblings. He had seen five monarchs on the throne and had invested in the industrial revolution which was taking the country by storm as the Victorian era came to life. When he fell in love with Sarah the concept of railways was unimaginable beyond the very basic use of tracks such as in mines. Now he had money in the new lines where trains were hauled by fire-breathing iron monsters!

How things had changed in his lifetime. But some things he believed in and tried to promote were many, many years off. Despite fears over the French Revolution spreading its ugly tentacles across the Channel, no such rebellion had taken place and social order reigned as it had done throughout his life. Grayan's concern for the welfare of the people had therefore done no harm and such philanthropy and care was being replicated by a few, a precious few, industrialists in this new age.

The improved role of women and acceptance of their equal status championed by the Master of Downsland, and fully supported by his wives at his side as well as many who worked for him, remained in the far distant future, and when he died he went to his grave regretting he had not been able to make more positive progress and influence many others.

David and Sarah continued with and improved on his philosophies to considerable success, the welfare of those who worked for them and of local people being priorities. Sarah was able to don Marie's mantle and actively encourage and promote those women who sought to demonstrate their abilities at a time when society frowned upon such ideas.

She helped Judith set up a small home on the estate where those suffering from mental illness could come. Once people were thought to be mad they were locked up and mistreated appallingly, but the new home gave a few the opportunity to see out their days in proper care, David overseeing the legal side. That was necessary as society thought the mad should be kept under lock and key. Judith successfully aided three to overcome their illnesses and return to normal life, but her premature death brought the healing to a halt although care continued.

Sarah ran the home with help from local girls keen to follow in her footsteps, and who supported the Grayans' ideals where women were concerned, especially knowing how Judith Winchell had risen to prominence under their patronage.

In time David ran into too many legal obstacles, most placed in his path quite deliberately by vociferous opponents, and sadly the home ended its days when the last resident died, the Grayans unable to fill the vacancies. With it went the legacy of Mrs Winchell, the renowned lady who healed with words.

Sarah was always an inspiration to local girls and her husband smiled on her efforts. As Mistress of Downsland she now had the power, influence and money to help those who wished to improve their education, work in different fields, and find their true selves even when convention was against such development. When her mother died she bequeathed, with her siblings' agreement, the smallholding to Lydia and her new husband knowing it would be maintained the way Catherine Brankly would've wanted it.

Sarah's own demise brought sadness once more to David Grayan, but this time he remembered all she had taught him and did not allow himself to sink into misery and despair, upholding her own good works so that they might continue beyond his death.

Downsland was inherited by Edward Handlen, Hester's eldest son, who moved in with his wife but proved a poor man of business and a reckless spender. Only now did the old Hall see the banquets and balls and other mighty social occasions largely denied it by the Grayans. Edward, despite his upbringing, failed to maintain the Grayans' principles where those employed by him were concerned and as debts mounted so he reduced his staff and stopped supporting Westlingstead in the philanthropic way it had enjoyed.

This Master of Downsland was readily accepted by those of social status and condemned by the ordinary people in complete contrast to the position with David Grayan. But finally financial issues overwhelmed him and he moved to more modest accommodation in London leaving Downsland in bad hands where it eventually fell into disrepair and ruin.

Lily Cowans remained in her corner of south-east Kent but was a frequent visitor to the Hall. She and Sarah were good friends and often set about tasks related to the home Judith ran, women united by capability and desire much to David Grayan's satisfaction. Shortly after Judith's demise Lily was taken ill in Dover and died at her parents' home with Sarah in attendance, the Mistress of Downsland losing two of her loveliest of friends in brief succession.

Happily David was the greatest comfort, returning the kindness Sarah had once shown him. They were generally a happy couple with Sarah earning the respect of all who knew her or knew of her. She died peacefully in her sleep, David instantly awake knowing instinctively what had happened. He kissed her, cradled her in his arms, said so many wonderful things about her and about their love, and laid her gently back on the pillow before going for the Housekeeper.

Within a few short years he joined his beloved wives and his child Charlotte in paradise, also dying peacefully and untroubled in his sleep.

Author's Afterthoughts

This is a work of fiction, possibly a flight of fancy.

Wealthy philanthropic and caring people existed in the 18th century but were few and far between. So David Grayan's character is not easily removed from truth, but what would have been considered outrageous and laughable were his views on all aspects of equality, not simply between men and women but also between the classes of society, and between employers and employees.

Having said that some women had enjoyed positions of prominence. Queen Anne reigned in the first part of the 18th century and she was not Britain's first queen. There were other notable and successful 'husbands and wives' in this era particularly amongst the aristocracy, but this story relates to the general picture, not the exceptions.

It would've been most unusual for the wealthy to mix so easily with the poor and certainly not with any degree of equality.

Grayan therefore represents idealism ahead of its time and not acceptable to his own class, so the background to the story is a kind of 'what if' scenario.

Certainly it is highly unlikely that a young girl, accompanied by a maid who was a friend, would've advanced upon the master of great house unannounced as Sarah and Ginny did, so that is an event that definitely belongs to the world of fiction. But stranger things may have happened in real life. By the same token it is unlikely a single lady of Lily Cowans standing would've called on a gentleman uninvited and without escort or chaperone.

Set in North Kent the actual locations of both Downsland and Westlingstead are deliberately vague, but the reader may have been drawn to the view that these fictitious places were above the North Downs perhaps somewhere between Sittingbourne and Faversham. The Belmont estate and the nearby village of Eastling were not the inspiration but easily could've been. It's a delightful part of rural Kent I love to walk.

The novel is set in a time when landscaping and the design of gardens in large estates was coming to the fore; indeed this was the time of legendary Lancelot 'Capability' Brown.

Real places are mentioned in the story, and Grayan's ride to the top of the Downs overlooking Lenham suggests his home was not far away. The description of the spectacular view from this point is very real indeed.

Although there is an historical backdrop to the tale, events of note are occasionally mentioned and not detailed. This might be an historical novel but is not a history book, and much that occurs within has been created to suit the story. I apologise if this offends any learned historians.

What is true is that north Kent (the River Medway and Sheerness) was invaded by the Dutch in 1667 and in the ensuing years there was further conflict culminating in the so-called fourth Anglo-Dutch war of the 1780s.

The role of medicine has a core part to play.

A necessary amount of research was carried out to add credence to these areas of the narrative and to ensure I did not step outside the confines of the age, but it will be appreciated that certain aspects have either been adapted for a purpose or taken to an extreme. Mental health issues, the work of women in medicine and so on, feature in this novel rather more boldly than they would have been seen in the 18th century. That is a vital part of the story.

The practice of gentlemen to refer to each other by surname has been largely ignored as the use of forenames seemed more appropriate in some contexts, and to eliminate confusion between the male Grayans.

James Parry-Barnard. Double-barrelled names were in use during this period, but normally to show that two families of high station were united, and a hyphen would rarely be employed. As hyphens are adopted today as the norm I have used one here.

The beautifully evocative word gay is used in the original sense as it would've been in the 18th century. The book is written in a style that reflects the modern day image of Georgian Britain and the novels of that and later eras, but the dialogue may be considered by purists to be more in the realms of TV's period dramas than rooted in reality.

Other books by Peter Chegwidden

Peter Chegwidden writes across various genres so there's bound to be something for almost everyone.

Short story collections

- Souls Down the River
- Sheppey Short Stories

Murder Mysteries

- The Chortleford Mystery
- Death at the Oast
- No Shelter for the Wicked
- Deadened Pain (a parody of crime novels)

Adventures of Tom the Cat

- Tom Investigates
- Tom Vanishes

Kent-based 18th century drama

- Kindale
- The Master of Downsland

Most of Peter Chegwidden's books are based in his home county, Kent. Three works (Deadened Pain, Tom Vanishes and Sheppey Short Stories) are available as e-books only. All others are available from Amazon as e-books and paperbacks.

Recent additions include **Souls Down the River**, described as a glorious and light-hearted romp down the imaginary Flemm Valley. The journey visits each village on the way and features a range of short stories, tales of sauciness and frivolity, of muddle and mayhem, of romps, scandal and rustic charm, as well as heroism, adventure, stupidity and love.

And **Death at the Oast** which follows in the footsteps of the highly successful *The Chortleford Mystery* and is also based in rural Kent. If you like your crime novels in a lighter and more cosy vein, where the book is as much about the characters as the murders, then these are for you.

You can preview all books on Amazon where the first chapters can be read. (*If you're in the UK best to search on Amazon UK*).

Printed in Great Britain
by Amazon

16323472R00180